STAR WARS®
THE WRATH OF
DARTH MAUL

STAR WARS®
THE WRATH OF
DARTH MAUL

BY RYDER WINDHAM

SCHOLASTIC INC.

New York Toronto London Auckland Sydney Mexico City New Delhi Hong Kong

www.starwars.com
www.scholastic.com

ISBN 978-0-545-38327-1
ISBN 978-0-545-43367-9

12 11 10 9 8 7 6 5 4 3 2 1   12 13 14 15 16 17/0

Cover illustrations by Mike Butkus
Printed in the U.S.A.   23
First printing, January 2012

For Allan Kausch, who introduced me to Darth Maul

TABLE OF CONTENTS

PROLOGUE

The prong-nosed rat knew that the dark heap lying in the tunnel was a dead man. He could tell by the incredible stench. Unable to detect any other predators in the tunnel, the rat's sharp nose twitched with excitement at his discovery, a large and easy meal, all for him.

The rat edged along the side of the tunnel, stepping over the skeletons of other creatures — many small skeletons, but others quite large — as it moved toward the corpse. Ragged scraps of broad, waterproof fabric were piled over the lower half of the dead man's body. His head, arms, and chest were exposed. A fine layer of dust covered his skin, barely concealing the bold, jagged tattoos that adorned his remains. His head rested at an odd angle against the ground because of the long, sharp horns that jutted from his skull. The rat slunk closer to the body and opened his jaws.

The rat never saw the fist that crashed down on the back of his neck. And then the man, who was very much alive, opened his yellow eyes as he rolled over and lashed out with his other hand to seize his prey. He kicked away the fabric scraps he'd been using as blankets, revealing the mechanical apparatus that formed his lower body.

The apparatus was affixed to the man's midriff, just below his rib cage, and consisted of a droid carriage equipped with six metal legs. The legs were unevenly jointed, cannibalized from the parts of ruined droids, each leg ending with a tapered point. As the prong-nosed rat writhed in his clutches, the man skittered out from under the blankets like a monstrous robotic spider, his metal legs clacking against the tunnel floor.

He had no recollection of how he'd lost his lower body or who had grafted his torso to the droid carriage. Although he knew the tunnels that had become his domain, he did not know that he was on a planet named Lotho Minor. Nor did he remember his own name. And for the moment he didn't care. His mind was on only one thing.

Food.

He tore into the rat and began eating it greedily. A few minutes later, as he licked the last of the gore from his lips, a familiar feeling returned to him. It was the only feeling he had, the only emotion he knew when he wasn't delirious with hunger. Hatred. Not just anger and rage, but pure and total hatred.

He hated his circumstances. Hated the tunnels and

all the vermin that ventured into them. Hated being hungry, and being unable to rest without some other creature trying to take a bite out of him. Hated that he knew all those distractions were meaningless. The primary object of his hatred was something far more significant, something he despised with such incredible intensity that he . . .

Can't remember.

Hated his bad memory too.

How had he arrived at this place? How long had he been living like a wild animal? His yellow eyes darted back and forth, sweeping the tunnel as if he might find a helpful answer in the shadowy nooks, amidst the gnawed bones of small creatures that littered the ground.

Nothing.

He grimaced. He wanted to remember. He wanted to know.

The frustration was like a painful itch that he knew he could never ever scratch. He lowered one hand to his side, and his fingertips brushed against one of his cold metal legs.

Wasn't always . . . like this.

He knew that he wasn't a man anymore, that he hadn't been one for years. He was just a creature in a filthy tunnel. And then he remembered the object of his hatred.

A man . . . the man who left me for dead.

The hatred surged through his veins, filling him with

the urge to kill anything within reach. He surveyed the skeletons and rotting carcasses on the tunnel's floor, then used his droid legs to launch several swift and vicious kicks that sent bones crashing against the walls. Finding a large rib cage, he seized it and brought it down hard across the back of one metal leg, then threw aside the splintered bones. He found no satisfaction in this petty destruction. He only hated more.

Why can't I remember?!

Balling his hands into tight fists, he felt his sharp, dirty fingernails dig into the bases of his leathery palms. He gnashed his teeth and squeezed his eyes shut as he struggled to conjure up a memory, any memory, that would help him recall his own identity.

It was then, while he felt his hatred burning within, that a spark ignited in his mind. And he saw a sea of fire. . . .

CHAPTER ONE

The boy named Maul had to stand on his tiptoes to peer through the thick window in his small room. The window was polarized to block heat and light, but the view was still so intense that it made the boy squint. The light did not come from the sky, which was choked with black, smoky clouds, but radiated from the river of lava that flowed below the facility where Maul lived. Turning his head slightly, he saw the lava empty into what looked like a wide, fiery sea.

The planet's name was Mustafar, according to the droid that looked after Maul. The droid also served as the boy's teacher and had shown him holograms that illustrated Mustafar's terrain and the planet's location in the galaxy. The droid had shown him holograms of other worlds too. Maul had a hard time understanding that the holograms represented actual planets, but he had to memorize their names and correctly indicate their locations or the droid would subject him to a painful shock.

Fortunately, Maul was alone. Looking through the window, he tried to spot any signs of life. Occasionally, he would glimpse Mustafar's armored natives riding lava fleas in the distance, heading for the northern region where they worked as miners. A few times, he had even seen ore haulers traveling across the sky. At the moment, he could not see any Mustafarians or vessels, just the never-ending flow of lava, fire, smoke, and clouds.

The droid had told Maul that he wouldn't last long on Mustafar's surface, but that didn't stop him from wanting to venture outside. After all, if the Mustafarians could move about freely, why couldn't he? He might need Mustafarian armor to protect him from the heat, and also some kind of breathing apparatus. He wondered how difficult it would be to acquire such things. He had no reason to believe a Mustafarian would just give him what he needed to survive. But he did imagine that going outside would be exciting.

Maul moved slightly and saw something shift across the window's surface. Maul realized it was his own reflection. He could see only the top of his head, which had multiple small horns. Like the rest of his body, his head was distinguished by red and black patterns. His eyes were bright yellow with small black pupils.

The first time he had seen his reflection, he had been startled, because he had thought he was seeing another person. For all he knew, his reflection *was* another person, another boy who looked like him and echoed his every movement. A boy who was semitransparent, suspended in the smoky air outside the room. A boy who was free to roam the planet's volcanic surface without fear of injury, who could leave Mustafar and go anywhere he wanted. A boy who could help Maul escape.

Maul wished he were that boy.

Bracing his hands against the seamless area where the smooth metal wall met the glass, Maul jumped up so he could see more of his thin body reflected in the window. He jumped again and again, fascinated by his leaping reflection as well as the sound of his bare feet smacking against the metal floor. He pushed himself away from the window as he jumped back, still facing the window, and continued jumping for several minutes. He didn't stop until well after his breathing had become short, his feet had gotten sore, and his leg muscles had begun stinging with pain.

Catching his breath, he turned away from the window and surveyed his room. The room's only remarkable features were a single door against the wall opposite the window and a cold-water faucet that was operated by a palm sensor, positioned over a small drainage hole in one corner. The door was made of thick metal, the same material as the walls, floor, and ceiling. The bottom of the door had a narrow horizontal slot, through which the droid would sometimes shove a small tray of food, usually bits of uncooked meat. Maul could not see through the slot, because it remained sealed when not in use, by a sliding sheet of metal. Above the door was a convex blister that housed an audio speaker and also a photoreceptor, which allowed the droid to watch Maul at all times. There weren't any controls to open the door from inside Maul's room, at least none that Maul had ever been able to find.

A chime sounded from the speaker, alerting Maul to begin his exercises. Even though his room was not very large and his legs were still tired from jumping, he knew better than to ignore the chime. He immediately began running in place.

At first, Maul kept his arms tucked by his sides. Then he started pumping his arms up and down to match the steady rhythm of his leg muscles. He wanted to close his eyes and pretend that he was somewhere else, perhaps a larger room, but he was not allowed to close his eyes while exercising. He forced his eyelids to stay open and pumped his legs faster.

The chime sounded again. Maul stopped running, fell back against the floor, and began doing a series of sit-ups and leg lifts. After several minutes, the chime sounded, and Maul rolled over to do his push-up exercises, alternating between one- and two-handed push-ups. Several more minutes passed before the chime sounded again, signaling the exercise session's end. Maul collapsed against the cold floor.

Someone's coming.

Maul pushed himself up and stared hard at the door.

Although he could not hear approaching footsteps, he knew the door would open in a moment, and a visitor would be standing in the chamber outside. He didn't know how he knew this. He just knew.

Maul could imagine only two possible visitors. One was the droid that looked after him. The other was the Man, who rarely visited. The Man wore a dark robe with a deep hood that left most of his features in shadow. Maul had never actually seen the Man's eyes.

Maul hated the Man even more than he hated the droid. The Man frightened him.

The door made a hissing sound as it slid up and vanished into a slot in the ceiling. Standing outside the doorway was the droid. Made of shiny black metal, the droid had a bulbous head with five red mechanical eyes called photoreceptors and a mesh-grille vocabulator for speaking, and a cylindrical torso that held four long, jointed pincers for arms. The torso rested on a swivel-hinged abdomen that had six spiderlike legs.

Maul never knew what to expect from the droid. Sometimes it brought food or medicine or sprayed Maul with antiseptic cleansers or escorted him to a larger adjoining chamber where it would chase him or let him run in circles. Other times, it would talk to him and teach him words.

Usually, the droid brought pain.

Once, the droid had delivered a bright green and yellow snake that wasted no time in attacking Maul, sinking its venomous fangs deep into the boy's arm. Maul screamed and then threw his own body down on top of the snake's to crush it. As ravenous as he was enraged, Maul had not been able to resist taking several large bites of the dead snake, which had been more than his small stomach could handle. After that incident, the droid had returned with medicine, bandages, and a stomach pump.

Now, standing before Maul in the doorway, the droid slowly extended one pincer away from its body and swiveled the tip in a broad circular movement. Maul kept his eyes focused on the rotating pincer as he felt his muscles tense, bracing himself to leap away from it. He didn't notice the small panel that opened below one of the droid's eyes. The opened panel exposed a socket that housed a telescopic arm tipped with a hypodermic needle. The arm lashed out, jabbed the needle into Maul's right shoulder, and then rapidly retracted into the droid's head. The droid had taken just a fraction of a second to make the injection — so little time that Maul barely comprehended that the needle had pierced his skin.

Maul blinked as he reached up and rubbed his shoulder. He realized that the droid had done something to him and had rotated its pincer only to distract him. And then he felt a strange, warm sensation spreading throughout his body. He frowned at the droid, and then his eyelids drooped and his legs buckled. The droid's arms extended, catching the boy before he could hit the floor.

The spider-legged droid picked up the unconscious boy and carried him out of the little room without any difficulty. The boy was not at all heavy. He was barely three years old.

When Maul awoke, he was lying on a metal bench in a large high-ceilinged chamber that he had never visited before. Three tall, narrow windows were set into one wall, illuminating the floor in front of Maul but leaving most of the chamber in darkness. Through the windows, he saw molten rock cascading past a black jagged cliff.

Maul did not remember falling asleep or leaving his own room. He suspected he was about to be disciplined. He wondered if he hadn't done all his exercises correctly or if he had made some other mistake. Not that it mattered. Sometimes he was disciplined without any explanation at all. He had been learning discipline since he had learned how to walk. One of the first things he learned was not to cry. Crying never made anything better. Crying only made things worse.

Maul slowly pushed himself up from the bench. He felt cool air against his back and suspected there was a vent or a doorway behind him. Looking around the chamber, he noticed five red lights glowing in the darkness of one nearby corner. He recognized the lights as the eyes of the spider-legged droid.

11

Maul rubbed his right shoulder. He remembered that the droid had struck him in the shoulder earlier, and suspected that the droid had made him fall asleep. He wondered what the droid might do next. Would it kill him?

The droid lurched out of the corner. Maul hit the floor with his bare feet, and began running as fast as his small legs could carry him away from the droid. Staying out of the light that stretched from the windows across the floor, he darted toward an inner wall, heading for the source of the draft he'd felt against his back. His vision adjusted to the darkness and he found a quadrangular doorway. He did not hesitate to run through it, even though he had no idea of what awaited him in the next chamber.

Darkness. A chamber without windows. Then he glimpsed a dim sliver of light ahead. Ignoring the droid's clattering footsteps behind him, he ran toward the light, which emanated from somewhere beyond a curved wall. He knew he couldn't outrun the droid, but he didn't dare stop.

Maul ran around the curved wall and entered a long, narrow corridor. Illuminated by small rectangular lamps embedded in the walls, the corridor was so long that he couldn't see the other end. Maul kept running. He heard the droid's footsteps pause at the corridor's entrance. He hoped the droid was too large to follow him into the corridor.

Risking a backward glance, he saw the droid had already tilted its body sideways so four of its legs tapped against the wall while the remaining two continued to scramble up the floor, propelling its metal body after Maul. Maul gasped as he turned his gaze forward, never breaking his stride.

He heard the droid's footsteps grow louder and knew it was gaining on him. He somehow sensed the droid was about to snare him with a pincer. Desperate and determined to evade the droid, Maul jumped to the side, planting one foot against the wall to his right, then sprang to the opposite wall, keeping his feet moving so that he traveled two steps across the vertical surface in a diagonal descent to the floor. Maul heard the pincer slam into the floor behind him, and he jumped up to make two more quick strides along the right wall before he flung himself back to the floor, still running forward. As he ran, he heard a loud and satisfying crash from behind, and he knew that the droid had tripped over its own legs in its failed effort to keep up with him.

Suspecting that the droid would not only recover but also be very angry with him, Maul ran faster. His heart was pounding as he saw that the corridor terminated at another quadrangular doorway. He exited the corridor fast and arrived in a chamber that was unlike any place he had ever imagined.

Broad tapestries hung from the walls, which were also decorated with strange sculptures. Carved furniture, made from strangely jointed and highly polished bones, rested on a wide rug that had once been an animal's hide. At the chamber's center, an enormous orb of transparent greenish blue liquid, nearly two meters in diameter, was suspended in the air above a circular dining table. Dozens of small, multicolored aquatic creatures swam within the orb, some so close to the surface that their swishing tails sent ripples around the orb's circumference.

Maul was so amazed by all the wondrous things in the room that he almost forgot that he had stopped running. He just stood there, looking from the swimming creatures to the decorations. But as he studied the carved furniture, he instinctively realized the chamber was a special place. It was a place where someone sat and looked at all the things in the room. It was a place where someone lived. He knew the droid did not require such luxuries. He was certain that this place was the Man's lair.

"Welcome, Maul," rasped a low voice from behind Maul. "I have been expecting you."

Maul froze at the sound of the Man's voice. He locked his eyes on the floating orb. He wished he could become invisible.

"I *had* expected that the droid would lead you here," the unseen Man continued. "The way you ran along the walls to evade the droid was *most* impressive. But then you always have been a clever boy."

Maul had heard the Man talk like this before.

Compliments were almost always followed by punishments. Maul braced himself as he kept his eyes fixed on the floating orb. As unnerved as he was by the Man's presence, he was more fascinated by the aquatic creatures inside the orb. He wondered if the creatures were edible.

A screech of metal sounded from the doorway that Maul had just entered, and the droid pushed its body out of the narrow corridor to emerge inside the chamber. After the droid righted itself so that all its legs touched the floor, it moved up beside Maul, stopping short of the animal-hide rug. Maul shifted his gaze from the floating orb to the droid and noticed two of its legs were now bent at odd angles. The droid swiveled its mechanical eyes to stare at Maul and said in a droning tone, "You should not have run away."

"Leave us," the Man snapped at the droid.

The droid tottered away from Maul, moving toward a wide doorway on the other side of the room. Maul wanted to leave with the droid, but instead he looked at the floating orb and remained where he stood.

"You may face me," the Man said soothingly.

More than ever, Maul wished he were the free-floating boy who appeared to exist beyond the window in his own room. He tried very hard not to tremble as he slowly turned and looked up to face the Man.

As usual, the Man was wearing his dark robe with the deep hood, but he had pushed the hood back so it was draped behind his head. Maul was surprised to see his exposed face. The Man had blue eyes, fair skin of a singular color, and a head of wavy hair. Maul was also taken aback by how different the Man's head was from his own. The Man didn't even have horns.

The Man lifted his eyebrows as he looked at Maul skeptically. "You can talk, can't you?"

Maul nodded.

"Yes?"

"Yes," Maul replied.

"You will address me as Master Sidious."

"Yes, Master Sidious."

Sidious smiled. "Excellent." He stepped past the boy and stopped beside the floating orb. Maul noticed that all the aquatic creatures within the orb swam to the far side, putting distance between themselves and Sidious. Sidious glanced at the creatures as if he found them only mildly interesting. "Maul, I have something important to tell you. I want you to listen carefully."

Maul listened.

Speaking slowly, Sidious said, "You . . . are . . . remarkable." Looking away from the watery orb, he faced Maul and added, "Very remarkable."

Maul did not know why he might be considered remarkable, or how Sidious expected him to respond. He decided to remain silent.

"Our galaxy is home to trillions of life-forms. Some are large, others small. But as diverse as they are, the truth is that most life-forms are just like these fish." Sidious gestured at the fish with a dismissive wave, and the fish appeared to shiver within the orb. "They seldom stray far from where they were born. They spend their time worrying about their next meal, about how they might avoid pain, and how long they might live. They live in fear of one another. And then, they die. It does not matter if they are an insect, a fish, a man, or . . . a snake."

Once again, Maul thought of the snake he had been forced to kill.

"You have already traveled great distances," Sidious continued. "You may have been born on the planet Iridonia, but you came to my attention on another world, Dathomir. There, the females rule and enslave the males. You were just an infant, and yet the most powerful beings on Dathomir were afraid of you. They wanted you dead because you were different." Sidious smiled. "Do you know what makes you so remarkable, Maul? So different from ordinary life-forms?"

Maul shook his head and answered meekly, "No."

Sidious raised his eyebrows slightly and pursed his lips. Shaking his head, he said, "That is not the correct response. The correct response is 'No, Master Sidious.'"

Maul swallowed hard, then said, "No, Master Sidious."

Sidious smiled again. "You are different because you are stronger. You have powers. You know things in advance. You look at the closed door to your room, and you know it is about to open. You have fast reflexes. Others only dream of anticipating moments as you do, or being able to move so fast. In this way, you and I are alike, Maul, except that my powers are much greater. My powers are greater because I know many things that you have yet to learn, such as how to make your powers work for you. Do you understand?"

"Yes, Master Sidious."

"Good. Good." Sidious walked around the watery orb until it was positioned between him and Maul. From Maul's point of view, the orb distorted Sidious's head and upper body. Sidious said, "I know you imagine a different life for yourself, Maul. An easier life than you have now."

Maul remained silent.

"I know you're upset about the snake that bit you," Sidious said, continuing around the watery orb until he had a clear view of Maul. "I know everything about you, Maul. Everything." Sidious edged around the orb until he was facing Maul again. "While you might think that your life is harsh and unpleasant, and that I am some-times cruel, there is a reason for you to endure such pain. The reason is that you must become strong in every way. You must learn to overcome pain. Someday, you might become stronger than I. You'd like that, wouldn't you? To be stronger than I?"

"Yes, Master Sidious."

Sidious beamed at the boy. "Good." He glanced at the watery orb. "Ah! Look there, at those two fish."

Maul followed Sidious's gaze and saw a small fish with red and black stripes hovering beside a larger dark gray fish that had moved away from the other creatures to the bottom of the orb. Maul replied, "Yes, Master Sidious." He noticed that the smaller fish had yellow eyes, the same color as his own. The small fish stared back at Maul.

"How amusing," Sidious said. "If I didn't know better, I'd say those two were pretending to be *us*. If they were, I wonder where that would leave the rest."

Maul looked at the fish in the orb's upper area and saw them begin to jerk and spasm. Several fish puffed up twice their original size, shuddered violently, and suddenly deflated. Others rolled erratically through the water, their eyes bulging as their gills pumped furiously. But after a few seconds, all the fish except for the two at the bottom stopped swimming entirely and began drifting off in different directions. Some floated toward the top of the orb, but most sank down beside the two surviving fish, who continued to hover next to each other. As the fish sank, Sidious recited a strange verse.

"Far above, far above,
We don't know where we'll fall.
Far above, far above,
What once was great is rendered small."

Maul wondered what the words meant. He knew Sidious had somehow selected the two fish and maneuvered them to the bottom of the orb and caused all the others to die. He didn't know how Sidious had done this, but suspected it was some kind of magic. Looking away from the dead fish, Maul faced Sidious and said hesitantly, "Master Sidious . . . is it possible . . . to learn this power?"

Sidious smiled broadly, showing his teeth. "It is possible. But not immediately. You must be patient. I've prepared a training room. And today, you will receive personal instruction . . . from me."

Maul was surprised to hear about a training room and was instantly curious to see it. He hoped it was larger than the training area outside his own small room. As he wondered how soon his Master would show him the new training room, the six-legged droid, its two damaged legs replaced by a shiny new pair, sauntered back into the chamber.

Sidious glanced at the droid, then looked back at Maul and said, "Legs are not easily replaced. You do realize you must be punished, do you not?"

"Yes, Master Sidious."

"Always remember . . . a punishment is a lesson, young Maul. Learn it well. Now, come along." As Sidious stepped away from the floating orb, he waved his fingers at a tapestry that hung against one wall. The tapestry slid silently up toward the ceiling and revealed an open doorway built into the wall. Sidious walked to the doorway, which Maul assumed was a passage that led to the new training room.

Maul tried to step away from the orb, but his legs suddenly felt like they were heavy weights, anchored to the floor. He knew he would be punished even more severely if he did not obey his Master, but it seemed his own body—independent of his mind—was refusing to move. But before Sidious noticed Maul's hesitation, the droid reached out with a pincer and gave Maul a sharp jab in the back of his left thigh, causing him to jump forward. The droid muttered, "Don't make things worse."

As Maul began to follow Sidious, he glanced back at the bottom of the orb for a final look at the two surviving fish. The small yellow-eyed fish was hungrily biting into a dead fish. The large gray fish hovered a short distance away and appeared to be watching the yellow-eyed fish with some interest before its eyes shifted to look at Maul. Maul hurried into the passage, followed by the droid.

The training room exceeded all of Maul's expectations. So did his punishment.

But he survived.

CHAPTER TWO

"Begin!" the droid said.

Maul ran fast across the training room floor, heading straight for the wall. Several months after his arrival in the training room, he was familiar with the routine. He launched off the floor with his left foot, hit the wall with his right, and ran several steps up the wall before he kicked away, flipping his body backward through the air. He landed on his feet, then sprinted back toward the wall and repeated the exercise again. And again.

And again and again.

The six-legged droid watched each move, making sure Maul performed the exercise exactly as Sidious had instructed. Sidious had told Maul that the exercise was designed to build strength, agility, and muscle memory. Sidious had also stressed that if Maul's timing was off and he flipped away from the wall incorrectly, he could wind up with a broken neck.

Maul continued the exercise until the droid told him to stop. As he landed on his feet, he felt his heart hammering within his small chest. He wanted desperately to rest on the floor, but resting was not allowed until the droid said so.

"Your timing has improved," the droid said. Rapidly extending one of its pincer arms, it swiped Maul with an electrode, giving the boy a shock.

Maul bared his teeth and snarled at the droid. Although he knew that the droid was simply carrying out Master Sidious's orders, teaching Maul to be prepared to deal with pain at any moment, he still resented getting shocks when he had not done anything wrong. The droid stared back at Maul through emotionless photoreceptors. Maul could anticipate many things, but he never knew when the droid was about to shock him. The droid was too fast.

However, Maul had learned much during his time with the droid in the training room. The room had special exercise equipment and weapons, as well as computer consoles that had been programmed to educate and challenge Maul's mind and mechanical abilities. He could identify hundreds of star systems, assemble complicated three-dimensional puzzles, and pinpoint the vulnerabilities of nearly every native creature on Mustafar. And in addition to running up walls, he could walk on his hands, climb swiftly up a rope, trot across a taut wire, and leap headfirst through an energy ring and come up standing.

"Go to console three," the droid commanded.

Maul went to the third computer console and seated himself before the computer's holoprojector. As he inserted both hands into the console's grip sockets, he wondered what the test would be about this time.

The holoprojector displayed a sequence of three different star systems and rotated each display so Maul could see the holographic stars and their respective orbiting planets from various angles. Then the computer cut off the projector, leaving Maul staring at empty air. The computer said, "Identify the second, first, and third systems, in that order."

"Malastare, Eriadu, and Denon," Maul answered quickly. He hoped the computer would next ask him to name the trade route that linked all three systems, because he knew the answer was the Hydian Way.

But the computer said, "The Malastare system includes three gas giants. Name the remaining planets that have more than one moon."

"Malastare and . . . Cogalle!" Maul said, his slight delay earning him a sharp sting in the palm of his left hand. Maul was still wincing in pain when the computer's audio speaker erupted with a recorded beast's roar.

"Identify the species," the computer droned.

"Tulrus." Maul suddenly felt searing pain in his right hand, and he corrected himself. "Northern tulrus!"

The questions continued for several minutes. Maul made only three more mistakes. When the computer was done, he removed his aching hands from the console sockets and massaged his knuckles. As he rose from his seat, the six-legged droid said, "Go to the ring."

The droid followed Maul to the ring, a circular platform that was elevated thirty centimeters above the training room floor. Maul hopped onto the platform while the droid ambled over to a nearby rack of weapons and selected a slender staff made of wood. Gripping the staff with a single pincer, the droid climbed onto the platform and faced Maul. "I will attempt to strike you. You will attempt to dodge the strike. Each successful strike or dodge counts as one point. Knocking an opponent off the platform counts as three points. The exercise ends when one of us has scored five points. Understood?"

"Yes." The word was barely out of Maul's mouth when the staff connected with the side of his left leg. He grunted in pain and anger.

"You forgot to jump," the droid said in a mocking tone. "My point."

The droid swung again, this time angling for Maul's right leg. Maul jumped. The droid let the staff's tip bounce off the platform and brought it up sharply to strike the bottom of Maul's right foot. Maul tumbled across the platform and came up standing, his eyes burning with fury at the droid.

"That must have hurt," the droid said. "The next strike will hurt more." The droid made a quick jab toward Maul, but the boy threw his body to the side and rolled, careful not to go over the edge of the platform.

"Your point," the droid said as it tossed the staff into the air. Maul ignored the airborne staff and kept his eyes on the droid. The droid caught the staff with a different pincer, then leaped forward. Maul dived under the droid, and as he somersaulted across the platform, he heard the staff whoosh past his head.

"Your point again," the droid said. "We are tied." The droid tossed the staff back and forth between three pincers, then seized it with a single pincer and rotated its arm so the staff spun like a propeller. The droid increased the speed of the rotation, transforming the staff into a barely visible blur.

Expecting the droid to advance toward him, Maul braced himself to jump away. He was not prepared when the droid threw the spinning staff directly at him, and he felt the slap of hard wood against the side of his face. The staff fell away from Maul and landed between him and the droid.

"I hope you are learning from this," the droid said. "The score is three to two." The droid stepped forward and reached for the staff.

Maul felt a rush of anger. The droid's pincer was still descending for the staff when the weapon leaped from the platform and flew toward Maul. Maul caught the staff with both hands as he glared at the droid.

The droid backed up. Maul held the staff out in front of him. He didn't know how the staff had sailed into his grip, and he wasn't sure what to do next. The droid had not mentioned that the staff could move by itself or said whether Maul would gain points if he obtained the staff or struck back at the droid.

"You've never done *that* before," the droid said, sounding surprised.

Maul didn't know what the droid was talking about. "The staff jumped. I . . . I only caught it."

"I must summon Master Sidious immediately." The droid's photoreceptors blinked and turned yellow as it transmitted a silent signal.

Maul wondered what he had done wrong. Then he wondered whether the droid might be trying to trick him by pretending to contact Sidious, and whether it might be preparing to attack again. The droid's photo-receptors flickered back to red, but it did not budge from its position on the opposite side of the ring. Maul continued clutching the wooden staff, his eyes locked on the droid.

Sidious entered the training room. Maul held tight to the staff but turned to his Master. Facing Maul, Sidious came to a stop at the edge of the elevated platform and said, "Tell me what happened."

"The droid and I were exercising, Master Sidious." Maul held the staff out before him. "This landed in the middle of the ring. Then it . . . it jumped up and landed in my hands."

Sidious nodded as if he understood. "Maul, what did you feel just before the staff jumped up?"

Maul glanced at the droid. "The score was three to two, Master. The droid was winning." He looked at Sidious. "I was thinking that the exercise isn't fair. The droid can hit me, but I can't hit back."

"Few things in life are fair, young one." Lowering his voice, Sidious continued, "But I did not ask you what you were *thinking*. I asked . . . what did you *feel*?"

Maul looked at the droid again. "I felt angry, Master."

Sidious smiled brightly. "Good. Good!" Without taking his eyes off Maul, he turned his head slightly and said to the droid, "Prepare my cruiser."

"Yes, Master Sidious," said the droid as it stepped down from the ring.

"Come along, Maul," Sidious said. "We're going for a ride."

Sidious's cruiser was a sleek vessel with a long prow, its aft area bracketed by angular fins that folded inward during landings. It raced through hyperspace, the dimension of faster-than-light travel. Sidious was on the cruiser's bridge and had left Maul alone, belted into the cruiser's passenger compartment. The boy sat quietly, his feet extending only a few centimeters over the edge of his seat.

Maul peeked through a rectangular viewport to see the luminous cascade of hyperspace. He had been excited to leave Mustafar, but he was also nervous, because he didn't know where his master was taking him or what the purpose of their journey was. Earlier, when they'd boarded the cruiser, Maul had briefly wondered if Sidious intended to take him to a faraway, extrasolar place to kill him. But after some thought, he decided it was unlikely that his Master would *take* him somewhere to kill him. If Sidious wanted him dead, he would not waste time traveling across hyperspace to get the job done.

The journey did not last long. Maul heard the cruiser's hyperdrive engine winding down. He continued gazing through the viewport. A moment later, the bright colors of hyperspace melted away and were replaced by a field of stars. The cruiser banked to port, and Maul saw they had arrived in the orbit of a small planet. He recognized a cluster of stars and realized they were still in the Atravis sector.

The cruiser descended to the planet's surface and landed. Sidious stepped into the passenger compartment, glanced at Maul, and motioned him to get out of his seat. As Maul unclasped his safety belt and lowered himself to the deck, Sidious passed his hand over a wall-mounted control switch, which simultaneously opened the starboard hatch and extended the boarding ramp. Maul followed his Master out of the cruiser.

"Welcome to Tosste," Sidious said.

A murky yellow sky hung over the bluish-gray terrain. Maul gazed across a wide area of mostly flat land and noticed some strangely angular rock formations in the distance. The ground was covered by sporadic clumps of stones and boulders. Maul saw no sign of movement.

"Take a good look," Sidious said. "We are standing upon what was once the bottom of an ocean. If it ever had a name, that name was lost to time many eons ago. Here, the only historic records are the geographic evidence." Sidious took a few steps away from Maul and looked toward the horizon. "It's hard to believe that Tosste was once home to billions of life-forms. While life on other worlds evolved and reached for the stars, Tosste's inhabitants were never so inspired. They stayed here. They died here. And what is their legacy? Nothing but fossils." He shook his head sadly. "To live without leaving a mark is a terrible thing. To die forgotten is even worse." He turned to face Maul. "It is . . . irresponsible."

Sidious's words chilled Maul. Was his Master implying that he was irresponsible? He wasn't sure. He stood very still and remained silent.

Sidious looked at the horizon again. "Walk with me."

Leaving the cruiser behind, they proceeded to a nearby outcropping of bedrock, which was bordered by a broad field covered by small stones. The tops of a few large boulders loomed over the stones. Sidious and Maul stopped at the edge of the bedrock. Surveying the stones, Sidious said, "What do you see?"

"I see rocks, Master Sidious."

Sidious frowned. Then he pointed to the center of the field of stones and said, "Go stand over there."

Maul always felt especially vulnerable when he could not see his Master, but he did as he was told, stepping across the stones until he reached the designated spot. He stopped.

"Turn around."

Maul turned to face his Master. Sidious stood with his legs apart, his hands clasped behind his back. Sidious said, "I suspect that every creature that ever lived on Tosste did not think much about rocks either. I had hoped that you would be smarter. I'll ask you again. What do you see, spread out on the ground all around you?"

Maul's yellow eyes darted back and forth. He saw only rocks. Some were pebbles, others large stones, and there were the tops of a few boulders. As ever, he did not want to disappoint his Master, but he did not know any other answer than the one he had already given. Returning his gaze to his Master's face, he said hesitantly, "I see rocks, Master Sidious. Thousands of rocks."

Something hard slammed into Maul's left shoulder blade. He ducked as he spun to confront his attacker, and as he moved, he saw the object that had struck him. It was a stone, which fell on the rocks near his feet.

Maul looked across the bluish-gray landscape. Not a trace of movement. No one had been standing behind him.

Another stone smashed into Maul's right bicep. He grunted as he spun again, this time to look back at his Master.

Sidious had not moved. His hands remained behind his back. But from the trace of a wicked smile on the Man's face, Maul suddenly knew the stones weren't flying by themselves.

Lifting his gaze to the sky, Sidious said, "The creatures that once roamed this now dead ocean, they lacked imagination. Ultimately, that is why they all perished. They failed to see . . . potential."

Potential?! Maul suddenly sensed a small stone whizzing toward his head. He raised his hand to deflect the stone as he ducked, but the stone sailed past his fingers and clipped one of his horns. "Weapons!" Maul shouted. "I see weapons!"

Sidious sighed. "The correct response is . . ."

"I see weapons, Master Sidious!"

"Not fast enough," Sidious said as a stone smashed into Maul's lower back.

Maul crouched and grabbed the nearest rock. He no sooner lifted it from the ground than he felt it burning into his hand. He yelped as he reflexively opened his fingers and let the rock fall. How could the rock have generated such intense heat? He suspected it was his Master's trickery.

"Oh, come now," Sidious said impatiently. "Almost any humanoid with fingers can do *that*."

Two stones smacked into the backs of Maul's legs, knocking him off his feet. He gasped as his small body fell on the hard rocks. Looking up, he saw two more stones rise from the ground. He twisted his body fast, trying to shield his head.

"Maybe I was wrong about you being special," Sidious said as he watched the two stones strike Maul. "Maybe you are just as useless and stupid as —"

Several stones hurtled up from the ground around Maul's body. Battered and bruised, Maul glared at Sidious. The stones sailed through the air, all heading straight for his Master.

Sidious whipped one hand out from behind his back and extended it before him. The rocks stopped in mid-flight, then fell to the ground. "Is that the best you can do?" Sidious sneered. "I should crush you now."

Maul snarled as he jumped to his feet and swiped at the air with both hands. Dozens of rocks launched up from around Maul and raced toward Sidious. Sidious moved his other hand out from behind his back and flexed his fingers. The approaching rocks rebounded as if they had struck an invisible shield.

Some of the rebounding rocks fell near Maul's feet.

Surprised, he stumbled back. He wasn't sure what had just happened.

"Well done, young one," Sidious said as the dust settled around him. "You passed the test." He began walking slowly toward Maul. "The droid told me that you moved the staff without touching it, but I had to see what you could do with my own eyes. Did you feel it? Did you feel the power of your anger?"

"Yes, Master Sidious," Maul responded automatically. Until that moment, he had not known that he had in fact been responsible for making the staff jump up from the ring in the training room. He looked at the rocks on the ground. He hadn't given any thought to launching them through the air either. He had just . . . done it.

Sidious came to a stop beside Maul. Looking down at the boy, he smiled and said, "I want to show you something. Stay close to my side."

Sidious extended his arms. Maul heard a rumbling sound and then saw stones sliding and bouncing away from two of the larger boulders that were about fifteen meters away, partially embedded in the ancient seabed. He realized the two boulders were rising slowly, as if an invisible giant were pulling them up from the ground. Dust and dirt fell away from both boulders as they tore free from the planet's surface. Maul watched with wonder as they ascended several meters into the air.

Sidious flicked his fingers. The two boulders launched even higher. He flexed his wrists, and the boulders spun around together like a pair of enormous dancers. He moved his hands apart, and the distance between the spinning boulders increased. Then Sidious clapped his hands together. Still spinning, the boulders swung into each other and collided with a thunderous crash. Shattered chunks and bits of rock exploded in all directions.

Watching the rocky debris rain down from the yellow sky, Maul said, "How, Master Sidious? How?"

"With the Force," Sidious said solemnly.

Maul looked at Sidious, hoping desperately to learn more.

"The Force is an energy field," Sidious continued. "It radiates throughout the galaxy. It is everywhere. It flows between all living things and every inanimate object. It is between us. It is between the stones, the cruiser over there . . ." He gestured to his starship. ". . . everywhere. Some beings—some very fortunate beings who are strong with the Force from the day they are born—are able to manipulate and control the Force. They can use its power to do incredible things. You and I, Maul, are such beings."

Maul looked at the two holes in the ground where the boulders had recently stood, then at the remains of the boulders strewn across the area. Knowing that such destructive power flowed through him made him feel very pleased. He smiled.

Seeing the boy's expression, Sidious said, "You and

I shall return to this world often. Here I will teach you the ways of the Force. But because the Force can be very dangerous to those who don't fully understand it, there is one rule you must obey. You must never reveal your powers to anyone else until I say you are ready. For now, the Force is our secret. No one else may know about it. Do you understand?"

"Yes, Master Sidious," Maul said, then quickly added, "But the droid saw the staff jump in the ring. Does the droid know . . . about the Force?"

"The droid knows just enough to help you in your training."

"Master Sidious, I meant . . . can the droid *use* the Force?"

Sidious chuckled. "No, boy. The droid is just a machine. Machines can't use the Force. But remember, the droid is a teaching tool. You are not allowed to use the Force against the droid."

"Yes, Master Sidious." Maul bit his lip.

"You have another question?"

"Master, you said I must not reveal my powers to anyone else. Who is 'anyone else'?"

Sidious pursed his lips, then said, "So far, you have lived a sheltered life, but it is only a matter of time before you encounter other beings. Most life-forms are oblivious to the Force. They don't realize that the Force binds the galaxy together. They cannot draw power from the Force." Sidious patted Maul's bruised shoulder. "Most people fear what they don't understand."

"Master Sidious, do you have to be angry to make the Force work?"

"Not all the time," Sidious said. "But it helps."

Maul stared at the ground. "Are there others like us, Master?"

Sidious knelt beside Maul so their eyes were on the same level. "Listen very carefully, boy. There are others who use the Force. But they are not . . . like . . . us."

CHAPTER THREE

"Tell me what you know about the Jedi, Maul."

Sidious and Maul were inside the training room in the Mustafar facility. Sidious stood beside the six-legged droid. The droid was operating a winch that controlled a long metal cable that extended to the ceiling. Maul was hanging upside down, his small body wrapped in chains, dangling from the winch's cable. Eight meters below Maul's inverted head was a large open vat of acid.

"I know only what I've learned from datatapes, Master," Maul gasped in response. Speaking was difficult because of the chain that was drawn tightly across his throat. His wrists were manacled behind his back, and as he struggled to free his hands, the droid began ticking at the winch's crank, slowly lowering Maul from the ceiling. He calculated that at the rate he was descending, he had about ten minutes to escape. "The Jedi," he continued, "are warriors who are strong with the Force. They use weapons called lightsabers. They are based on the planet Coruscant. They serve the Galactic Republic as peacekeepers."

Sidious smiled. "That's according to the data-tapes. But what I am about to tell you is the *truth*." He stepped away from the droid and began walking in a wide circle around the vat of acid. "The Jedi Order was founded twenty-five thousand years ago by a group of beings who were strong with the Force. Before the Jedi Order, such Force-sensitive beings were isolated instead of united. Some were regarded as wizards. Others as demons. There were not many. Nearly all were considered unique on their own worlds. They were strong, powerful individuals. Free to live and die as they wished.

"But the Jedi Order changed all that. They started by analyzing the Force to understand its power. They found it had a wide spectrum that was influenced by emotions. They debated their findings. Over time, they discovered there was much they could not under-stand, and they chose to believe what they wanted to believe. They believed some mysteries were best left unsolved. They believed that the Force itself was testing them. Like narrow-minded, superstitious children, they *created* explanations for the Force.

"And rather than embrace the full spectrum of the Force, the Jedi ignored the infinite shades of gray that stretched between light and darkness. They declared the light side of the Force was good and the dark was evil. To them, there could be no in-between, no middle ground." Sidious let out an exasperated sigh. "It's one thing to examine an energy field that permeates the galaxy. But to give an energy field characteristics of good and evil? One might as well say, 'That cloud wants to protect us from solar radiation, but that other cloud wants to strike us dead with lightning.'

"And then the Jedi declared that to be born with Force powers was not a gift or a curse. They insisted it was a *calling*. They proclaimed the Force should never be used for selfish purposes, that all Force-sensitive beings were obligated to use their powers for the benefit of others." Sidious shook his head ruefully. "Many Force users joined the Jedi Order, but the Jedi were not satisfied with their numbers. They sought out the so-called wizards and demons, and gave them three options. Join the Jedi, cease using Force powers, or die."

Sidious paused to look at Maul. Maul had traveled almost halfway to the acid vat. He had already wriggled his left hand out of the manacles and was now working to free his right.

"Join the Jedi," Sidious said. "Relinquish your individuality and freedom, and fight only when the Jedi tell you to fight. *Cease using Force powers*. One might as well tell an ordinary life-form to stop living. *Die*. . . . Well, I don't believe that requires an explanation. And

so, the Jedi not only increased their ranks but destroyed those who disagreed with them.

"The Jedi convinced the Galactic Republic that they could be the Republic's guardians. The Jedi Order thrived, and they expanded their authority beyond the Core Worlds. They used their powers and their lightsabers to vanquish those who opposed them. For many millennia, the Jedi were unchallenged. And they grew confident. So confident that they could hardly imagine the possibility that some Jedi did not *want* to be Jedi.

"But almost seven thousand years ago, a group of Jedi rebelled against their own kind. The battle that ensued lasted one hundred years. The so-called peace-keepers believed the war was over when they banished the surviving rebels to an uncharted region of the Outer Rim Territories. But the exiles did not meet their end in the Outer Rim. They discovered the Sith species, and they used their powers to conquer the Sith. They became the Sith Lords."

Sidious raised his right hand slowly and examined his fingernails. "Maul, in your studies of history and the galaxy, have you ever come across any datatapes about the Sith Lords?"

Maul had freed his other hand and was now bent at the waist, lifting his torso so he could work on the chains that were biting into his ankles. He glanced at Sidious and replied, "No, Master."

"That's because the Jedi destroyed many records."

Sidious flexed his fingers, then lowered his hand to his side. "The early Sith Lords had one ruler, the Dark Lord of the Sith, and their armies were legion. Eventually, they discovered the path back to Republic space and fought the Jedi in the Great Hyperspace War. They lost. But the Sith Lord Naga Sadow survived and managed to preserve his spirit in a tomb.

"Hundreds of years after Sadow's death, a Jedi named Freedon Nadd revived Sadow's spirit. Nadd became the new Dark Lord, and he used his powers to conquer the world Onderon. Following Sadow's example, Freedon Nadd also preserved his own spirit in a tomb. Many centuries later, Nadd's spirit was awakened by the Jedi Exar Kun, who became the next Dark Lord. Exar Kun allied with a wayward Jedi named Ulic Qel-Droma, and together they established a Sith Order ruled by two, a Master and apprentice. These two Dark Lords of the Sith failed to conquer the Jedi because they wound up fighting each other, as did their successors, another pair of former Jedi, named Revan and Malak. History, it seemed, was repeating itself." Sidious looked at Maul. "Am I going too fast for you?"

"No, Master." He was having some difficulty with the chains at his ankles, and he was close enough to the acid that the smell of it was burning his nostrils.

"I neglected to mention that Revan and Malak renamed themselves Darth Revan and Darth Malak. Some historians believe Darth is a contraction of *dark* and *Sith*, while others suggest it was a corruption of *daritha*, an ancient Rakatan word for 'emperor.' In any event, the honorific Darth was introduced to the Sith Lords. Following Revan and Malak, other former Jedi assumed the mantle of Dark Lords . . . and none learned from their predecessors' mistakes.

"History took a different turn about a thousand years ago, when yet another former Jedi, named Kaan, rose through the ranks of a new order of self-proclaimed Sith Lords. After Kaan became Dark Lord and united thousands of followers, he tried to avoid the mistakes of his predecessors. To avoid infighting, Kaan proposed that all Sith Lords were equals. Kaan's army became known as the Brotherhood of Darkness."

The droid's pincer lost its grip on the winch's crank. The metal cable slipped half a meter before the droid stopped the crank with another pincer. Maul's body fell and jerked violently in the air. He did not cry out but stayed focused on his shackles as he resumed his slow descent to the acid, which was now closer than he'd anticipated.

"At the Battle of Ruusan," Sidious continued, "the Jedi overwhelmed the Brotherhood of Darkness. With surrender not an option, Kaan crafted a Force-fueled weapon called a thought bomb, which would destroy all Force users within its blast radius. The thought bomb killed Kaan, his army, and many Jedi.

"But one Sith Lord survived. Darth Bane. Bane knew

that Kaan had been wrong to believe in strength in numbers. Bane knew that too many Sith Lords resulted in too much envy and competition. Everyone wanted to be the leader, the Dark Lord, and nearly everyone was willing to kill other members of the Brotherhood in order to achieve that goal. And so Bane established the Rule of Two. One Sith Master. One Sith apprentice." Sidious looked at Maul, who was still struggling with the chains, and added, "Any more would be to lose control."

Maul broke free, gripped the chain, and swung out, twisting his body in midair so he landed on his feet beside the acid-filled vat. He faced Sidious. Although he did not know his own age, he was now nearly as tall as Sidious's hip. He said, "Master, do the Sith Lords still exist?"

"I would not rule out the possibility," Sidious said. "Just remember, the Jedi do not tolerate Force users outside their order. It is because of them that you and I live in secret. Had they discovered you on Dathomir before I, they would have attempted to mold you into one of their own. A mindless, obedient servant for the Republic. Had they failed, they would have destroyed you. Now that you know the truth, how would you describe the Jedi?"

Maul thought for a moment, then said, "They are cowards, Master. Cowards and tyrants. They are weak."

Sidious smiled. "Do not underestimate the Jedi. Even though they have a fatal flaw, they are formidable."

"What is their fatal flaw, Master?"

"Compassion." Sidious looked at the chain that Maul had left swinging back and forth over the vat of acid. "You took much too long to free yourself. You will do the exercise again. But this time, the droid will lower the chain faster."

Maul bowed. "Yes, Master."

CHAPTER FOUR

"I have a surprise for you, Maul," Sidious said as he handed a cylindrical metal object to the boy. "Do you know what it is?"

"Yes, Master Sidious," Maul said as his eyes widened with awe. "It's a lightsaber. I've seen them on holovids."

They were on the planet Tosste, standing at the center of a grove of gnarled black trees at the edge of a desolate field, not far from Sidious's cruiser. Sidious had been bringing Maul to Tosste regularly over the past year, as the wide-open spaces allowed opportunities for training that could not be conducted on Mustafar's volcanic surface. Maul would run for great distances and perform long jumps. Under his Master's supervision, he fired ranged weapons and explosives and also practiced using the Force to lift and move objects. Maul never knew when Sidious would bring him to Tosste, or what plans Sidious might have for him there, but he always looked forward to any trip away from Mustafar.

Even if he was required to do rigorous exercises at their destination, he still regarded such excursions as adventures.

Maul turned the lightsaber over in his hand, testing its grip. He held it away from his body, just as he had seen Jedi hold their weapons in the educational holovids he'd studied in Mustafar's training room.

Sidious said, "What do you think?"

"It weighs less than I thought, Master."

"It's a training saber. The same kind used by Jedi younglings."

Maul wondered how his Master had obtained the weapon. But he didn't ask.

"That's the activation switch," Sidious said, pointing to a green switch on the lightsaber's grip. "Press it with your thumb."

Maul thumbed the switch. A brilliant amber blade of pure energy flashed out from the emitter at the end of the grip, accompanied by a loud hum. Holding tight to the grip with both hands, Maul could feel the power of the weapon. He grinned, unable to conceal his delight.

"That's it," Sidious said. "Feel the energy? Now, go on. . . ." Sidious made a waving gesture. "Test it."

Stepping away from Sidious, Maul made a tentative jab at the air, then swung the lightsaber back and forth. The weapon's hum changed pitch as the blade moved. Maul also noticed how the lightsaber illuminated the surrounding trees. He shifted his stance and faced a thick, twisted limb that jutted out from one of the gnarled trees. He looked to his Master.

"I know what you're thinking," Sidious said. "Will a training saber cut through that tree?" Sidious shrugged. "A Jedi would hesitate to share this information, but . . . well, I am not a Jedi. Training sabers *can* be adjusted for greater power, but the process is a bit time-consuming. You might try this instead." Sidious reached into a deep pocket, removed another lightsaber, and held it out to Maul.

Maul looked at the weapon in his Master's hand. He switched off the training saber, barely noticing how its humming sound fizzled out, and exchanged it for the proffered lightsaber. He noticed that the grip was heavier than the training saber's. He thumbed the activation switch.

A red beam flashed from the weapon's emitter and hummed to life. Maul immediately sensed that the blade was even more powerful. He looked again at the gnarled tree's limb, then glanced at Sidious. Sidious nodded. Maul jumped forward and sent the lightsaber's blade in a downward slash through the limb. He had expected at least to hear some kind of a cracking noise as the limb separated from the tree, but the blade sliced through the limb with a continuous whoosh, as effortlessly as a bird's wing slicing through air. And then the severed limb crashed loudly against the ground.

"Well done," Sidious said.

Maul swept the blade through the fallen limb again and again. With each sweep, he marveled at how cleanly the blade sliced through wood. From what he'd seen on the holovids, he knew the weapon was just as effective with dense rock and thick metal.

After he had reduced the tree's limb to diced chunks, he turned his attention to the tree's trunk and kept swinging. Sidious did not stop him.

When Maul finished with the tree, he reluctantly returned the lightsaber to his Master. Sidious said, "Now, it is time for you to meditate."

"Yes, Master." Maul turned and walked out of the grove, heading into the neighboring field. Sidious had trained him to relax his mind and body by closing his eyes and visualizing a dark, comfortable nothingness, leaving himself open to the power of the Force. Maul enjoyed meditating. It always left him feeling stronger.

He had taken only a few steps into the field when his foot struck something that moved. He looked down and saw a dinko.

From his studies, Maul knew about dinkos. They were nasty palm-sized creatures—not that anyone would want to pick one up. The dinko had powerful, perpetually moving rear legs that were naturally equipped with serrated spurs, two pairs of grasping claws on its chest, and extremely sharp fangs. The grasping claws were especially feared, as dinkos used them to grab on to a victim's finger or nose and would not let go unless surgically removed or killed. Even more notorious was the dinko's stinking venom. Because dinkos were native to Proxima Dibal, a planet situated on the far side of the galaxy, Maul wondered how a dinko had ever arrived on Tosste.

The dinko sprayed venom directly into Maul's face. Maul flinched as the venom hit him, stinging his eyes. He howled, then brought his boot down hard on the creature. He felt a certain satisfaction as he removed his heel from the crushed dinko and inspected its remains. Pleased at the way he had dealt with the dinko, he turned to look back at his Master.

"You flinched," Sidious said without pleasure. "You were afraid of the dinko?"

"Yes, Master. But I controlled my fear." Maul stated his claim with great certainty.

Sidious responded with a nod. But from experience, Maul knew his Master was displeased. He also knew a punishment would come.

They returned to Mustafar. Maul ate his evening meal as usual. He was not confined to a sensory-deprivation suit or forced to sleep on a hard floor. The atmosphere controls in his quarters were not turned off.

No punishment came the next day, or the next, or anytime soon. Eventually, Maul forgot about the dinko incident on Tosste.

And then one night, after a particularly exhausting series of exercises, Maul went to his quarters in the training room. After he entered his quarters, the door hissed closed behind him. He undressed in the darkness. Then he turned back the coverlet that was draped over his sleep mat, and a dinko jumped straight at him.

Maul was startled. He batted the dinko away but missed when he tried to stomp it to death. He hesitated, fearing that its claws would tear into his bare foot.

Another dinko jumped out from a corner. That dinko was followed by another, and then another. Maul realized the room was filled with the creatures.

The boy ran to the door and slapped the button to open it. The door remained shut. He tried to turn on the lights. The lights stayed off. In the darkness, one dinko jumped onto Maul's shoulder and dug its claws into his ear. Another latched on to one of his toes. Maul cried and screamed as he tried to shake them off. The dinkos sprayed their venom and blinded him. The stench was nauseating. Maul threw his body against the walls in a desperate attempt to crush them.

It took Maul almost an hour to kill all the dinkos. When he was done, he passed out on the floor of his gore-filled quarters.

The door did not open until the next morning. It slid back to reveal Sidious standing in the doorway. He looked at Maul's inflamed skin, swollen eyes, and bloody hands and feet. He said, "Do not flinch again."

Maul understood. He learned. He obeyed. And after his test against the dinkos, he never ever flinched.

CHAPTER FIVE

"Hold still," said the six-legged droid as it wiped blood from Maul's rib cage.

Maul squirmed on the edge of the metal table and said through clenched teeth, "You have the bone-knitter on the wrong setting."

"No, I don't," said the droid as it moved the medical tool deeper into the wound on Maul's left side. Then it repeated, "Hold still."

They were in the expansive training room in the Mustafar facility. Five months had passed since Sidious had begun training Maul in lightsaber combat. In recent days, the droid had been teaching him how to throw blades with great accuracy, and also how to dodge and catch blades that the droid threw at him while he did his exercises. As for running up walls and flipping backward to the floor, Maul had become so adept that he could do it with his eyes closed. However, he had been unprepared when, a few minutes earlier, he had kicked away from the wall and straight into one of the droid's waiting pincers.

The droid set aside the bone-knitter, then sprayed an exotic salve over Maul's skin. "You should be relieved that Master Sidious was not present when you allowed me to break two of your ribs," the droid said. "He would have been most displeased."

"I didn't *allow* you to break my ribs," Maul said as the droid began wrapping a bandage around his torso. "I thought you were standing near me to watch me exercise."

"Well, you know what Master Sidious would say." Adjusting the pitch and tone on its vocabulator to perfectly mimic Sidious, the droid rasped, *"To leave yourself vulnerable is an open invitation to death."* Switching back to its usual voice, the droid said, "Still, I'm sorry. I didn't mean to hurt you. It was an accident."

The droid's words surprised Maul. The droid had never before imitated Sidious or apologized to Maul. No one had ever apologized to Maul before. Maul said, "I will be more careful next time." Then he looked at the droid's red photoreceptors and added, "Do you have a name? I learned from the computer that many droids have names."

The droid responded with a chittering noise that sounded like a cross between grinding gears and laughter. "I was programmed and engineered for training and discipline. My designation is TD-D9. If you wish, you may call me Deenine."

"Thank you, Master Deenine."

The droid chattered again. "No. Just Deenine."

"Oh." Maul was suddenly curious about the droid. "Have you always been on Mustafar, Deenine?"

"No, I've visited other worlds. I've been to Coruscant, Naboo, and . . ." The droid flicked its photoreceptors to face Maul and said, "Forget I said that. You didn't hear that from me."

"I won't tell."

"Good. You may put on a shirt now."

Maul eased himself off the table and reached for the shirt he'd been wearing earlier. It now had a hole in it, where the droid's pincer had torn through the fabric, and was stained with blood. But before Maul could pick up the shirt, the droid snatched it and added, "You may put on a *clean* shirt."

Maul walked across the training room and stepped through a doorway to enter his quarters. Nearly twice the size of his former room, his quarters had a lighting system that he could control, a sleep mat with a coverlet, and a small trunk for storing clothes. It also had a door that he could open from inside or outside. Except when Sidious or the droid locked him up, he was generally free to go to the training room at any time.

But there was one thing his quarters lacked. A window.

Maul's former room had been in almost every way unmemorable, but it had had a view. He had spent many hours scanning the rocks for Mustafarians and their lava flea mounts, but his memories of that time seemed increasingly dim. Back then he had wished for a view of a different world. Now he wondered if he would ever see the lava flowing into the fiery sea again.

He reached into his trunk and removed a clean black shirt. He thought it was strangely kind of the droid to suggest that he should wear a clean shirt. He had learned about friendship from an educational recording, which showed how some creatures lived and worked together without harming each other. He wondered if the droid might be his friend.

Maul pulled the shirt on and felt a stab of pain at his left side. He gnashed his teeth and took a series of quick and shallow breaths through his nose, careful not to expand his lungs so much that they'd make his ribs hurt. He wondered how long it would take for his ribs to heal.

As he exited his quarters, he said, "Deenine, when will my ribs — ?" He stopped short when he saw Sidious standing beside the droid. He had not heard Sidious enter the training room.

Sidious was holding Maul's torn, bloodied shirt. Sidious looked from the droid to Maul and said, "Maul, tell me what happened."

Maul glanced at the droid, then said, "I was training, Master Sidious. I ran up the wall, and when I jumped away from it, Deenine stuck out a pincer and broke two of my ribs. It was an accident. Deenine didn't mean to hurt me."

"Really?" Sidious said. "I didn't know the droid was capable of doing anything accidentally. Or that you and . . . 'Deenine' were on familiar terms." Still holding the torn shirt, Sidious faced the droid. "Is it true? Did you injure Maul by accident?"

"No, Master Sidious," the droid said. "When Maul leaped from the wall, I raised my pincer knowing that it would break his ribs if he did not adjust his body in midair."

"So why did Maul think it was an accident?"

"Because I told him it was an accident, Master Sidious."

"In other words, you lied?"

"Yes, Master Sidious. I lied."

Sidious looked back at Maul. "Have you learned anything from this, Maul?"

Maul glared at the droid. He felt betrayed and angry. He could not believe he had trusted the droid. Looking back at Sidious, he said, "Yes, Master Sidious. I have learned I must not trust anyone. I must be ready to attack and fight back at all times."

"Excellent," Sidious said as he tossed the torn shirt onto the metal table. "And because 'at all times' includes right now, you will now repeat the exercise you were doing with the droid. Only this time, you will avoid breaking any more ribs." Sidious gestured to the nearest wall. "Begin at once."

The droid made a chittering noise, then said, "I beg your pardon, Master Sidious, but I suggest you allow Maul's ribs to heal before he attempts to—"

"I do not recall asking for anyone's opinion," Sidious said, keeping his eyes on Maul. "Especially an opinion from someone who is an admitted liar."

The droid offered no response.

"Now, Maul," Sidious continued, "what *you* said is absolutely true. You *must* be ready to attack and fight back at all times. If your bones were broken during a fight with an actual enemy, do you think that enemy would wait for you to heal before attacking you again?"

"No, Master Sidious."

Sidious gestured again at the wall. "The droid will stand near while you run up the wall and leap back to the floor. At any given moment, the droid might attack. And the droid will not hold back because you are already injured. Do you understand?"

"Yes, Master Sidious."

Glancing at the droid, Sidious added, "Do you understand?"

"Yes, Master Sidious." The droid shuffled over to the wall and waited for Maul to run.

Maul went straight for the wall. He tried to ignore his broken ribs, but with each step, he felt the sharp pain intensify. He did not cry out. He would give neither his Master nor the droid the satisfaction of hearing him cry. He was angry at both of them, especially at the droid. He let the pain feed his anger, let his anger feed his strength. He ran up the wall several steps before he kicked off, keeping his left arm close to his side to prevent the droid from striking his rib cage again.

Maul did not think the droid would attack on his first flip away from the wall. He was still in midair when the droid lashed out with violent force. Maul felt his left arm snap as the droid's swat knocked him clear across the room. Maul crashed into the opposite wall and then everything went dark.

When Maul opened his eyes, he was lying on the sleep mat in his quarters. His upper left arm was heavily bandaged. He pushed himself up carefully. Every part of his body hurt. Moving his right hand over to his left side, he felt that the bandages were wet with blood. And then he noticed a familiar shadow fall across the floor from the doorway.

"Master Sidious is very displeased," said TD-D9 as it stepped into Maul's quarters. "Very displeased with both of us."

Maul noticed the droid was carrying a medkit. He looked away from the droid and faced the wall. "Go away and leave me alone."

"Your bandages need to be changed."

"I said go away!"

"But if don't apply bacta, your wounds won't heal. They'll become infected and—"

"You keep your claws off me! I'll take care of myself!"

The droid chattered a mechanical sigh, then placed the medkit on the floor beside Maul's sleep mat. But as the droid retreated for the doorway, it paused and said, "There's something I want to tell you, Maul. I want you to know that I—"

"I don't care what you have to say," Maul interrupted. "You're a liar."

"That's right, I lied," TD-D9 said. "But I didn't lie to you. I lied to Master Sidious."

Maul listened.

"When I told Master Sidious that I lied to you, that was a lie. The truth is that I accidentally broke your ribs. But if I had told Master Sidious the truth, he would have destroyed me."

Maul looked away from the wall and scowled at the droid. "Are you also going to tell me that breaking my arm was an 'accident' too?"

"No, Maul. I did that on purpose. It was the only way to immediately end the exercise. I did not want to prolong your pain. I did not want to hurt you. I hit you so hard that I knocked you out because I did not want Master Sidious to hurt you more than that."

"You broke my arm!"

"I'm sorry for that. But I believe Master Sidious would have done worse."

Maul thought about this, then said, "What makes you think I won't tell Master Sidious that you lied to him?"

"If you do, he'll replace me with another droid. Maybe he'll replace me with a droid who actually enjoys inflicting pain." The droid sighed again. "I told you I'm sorry. Your bandages really do need to be changed."

"I'll do it myself," Maul said sullenly. "I don't want to talk with you anymore."

The droid walked out through the doorway, leaving the medkit behind. Maul looked at the medkit and wondered if his Master or the droid had done something to the bandages so he would be in even more pain after he put them on.

He faced the wall that was opposite the doorway. He thought of the tapestries that decorated the walls in Sidious's chamber, and how one tapestry concealed the passage to the training room. He wondered if a secret passage might be hidden behind the wall right in front of him.

Too weak to walk, he crawled over to the wall and pressed his right hand against it. The wall did not yield to his pressure, but as he removed his hand from its surface, he saw he had left traces of blood. He had forgotten that he had touched his wounded side earlier.

He recalled his Master's words on Tosste: *To live*

without leaving a mark is a terrible thing. To die forgotten is even worse.

Maul reached to his wound again, then extended his index finger and drew a vertical smear of blood directly onto the wall. He then drew another vertical line to the right of the first one and then added two horizontal lines that connected with the vertical lines to form a rectangle. Next Maul concentrated on the area within the rectangle. It took him just over twenty minutes to fill the rectangle with a drawing of what he remembered of Mustafar from his view through the window of his old room. By the time he was done, he felt very tired.

Maul crawled back onto his sleep mat and lay down again, positioning his head so he could look at the drawing he'd made with his own blood. He wished he could leap into the drawing and run away. He was still looking at the drawing as he drifted off to sleep.

When Maul next awoke, he was still in his quarters but dressed in fresh bandages. He realized that TD-D9 must have taken care of him while he was sleeping. He also noticed that all the walls had been cleaned, and that his drawing had been completely erased.

TD-D9 appeared in the doorway. Maul frowned at the droid. TD-D9 said, "Master Sidious instructed me to bring you to him now."

Maul decided it was best to not mention the drawing. He thought it would hurt for him to get up, but he felt surprisingly better than he had earlier. He suspected the droid had given him medicine while he had slept. Leaving his quarters, he followed the droid out through the training room and up through the passage that led to Sidious's private chamber. As they walked, Maul said, "Deenine, do you know if Master Sidious intends to kill me?"

"I don't think so," TD-D9 replied. "He has invested so much time into your training that I suspect he wants you to stay alive. But I don't think you should have drawn that picture on the wall."

Maul's steps did not falter as he continued following the droid, but his mind was suddenly racing. He wondered what consequence he might suffer because of the drawing. He said, "Did Master Sidious see the drawing?"

"I don't know. I erased it right after you fell asleep."

"Then how would he even know about the drawing . . . unless you told him?"

"I didn't have to tell him," TD-D9 said. "You should know by now, child . . . Sidious knows everything."

Before Maul could ask the droid any more questions, they exited the passage. They found Sidious standing beside the hovering watery orb. Maul noticed that the orb had been restocked with living fish. He spotted the two survivors of the previous menagerie lurking at the bottom of the orb. The big gray fish was looking away from Maul, but the smaller one with red and black stripes had one yellow eye fixed on the boy.

The striped fish had grown larger since the last time Maul had seen him.

Sidious looked at Maul, then frowned. "Tell me, do you think I've been rough on you?"

"No, Master Sidious."

"You do understand that your training serves a greater purpose?"

"Yes, Master Sidious."

Sidious smiled. "I suspect that others might question my teaching methods, but I am glad you do not. I can assure you that you are an excellent pupil. Not once did you cry out during your recent exercises. Not once. You are an exceptionally strong boy, and you are becoming stronger every day."

"Thank you, Master Sidious," Maul said as he bowed, ignoring the pain of his aching ribs.

Sidious raised his eyebrows. "Now, there is another matter that has come to my attention. Evidently, you are not entirely satisfied with your quarters. You miss the view that you once had of Mustafar. Is this correct?"

Without hesitation, Maul replied, "I was not thinking clearly when I drew a picture on my wall, Master Sidious."

"You have no wish to return to your former room?"

"No, Master."

Sidious smiled again. "I didn't think you would want to go back to that little box. But if you missed the sight of Mustafar, you should have told me. After all, seeing

Mustafar is something that can be easily arranged." Sidious waved a finger at TD-D9.

The droid responded by firing a tranquilizer dart into Maul's neck. Maul collapsed to the floor. TD-D9 did not attempt to break his fall.

A loud roar awakened Maul. He coughed as he inhaled hot, acrid fumes, and his eyes stung as he opened them. He saw darkness overhead, and for a moment, he thought he was in a cave. But then he noticed the darkness was moving and alive with dancing bright red stars. And he suddenly knew what he was really looking at.

Dark clouds. And drifting, burning ashes.

He pushed himself up. He was on a broad slab of rock on Mustafar's surface. The loud roaring sound came from a nearby rocky vent that was spewing lava. He didn't know how long he'd been outside or even how far he was from Sidious's facility. But he knew he had not arrived at this place on his own.

He looked around. He saw no sign of TD-D9 or Sidious, or of any kind of shelter. Although they had not taken away the clothes and bandages he was wearing, they had not left him with any provisions. But he did have something to his advantage. He had his training.

Maul was not scared. He felt free. He could live or perish on this hostile world without anyone to tell him what to do. And then he realized he was not in any way eager to die. He became resolved to survive. He would do anything and everything necessary to stay alive.

He saw a dark shape move past the lava vent. Crouching low to the ground, ignoring the pain from his ribs and left arm, he watched with wonder as a tall, masked Mustafarian rode by on a massive six-legged lava flea. Two more flea-mounted Mustafarians followed.

Maul had no idea where the Mustafarians were headed, whether they were going to a mining camp or back to their remote village. He would track them, find their food, and steal it. If it became necessary to kill them to ensure his own survival, he would gather rocks to strike them dead or strangle them with his own bandages and broken bones. And then he would find his way back to Sidious and prove that he was indeed a strong boy. He would prove that he feared nothing.

He would earn the respect of his Master.

The three Mustafarians moved off. Maul followed them.

CHAPTER SIX

"Ah, you have returned," Sidious said to Maul, who stood before him in the tapestry-decorated chamber in the Mustafar facility. Sidious was holding a small container of food pellets, which he had been gently pushing into the hovering watery orb to feed the fish. Maul's head was covered with soot and dirt, and his torso was adorned with ill-fitting, bloodstained Mustafarian armor. Looking at the armor, Sidious smiled. "I see you kept busy during your little outing."

The spider-legged droid TD-D9 stood a short distance behind Maul. The droid's right front leg was missing, and one of its left legs was mangled. "I found him outside, Master Sidious," TD-D9 said, "not far from the landing pad. He'd set a trap. I walked right into it." Raising one of its pincer arms, the droid held out the shattered remains of its front right leg. "Maul could have destroyed me."

Sidious set aside the fish food and looked at Maul

skeptically. "Is this true? You could have destroyed the droid?"

"Yes, Master Sidious," Maul replied.

"Then why didn't you?"

Maul tilted his chin toward the droid. "Because I wanted to bring this thing back to you in pieces."

Sidious smiled again. "Maul, do you know how long you were running around on Mustafar's surface?"

Maul grimaced. "I'm not certain, Master Sidious. I fell asleep twice while I was outside."

"Well, I'll tell you, then. You survived outside for seventeen standard days. I doubt very much that many boys your age—and that includes young Mustafarians—could accomplish such a thing without a wealth of provisions and emergency equipment. I commend you."

Maul bowed, holding his left arm away from his side as he did so.

Sidious noticed the angle of Maul's arm. "You didn't heal properly. Your arm must be broken again and reset. Is it painful?"

"Yes, Master Sidious," Maul said flatly, his tone not even slightly betraying his extreme discomfort. Out of the corner of his eye, he spied the red and black striped fish with yellow eyes swimming near the larger gray fish at the bottom of the nearby orb that was suspended above the circular dining table. The yellow-eyed fish appeared to have grown bigger again.

Sidious looked to TD-D9 and said, "Take Maul to the training room. Attend to his arm. Clean him up. And then bring him back to me."

"Yes, Master Sidious," the droid said, then added, "Afterward, do you wish for me to repair my own legs?"

"Yes, of course," Sidious said.

Leaving Sidious, TD-D9 hobbled after Maul to the training room. Neither spoke once, not even while the droid reset Maul's broken arm. Thirty minutes later, they returned to Sidious's chamber. Maul was wearing fresh clothes. His left arm was wrapped in a bacta splint.

Sidious was seated at the dining table beneath the watery orb. Fine cutlery, dinner plates, and drinking goblets were on the table. Facing TD-D9, Sidious said, "You may repair yourself after you bring us dinner."

"Yes, Master Sidious," said the droid, hobbling out of the chamber again.

Sidious looked at Maul as he gestured for the youth to sit in the chair across from his own. Maul was surprised. His Master had never before invited him to dine in the chamber. And because he was extremely hungry, he also felt grateful. Maul bowed to his Master before he sat down. The fish swimming in the watery orb overhead made shimmering shadows across the table's surface.

"This is a momentous occasion," Sidious said solemnly as he dragged his finger around the rim of his goblet. "Because my presence is increasingly required on other worlds, I have arranged for you to attend the Academy on the planet Orsis. It is an institution for training paramilitaries for planetary governments. They also train intelligence agents, mercenaries, and assassins, as well as supplying professional combatants for the gladiatorial arenas. It's a very exclusive school. To be an Orsis cadet is considered quite an honor."

Maul was astonished. The prospect of leaving Mustafar and attending a school with other students was almost overwhelming.

"The director of the Academy," Sidious continued, "is a Falleen named Trezza. He's a bit short and almost two hundred years old, but do not let that fool you. He is as tough as they come, and mind tricks will not work on him. But there are a few minor challenges. Trezza does not know my name and he never will. And to protect my identity, I shall wear a disguise. Understood?"

"Yes, Master," Maul said, although he could only imagine why his Master wanted to protect his identity.

"You may use your own name, but there is one catch, and this is very important. You are not allowed to use your Force powers on Orsis unless you are alone with me, and unless I grant you permission. When time allows, I will continue to train you in the ways of the Force while you are on Orsis, but you must never use your powers against any other students or faculty members under any circumstances. You must never even talk about your powers to anyone else on Orsis. If you disobey this command, the consequences will be most dire. Understood?"

"Yes, Master." He knew what *dire* meant.

Sidious poured a dull-colored liquid into the goblet set before Maul and then his own. Raising his goblet to Maul, Sidious said, "To future endeavors."

As Sidious and Maul drank, TD-D9 hobbled back into the chamber carrying a tray that held plates covered by domed lids. The droid set the covered plates before the seated figures, then said, "Are you finished with me, Master Sidious?"

"Most definitely," Sidious said. Keeping his eyes on Maul, Sidious waved at the droid. TD-D9 lifted off the floor, flew across the chamber, and smashed into the wall. The impact was so great that Maul noticed small shock waves ripple across the suspended orb. The droid's photoreceptors went dead as its ruined body collapsed in a loud crash.

Maul didn't flinch. He thought of all the time he'd shared with the droid, how it had reared him and punished him, and how he'd never expected his Master to destroy it. He wouldn't have the chance to say goodbye, or to destroy the droid himself. All these thoughts raced through his mind, but he didn't flinch.

Smoke began rising from the droid's shattered head. Sidious grinned. "Not the most efficient way to eliminate an old droid we don't need anymore, but that *did* feel good. Now, let's see what's for dinner." Ignoring the smoldering droid across the chamber, Sidious lifted the lid off his plate and revealed there was nothing on it. He sighed. "Oh, well, I wasn't very hungry anyway. How about you, Maul? What's on your plate?"

Maul had no idea what kind of game his Master was playing. He hoped he would find food on his plate but braced himself for disappointment. He removed the lid from his plate to reveal the red and black striped fish he'd watched grow over the past four years. Lying on its side, the fish stared back at him through one eye. Maul saw the fish's gills flex and realized it was still alive.

Maul didn't flinch.

The fish's eye shifted to look at its former home, the orb above the table, where other fish continued to swim. Maul doubted that Sidious expected him to pick up the fish and insert it back into the orb.

"Go on," Sidious said. "Dig in."

Maul obeyed. He tore into the fish, starting with the head. As he ate, Sidious said, "We will leave for Orsis tonight. Do you have any questions?"

"Yes, Master," Maul said between mouthfuls. "What will be your disguise on Orsis?"

"Naturally," Sidious said, "I shall present myself as a man with a lack of vision."

CHAPTER SEVEN

"Welcome to Orsis Academy," hissed the short male Falleen, a reptilian humanoid with green skin, as he stepped away from the massive desk in his office to greet the two people, a man and a boy, who had just entered. "I am Trezza, the Academy's director."

"Thank you for receiving us," said the man, who wore a bulky old set of cybernetic goggles, a sensor-laden metal bracket that completely concealed his eyes and most of his forehead. He clutched a walking stick in one hand and had his other hand placed on the shoulder of his young companion, who wore loose-fitting black clothes. "Allow me to introduce you to Maul."

Trezza had already noted the boy's horns and tattooed visage, and assumed he was a Zabrak. Trezza bowed slightly and said, "Greetings, Maul. You may call me Master Trezza."

Maul bowed deeply. "I am honored, Master Trezza."

Returning his attention to the sensor-goggled man, Trezza said, "And how shall I address you, sir?"

Sidious sighed. "With all due respect, I prefer to remain nameless. For practical purposes."

"Very well," Trezza replied with a smooth smile, making it evident that he was no stranger to clients who valued privacy above all else. "So, you came here to discuss . . . ?"

Sidious smiled. "As I mentioned in the holomessage that I sent, I am a modest businessman. But I anticipate my business will expand greatly in years to come and that competition will increase. I shall require a very dedicated bodyguard. One with a good set of eyes. You may have noticed I am somewhat ocularly challenged." Sidious lifted his walking stick and tapped its handle twice against the side of his sensor goggles. "Maul's vision is exceptionally good, and his loyalty is beyond question."

Trezza glanced at Maul again, then returned his attention to the goggled man. "Do you have a certain time frame for when you expect Maul to be . . . sufficiently *grown* for such a job?"

Sidious chuckled. "My mind is quite made up about Maul. I can afford to wait. I trust you have received the credits I sent for his registration and tuition?"

"Yes," Trezza hissed. He picked up a datapad and examined a readout. "Your payment is in order. However, Maul does have to take a standard physical examination.

Also, his age was not indicated on the registration. Our administration would like to know that and some other data for placement purposes and general record keeping."

"For confidentiality reasons," Sidious said smoothly, "I would prefer not to divulge Maul's age. I also request that he not be prodded by any medical droids unless he receives injuries that require immediate attention. I have already made a contribution in addition to the other fees, but I am quite willing to pay more to ensure . . . privacy."

"That won't be necessary," Trezza said. "Your contribution was exceedingly generous, and very much appreciated. If it is your wish that we keep no records of the boy's enrollment, I personally guarantee that there shall be no records. However, there is one thing we must address. Even though we're a long way from Coruscant, the Jedi Order forbids Orsis Academy from training Force users."

Neither Sidious nor Maul flinched. Sidious smiled and replied, "You are most perceptive, Master Trezza."

Trezza tapped the side of his nose. "My nose and I have been around a long time, and we've met all types. I can smell Force users. I suspect you're aware of the Jedi Order's rules and regulations, that they expect me to report any Force-sensitive applicants, but here's another fact for you. I really don't care much for the Jedi. The way I see things, if a cadet is Force-sensitive, that's the cadet's business. Just don't make it *my* business." He looked at Maul. "I don't know what kind of powers you have, son, but while you're on my property, no use of the Force. If you can't handle that, you will be expelled. Am I clear?"

Maul bowed. "Yes, Master Trezza."

"You are most accommodating," Sidious said with a polite nod.

"We shall take excellent care of Maul."

Sidious grimaced. "I wouldn't want you to show him any favoritism."

"Of course not," Trezza said. "I meant only that he will receive the very best education in the arts of combat." Trezza redirected his gaze to Maul. "Would you like to have a look around the school?"

"Yes, Master Trezza."

Sidious smiled as he patted Maul's shoulder. "I believe I'll join you." As they exited Trezza's office, Sidious moved his walking stick back and forth, tapping at the floor in front of him.

Orsis Academy was a sprawling compound. Bordered by a tall wall that was topped by security sensors and automated weapons placements, the school consisted of nine interconnected buildings, three large open courts, and an open field beside a starship landing pad. Sidious's cruiser rested on the pad next to a drop ship that had just arrived from the aptly named Orsis Orbital Station, the large space station that traveled in a geosynchronous orbit with the planet. In broad daylight, the station was visible as a point of light in a fixed position in the sky.

As Trezza guided Maul and Sidious to a wide walkway that spanned two buildings, Maul spotted a stairway that led down to a beach along the seashore. He felt a pang of excitement as he took in the view. He was still having a hard time believing that his Master had brought him to Orsis, that his years of isolation on Mustafar might actually be behind him.

Maul glanced at his Master. Sidious had explained that the sensor goggles were a necessary disguise because he did not want to be recognized on Orsis. Maul wondered, *Why would anyone here recognize Master Sidious?*

Trezza led Maul and Sidious across the walkway, which overlooked one of the open courts. Trezza said, "We place as much importance on computer skills as we do on poison production and assassination techniques. And Orsis offers many opportunities for training programs beyond the walls of the Academy. As cadets mature and progress, they learn to fight and survive in the mountains, forests, deserts, and seas. We have hunting grounds and . . ."

A loud clattering sounded from the court below. Sidious stopped short with Maul and said, "What's that racket?"

"Some of our younger cadets are exercising with combat staffs," Trezza explained. "If you step closer to the rail, you can see them . . ." Remembering his guest's sensor goggles, he added, "Oh, please forgive me."

"That's quite all right," Sidious said, his mouth twitching into his smile as he reached up to adjust his goggles. "I can usually see shapes well enough, just not much detail."

Trezza motioned for Maul to guide Sidious closer to the railing. Maul looked down and saw several dozen cadets, mostly humanoid adolescents, swinging wooden combat staffs at each other. Thanks to his studies on Mustafar, he could identify each cadet's species. A pair of bug-eyed Rodian boys seemed to be the noisiest with their weapons. Both Rodians were testing their staffs against a Nautolan girl, an amphibian with tentaclelike tresses extending from her head. The Nautolan moved quickly and appeared to be very capable of defending herself.

"Right now," Trezza said, "we have just over five hundred cadets. As you know, we offer programs for ages eight years old and up. Most have enrolled for four- or eight-year programs. We also have a good number of 'floaters,' temporary students who come here to refine their skills. Graduates also come back from time to time for the same reason."

Sidious said, "Bounty hunters?"

"Occasionally. Do you object?"

"Not at all. On the contrary, I've met a few very accomplished bounty hunters in my time." Sidious stroked his chin thoughtfully. "I've heard your instructors include a Mandalorian who once fought Jedi. I believe his name was Krakko. Meltch Krakko. Is it true he's the best?"

Trezza stared quizzically at Sidious's goggles, then looked back at the cadets below. "He's still *among* the best, but I regret to inform you that your information is dated. Commander Krakko left us some time ago, returned to his clan. As you may be aware, the Mandalorians are engaged in a civil war."

"Oh, now that *is* unfortunate," Sidious said as he patted Maul's shoulder. "I really had hoped the boy might receive training from a Mandalorian. You see, Maul has been in a few fights, but . . . well, he can be a bit wild. He lacks finesse. He needs to learn how to make each move count. I don't suppose you have another Mandalorian about?"

Maul was surprised and embarrassed by his Master's description of him, but he kept his expression neutral. He almost missed the irritation in Trezza's voice as the Falleen replied, "Commander Krakko was our *only* Mandalorian instructor. But I'm confident that we can still teach young Maul here some things that he can't learn anywhere else." Trezza looked at Maul. "I've already agreed to forgo the standard physical examination for you, Maul. But now that I'm aware you've 'been in a few fights,' I would appreciate a demonstration of your abilities."

Maul looked to Sidious. Sidious adjusted his goggles and said, "A demonstration? I suppose that does sound like a practical way for you to evaluate Maul."

Trezza led Maul and Sidious into a lift tube and they descended to the court. As Maul stepped out onto the same level as the cadets, he suddenly realized they were all taller than he. Every one of them.

Seeing Trezza, the cadets halted their exercises, lowered their combat staffs, and bowed to him. Trezza gestured to Maul and said, "We have a new cadet. His name is Maul. I'm told he can fight."

One of the Rodians laughed out loud. Trezza shot him an icy look. The Rodian shut his snout.

Trezza cleared his throat. "I'm looking for a volunteer. Will any one of you fight the new cadet?"

Maul did not expect every cadet to raise an arm, tentacle, or equivalent limb into the air and shout in unison with the others, "I volunteer, Master Trezza!"

Trezza looked at Maul. "Remember what I said about the rules on my property, son."

"Yes, Master Trezza." Maul looked at Sidious.

Sidious adjusted his goggles, leaned close to Maul, and whispered, "Select the largest and most muscular student. Introduce yourself. Hurt him. No killing."

As Maul's gaze traveled across the cadets, he peeled off his black shirt, exposing his lean, tattooed torso. He was aware of the many eyes gazing at the bold red and black patterns on his bare flesh. He placed his shirt neatly on the ground. Stepping away from Sidious and Trezza, he overheard one cadet whisper, "Check out his ribs."

Maul breezed past the malodorous Rodians and came to a stop before a teenage Abyssin, a hulking native of the planet Byss. Distinguished by a broad head that held a single eye with a slit pupil over a broad, fleshy nose and a mouth full of sharp teeth, the Abyssin stood nearly two meters tall. Maul tilted his head back, looked up into the Abyssin's eye, and said, "I am Maul. Your move."

The Abyssin's nose twitched, and then he blinked his eye in disbelief. When he had volunteered to fight the boy less than a minute earlier, he had never imagined the boy would actually choose him. His eye flicked to see Trezza. Trezza nodded to him.

The Abyssin shifted his feet. Maul stood his ground. All the other cadets stepped back, leaving room for the combatants.

The Abyssin launched a sweeping kick that knocked Maul off his feet, and then lashed out with one hard-muscled arm that connected with Maul in midair. Maul flew across the courtyard and crashed to the ground. Both Rodians roared with laughter. Trezza did not reprimand them.

The Abyssin leaped forward, landing on his powerful legs a short distance from his opponent, and waited for Maul to rise. Maul shook his head as if he were making sure nothing was loose as he slowly pushed himself up from the ground. Once he was on his feet, he turned to face the Abyssin again. Maul threw a jab at the Abyssin's left thigh, just above his knee.

If the Abyssin felt the jab, he didn't show it. He pivoted on one foot and kicked out with the other, catching Maul in the stomach. The sound of the impact made a few cadets wince. Maul was again lifted off his feet. Hitting the ground, his body rolled like a broken doll past several cadets until he came to a stop near the feet of the female Nautolan. The Nautolan looked down at Maul's small, tattooed back, then turned to face Trezza and said, "With all due respect, Master Trezza, this is *not* a fair fight."

"What's that?" Sidious said as he tapped his walking stick against the ground. "Did Maul do something unfair?"

"Not at all," Trezza said. "He simply chose to go up against an older cadet."

"He does have spirit," Sidious said. Then he muttered, "Curse these old goggles. I can't see a thing."

Maul braced one palm against the ground. His arm trembled as he pushed himself up. The Abyssin stepped closer to Maul, moving up behind him. Maul started to turn to face the Abyssin, but then his legs buckled and he collapsed. Maul squeezed his eyes shut, then opened them. He looked at a cloud overhead, then shifted his gaze to see the Abyssin. Maul gasped, "What's . . . your name?"

The Abyssin blinked at the boy for a few seconds but finally replied, "Dalok."

Maul twisted his neck away from the Abyssin and his horns dug into the ground. His chest shuddered and then his limbs went slack. He turned his head again, and his eyes rolled up into their sockets before they shifted back to stare in the general direction of the Abyssin. "Your name," Maul repeated. "Please . . . tell me . . . what's your name?"

The other cadets quietly moved in around the Abyssin to get a closer look at the defeated boy. Seeing that Maul was thoroughly beaten, the Abyssin knelt beside him, leaned over his face, and said, "I just told you. My name's Dalok. Are you all ri—"

Maul grabbed the back of Dalok's head, pulled Dalok's face up against his own, and sank his teeth into Dalok's fleshy nose. The startled Abyssin screamed. With his teeth and one arm, Maul held tight to Dalok's head while he moved his other hand to grab Dalok's throat.

The surrounding cadets recoiled. Dalok tried to roll away from Maul, but Maul stayed on him, slamming and driving his knees into the nerve clusters in the Abyssin's shoulders. Dalok was flat on his back as he convulsed, his arms flopping uselessly beside him. Dalok passed out.

Maul rose to stand beside Dalok's unconscious body. Turning slowly, he looked at every one of the surrounding cadets, letting them see the Abyssin's blood dripping down his chin and notice that he wasn't even breathing hard. He thought he smelled fear from the female Nautolan who had tried to call off the fight. He didn't know how old she was, but noted she was slightly taller than he. When his yellow-eyed gaze fell on the Rodians who'd laughed at him, he spat at the ground.

An astonished Trezza looked at the goggled man beside him. "You said Maul has been in a few fights. Just how many is 'a few'?"

"I'm not sure, really," Sidious said with a shrug. "Obviously, I never actually *saw* any of his fights. Tell me, did he win this one?"

"He almost beat his opponent to death."

"Did he, now?" Sidious chuckled as he elbowed Trezza. "I *told* you he was a bit wild."

The Nautolan moved past Maul, and one of her head tresses brushed against his arm. She knelt beside Dalok and checked his pulse. Looking to another cadet, who stood gaping nearby, she said, "His nose will heal but he needs a medpac." As the cadet went for the medpac, the Nautolan turned to face Maul. Maul could see his own reflection in the Nautolan's large black eyes. Although he could not comprehend why, he did not want her to be afraid of him.

Keeping her eyes fixed on Maul, the Nautolan said, "You *did* know that Dalok's an Abyssin, didn't you?

That Abyssins have regenerative abilities?"

In fact, Maul was already aware of this, but that particular bit of knowledge had not crossed his mind when he'd challenged the Abyssin. He'd simply selected the largest and most muscular student, just as Sidious had instructed. Maul looked away from the Nautolan and let his gaze flick back and forth at the Rodians' snouts. "No," he lied. "I didn't know."

The Rodians trembled. Maul knew he was going to enjoy his time at Orsis Academy.

CHAPTER EIGHT

"I want to go swimming," said the female Nautolan, whose name was Kilindi Matako.

Maul did not know why Kilindi was talking to him. He had been at Orsis Academy for almost three years, and the other cadets always kept their distance from him during his recreation hours. He continued dragging his vibroblade along the edge of the long branch he was carving into a spear. But when Kilindi didn't walk away, he realized she might be expecting a response, so he said, "Then you should go swimming."

They were in the open courtyard closest to the sea at Orsis Academy, near a gateway to a path that led down to a rocky beach. On the far side of the courtyard, a group of cadets was preparing for the upcoming martial arts competition against a rival military school.

"I thought you might want to come with me," Kilindi said.

Surprised, Maul cast a sidelong glance at her and said, "Why?"

"I don't know. I just thought you might. I thought maybe you liked to swim."

Maul's jaw tensed as his memory flashed back to Mygeeto, a planet of ice and snow in the Outer Rim Territories. During a break from the Academy, Master Sidious had brought him to Mygeeto to exercise and test his Force powers. They had been walking by a lake that was covered by a sheet of dark ice. Even though Maul had worn heavy, insulated clothes, the frigid winds cut like lasers against his skin. He had just completed a series of exercises that had him running up sheer, icy slopes and then coming down as fast as he could. He knew he had performed well, and he'd hoped that his Master might praise him.

Instead, his Master raised a hand and used the Force to lift Maul's small body, tossing him into the middle of the lake.

Maul crashed through the ice and sank, his heavy clothes and boots pulling him down. As the freezing water bit into his face and chilled his blood, he feared he would die. And then his Master's words came to him. . . . *Turn your fear into anger.*

It was easy for Maul to be angry, especially with his Master. The dark side ignited and fueled his anger. He was enraged by the icy water and by the entire planet Mygeeto. He fought his way to the surface, kicking and clawing and bursting through the ice. And after he broke through the ice, while he was still gulping freezing water and struggling to keep his face above the surface, he saw his Master on the shore.

His Master made no move to help him.

Maul's rage was incredible. His fury propelled his arms and legs, made him push through the water, kick his booted feet, and swim to shore. The dark side had set an inner fire to keep him alive, but he quickly realized that same fire did little to keep him warm. He was shivering fiercely as he arrived before his Master.

And even then, his Master did not praise him, but merely continued their walk by the lake, with Maul staggering along at his side, hating the cold, hating the water, hating everything. . . .

"Well," Kilindi said, "I guess I'll see you later." She turned away from Maul and began walking toward the courtyard's gate.

"Wait," Maul said. He switched off his vibroblade and set it down beside the spear he'd been working on. He said, "I like to swim."

Maul marveled at the way Kilindi moved through the sea, her long head tresses trailing behind her. He thought she was even more graceful in the water than she was on land. Not that he would ever tell her.

He was standing in the sea, not far from the shore, just up to his waist, his bare arms held out stiffly at his sides. Kilindi was swimming about thirty meters beyond him, her strong legs cutting through the water without any obvious effort. He watched her submerge and was surprised when just a few seconds later she broke the surface a meter away from him.

Gazing at Maul with her large, dark eyes, Kilindi said, "Is something wrong?"

"No," Maul said.

"But you said you liked to swim, and you're just standing there."

Maul grimaced. "It's been a long time. Since I've been in water."

"Oh." Kilindi glanced at the shore. "Do you want to go back?"

"No." Maul moved his hands back and forth in the water. "I . . . I like being here."

Kilindi lowered her body so just her head and shoulders were above water. "I like it here too. There weren't any seas like this where I grew up."

"I don't understand," Maul said. "You are a Nautolan. Your homeworld is Glee Anselm. An ocean planet."

"But I didn't grow up there," Kilindi said flatly. "You knew that, right?"

Maul shook his head. Because he had not grown up on Iridonia or Dathomir, he felt foolish for having assumed Kilindi came from her people's homeworld.

"I thought it was common knowledge," Kilindi said. "I've heard other cadets talking about it, so you were bound to find out. Before I came to the Academy, I was on Orvax Four. I was a slave."

Although slavery was outlawed on Republic worlds, Maul knew that it existed throughout the galaxy. His mind was suddenly filled with many questions about Kilindi's past, but he said nothing, because he had no reason. He didn't need his Master to tell him that the girl's life should not be of any interest to him. And yet he was interested.

"But all that's behind me now," Kilindi continued as she tilted her head back and looked up at the sky. "My owners are dead."

Without thinking, Maul blurted out, "You killed them?"

Kilindi lowered her head so she faced Maul again. "Yes. They were a large family. I killed them all."

Maul thought, *Good.*

"Killing them was easy, but leaving Orvax was hard. Lots of slavers were hunting me. But Master Trezza heard about the killings and . . . well, he found me before anyone else did. He's the reason I'm at the Academy. I'm his ward. You knew *that*, right?"

"I knew you were Master Trezza's ward," Maul said. "That's all."

"So now you know about me. What about you? Where are you from?"

Maul looked down and watched the water ripple at his fingertips. "I can't say."

Kilindi tilted her head curiously. "Because you can't say, or because you won't?"

"Both," Maul said, then shook his head. "We can't talk about . . . me."

Kilindi shrugged, the movement making her head tresses jiggle. "Never mind. I won't ever ask personal questions again. But I do have some advice for you."

Feeling suddenly irritated, Maul said, "Why should I want *your* advice?"

"Because I know why you're making your own wooden spear."

That got Maul's attention. "I'm listening."

"Master Trezza invited you to go hunting wild kaabores with him and told you it's a tradition at Orsis Academy for cadets to make their own wooden spears for their first kaabore hunt. But it's really a test to see if you're prepared for the unexpected. I'm guessing he'll lead you straight to a pack of armored chargrecks. That's what he did to me on my first hunt. See these scars?" Rising so her upper body was above the water's surface, Kilindi turned to show Maul the three jagged marks across the back of her left shoulder. "A chargreck did that. Your wooden spear will be useless."

Maul eyed Kilindi suspiciously. "Would Master Trezza be very angry with you for telling me this?"

Kilindi nodded. "Very."

"Then why? Why tell me?"

Kilindi grinned. "Because I'm hoping you will tell me about the look on Master Trezza's face when you pass his test." And then Kilindi sent her body backward, sliding into the water and launching away from Maul. She took care not to splash him as she left.

Maul lowered his body into the water up to his neck, then held his breath and kept his eyes open as he dropped below the surface. He could clearly see Kilindi, illuminated by shafts of sunlight as she undulated past a school of fish. He still hated the waters of Mygeeto, but he decided the sea of Orsis was not entirely unpleasant.

He thought about what Kilindi had told him. He had been looking forward to his hunting expedition with Trezza, but now, even more so.

Four days later, Maul was with Trezza in an outback to the north of Orsis Academy when Trezza pointed to the ground and whispered, "Look there. Kaabore tracks, and they're fresh. I'm guessing there's one just beyond those trees."

Maul shifted his long spear in his hands as he looked toward the trees. Keeping his voice low, he said, "Shall I try flushing it out, Master Trezza?"

Trezza smiled. "Be my guest."

Holding his spear with one hand, Maul moved past the trees, down a short hill, and around some tall shrubby growths before he saw the five armored chargrecks that were waiting for him, just as Kilindi had anticipated.

Each chargreck's body was protected by incredibly strong segmented plates lined with sharp spikes.

Maul reached to his belt with his free hand and grabbed a small packet. All the chargrecks hissed and lunged at him at the same time. He threw the packet at them as he flipped backward. He was still arcing through the air as the packet exploded open with a quiet pop and deployed a wide electroshock net. The chargrecks hit the net and were instantly stunned. They thudded to the ground a split second before Maul landed on his feet.

Maul glanced behind him. No sign of Trezza. He set his spear aside and moved fast. He deactivated the net, which he had taken from the Academy's munitions room, then bunched it into a tight ball and stuffed it between the branches of one shrubby growth. He gathered his spear, then walked back up the hill and past the trees before he found Trezza. Trezza said, "Find anything?"

"No kaabore, Master Trezza," Maul said casually. "Just a few chargrecks."

Trezza's reptilian gaze bore into Maul's eyes. "Chargrecks? Out here? Are you sure?"

"I think so, Master Trezza. That is, they *looked* like chargrecks."

"What happened? Did they run away?"

"Oh, no, Master Trezza." Maul shifted his spear from one hand to the other. "I killed them. I just didn't think anything of it because I was looking for a kaabore."

Trezza glanced at Maul's spear and then back at the boy's face to see if he was lying. Trezza said, "You killed them? With that spear?"

"No, Master Trezza. I killed them with my hands."

Trezza's nose twitched, and he looked very confused as he said, "You didn't use the Force. I'd have smelled it on you."

"I know you would have, Master Trezza."

Maul could hardly wait to tell Kilindi about how he had used the electroshock net, and also about Trezza's reaction. But he wouldn't tell her what Trezza had said about the Force. He always kept in mind his Master's warning, that no one other than Trezza could know about his powers, because if anyone found out . . .

The consequences will be most dire.

CHAPTER NINE

Crouched behind the wide trunk of an ancient tree, Kilindi Matako stayed in the tree's shadow as she surveyed the steep, rocky cliff at the edge of the forest. She glanced at Maul, who was hunkered down beside her, and whispered, "Ready?"

Maul nodded. Six years had passed since his arrival on Orsis. Taller and stronger, he still did not know his own age, but based on his observations of similar humanoids, he assumed he was about thirteen years old. Although he was already considered a master of numerous martial arts, he still had difficulty working as part of a team.

Except when he was partnered with Kilindi.

Kilindi moved first, diving away from the tree so she rolled across dead leaves and came to a stop behind another trunk. A sudden burst of blaster fire tore at the ground between the two trees. A second burst pounded into the opposite side of the tree that Kilindi had moved behind. The trajectory of the blaster bolts indicated the shots came from the top of the cliff, about six meters above Kilindi's position. She glanced back to where she'd left Maul, but he had already vanished. She waited.

Barely ten seconds later, Kilindi heard a horrific scream from atop the cliff. A blaster fired, and then another voice wailed across the forest. When the screaming stopped, a third voice called out, "Mission accomplished. All clear." The third voice was Maul's.

Kilindi moved around the tree and walked out into the open, heading for the base of the cliff. It took her almost a full minute to scale the wall of rock. As she climbed, she sighted three spherical remotes hovering out of the forest and rising into the air. She knew that the remotes belonged to Master Trezza, and that he used them to track cadets during exercises.

When Kilindi reached the top of the cliff, she found Maul standing a short distance from two fellow cadets, the Rodians Hubnutz and Fretch. The Rodians were clutching at their respective right arms, sitting on the ground beside the shattered pieces of their blaster rifles.

"Thanks a lot, Maul," Hubnutz snorted sarcastically. "Nice of you to only fracture our arms this time."

A repulsorlift engine sounded from overhead, and Kilindi and the Rodians looked up to see Master Trezza's shuttle approaching from Orsis Academy. The three remotes glided up to the shuttle and secured themselves to a rack on the vessel's sensor array.

"Oh, isn't that terrific?" Fretch said. "Now we get to listen to Trezza lecture us on how we messed up."

"Yeah, Maul, you're a real prince," Hubnutz said as the shuttle landed.

Maul ignored the Rodians and the shuttle as he stood at the edge of the cliff, gazing over and beyond the forest canopy, staring in the direction of the distant mountain range that was broken by Blackguard's Gorge, where Sidious had acquired an old fortress to be used as his private retreat during visits to Orsis. With Trezza's permission, Maul was allowed to travel by speeder bike to the fortress, where his Master continued to train him in the ways of the Force and also lightsaber combat.

My Master is there now. Waiting for me.

Fretch saw Trezza climb out of the shuttle, then angled his snout at Kilindi and added, "Hope you had fun showing off for your pet slave."

"I'm not a slave!" Kilindi said, her head tresses whipping off her shoulders as she whirled to face Fretch. "And I'm no one's pet!"

"Good one, Fretch," Hubnutz said. "You hit a nerve in Maul's slave." The two Rodians laughed wheezily.

Maul kept staring at the mountains on the horizon.

Kilindi scowled. It was common knowledge that she had served as a slave before she arrived at Orsis Academy. If she had any inclination to respond to the laughing Rodians, she refrained when she saw Trezza walking toward them. Hubnutz and Fretch rose to their feet, grunting from the pain of their injured arms. Kilindi noticed that Maul had not budged, that he was still gazing over the forest. She whispered, "Master Trezza's here."

Maul turned and directed his gaze to Trezza, who was carrying a datapad. Trezza came to a stop beside the Rodians, and the four cadets bowed to him. Trezza bowed his head slightly, then said, "Hubnutz and Fretch. You failed to defend the cliff."

"Maul busted our arms again," Hubnutz whined.

Trezza frowned with disappointment at the Rodians. "If you can't defend yourselves against an opponent you already know, how do you ever expect to deal with the unknown? You must be—"

"But Maul's not like other people!" Fretch protested.

Trezza's green brow furrowed. "You interrupt me again, young Fretch, and you'll find yourself in solitary confinement for a week."

Fretch bowed. "Forgive me, Master Trezza."

"As I've told you too many times before, you must be more mindful. You must learn to think like your enemy, to anticipate every measure with a countermeasure. If you are not prepared for the unknown, the unknown will strike you dead."

"Yes, Master Trezza," the Rodians said in unison.

Turning to Maul and Kilindi, Trezza said, "You are to be commended for your stealth. I confess, I could not keep track of you two. My remotes lost sight of you after you evaded the third patrol in the canyon, before you reached the forest. I know that canyon well. Did you stray into a cave?"

"Yes, Master Trezza," Kilindi answered.

"Why?"

Kilindi glanced at Maul. Maul said, "Because the remotes were revealing our position to our opponents. Before the exercise, I overheard Hubnutz and Fretch talking. They placed trackers on your remotes."

"You couldn't have overheard us," Fretch said. "Hubnutz and I were alone in the barracks when we talked." And then Fretch noticed Trezza glaring at him.

Hubnutz said, "It was Fretch's idea!"

Trezza sneered at the Rodians. "I'll deal with you two later." Returning his attention to Maul and Kilindi, he said, "Come with me. We have a very special appointment." Trezza began walking back to his shuttle.

Special appointment? Maul's expression remained passive, but his mind raced as he wondered what Trezza wanted with him and Kilindi. He started walking with Kilindi, following Trezza, and was halfway to the shuttle when he said, "I forgot something." He went back to the Rodians.

Seeing Maul approach, Fretch said, "Thanks for squealing on us."

"Yeah," Hubnutz said. "You're a real pal."

"Don't make things worse," Maul said. "Trezza wants to see us shake hands."

"Why?"

"He didn't say."

As Fretch carefully extended the hand at the end of his fractured arm, he glanced at the shuttle and said, "But Trezza's not even looking at us."

Maul grabbed three of Fretch's long green fingers and twisted them sharply. The noise of rapidly snapping bones made Fretch gasp and Hubnutz cringe. Fretch made a sick gurgling noise.

"Either of you ever call Kilindi a slave again," Maul said, "I'll tear your arms off and feed them to you."

Maul released Fretch's broken fingers and headed back for Trezza's shuttle. He boarded the shuttle and took a seat in the passenger compartment across from Kilindi and Trezza. Trezza was consulting a timetable on his datapad, oblivious to what Maul had just done to Fretch. After the shuttle lifted off, Maul was not at all surprised to see they were headed for Blackguard's Gorge.

Trezza looked up from his datapad and said, "Kilindi, have you met Maul's Master before?"

"No, Master Trezza. But I have seen him on occasion, when he's visited the Academy. May I ask . . . are we going to his retreat?"

"Indeed, we are." Trezza looked at Maul and said, "I remain astonished that your Master managed to obtain Blackguard's Castle. The previous owner made it clear to everyone in the Orsis system that he had no intention to sell."

If Trezza had asked Maul how his Master had obtained the castle, Maul would have respectfully and truthfully answered that he did not know. Because Trezza's comment had not been a question, Maul remained silent. He knew Kilindi was also wondering why they were traveling to meet with his Master. He glanced at Kilindi, who was peering through a viewport to see the land below.

Snaking between the treacherous cliffs of two snow-capped mountains, Blackguard's Gorge was a long valley that had been named, according to legend, after an ancient space pirate who had used the gorge as his hideout for decades. The only structure in the gorge was Blackguard's Castle, a modest fortress that hugged the shadowy vertical slab of a steep cliff. The castle was essentially invisible to the naked eye, because its rough exterior blended in perfectly with the colors and textures of the mountain. Even the landing pad, at a glance, resembled nothing more than a wide shelf of broken rock.

Trezza's shuttle touched down on the landing pad, and a tall, wide rock made a rumbling sound as it traveled on ancient mechanisms, sliding back from the mountain wall to reveal a concealed hangar. Exiting the shuttle, Kilindi was the first to spot Maul's Master. He was standing in the spacious hangar's entrance, holding a walking stick in one hand and wearing the sensor bracket that concealed the upper half of his face.

"Greetings," Sidious said to the group. "Please, come with me. Our guest is waiting inside." He tapped his walking stick across the landing pad, motioning the others to follow him.

Guest? Maul was intrigued. Except for him and occasionally Trezza, Maul was unaware of anyone ever visiting his Master at the castle.

Sidious's cruiser was parked on the far side of the hangar, which also housed a technical station, assorted tools and supplies, and a few empty cargo containers. The walls were solid rock. Sidious grinned impishly as he led Trezza, Kilindi, and Maul to the center of the hangar. Maul had a strange feeling inside the hangar, a feeling he couldn't quite define. *Almost like . . . we're being watched.*

"You didn't tell them about our guest, did you?" Sidious said to Trezza.

"No," Trezza said, shifting his datapad so he held it behind his back. He looked at Maul and Kilindi. "Recently, the Orsis Academy faculty and I realized we had a problem. A problem concerning you two."

Maul sensed Kilindi was alarmed by Trezza's announcement. He found it hard to understand why she couldn't at least pretend to remain calm.

"Perhaps I should rephrase that," Trezza continued. "The problem was not with you, but with our existing faculty. There was little more that the instructors could teach either of you about stealth tactics or hand-to-hand combat techniques, and yet you have two more years ahead of you at the Academy. In short, you require greater challenges than the other cadets. Now, I mentioned this problem to a certain businessman." Trezza gestured to Maul's Master, who smiled sheepishly. "Maul, your Master suggested a former instructor who only recently became available again. Your Master also made a generous donation to enable Orsis Academy to secure this instructor. And now, it is my honor to introduce both of you to — "

Sidious cleared his throat loudly. Reaching up to adjust his sensor bracket, he said, "Excuse me, Master Trezza, but I'm very curious about something. I wonder how Maul and Kilindi will react if they meet their new instructor *without* knowing any more details in advance."

"But of course," Trezza said. "Why don't you and I move over beside your cruiser and give these young people some room? May I guide you?"

Sidious tapped his walking stick against the floor

and said, "That's very kind of you, but I *do* know my way around here."

Leaving Maul and Kilindi at the center of the hangar, Sidious and Trezza went to the cruiser and turned to face the cadets. Sidious leaned close to Trezza and said, "Let me know when anything interesting happens."

Kilindi said, "I have a bad feeling about this." And then she gasped and grabbed the back of her neck, her knees buckling. Maul caught her around the waist and pulled her against his body as he launched sideways, carrying her with him. In midair, his right hand swept up Kilindi's back until his fingers touched a small dart in her left shoulder blade. He hit the floor with the girl on top of him, absorbing the impact as he plucked the dart out from her shoulder. He rolled away from her and was still clutching the dart as he rose to stand, gazing in the direction of the dart's trajectory.

He saw a figure, a man who wore dark gray body armor and whose head was concealed by a helmet with a distinctive T-visor. The armored man held a dart pistol in one hand and had a missile launcher secured to his back.

A Mandalorian.

Maul knew about Mandalorians, whose warrior heritage dated back thousands of years. He also knew that two factions of Mandalorians had battled each other in a long civil war, and that the war had ended recently. And he recalled that his own Master, after their arrival on Orsis six years earlier, had talked with Trezza about a former Academy instructor, a Mandalorian who had once fought Jedi.

Maul was fast enough to see the Mandalorian's incredibly swift approach. He was also fast enough to dodge the first kick that came at his head. But he wasn't fast enough to stop Meltch Krakko's fist from knocking him out cold.

CHAPTER TEN

Running fast along the volcanic mountain slope on Orsis, Maul gnashed his teeth as another low-energy blaster bolt tore through the thin fabric of his utility suit and slammed into his back. He ignored the pain and kept running.

His pursuers were Meltch Krakko and the two Rodian cadets, Hubnutz and Fretch, and the goal of their exercise was to capture Maul. Krakko and the Rodians were wearing mimetic suits, energy-powered cloaks that allowed for almost perfect camouflage in any environment. Since Krakko's return to Orsis Academy two years ago, he had not only taken a special interest in training the Rodians in tracking and sharpshooting, but also in tormenting the fifteen-year-old Zabrak.

For Maul, the current exercise was merely a warm-up for a bigger challenge on Orsis, an Academy rite of passage called the Gora. Named after the challenge's location, an immense volcanic crater filled with dense forests, vast swamps, and bloodthirsty beasts, the Gora required a cadet to traverse the crater for seven days, surviving without food or equipment except for a single vibroblade. From what Maul had heard, being chased by camouflaged hunters was nothing compared to surviving the Gora.

Maul approached the rim of the mountain's valley, where glacial water and wind had carved a maze of tall, rocky formations. He darted into the labyrinth, never pausing to catch his breath. More blaster bolts zinged past his body. If his pursuers' blasters had been set to kill, he would have been dead already, a fact that infuriated him. But because Sidious and Trezza had forbidden him from revealing his Force powers to Orsis faculty and cadets, he was obliged to let his pursuers shoot him occasionally. If he'd dodged *every* blaster bolt, they would have had ample reason to suspect he was a Force user.

Without glancing back, he drew his own blaster, which was also set at nonlethal power, and returned fire. He felt his rage increase as he deliberately missed his attackers. Although their mimetic suits rendered Krakko and the Rodians practically invisible, Maul had no difficulty sensing their exact positions behind him. He could have shot each one of them with his eyes closed, but that would have been against the rules that Sidious and Trezza had established. And so he pretended to miss Krakko and the Rodians, let them believe he was an ordinary Zabrak, and sometimes allowed himself to be hit.

A blaster bolt slammed into his calf, and another into his right shoulder. The pain did not slow Maul but he pretended to stumble anyway, all in his ongoing effort to conceal his powers. But as he ran forward, he saw he was heading straight for a deep chasm. Although he was confident that his incredible strength and agility would have enabled him to leap to the other side of the chasm, he knew it would be a mistake to make such a jump with Krakko and the Rodians watching. However, he was also determined to evade his pursuers, to show them that he was more daring than they could ever imagine.

I'll earn their respect.

Maul kept running right up to the chasm's upper ledge, then flung his body into the gap, aiming not for the opposite ledge but for the wall below it. He used the Force to cushion his impact against the wall, then extended his arms to hook his hands over an outcropping a few meters below the ledge. With his legs dangling in the air below him, he made every movement look desperate, even though he was not in the least afraid.

He sensed movement above, and knew Krakko and the Rodians were searching for a narrower gap so they could follow him across the chasm. They succeeded less than a minute later, and Maul looked up to see them leaning out over the ledge. He assumed the exercise was over, that they would lower a rope to bring him up.

A rock struck his horned head, and another hit his shoulder. He heard a scuffing noise from above and realized his pursuers were kicking rocks over the rim. As a rock struck the back of one hand that clung to the overhang, he knew he hadn't earned their respect at all.

They're trying to kill me.

Maul was done with restraining his powers, and pretending to be something that he wasn't. Summoning the Force, he launched himself from the overhang and sailed up and out of the chasm. He somersaulted and twisted in midair, flipping his body over the three camouflaged hunters so that he landed on his feet, facing their backs. Startled, Krakko and the Rodians turned fast. Maul had already drawn his blaster and opened fire at them at point-blank range.

Krakko grunted and the Rodians cried out in pain as the blaster bolts hit them. They jumped and rolled away from the chasm's edge, firing back at Maul. For a moment, they moved as if their mimetic suits still gave them an advantage over their prey. Maul used the Force to avoid being hit while he rapidly squeezed and released his blaster's trigger, moving his arm back and forth to aim and fire at each of his cringing targets. He didn't miss once.

Hubnutz and Fretch tried to find protective cover. Maul shot at their legs and continued shooting them after they fell and began screaming. Krakko deactivated his own mimetic suit so he was fully visible. Facing Maul, he shouted, "Stand down!"

Maul fired at Krakko.

"Stand down!"

Maul pretended he didn't hear Krakko over the blaster's report. He felt the blaster start to overheat but kept firing.

And then an amplified voice from above bellowed, *"Cease fire!"*

Maul lowered his blaster as he looked up. He saw an airspeeder approaching. Trezza was behind the airspeeder's controls. The Falleen's expression was outraged.

Maul knew Master Sidious would be even less pleased.

"You're not entirely to blame for what happened," Sidious said, his face lost in shadow beneath his dark blue cloak.

Maul stood before his Master on the stone floor in the cavernous main hall of the fortress at Blackguard's Gorge. After Trezza had treated Maul's wounds and informed him that his Master had already arrived on Orsis to observe the exercises, he had traveled by speeder bike from the academy to the fortress. Because he had been repeatedly told not to reveal his powers, he knew his punishment would be terrible.

"The dark side has taken a serious interest in you," Sidious continued. "And is gauging if you might be a proper vessel for its power. Seeking expression and loathing restraint, the dark side tests us continually, competing with our will and our need for secrecy."

"Yes, Master," Maul said. "I was overcome."

"Overcome?" Sidious's eyes blazed beneath his cowl. Maul looked down at the stone-cold floor.

"I said that you weren't *entirely* to blame," Sidious said bitterly. "The willingness of the dark side to cooperate in your pitiful demonstration doesn't exonerate you from breaking your vow to me and from jeopardizing my plans."

Maul had not wanted to disappoint his Master. He wanted to apologize and ask for forgiveness, but he knew if he did, his punishment would be even worse. And then he thought of how long he had suffered on Orsis because he had not been allowed to use his powers, and he felt his shame transform into rage. He looked up at Sidious and was about to speak but his Master made a pinching gesture. Maul felt his throat constrict.

Sidious walked a few steps away from Maul before he released his remote grip on Maul's throat. Looking back at Maul, he continued, "You have called unwanted attention to yourself. The Jedi have been continuing to harass Trezza for creating assassins and proxy armies, so consider what might have happened had a Jedi been present during the exercise. A Jedi would not only have grasped that you are strong in the Force, but that you have received training in the dark arts, endangering *my* position."

Maul felt crushed. He thought of all his years of training, his constant effort to please his Master. He reflected on the exercise that had ended at the chasm, tried to imagine escaping his tormentors *without* using the Force, but he knew his thoughts were pointless. He could not undo his actions.

"Now," Sidious said, "what did you wish to ask me earlier?"

Speaking tentatively, Maul said, "How long must I go on being one thing here and another there? Trained in the Force here, and trained to do without it there? What are your plans for me, Master? What *am* I to you?"

Sidious sniffed. "You are my student, Maul, and one day you may become my apprentice."

Despite all that his Master had taught him, Maul knew practically nothing about Sidious. How had Sidious obtained his wealth or gained so much knowledge of the Force? It was a mystery to Maul. For all he knew, Sidious was a warlord, a sorcerer, a monarch, or even a banished Jedi Master. Maul said flatly, "Your apprentice."

"Perhaps. But if that is meant to be, it will come at the end of many trials that will make these present ones seem insignificant. Removed from the shelter of Orsis, you will begin to understand that the Republic is built on deceit, and that it only survives because the Jedi Order wishes it to survive. You will need to be resolute in your allegiance to the dark side of the Force."

Maul nodded. "I understand, Master."

"No," Sidious said. "You only think you do." From the folds of his dark robe, he produced two lightsabers. He tossed one to Maul, then ignited the weapon that remained in his own hand.

Maul ignited his lightsaber. From the look in his Master's eyes, he guessed that the burns he was about to sustain would be much more painful than the ones he'd received from Meltch Krakko's blaster.

He guessed right.

A week later, most of Maul's wounds had healed as he prepared for the Gora. He was in the Academy barracks, modifying his combat vibroblade's ultrasonic vibration generator, when Kilindi and another female cadet, Daleen, walked in. Daleen was a dark-haired human, slightly younger than Kilindi, and rumor had it that she was the princess of a royal house.

Kilindi said, "Meltch came looking for you."

Maul glanced at the doorway. "Where is he now?"

"Up top, I think," Daleen said.

Maul knew "up top" meant Orsis Orbital Station. He also knew it wasn't unusual for Meltch Krakko to be there, that the Mandalorian instructor occasionally met with off-worlders at the station. But in the past week, Maul had begun to wonder if Sidious and Trezza had conspired against him, if they had encouraged Krakko to push him beyond his limits, all in an effort to find out whether Maul would break his agreement and use the Force. Now, he wondered if Sidious and Krakko ever crossed paths on Orsis Orbital.

Kilindi said, "Want any tips on what to watch out for in the Gora?"

Maul shook his head as he returned his attention to modifying his vibroblade. "I'll make do."

Kilindi laughed. "That's what *I* said, and look where it got me." Turning around, she shifted her head tentacles to display a relatively recent set of scars that crisscrossed her muscular arms and shoulders. Although bacta treatment would have erased all her scars, Kilindi kept them as proof of her experience.

Grinning at Maul, Daleen said, "Just don't get lost out there." She reached out and gently rubbed the back of his head, careful not to touch his horns. "We're cooking up a surprise for your return."

Kilindi and Daleen walked out of the barracks, leaving Maul wondering what they might be up to. Generally, Maul did not like surprises, as few in his life had been pleasant. But as much as he had been looking forward to the Gora, he now looked forward even more to seeing Kilindi and Daleen when the Gora was over.

The first day of the Gora was beyond intense.
The second day was even more brutal.

The third, fourth, fifth, and sixth days were increasingly bloody. And Maul was having the time of his life.

Countless wild predators kept him constantly occupied as well as sleepless. Except for his heightened senses and physical strength, he did not use the Force in any obvious way. With his vibroblade more often in his hand than in the sheath strapped to his upper leg, he moved like a jungle animal through the forests and grassy swamps that filled the enormous crater, killing some beasts in self-defense, some for food, and others for sheer sport.

Never had he known such freedom. After years of obeying others while containing his rage, he was able to run and hunt and kill as he pleased. By the seventh day, he almost regretted that his journey across the Gora would soon be over.

And then the storm hit. The clouds seemed to roll in from out of nowhere. Within minutes, torrential downpours and hurricane winds hammered at the jungle, turning ground to mud and tearing trees from the ground. The Gora had been dangerous enough with bloodthirsty creatures lurking everywhere, and Maul began to wonder if nature itself were trying to kill him.

Scrambling over fallen trees and trudging through flooded swamps, he made his way through a thorn forest to a rustic outpost, his final destination in the Gora. Once he reached the outpost, he could call for an airspeeder to return him to the Academy. He was eager to see Kilindi and Daleen again.

The storm began to die as Maul left the thorn forest and emerged at a broad savannah. He knew the outpost wasn't far, just beyond the grasslands that stretched out before him. But as he began to move across the savannah, he heard footfalls from the forest.

Llian beasts, he determined. Llians were large creatures with spined tails, and although they didn't travel in herds, it sounded as if at least three were heading straight for him. As he drew his vibroblade, he scanned the grasslands, searching for a length of wood so he might quickly improvise a lance. But no such wood or deadfall was in sight.

Four llians burst from the forest, and Maul was surprised to see each beast bore a rider. The riders were slim humanoids dressed in red, hooded garments. Each was armed with an energy bow and pike.

Maul did not recognize the riders, but knew at a glance they were formidable warriors. Although he felt the dark side of the Force swell within him, he did not summon his powers to defend himself. He suspected that Master Sidious had sent the warriors to test his loyalty and commitment.

The llians moved around Maul. Three warriors drew their energy bows and fired glowing arrows at Maul, not to strike him but to drive him back to the fourth mounted warrior who had moved up behind him. Maul dodged the arrows but was knocked backward by an invisible force, and then yanked off his feet so he was suspended upside down in the air a full meter above the ground. The vibroblade fell from his hand.

Inverted and immobilized, he saw the fourth warrior dismount. From his upside-down perspective, he saw a tall, silver-eyed female with a pale face that was adorned with angular black tattoos. Below her high-peaked red hood, a shieldlike hexagonal medallion appeared to be affixed to her unusually high forehead. A trove of talismans and amulets dangled around her thin neck. As she walked toward Maul, tapered streamers shifted behind her robe, moving like tendrils with a life of their own. "Don't resist, Nightbrother Maul," she said. Her voice was deep, with a most unusual accent.

Maul sensed the Force about her. He was certain she was in league with Sidious, possibly an apprentice. Before he could respond, she made a gesture with her hands and then extended one long finger to touch his forehead.

Maul plunged into unconsciousness.

He awoke groggily, feeling drained, as if he had been robbed of the Force. From the noise and vibrations around him, he knew he was inside a small spaceship. Shifting his fingers to his upper leg, he felt the empty sheath to confirm his vibroblade was gone.

He opened his eyes. He was lying on an accelerator chair in the main cabin of a drop ship. Pushing himself up, he saw the woman who had rendered him unconscious. Apparently, the woman and her fellow warriors were so confident in their strength that they had not bothered to cuff or shackle him.

"You are skilled, Maul," the woman said from her own seat, "but perhaps not as skilled as I was led to believe."

Maul sneered. "That seems to be the common opinion lately."

The woman's eyes widened slightly. "Very revealing. A few moments ago I was thinking that I erred in coming so far and in risking so much to return you to your clan brothers. And yet I sense that you are strong in the Force."

"I have no brothers," Maul said sharply, as if he found the word distasteful.

"Ah, but you do. And once among them your life will be very different. On Dathomir, you will be nurtured and trained as the Winged Goddess and the Fanged God meant you to be trained. When the time is right you will face the Nightbrothers' equivalents of the Tests of Fury, Night, and Elevation. And should you pass those trials, you may be fortunate enough to be transformed into an extraordinary warrior. Your strength will be enhanced tenfold, and those puny horns that stipple your head presently will become long and lethal."

Maul had stopped listening as soon as she'd mentioned Dathomir. Sidious had told him about the Nightsisters, the Force-using witches who ruled that world. He thought of his most recent meeting with his Master, a week prior to the Gora, when Sidious had cautioned him that "beings of all nature" would attempt to deceive him, to fill his head with lies. There was no question in his mind that the witch who had captured him was associated with Sidious, that she was either deliberately or unwittingly testing Maul. He refused to become a pawn in their game.

"I won't be going to Dathomir."

The witch raised an eyebrow. "You've no interest in seeing your birth world or meeting the members of your Nightbrother clan?"

"Neither."

The witch frowned. "You are fated to serve us, Maul, one way or the other. It has always been thus."

Staring hard at the witch, Maul said, "I serve only one Master."

The witch smiled without mirth. "The Falleen you answer to will have to find another."

The Falleen? Maul was confused. Was she under the impression that Trezza was his only Master, or was she toying with him? He considered mentioning Sidious by name, but decided against it.

A red-garbed Nightsister stepped into the cabin. She was armed with an energy bow and a sheathed energy sword, a fixed-blade weapon that resembled a glowing lightsaber. Maul recognized the Nightsister as one of the warriors who'd attacked him in the Gora. Like the seated witch, she had pale white skin and a tattooed face, but Maul noticed she was younger and did not have such a high forehead. The Nightsister said, "Mother Talzin, we are approaching the station."

Talzin nodded but kept her eyes on Maul. "Can I trust you to behave while we transfer to our vessel, or do you wish simply to awaken aboard it?"

Maul glanced at the young Nightsister's weapons. "For the moment, you have the upper hand. I won't make trouble."

"Of course you won't," Talzin said soothingly.

Maul looked out a viewport and saw they were approaching Orsis Orbital Station. A moment later, the drop ship shuddered as a tractor beam locked onto it. As the tractor beam eased the ship into one of the station's docking bays, Maul considered his limited options.

He knew that the station's cargo and passenger hubs were linked at several points by air lock corridors. If he could break away from the Nightsisters and get to another ship, he might be able to return to Orsis before anyone at the Academy realized he had left the Gora. He would prove to Sidious that he would not be taken so easily.

The drop ship touched down in the space station's large, dimly illuminated cargo bay. As Maul walked with Talzin and the three Nightsisters down the drop ship's boarding ramp, he was struck by a sudden feeling of apprehension. Talzin must have sensed something as well, because she turned to look at him, as if he might be the cause of her concern.

Maul said, "Trouble."

CHAPTER ELEVEN

Sensing he was being watched by hidden life-forms, Maul scanned the shadowy corners of the high-walled cargo bay. Without any prompting from Talzin, the three Nightsisters drew their swords and enabled their energy bows. Talzin stepped away from her group, moving out into the middle of the cargo bay as if she were not worried in the least.

"Stay right where you are and lower your weapons," a gruff voice barked from the cargo bay loudspeakers. And then the life-forms emerged from shadows. Leathery-skinned Weequays stood amongst large-headed Siniteens, all armed with blaster rifles that were leveled at Maul and the Nightsisters.

A towering figure clad from head to foot in garish battle armor moved to the center of the cutthroats. He was a Vollick, a native of Rattatak, an Outer Rim world infamous for its gladiatorial death matches. A remarkably large blaster was holstered to his hip.

Each of his arms looked as if they weighed more than Maul's body.

"You won't be returning to Dathomir, Mother Talzin," the Vollick said. "The five of you are going to be my guests on Rattatak, where you will eventually become members of my elite army." He drew his enormous blaster from its holster and fired a shot at the bay's tall ceiling. "Our weapons are set on stun, but we'll shoot to kill if you decide to refuse my invitation."

Maul wondered how the Vollick warlord and his soldiers had known Talzin would be arriving on the space station, and then he wondered if the Vollick might be Talzin's accomplice. Talzin said nothing. She raised her hands as if in surrender, then extended her fingers.

Maul was surprised to see dozens of Nightsister warriors materialize from the sidewalls and upper levels of the docking bay. However, he instantly sensed they were insubstantial, that the new arrivals were nothing more than a powerful Force illusion created by Talzin. The warlord and his soldiers fell for it. They rapidly reset their blasters' selector switches from stun to full power, angled their weapons away from Talzin, and opened fire at the apparitions. Genuine blaster bolts and illusory arrows began crisscrossing the bay.

The real Nightsisters drew their energy bows and began launching very real arrows at the Weequays and Siniteens. They dropped several soldiers before Talzin's conjured illusion evaporated unexpectedly.

Maul glanced at Talzin, saw her frustrated expression, and wondered if she had complete control of her powers.

"Cease fire!" yelled the startled Vollick. "Cease fire!" But his men ignored him and turned their weapons on the genuine Nightsisters who remained in the bay. As Maul ducked for cover, he saw a Weequay blast one of the Nightsisters at the same moment that a Siniteen fired a shot that tore through Talzin's thigh. The Nightsister dropped her energy bow as she collapsed. Talzin stumbled and fell on the deck several meters away from Maul.

Maul considered running back into the drop ship, but he doubted that it had sufficient power to escape the bay's tractor beam array. And looking at Talzin sprawled on the deck, he also began to wonder whether Sidious wanted her dead. He thought, *If this is a test, it's for keeps.*

He ran toward the fallen Nightsister, leaping and tumbling across the deck until he reached her energy bow. He didn't have to look at her to know she was dead. Snatching up her weapon, he darted back to the drop ship, took cover behind one of the landing struts, and began firing back at the warlord's men. Talzin was still lying on the deck. The two remaining Nightsisters had moved beside her and were unleashing a barrage of arrows at their opponents.

Maul scanned the cargo bay. Recalling the space station's layout from previous visits, he visualized the shortest route to a neighboring bay where he hoped to find another drop ship. He was still working with his rough plan to return to Orsis before anyone discovered he was missing. Although he would have accomplished this goal more easily if he used the Force, he did not want to disappoint his Master again. He was about to make a break for the nearest hatchway when he heard Talzin call out, "Don't leave us, Maul!"

Talzin was on her feet, supported by one of the Nightsisters while the other was covering them. Blaster bolts whizzed past them. Talzin cried, "Maul!"

Maul didn't know what to do. Would Sidious expect him to show sympathy? Was Talzin even one of Sidious's agents? Either way, how would he better serve the dark side of the Force? By helping the Nightsisters, or leaving them to die?

Maul cursed through his gritted teeth. He hooked the energy bow over his right shoulder, then ran through a hail of blaster bolts to reach Talzin. He heaved her up from the deck, flung her over his left shoulder, and raced for the entrance of a cylindrical corridor that led to the safety of an adjacent bay. The two Nightsisters followed, firing arrows at the warlord and his soldiers behind them as they moved after Maul.

Maul was fifty meters shy of the connector's entrance when a hail of blaster bolts cut him off. He carried Talzin behind a large cargo container for cover, then propped her up on the deck beside the container. The other two

Nightsisters arrived, positioned their bodies to protect Talzin, and returned fire. Maul looked at Talzin.

"Our magicks don't work in this sterile place," Talzin said bitterly as blaster bolts ricocheted off the container. "That's why I could not sustain the illusion."

"The illusion that nearly got all of us killed," Maul said.

Talzin winced as she moved her hand over the deep wound in her outer thigh. "On Dathomir, I would be able to heal myself."

"No one asked you to come here," Maul said, but then thought maybe she had responded to an invitation from Sidious.

"We came for your sake."

"That's a lie."

Talzin's silver eyes flared. "You fail to grasp that you belong to a great heritage, Maul. That you were spirited away from Dathomir doesn't alter the fact that you are a Nightbrother, and that your fate is joined with ours."

Maul snorted. "Everyone has a plan for me."

Talzin's brow furrowed, then she said, "I don't understand."

Maul ignored her as he tried to find a way out. Looking to the area between the cargo container and the soldiers, he saw a dozen automated load-lifter droids. Apparently oblivious to the firefight, the simple-minded droids were hauling similar cargo containers to different areas of the bay. The containers were drifting slowly into the bay on powerful tractor beams from a cargo ship that was too large to be berthed inside the station. Maul knew enough about starship technology to know that a computer housed in the bay's upper-level control room was guiding the droids and tractor beams. Looking up, he found the control room's window.

"We've one chance to make it through the connector and into the passenger pod," Maul said. He looked at Talzin. "I'm going to need one of your energy swords."

"You've no training in the use of that weapon," said Talzin.

Maul shrugged the energy bow from his shoulder. "I'll just have to improvise."

Talzin grabbed an energy sword from one of the Nightsisters and handed it to Maul. Taking the sword, he leaped away from the cargo container, hit the deck, and then sprinted for the control room's bulkhead.

The soldiers turned their weapons and fired at Maul. Gripping the energy sword with both hands, he sprang from the deck, launching himself up toward the control room. He plunged the sword through the control room's window, creating a vertical hole, then flipped his body to kick the window and shatter it. As he landed inside the control room, the soldiers fired more blaster bolts after him, and the bolts ricocheted off the room's walls. One stray bolt grazed the side of Maul's upper right arm, drawing blood.

Ignoring the pain, Maul dropped to the control room's floor until he reached the main control board. His education at Orsis Academy had included learning how to override computers, and he quickly reprogrammed the cargo bay's tractor beam array.

Almost instantly, the cargo containers that had been drifting slowly into the bay were suddenly soaring in at rapid speed. Although the increased speed had no effect on the cargo ship parked outside the space station, the containers began piling up inside the bay faster than the load-lifter droids could catch them. The pile quickly accumulated into a wall of containers that separated the soldiers from the Nightsisters, but left the Nightsisters with a clear passage to the connector that led to the space station's passenger hub.

Rising from the control room's floor, Maul glanced down to see several soldiers trying to run to the far side of the bay before the incoming containers cut them off. The containers moved faster than the soldiers could run, and they were crushed. The remaining soldiers retreated.

Maul jumped down from the control room and returned to Talzin and the two Nightsisters. He wrapped his arm around Talzin's waist and helped her to her feet. The Nightsisters followed Maul and Talzin into the air lock corridor.

With the Nightsisters bringing up the rear, the two of them hurried to the entrance of the cylindrical corridor.

Maul saw the entrance's sealed hatch, but because he didn't want to lose his hold on Talzin, he used the Force to open the hatch. After they all moved through the hatch and into the corridor's first airlock, Talzin used the Force to seal the hatch behind them, and the pair of Nightsisters launched their energy quarrels to destroy the hatch's control panel. An alarm began blaring. Maul ignored it and kept moving.

Working as a team, they repeated their actions as they moved through several more hatches until they reached the station's passenger hub. Maul wasn't sure what Sidious would think of his use of the Force, but as they moved into the passenger hub, he became absolutely certain that his Master was testing him. He was so certain that he stopped in his tracks.

"Why are you waiting?" Talzin said. "Our ship isn't that far."

"You can stop pretending," Maul said.

Apparently confused, Talzin shook her head. "About what?"

"About Dathomir, the Nightbrothers, and the rest. I know that you were sent by my Master. I know, because I sense him. My Master is here."

Moving through a maintenance level to avoid more soldiers, Maul, Talzin, and the Nightsisters finally arrived in the hangar that housed Talzin's starship. Maul had expected to find the warlord's soldiers stationed in the hangar to prevent Talzin from reaching her ship, but he had not expected to find over a dozen Weequays lying dead on the hangar's deck.

Although none of the Weequay bodies bore obvious wounds, Maul knew how they had died, and also the identity of their killer. Leaving Talzin standing with her Nightsisters, he moved across the hangar to face a dark alcove. He stopped, dropped to one knee, and bowed his head.

"Master."

Sidious stepped out from the alcove. He wore his dark robe, and his face was concealed by the shadows beneath his deep hood.

Talzin and the Nightsisters fell back a step. Evidently, they could sense the man's power in the dark side of the Force. As the Nightsisters kept their energy bows aimed at the deck, Sidious turned slightly toward them, gestured to Maul, and said, "This one does not belong to Dathomir. He is mine."

Talzin said, "Then you didn't merely abandon him to the Falleen."

"On the contrary," Sidious said.

Talzin glanced at Maul. "You have trained him well."

Sidious motioned to Talzin's ship. "You'll find the body of your fallen Nightsister aboard."

Talzin nodded her head in gratitude. Sidious folded his hands into the opposite sleeves of his robe and said, "Now, be gone from here before I have a change of mind."

Talzin was unaccustomed to taking orders, but she gestured to the Nightsisters to board the ship. The Nightsisters walked past Maul, who was still kneeling with his head lowered. As Talzin limped past Maul, she casually allowed her dangling left hand to brush the bloody wound that had been opened in his upper right arm. She proceeded up the boarding ramp. Neither Maul nor Sidious noticed her move her left hand to one of the talismans that dangled from her neck, and press Maul's blood upon the talisman before she entered her ship.

Talzin's ship lifted from the deck and glided out of the hangar. Sidious moved to an observation window that overlooked Orsis. Maul followed obediently, then dropped to a kneeling posture and waited for his Master to speak.

Staring out the window, Sidious said at last, "You did well, Maul. It pleases me that you showed restraint and betrayed none of your training in the dark side of the Force."

Maul bowed his head. "I did so in the hope of one day becoming your apprentice."

Sidious glanced back at Maul. "Then consider yourself one step closer."

"Thank you, Master."

Sidious stepped away from the window. "The time has come for you to learn certain things about the nature of our undertaking. As I told you, I have been putting into motion the stages of a Grand Plan, a plan you may play a part in if you can continue to demonstrate worthiness and loyalty. You should know, though, that this plan has in fact been in the making for a millennium. It springs from the minds of many who serve a great tradition." He paused to look at Maul. "A tradition of far greater import than the Dathomiri brotherhood Talzin surely told you about. It is the tradition of the ancient order known as the Sith."

Surprised, Maul narrowed his eyes. "You told me of the Sith when I was young, Master."

"What I kept from you then is that I am the Sith Lord, *Darth* Sidious. My Master both named and conferred the title on me, and at my discretion, you may one day be afforded the same honor by me."

Maul swallowed hard. "I will strive to prove my worth to you, Master."

"Yes, you will," Sidious said. "From this point on I will begin to tutor you in the ways of the Sith. We are opponents of the Republic, and the sworn enemies of the Jedi Order. It will be our task to see the former brought down and the latter expunged from the galaxy. Where I will remain the guiding hand in this, it will fall to you to execute missions that could pose a risk to my position should the true purpose of our acts be discovered."

For years, Maul had wondered the purpose of all his training. Now he knew. His heart pounded.

"Nothing less than perfection will be sufficient, Maul," Sidious said. "Do you understand?"

Maul bowed his head again. "I understand, Master."

"Then let's put that to the test, shall we?"

Maul looked up. "Another?"

Sidious's brow furrowed. "Another?"

"As you engineered with Mother Talzin?"

Sidious grinned faintly. "What happened on Orsis and aboard this station was not set in motion by my hand, Maul. In fact, you were betrayed by one who told Talzin where to find you, and then aided and abetted her plan to capture you."

Maul's eyes widened with surprise, and then he felt a wave of anger. "May I know the identity of my betrayer, Master?"

Sidious looked at the ceiling for a moment as he considered Maul's request, then replied, "Meltch Krakko."

Krakko?! Maul scowled, wondering how long the Mandalorian had been plotting against him. "Did Trezza know, Master?"

Sidious shook his head. "Trezza knew nothing. However, I fear that we may not be able to contain the damage that has been done. We can't risk that word of your disappearance and all that followed may spread." He stroked his chin thoughtfully. "I will deal with the Vollick warlord. But it will be your task to deal with Trezza and the others at the school."

The others? Maul thought of Trezza, who had

always treated him with a degree of respect that Sidious never had. He thought of Kilindi and Daleen, who had shown him kindness. And then his pounding heart turned to stone and he said, "I live to do your bidding, Master."

Sidious nodded. "And as long as you do, you will continue to live."

Maul rose.

"Be discreet," Sidious said.

Leaving the space station, Maul traveled by drop ship back down to Orsis. On his way, he visualized what he had to do. He knew the layout for every building at the Academy, knew every entrance and exit. He thought of all the things he hated about the place, especially the rules that forbade him from using the Force.

Night had long fallen by the time he reached the Academy's perimeter, and he felt very different from the cadet he had been when he left to begin the Gora. Now, his education seemed ages behind him. He felt he was one with the dark side of the Force.

He moved quickly and quietly through the court-yards and buildings. First, he killed the Academy's sentries, and then the security guards posted outside the training rooms and barracks. He used the Force when it was most efficient, and his bare hands whenever it pleased him. Knowing that most of the cadets would already be asleep in the barracks, he went noiselessly from one darkened room to the next, leaving a trail of death.

He entered the room shared by Kilindi and Daleen. Kilindi's bunk was empty. Daleen's wasn't. Daleen was snoring lightly. A moment later, her life had ended, and Maul was moving out the door. He took no comfort from Kilindi's absence. He knew he would find her.

When he arrived upon the sleeping forms of the Rodians Hubnutz and Fretch, he woke them before he broke their necks.

Not every cadet was sleeping. Maul found a group of older cadets practicing martial arts in a training room. He locked the doors, switched off the lights, and moved through the group like a furious beast of prey.

Covered in blood, he proceeded to the building where the instructors had their own quarters.

Approaching the door to Trezza's office, he heard voices inside. He recognized the voices. Kilindi and Trezza. Kilindi was demanding that Trezza explain why Maul had not returned from the Gora. She sounded worried and angry. But as far as Maul was concerned, she was talking about someone else, someone he didn't know.

Maul opened the door and stepped into the office. Trezza was seated behind his massive desk. Kilindi stood before him. And Meltch Krakko stood on the far side of the room, near an open fireplace.

Kilindi gasped at the sight of Maul's blood-soaked

body. Maul fixed his gaze on Krakko and walked straight toward him. Even though Maul was not carrying any weapons, Krakko drew his blaster and fired at him. Maul jerked his body to the left, dodged the blaster bolt, and kept walking toward Krakko. Krakko fired two more shots. Maul dodged those too before he grabbed Krakko's gun arm with one hand, and his neck with the other. Krakko sputtered angrily. What Maul did next made Trezza gasp and Kilindi cover her mouth with her hands.

Maul kept his eyes on Trezza as he hurled Krakko's lifeless body into the fireplace. Trezza raised his hands to show he wasn't holding any weapons and said, "Maul, please calm yourself. We can talk about this." Keeping his hands raised, he looked anxiously at Kilindi.

Maul sensed Trezza's anxiety and knew Trezza was just trying to stall and distract him. He was not surprised to see the flat metal knife pop out of Trezza's sleeve.

Catching the knife between his fingers, Trezza threw it at Maul. Maul's left hand flew in front of him to catch the knife by its handle, then whipped it back with blinding speed at Trezza's upper chest. Trezza gasped, clutched at his chest, and collapsed upon his desk.

Maul looked at Kilindi. She was staring at him blankly, but she radiated fear like a child in the presence of an enormous monster. Maul walked toward her. He never paused to wonder how his life might have been different if he had not revealed his Force powers to Meltch

Krakko. He never paused at all. His only purpose was to serve his Master.

Kilindi didn't run. She did try to smile. She said, "I guess you're not interested in the surprise that Daleen and I had for you."

"Not anymore," Maul said.

Soon after the destruction of Orsis Academy, Maul learned why Sidious had been so protective of his own identity for so many years. Evidently, Sidious had long maintained another identity as a public figure, a Senator from the planet Naboo. In his Senatorial guise on the planet Coruscant and other worlds throughout the Galactic Republic, Sidious was known as Palpatine. Most people who knew Palpatine regarded him as a polite, quiet man, as modest as he was harmless.

Maul moved with Sidious to Coruscant, where Sidious had long kept a secret lair in a skyscraper in an industrial area. Maul spent the next two years carrying out a series of secret missions for his Master. The missions were conceived to help Sidious gain power without others ever knowing of his existence. By the end of those two years, Maul had repeatedly proven that he was as strong as he was fast, and that he would never break. He also sensed that his control of the darkness that fueled the Force was close to perfect.

CHAPTER TWELVE

Sidious and Maul returned to Mustafar. For fourteen days, Sidious put Maul through a series of grueling physical tests. Maul defended himself against lightsaber-wielding droids in the training room. Blindfolded, he threw daggers at robotic targets, which threw the daggers back at him. He was blindfolded again before he climbed into a starship flight simulator wired with disciplinary electrodes. He wore a sensory-deprivation suit when he ran through a maze that was lined with razor-edged walls, and also when he was deposited into a previously unexplored Mustafarian cave. In locked chambers, he was exposed to extreme temperatures and deprived of food. For each test, he drew strength from the dark side of the Force.

When the fourteen days were over, Maul was exhausted. His entire body ached as he stood before Sidious in the meeting room. Not only had he passed every test, he had destroyed every test. However, his

Master always expected more from him, so he was not entirely surprised when Sidious said, "Because you have survived the preliminaries, you may proceed to the actual test to become a Sith Lord."

Maul willed his body to remain standing.

"I am sending you to a planet in the Outer Rim," Sidious continued. "It is made up of three kinds of terrain. Desert, swamp, and mountains. You will have at least three matches on each terrain. I have sent a fleet of assassin droids to attack you. Each is programmed with different strategies. Some will work together. Some will work alone. They are all programmed to kill."

Maul turned to face his Master. Although Maul remained silent, the fire in his eyes betrayed his surprise. And his excitement.

Sidious noticed Maul's reaction. "That is correct. I am prepared to lose what I most value. So must you be to become a Sith. You must be prepared to lose your own life in order to win."

Maul nodded. "I understand, my Master."

"You will have to survive for a month," Sidious added. "You will have only a survival pack."

Despite his exhaustion, Maul felt exhilarated. He was determined to prove he was the best apprentice in the history of the Sith.

Sidious did not accompany Maul in the droid-piloted cruiser that left Mustafar, nor did he inform Maul of the cruiser's destination. But while the cruiser was traveling through hyperspace, Maul tapped at a keypad at the navigation console until he accessed and bypassed the coded coordinates that identified his destination as Hypori, a planet in the Ferra sector of the Outer Rim Territories. He had never been to Hypori before, but he had not expected his Master to send him to a familiar world.

The droid pilot emerged from the cockpit and noticed Maul examining a scope at the navigation console. The droid said, "I don't think Master Sidious will be pleased to know that you accessed restricted data from the navicomputer."

Without looking away from the scope, Maul replied, "When Master Sidious learns that you used dated encryption codes for the destination coordinates, he'll feed you through a shredder for a full week."

"Oh," said the droid pilot. "If you'll excuse me, I'm going to erase my memory of the past minute."

Good idea, Maul thought as the droid returned to the cockpit. But then it occurred to him that the droid pilot might actually be an assassin droid. He could only imagine how many assassin droids were already waiting for him on Hypori, and it was possible that the pilot droid would deliver him straight into a massive ambush.

The cruiser dropped out of hyperspace to arrive within view of Hypori. It was a small world, and scattered clouds were visible in the upper atmosphere. Even from space, Maul could make out some wide areas of desert, small oceans, and shadowy mountain ranges, which were consistent with Sidious's description of the varied terrain.

The cruiser descended through the planet's atmosphere. Maul grabbed the survival pack that Sidious had given to him and strapped it to his back. He leaned into the cockpit, looked through the window, and saw they were angling down over a body of water, heading toward a rocky beach.

The droid swiveled its mechanical eyes to face Maul and said, "Please don't ask me where we're going to land. I'm not authorized to tell you."

Ignoring the droid, Maul examined the ship's readouts for flight speed and altitude, then cast a final glance through the window, noting the distance to the beach, before he pulled out of the cockpit. As he mentally calculated the cruiser's approach to the beach, he dropped to a crouch beside the main hatch, wrapped one arm tightly around his legs so his knees were clasped against his chest, and used his free hand to hit the lever for the emergency exit.

The hatch exploded open. Maul kept his head pressed against his knees as he sailed out of the cruiser, fifty-five meters above sea level. He tumbled through the air, the cruiser's engines whining away from him as it veered across the sky. Automatically recalculating his descent, he twisted at the waist before he straightened and extended his legs skyward. His fists braced before him, he knifed into the water.

The water was cold. Holding his breath, Maul made sure the survival pack was still secured against his back, then began swimming to shore, staying below the water's surface. He suspected the droid pilot would tell Sidious about his leap from the cruiser, but that did not concern him. His test required that he survive for a month on Hypori. Sidious had never told him to remain on the cruiser until it landed.

When Maul neared the shore, he broke the surface with his mouth and nose but kept his body underwater. He reached out with his senses. He could not detect any movement on the rocky beach, but he knew it was only a matter of time before the assassin droids found him.

And then they found him.

The assassin droids were relentless. Programmed to fight to the death, they had blasters built into their chests and hands. No matter how hard Maul tried to conceal himself or his desperately improvised camps, the droids found him. They never slept, never allowed Maul to sleep for very long, never hesitated before they pounced. When Maul did manage to rest and recover, he fell asleep *knowing* he would be awakened by an attack.

The droids drove him into the frozen mountains and across the burning deserts. Maul's survival pack was torn from his back and lost in one battle. And after twenty days, Maul realized he was at risk of losing something else. His mind.

Because the attacks never stopped.

Maul was beyond paranoid. He had reason to believe that every sound, every shape, and every shadow on Hypori was a potential threat.

He grew thin and his strength began to ebb. He foraged for food when he could. Life was scarce on Hypori, but he found a few small animals, killed them, and ate them raw, because he dared not risk building a fire that would attract more droids.

It was while he was trying to eat a tough-skinned lizard at the base of a cliff that two droids attacked. Maul defeated both droids but sustained a blaster wound to his thigh. Limping into a ravine, he found a large cave and hauled his body into it. Maul knew he had to recover before he could fight again. But without his survival pack, he had no healing bacta or bandages.

The wound festered. The pain was blinding. He listened for approaching droids but heard none. The days blurred, but Maul was almost certain that a full month had passed since he had arrived on Hypori. As he fell into and out of restless sleep, Maul began to wonder if his Master had forgotten him.

His wound became worse. The pain was beyond excruciating. He had no doubt that death would come soon. He thought he was hallucinating when he saw a cloaked figure appear at the mouth of the cave.

It was Sidious.

Maul could not believe his eyes. He felt not only relieved to see his Master, but genuinely glad. His Master would help him.

Sidious moved into the cave. He came to a stop near Maul. Smiling as he looked down at his apprentice, he said, "Now it is time for your final battle."

Maul wondered if he had heard correctly. He knew his Master must have been able to see plainly that he was not fit to stand. And yet he also knew his Master never tolerated weakness of any kind. Maul scrabbled at the cave's walls and pulled himself up. His balance was off. Searing pain shot through his leg as he lurched forward.

Sidious handed Maul a lightsaber. Maul fumbled with the weapon and activated it. The cave's walls shimmered with light.

Maul did not realize how parched his throat was until he rasped, "Where is the assassin droid, Master?"

Stepping back from Maul, Sidious drew his own lightsaber and ignited its red blade. "I will be your opponent."

Maul stared at his Master with disbelief. And then his disbelief changed to anger. He summoned up the dark side of the Force. He felt a burning sensation flicker and grow within him, a trickle of strength. He took a step toward his Master.

Sidious sneered. "You cannot be as pathetic as you look." He raised his lightsaber and attacked.

Maul parried the blow and reversed, coming at Sidious from the opposite side. But Sidious had already vanished, leaving Maul to lunge at empty air. As Maul lost his balance, his body fell against the cave's wall.

Sidious said from behind Maul, "You *are* that pathetic. You are weak. Not worthy of being a Sith Lord. I have misjudged you."

Maul's anger turned to rage. He spun fast and swung his lightsaber again, but again he failed to strike Sidious, who moved faster than he could follow. He fell against the opposite wall and gasped for breath.

Sidious howled with laughter. "I expected your failure. I saw your weaknesses long ago. Your doubts in your own abilities. Your *lack of faith* in my teaching. Your *inability* to embrace the dark side. And that is why, over these long years, I have secretly trained another apprentice."

Maul stared hard at Sidious.

"Oh, poor Maul. All he ever wanted was a friend. Does it please you to know I have another apprentice? Does it make you feel less alone?"

Still trying to catch his breath, Maul said, "More than one apprentice . . . is against the rules of the Sith."

"You are right," Sidious said with a grin. "A spark of intelligence, at last." He gestured to the mouth of the cave. "My second apprentice is on the other side of the planet. He conquered all the assassin droids sent after him. He only sustained a flesh wound. He is healthy. He is strong. Unlike the pathetic weakling I see before me."

Maul realized his opponents had not really been the assassin droids. He thought of all the punishment he had endured over the past month, and then of the unending punishments of his entire life. He thought of his true opponent, the unseen adversary, chosen by Sidious to become a Sith Lord. Maul felt robbed of his past and future. And then a rage unlike anything he had ever felt before swelled through him. The rage was so over-whelming that he thought it might consume him.

No. I can direct it. My rage will consume my enemy. It will consume my Master. Glaring at Sidious, Maul saw the true face of his enemy.

Sidious snickered. "Can you understand? Focus. If there can be only one apprentice, then one of you must die. Who do you think I have chosen to die, Maul?"

Maul felt his rage flowing through his veins, pumping energy into every muscle. He felt so powerful that he believed he could accomplish anything. And more than anything else, he wanted his Master's blood.

Maul sprang at Sidious. Sidious barely missed the first blow from Maul's lightsaber, an upward swing that aimed to rip Sidious in half. Maul swung again but Sidious deflected the blow and retreated. As Maul moved across the rough cave floor, sweat stung his eyes, but he did not stumble. He somersaulted through the air, his lightsaber whirling in the darkness. Sidious raised his lightsaber to parry the next blow, which was so powerful it made him stagger backward. As Maul struck again, he thought, *I'm going to kill him.*

Sidious parried every blow, but Maul could tell his Master was working hard to keep him at bay. As Sidious backed up against the wall, he said, "You want to kill me? You want to kill your Master?"

"Yes," Maul grunted.

"You hate me?"

"Yes!" Maul screamed through clenched teeth.

Sidious shifted like a liquid shadow, maneuvering around his apprentice. Maul was suddenly up against the wall, gasping for breath as his vision blurred. His strength was evaporating. He turned fast to see Sidious. Sidious lashed out with his lightsaber. Maul parried the blow, but then his lightsaber suddenly flew from his hand.

As Maul heard his lightsaber deactivate and clatter across the cave's floor, Sidious raised his own lightsaber and advanced. Maul knew he was about to die, but he did not cringe. As Sidious swung his lightsaber, Maul leaped forward, grabbed Sidious's wrist, and sank his teeth into his hand. Maul tasted blood and spat it back at Sidious.

Sidious brought the lightsaber down on Maul. Maul waited for the pain and the shock of death.

He was surprised when the lightsaber's blade bounced off his shoulder.

Sidious cackled merrily. He stood and looked at Maul. Then he tossed the lightsaber aside. Maul realized his Master had been using a harmless training saber.

Maul leaned back against the cave wall. The rock bit into his back but he concentrated on the pain while his Master continued to laugh without mercy. When Sidious was done, he faced Maul and said, "Do you feel the hate?"

Maul nodded.

"Good. It is the source of your strength. You still hate me. No matter. Today you have delivered yourself into my hands. I have the power of life or death over you, Maul. Someday you will hold that power over another. It is the honor of the Sith. You will devote yourself to the idea of domination."

"But . . . what about the other apprentice?"

"There is no other apprentice."

Maul was astonished. He didn't know what to say.

"You have passed the test."

Maul could still taste his Master's blood on his lips, but his rage was rapidly ebbing. He shifted his feet and realized he was standing on his lost lightsaber. He picked it up and shoved it into his belt.

"From this day forward," Sidious said, "you are a Sith Lord. You have chosen a path of darkness, the path of power. You are Lord Maul. You are my instrument."

"Yes, Master."

Sidious smiled proudly. "Your rage. You enjoyed it? You enjoyed wanting to kill me?"

"I took pleasure in it."

Sidious laughed again, but it was not a mocking laughter. "You will do well, Lord Maul."

Maul realized he no longer felt any anger toward Sidious. He felt only . . . loyalty.

Sidious and Maul returned to Coruscant, where a medical droid tended to Maul's injuries. Maul had felt drained by his trials on Hypori, but within several days, he felt stronger than ever before. Now that he was a Sith Lord, he was empowered by a sense of purpose.

He was fully recovered when Sidious summoned him to his private library. He found Sidious examining an ancient pyramidal holocron. Maul knew from his studies that the holocron was a Sith artifact, used to preserve data.

Sidious glanced at his apprentice. "You are a formidable warrior, Lord Maul. Now you need a weapon to match. I have spent many hours perusing the Sith archives, and I believe I have found something appropriate for your fighting skills." He brushed his fingers along one edge of the holocron, and a moment later, the holocron projected a hologram of a double-ended lightsaber.

Maul stared at the hologram, fascinated by the weapon's appearance. Imagining the damage it would inflict, he suddenly felt eager to wield such a lightsaber.

"This will be your weapon, Lord Maul. In order to serve me well, you must be invincible." Pointing to the hologram, he continued, "You must build the lightsaber yourself so that you know it intimately. It will be fitted for your hand, balanced for your stroke. You shall train with it until it is a part of you. And then you shall join me on the greatest mission of all."

"What is that, Master?"

"The domination of the entire galaxy."

CHAPTER THIRTEEN

Maul was exercising in his training room on Coruscant and had just completed a triple backward flip when he heard the signal on his comlink. He pressed a button on the comlink and heard his Master's voice. "Strategy room. Now."

Maul strode fast to a turbolift and ascended to his Master's strategy-and-communications room. Maul suspected his Master wanted to give him an update about his plan that involved the Neimoidian Trade Federation.

Although Maul did not know every detail of his Master's current project, he was aware that Sidious had established an alliance with the greedy Neimoidians. The Neimoidians were angry because the Galactic Senate had imposed taxation on the former Free Trade Zones of the Republic's outlying star systems, but then Sidious told the Neimoidians how they could force an end to the new regulations, allowing them to reap even greater profits. Sidious had instructed the Neimoidians to use their battleships to form a blockade around the planet Naboo, and then deploy battle droids to invade the world. After the invasion, the Neimoidians would force Queen Amidala to sign a treaty with the Trade Federation, a treaty that would convince the Republic Senate that the Neimoidians had assumed control of Naboo legally. Maul trusted that this project was part of a larger scheme, and that his Master would explain everything in time.

Exiting the turbolift, Maul found Sidious waiting in the center of the strategy room, in front of the holocomm station. Sidious was wearing his robe with the hood draped across his back. He did not look pleased.

"The Neimoidians are signaling me," Sidious said, the irritation evident in his voice. "I want you to hear the transmission." Raising his hood to conceal his face, he continued, "No doubt they have contacted me because of some ridiculous setback that has sent them into a panic. Stay out of sight."

Maul moved to the side, stepping into a shadowy alcove near the comm console.

Maul watched as holograms of two Neimoidians materialized in the air before Sidious. Humanoids with lumpy grayish-green flesh and eyes with horizontal irises, the Neimoidians were Viceroy Nute Gunray, the leader of the Trade Federation, and Daultay Dofine, the captain of the Trade Federation's flagship vessel. Nute was distinguished by a tall, crested tiara. Daultay's head was topped by a command officer's gray miter, and his face wore an especially worried expression.

Sidious said, "What is it?"

"This scheme of yours has failed, Lord Sidious," Daultay replied, trembling. "We dare not go against these Jedi."

Jedi?! Maul saw his Master stiffen in anger, and then another hologram appeared in the air. Transmitted by the Neimoidians, the hologram showed a pair of Jedi — a bearded Jedi Master and his younger Padawan apprentice — seated in a meeting room in the Neimoidians' battleship.

Sidious sneered as he said, "Viceroy, I don't want this stunted slime in my sight again."

The cowardly Daultay ducked and shuffled out of view. Still facing Nute Gunray, Sidious continued, "This turn of events is unfortunate. We must accelerate our plans. Begin landing your troops."

Nute gasped. "My lord, is that . . . legal?"

"I will *make it* legal."

Nute's lumpy brow furrowed. "And the Jedi?"

"The Chancellor should never have brought them into this. Kill them immediately."

"Yes. Yes, my lord," Nute said hesitantly. "Uh . . . as you wish."

Sidious broke the connection and the holograms faded out. A question formed in Maul's mind. He knew that he should remain silent, that to interrupt his

Master's thoughts almost always brought harsh conse-
quences. Unable to wait, Maul said, "Do you think the
Neimoidians are capable of destroying the Jedi, Master?
They are fools."

Sidious nodded slowly. "Yes, they are fools. But even
fools are sometimes lucky."

Maul returned to his training room. He moved his
hand over a sensor on a curved wall, and then the wall
panel slid back to offer a sweeping view of Coruscant.
The city appeared to spread out above, below, and around
Maul. The sun was setting, and he watched the sky shift
to crimson. As millions of gleaming windows and passing starships reflected the color of the sky, Maul thought
the entire world looked as if it were bathed in blood. He
thought it was beautiful.

And then he thought of the two Jedi who had arrived
at the Neimoidians' blockade at Naboo. He hoped the
Neimoidians would fail to kill the Jedi. By the Force,
he *knew* they would fail. And after all his years of training, he would be called into service to strike against
the Sith's greatest enemy.

Maul grimaced. He realized that by wishing for the
Neimoidians to fail, he was also wishing for his Master's
order to fail. Maul did not like this contradiction, the
conflict it presented. He did not want to be disloyal, but
he couldn't stop the feeling that gnawed within him. . . .

The Jedi are mine. Mine to hunt. Mine to destroy.

The feeling wasn't purely selfish. Maul wanted his Master to see that he was a worthy apprentice. As far as Maul was concerned, all his previous tests had been trivial. To fight the Jedi would be his first true test. The *ultimate* test.

From Maul's vantage point in Sidious's lair, the Jedi Temple was not visible. He closed his eyes and visualized the Temple in his mind and saw a smoking ruin. The bodies of fallen Jedi Knights and their small Padawans littered the stairwells and hallways. He saw himself standing in the rubble, surrounded by Jedi corpses. He envisioned his Master arriving to meet him at the scene.

Here is what I have done for you, Master.

I am pleased, Lord Maul.

Maul opened his eyes. His vision had been so realistic he could smell the blend of rising smoke and spilled blood. He had no doubt that he had seen something more than a dream. He knew he had glimpsed the future.

It wasn't long before Sidious once again summoned Maul to his strategy room. When Maul arrived, he found his Master wearing a quilted blue cloak with Naboo-style bloused sleeves. Sidious shrugged out of the cloak and donned his dark hooded robe.

With his face lost in shadows beneath the hood, he glanced at Maul as he gestured to the dark alcove a short distance behind the single seat at the communications console. "Stand over there," Sidious said. "Remain in the background. I may need you. Who knows what those Neimoidian slugs have managed to bungle this time?"

Sidious seated himself in front of the holoprojector and initiated a transmission to Nute Gunray's battleship. Maul watched from the dark alcove as a hologram of Nute and his diplomatic attaché Rune Haako materialized in the air before Sidious.

Eyeing the two Neimoidians, Sidious said, "What is your report of the invasion?"

"We control all the cities in the North," Nute replied, "and are searching for any other settlements."

"And Queen Amidala, has she signed the treaty?"

"She has disappeared, my lord," Nute said ruefully. "One Naboo cruiser got past the blockade."

Sidious snarled. "I want that treaty signed."

"My lord, it's impossible to locate the ship. It's out of our range."

"Not for a Sith," Sidious said. With a discreet motion of his hand that only Maul could see, Sidious gestured for Maul to approach. Maul stepped forward so he stood just behind his Master. He braced his arms across his chest and stared down at the Neimoidians' holograms.

Sidious continued, "This is my apprentice, Darth Maul. He will find your lost ship."

Maul saw the look of surprise and dismay on the faces of both Nute and Rune Haako as they shifted their gazes from Sidious to him. He thought, *Yes, you fools. There are two of us.*

Sidious broke the connection with the Neimoidians. Turning to face Maul, he said, "Those incompetents have performed worse than my lowest expectations. Queen Amidala *must* sign that treaty." He clenched his teeth. "The Jedi are behind this, of course. They are becoming a nuisance and must be eliminated. Find them."

Maul bowed. "I will find them, Master. I will not fail."

Sio Bibble, the governor of Naboo and chair of the Naboo Royal Advisory Council, was among the many citizens captured by the Neimoidians during the invasion of Naboo. Maul scavenged holographic datatapes to replicate Sio Bibble's likeness and voice and created a fragmented message from the white-haired, bearded governor. Reviewing the message, Maul watched Bibble's simulated likeness say urgently, ". . . cut off all food supplies until you return. The death toll is catastrophic. We must bow to their wishes. You must contact me."

Maul's plan was to transmit the message and establish a connection trace to pinpoint the location of Queen Amidala's starship. He routed the transmission so it would appear to originate from the Royal Palace on Naboo. And then he waited.

It did not take long for Maul to intercept a response, a brief encrypted message that said the Queen was safe and would soon return to Naboo. The response came from a small sand planet in the Arkanis sector, in the Outer Rim Territories. The planet's name was Tatooine.

Maul found Darth Sidious standing on a balcony that curved around the outside of their secret lair on Coruscant. Sidious was apparently oblivious to the airships that whizzed past the balcony as he gazed out over the skyscrapers that illuminated the night. As Maul approached, he heard his Master mutter . . .

"Far above, far above,
We don't know where we'll fall.
Far above, far above,
What once was great is rendered small."

Sidious glanced at Maul. Maul recalled the verse from his childhood and wondered why his Master had recited it, but he did not ask.

Sidious began walking on the balcony and Maul fell into step alongside him. Maul said, "A connection trace suggests the Queen is on Tatooine. She might be hiding there while she plans to retake her planet."

Sidious shook his head. "She is not so brave. She still trusts the power of the Senate. No, that is not why they landed on Tatooine. And the reason is not your concern. Just find them."

"Tatooine is sparsely populated," Maul said. "If the trace was correct, I will find them quickly, Master."

"Move against the Jedi first. You will then have no difficulty taking the Queen to Naboo to sign the treaty."

Sidious came to a stop at the edge of the balcony. Maul stopped beside him and said, "At last we will reveal ourselves to the Jedi. At last we will have revenge."

"You have been well trained, my apprentice. They will be no match for you."

Leaving his Master on the balcony, Maul proceeded to the hangar that housed his personal starship, the Sith Infiltrator named *Scimitar*. Sidious had given him the vessel, which was equipped with a powerful hyperdrive, weapons, and a rare cloaking device that rendered the ship completely invisible. Maul had used the ship on numerous missions on behalf of his Master, including recent attacks on the interstellar criminal organization Black Sun and Bartokk assassins on the planet Ralltiir.

After boarding the ship, he entered Tatooine's coordinates into the starship's navicomputer to plot his course through hyperspace, a course that would have him leave Coruscant via the Corellian Run and then shift to the Triellus Trade Route to reach Tatooine's binary star system in the Arkanis sector. Minutes later, seated behind the *Scimitar*'s controls, he was rising away from Coruscant when he realized his entire body was tingling with excitement.

He could hardly wait to kill Jedi.

CHAPTER FOURTEEN

The *Scimitar* dropped out of hyperspace. Maul glanced through a shielded viewport to see the twin suns of the Tatoo system, then spotted a third point of light that was so bright it could have easily been mistaken for a small star. Maul checked the nav console and confirmed the third body was Tatooine.

Although Maul did not expect to spend much time on the sand planet, he had briefed himself about what he would find there. The Republic had no functional presence on Tatooine, which was essentially run by the Hutts, large sluglike beings whose criminal enterprises spanned the galaxy. Because water on Tatooine was so scarce, most colonists were moisture farmers. Indigenous natives included bright-eyed Jawas, hooded scavengers who drove enormous sandcrawlers through the desert in search of scrap metal and abandoned vehicles. There were also nomadic masked savages called the Tusken Raiders, known to moisture farmers as Sand People, who rode large creatures called banthas. From what Maul had gathered about the Sand People, he doubted that Queen Amidala and the Jedi would seek refuge with them. Everyone avoided Sand People.

A light flashed on the comm console. The *Scimitar* had picked up a distress signal from a nearby ship. Maul sighted the ship on his viewscreen, saw it was a small space cruiser that had stalled in a shipping lane. He ignored the distress signal, but as he passed by the ship, the signal grew louder, and then a voice cried from the comm, "Help us! Please, help us!"

Maul saw a large bulk freighter tumble out of hyperspace, and he assumed the freighter had arrived to assist the stalled ship. But then the stalled ship's engines fired and it raced after the *Scimitar* while the freighter came up fast on Maul's other side. Through his viewport, Maul saw panels slide back on the freighter's hull to reveal proton-torpedo launchers.

Pirates. Maul brought his fist down on the edge of his console. He felt foolish and furious for letting down his guard, for letting his ship be sighted, for leaving himself open to an attack. He did not want any witnesses to his arrival on Tatooine. His mission was too important. But he knew that the pirates had never seen a ship like his before, that they were fully intent on seizing it. He dared not activate the *Scimitar*'s cloaking device, because that would only draw more attention to the ship's existence. The pirates would love to get their hands on an exotic cloak, and if they couldn't, they would doubtlessly talk about the ship, and their talk might reach the Jedi on Tatooine. All these thoughts raced through his head in just a few seconds.

Maul knew he would have to kill the pirates. Every one of them.

He increased energy to the *Scimitar*'s deflector shields as he angled away from the other ships, but they veered along with him and cut him off, just as he had expected. Then the space cruiser opened fire and the *Scimitar* was rocked by the blast, a warning shot. He responded by cutting power, letting his deflector shields fall. The *Scimitar* came to a dead stop in space.

Anticipating that the pirates would board the *Scimitar*, he went to the back of his ship and climbed into a cramped escape pod. As the pod's hatch sealed with a hiss, he consulted a monitor to watch the bulk freighter draw closer. An armored docking tube extended from the freighter.

Maul slid the pod's release mechanism as he activated its engine, keeping it set on low power. The pod drifted a short distance away from the *Scimitar*'s hull, and he maneuvered so the *Scimitar* concealed his position from the approaching freighter. He was not about to let anyone claim his ship. When he was certain the pirates had boarded the *Scimitar*, he guided the pod straight for the bulk freighter.

The freighter was an unremarkable model,

essentially an enormous box with a hyperdrive. Maul saw the hull was covered with grime and space dust as well as scorched by cannon fire. The freighter's docking bay was open, apparently in preparation to receive the *Scimitar*.

Maul guided his small pod into the freighter's docking bay, which was large enough to contain both the *Scimitar* and the pirate's cruiser. Illuminated by bright lamps, the docking bay was cluttered with debris and piles of rotting food. As he looked for a clear spot to land, he spotted two pirates. They were Togorians, tall beings covered with matted fur, their powerful arms ending in incredibly sharp claws. The Togorians were using their claws to tear open large metal crates, and Maul assumed the crates had been seized from some previous victim. Togorians were notoriously greedy as well as murderous.

Both Togorians glanced at the escape pod as it landed neatly in the cluttered docking bay, then returned their attention to opening the crates. Maul knew that they assumed a fellow pirate had landed the pod.

Maul opened the pod's hatch, leaped out, activated his lightsaber, and charged the two Togorians. One pirate unsheathed a vibroblade while the other snared a vibro-axe. Maul immediately evaluated that the one with the vibroblade favored his left side, and that the other pirate was clumsy. They meant nothing more to him than any other targets.

Maul flipped through the air and his blade swept

through the right side of the first pirate. The arm holding the vibroblade fell upon the deck with a sickening thud, and then the stunned Togorian collapsed beside it. Maul drove his lightsaber through the fallen pirate's chest but did not pause to watch the Togorian's body jerk and die. He was already racing toward the second pirate, who was bigger than the first.

But instead of standing his ground, the Togorian bolted away from Maul and ran for a comlink station beside a nearby hatch. Not wanting the entire ship alerted to his presence, Maul summoned the power of the dark side and focused it on the pirate. The Togorian was thrown off his feet. He flew past the comlink station and smashed into the bulkhead. Maul had intended for the impact to kill the Togorian, but the pirate, still clutching his vibro-axe, staggered back from the bulkhead and roared with rage as he turned to face his attacker.

The Togorian ran for Maul. Maul spun his lightsaber and the Togorian's wrist separated from his arm. The Togorian saw his hand and vibro-axe fall to the deck, and he howled. Maul's blade spun again, and connected with the Togorian's neck. The pirate's body collapsed.

Maul's pulse had not increased during the fight. His breathing remained steady. Deactivating his lightsaber, he stepped through a hatch and raced down a filthy corridor, littered with discarded junk, heading for the bulk freighter's bridge.

Unlike the docking bay, the bridge was dim,

primarily illuminated by sensor scopes and datascreens. Maul blinked his eyes, letting his vision adjust to the darkness, then he slunk into the bridge without a sound. Overhead, large metal cages dangled from the ceiling. The cages were filled with the motionless forms of many creatures, their faces gaping in wide-eyed agony. Maul realized the creatures had been killed but their bodies preserved, their expressions frozen at the moment of their deaths. He was disappointed that the corpses didn't include any Jedi.

Below the cages, four Togorians were staring at a console, watching a monitor that displayed another Togorian, who was standing within the *Scimitar*. The on-screen Togorian's fur was elaborately braided and ornamented with glittering objects. Over the comlink, the pirate with the boarding party reported, "I'm telling you, there's no one on board!"

One of the four Togorians who stood before the monitor wore a necklace made from assorted skulls. Maul guessed him to be the captain and knew he was correct by the way the Togorian barked, "You looked for hidden compartments?"

Sounding exasperated, the Togorian on the monitor replied, "Of course we searched for hidden compartments, we're not fools! It's an unmanned ship. The course was set for Tatooine. That's why it didn't answer the distress signal. Have you ever seen a ship like this? I haven't!"

The captain appeared to be weighing his options, then growled, "All right, idiot. Bring both ships into the loading dock. The bay is still open. If you do find any passengers, kill them."

The captain broke the connection and the monitor went dark. One of the other pirates growled, "Hela-Tan is a fool. They could be in hiding."

"Then we'll find them," the second pirate said.

"Or they could have escaped," added the third.

"Shut your flapping mouth," snorted the Togorian captain. "What's the difference? We have the ship." He turned away from the others.

Maul moved fast. He activated his lightsaber and cut the nearest Togorian in half. The Togorian did not cry out, but the noise of his collapsing body caused his fellow pirates to turn. The captain faced Maul, baring his fangs. Drawing two vibro-axes from his belt, the captain roared, "Prepare to die, scum!"

Maul wondered why so many opponents felt compelled to announce their intentions with threats and taunts. Deciding to save the captain for last, he flipped across the bridge, kicked the second pirate in the throat, and then drove his lightsaber through the pirate's chest. The second pirate fell.

The third pirate whipped out a vibroblade. Maul charged him. As Maul's lightsaber cleaved through his target, he sensed that the captain was taking aim at his back. Leaping from the third pirate's dead body,

Maul soared backward over the captain's head just as the captain's vibro-axes met with a loud, energized shriek where Maul had been standing just a fraction of a second earlier. Maul grabbed hold of the bars on an overhead' cage and swung himself to land behind the captain.

The clashing vibro-axes ignited, illuminating the remains of the caged wretches and casting ghastly shadows throughout the bridge. Prying his vibro-axes away from each other, the captain turned to face Maul again. Blood pounded in Maul's ears as he spun his light-saber, slashing the captain's arms before delivering a killing blow.

From the comm console, a Togorian's voice crackled, "Approaching docking bay."

Maul stepped to the console. He did not activate the visual monitor as he lowered his face over the comm and said, "Proceed to the bridge." Then Maul turned his attention to the freighter's computer. He knew Togorian pirates always fled the scene of a crime immediately to avoid capture. And thanks to his mechanical training with Sidious, it took only a few seconds to interface the freighter's propulsion units with the proton torpedoes. The moment the Togorians punched the ignition for their engines, the entire ship would blow up.

Leaving the bridge, Maul ran back to the docking bay. He heard the pirates approaching and ducked into a side corridor. He watched the pirates stagger past his position, heading toward the bridge. They were already arguing about how they should divide the spoils from the strange, newly acquired starship.

After the Togorians were gone, Maul hurried across the brightly lit bay. The *Scimitar* rested beside the pirates' space cruiser. He ran past the escape pod that had delivered him to the docking bay. He had already resolved that he did not have time to recover the pod.

The *Scimitar*'s boarding ramp was down. Maul ran up the ramp and nearly collided with the Togorian whose fur was decorated with glittering objects. Up close, Maul saw that the objects were sharp razors, and that this Togorian was bigger than the others. Much bigger.

Maul surmised the pirate had remained on the ship so he could take what he wanted before the others had their chance. The pirate was holding two fistfuls of credits that Maul kept aboard for emergencies, and was about to deposit the credits in an open satchel at his feet. Maul saw the satchel was bulging, and suspected the pirate had also found his stash of crystals, which he kept for worlds that did not accept credits.

Maul activated his lightsaber. The pirate tossed the credits aside and removed his vibro-axe from his belt. Eyes fixed on Maul, the pirate said, "There you are." He stuck out his thick purple tongue and dragged it across his lips. "Think you can escape me? Think again. I'll finish the job."

Maul was irritated by the Togorians' tendency to taunt before striking. He was also eager to leave the freighter, as he expected the other pirates would start the engines at any moment. He whirled in an arc and went for the hulking Togorian's chest.

Incredibly, the pirate sidestepped the attack. His vibro-axe swept past Maul's shoulder but smashed into the *Scimitar*'s auxiliary control console. Maul saw the damage was minimal, but seethed with rage. Hoping to prevent further damage to his ship, he leaped past the pirate and flipped down the *Scimitar*'s boarding ramp. The pirate followed.

Jumping to the docking bay's deck, the pirate shook his fur, and his glittering, decorative shards reflected the lights from the bright lamps that illuminated the docking bay. The light momentarily dazzled Maul's vision, causing him to lose focus as the pirate swung his vibro-axe. Maul jumped away, but not before the vibro-axe's blade caught his leg. Maul felt the blade slice into his flesh. He bared his teeth as if he were biting on the pain itself.

He glared at his opponent, then leaped and twisted in midair, spinning his lightsaber at the pirate. Maul's blade took off the pirate's arm before landing. The pirate collapsed, and Maul struck him again, but it was not a killing blow because he did not wish for the pirate to die immediately. He wanted the pirate to die in agony.

Ignoring his own wound, Maul deactivated his lightsaber, jumped over the pirate's body, and raced back up the *Scimitar*'s boarding ramp. Although he wished he were already seated behind the controls on the upper deck, he didn't dare waste the few seconds it would take for the lift to carry him to the bridge. As the boarding ramp automatically retracted, he went straight to the auxiliary control console that the Togorian had struck earlier. He was checking the console to make sure it was fully operational when he heard a loud hum outside his ship. He knew the noise was the freighter's preliminary ignition warming up. He tapped at the console's controls and powered up the *Scimitar*'s shields and engines.

A warning light flashed. The *Scimitar*'s ramp had retracted but the hatch was still open. Maul heard an inhuman roar from behind and turned to see that the hulking pirate—minus one arm, and with his face covered in blood—had wedged himself into the boarding hatch, his body pinned between the hatch's doors. Clutching to the inner hatch with his remaining hand's bloodied claws, the Togorian wasn't about to let go on his own.

The pirate's legs were still dangling out of the hatch as Maul pushed the *Scimitar*'s engines to full power and blasted out of the freighter's docking bay. Alarms wailed as air rushed out the open hatch. As the *Scimitar* soared into space, Maul was yanked off his feet and hurled toward the pirate in the hatch.

Maul's wounded leg slammed against the bulkhead inside the hatch. Air was torn from his lungs as his fingers seized a metal rung. His face was mere centimeters from the Togorian's, and he could see from the pirate's frenzied expression that he had every intention of making sure Maul died with him.

. Maul rammed his horned head into the pirate's skull. The pirate's one-handed grip loosened. Maul twisted his body and kicked the pirate's midsection. The pirate roared and sank his claws into the inside of the hatch's frame. The dark side surged through Maul, and he kicked the pirate in the face.

Behind the *Scimitar*, the bulk freighter exploded, spraying burning fuel and shredded metal in all directions. The resulting shock wave rocked the *Scimitar*, and the Togorian was blown away from the hatch. Maul hit the hatch's emergency button and it sealed instantly, sending him rolling back into the *Scimitar*.

Emergency air flooded into the lower deck. Maul gasped as he scrambled onto the lift. Arriving on the upper deck, he did not limp as he went to his seat and settled behind the controls. He took a deep breath. He felt good to be alive after his enemies were dead.

Angling away from the wreckage of the pirate ships, he guided the *Scimitar* toward Tatooine. He knew he should treat his wound soon but decided to wait until after he'd landed. Meanwhile, his pain gave him something to focus on.

He was looking forward to finding more enemies.

From space, Tatooine looked like a scorched sphere with just a few small, scattered clouds. The *Scimitar*'s sensors directed Maul to the planet's larger spaceports and settlements, and he was pleased to see that night had fallen over those areas. From experience, he had come to prefer night landings, because most so-called civilized beings liked to have their lights on at night. They revealed themselves. Even Sand People and Jawas were known to huddle around open fires after the twin suns set.

As the *Scimitar* descended to the sand planet's dark hemisphere, Maul began to see the lights of the more populated areas as well as solitary moisture farms. Queen Amidala's ship could be anywhere on Tatooine, but he was confident he would find it.

He landed his ship on a mesa. He did not leave the *Scimitar* until he was certain that no detectors were aimed in his direction and that he had arrived unnoticed. Carrying his electrobinoculars, and wearing a programmable wrist link above his left hand, he stepped down the boarding ramp and onto the hard-packed sand. The air was cool and incredibly dry, and a few stars were already visible in the evening sky.

Maul came to a stop. From where he stood, he could see the distant lights of three settlements. His electrobinoculars were equipped with radiation sensors for night vision and powerful light-gathering components for long-distance scanning. He raised the electrobinoculars to his eyes and scanned the terrain to his left. According to the data display on his electrobinocular viewscreen, he was looking at Mos Espa, one of Tatooine's largest spaceports.

Turning almost completely around, Maul viewed the city of Mos Taike, which was located between the Northern Dune Sea and another broad area of barren desert, the Xelric Draw. Shifting to his left, he viewed another spaceport, Mos Entha.

Maul lowered the electrobinoculars, tapped a command into his wrist link to summon his probe droids, and turned to face the *Scimitar*. He watched three bulbous, black Dark Eye probe droids hover out of the aft hatch. Each sensor-laden probe droid had been programmed to seek out Queen Amidala, her ship, and the two Jedi who had escaped with her from Naboo.

The three probe droids glided past Maul before they separated, each veering off toward one of the three populated areas. After they were gone, Maul trudged back to the *Scimitar* so he could monitor the droids' progress. The sand sucked at his boots, making every step an effort.

Sweat beaded on his tattooed forehead. His wounded leg was practically screaming for treatment. But even after he was back inside the *Scimitar*, he delayed reaching for a medpac. He worked with the pain, manipulating it, shaping it into desire. He craved revenge against the Jedi. They were the reason he had traveled to Tatooine. If not for their existence, his encounter with the Togorian pirates never would have happened. His desire for vengeance grew like a blanket of darkness around him. Only after he felt consumed by anger did he dress his wound.

Maul grinned. The pain was nothing compared to what he would do to the Jedi.

CHAPTER FIFTEEN

Maul unloaded his speeder bike from the *Scimitar*'s underside cargo hatch. It was the day after his arrival on Tatooine, and the twin suns were blazing in the sky. He had already received significant transmissions from his three probe droids.

The first probe droid had sighted a tall, bearded man carrying a lightsaber at Mos Espa Grand Arena after a Podracing competition. The second probe droid had been destroyed — possibly by a lightsaber — before it transmitted an image of a run-down light freighter named the *Dusty Duck*, which had simply been in the wrong place at the wrong time. Fortunately, the third probe droid had discovered the location of Queen Amidala's starship in the Xelric Draw. Now Maul was waiting for the first probe droid to return with a full report from Mos Espa. And he wanted his bike ready if he needed it.

The bike was a custom Razalon FC-20 repulsorlift speeder, equipped with a quiet but powerful rear thrust engine, ideal for covert missions and sneak attacks. The bike had no built-in weapons, sensors, or shields, as Maul believed his own skills and lightsaber were sufficient to overcome any enemy.

Thanks to the combination of his discipline and remarkable powers of recuperation, Maul did not limp as he walked, using one hand to nudge his bike through the arid air, away from his ship. He had treated his leg with bacta and wrapped it in bandages. When he was fully healed, not even a scar would exist as evidence of his fight with the Togorian.

But his leg still ached. Earlier, after discovering bantha tracks near the *Scimitar*, he had had a brief encounter with Sand People. He suspected they had intended to lure him away from his ship and kill him. He had refrained from slaughtering them because a pile of dead Sand People might have drawn unnecessary attention. Still, running back to the *Scimitar* had not been good for his leg.

I'll rest after the Jedi are dead.

Maul left his bike hovering in the air behind him and came to a stop at the edge of the mesa. He gazed toward Mos Espa. And then he saw the probe droid zipping over the sand, approaching his position. The probe droid came to a stop less than a meter away from Maul's face. The droid uttered a few words in its own language, but Maul understood.

A Jedi had left Mos Espa and was returning to the Queen's ship.

Maul walked back to his bike, climbed onto its saddle, and launched off the mesa, leaving the watchful probe droid with the *Scimitar*. Maul's black cloak whipped at his back as he raced over the desert floor and into the Xelric Draw.

He soon saw the Queen's starship, still resting where his droid had sighted it earlier. Despite a layer of dust, the ship's highly polished silver exterior gleamed under the bright desert sky. The ship's boarding ramp was lowered.

And then Maul sighted two figures in front of him, both running toward the ship. The nearest figure appeared to be a child, a young boy. Beyond the boy was the tall Jedi.

Maul sensed something about the boy. The boy seemed to emanate ripples in the Force, but the ripples were unfocused, uncontrolled. This surprised Maul but did not distract him. He stayed focused on his target, the Jedi. If he happened also to mow down the boy in his path, so be it.

Maul accelerated. He was almost on top of the boy when the Jedi turned and shouted, and then the boy fell flat to the ground. As Maul's bike passed over the boy's prone body, Maul realized the Jedi must have commanded the boy to fall. He was intrigued by the fact that the boy had obeyed without hesitation, without looking back. Most boys would have stopped and turned.

Dismissing the boy as insignificant, Maul cut the bike's engine and leaped from it, sailing over the Jedi's head as he activated his lightsaber in midair. The Jedi activated his own green-bladed lightsaber and raised it fast to block Maul's sweeping blade. The lightsabers met with a bright flash of energy before Maul landed on his feet in a tight crouch.

The pain in his leg was exquisite.

Up close, Maul saw the Jedi was a big man. The Jedi shouted at the boy to go. Maul swung hard with his lightsaber but the Jedi blocked the blow. The Jedi shouted, "Tell them to take off!"

As the boy ran for the Queen's ship, Maul lashed out at the Jedi again and again, but the Jedi blocked each blow. Maul was suddenly aware that the Jedi seemed to anticipate each lunge and jab, as if he knew how Maul would move before Maul himself knew. Maul drew from the dark side of the Force and began to move faster, increasing the speed of his lunges along with his footwork. The Jedi kept up with Maul, but Maul soon sensed . . .

He's getting tired.

Maul felt the pain in his leg become more intense. He became angry at himself for being wounded, used the anger to fuel the dark side, and directed his rage at the Jedi. Maul was certain he would defeat his opponent.

He will fall heavily, like a monument.

But the Jedi did not falter. As Maul spun and moved around the Jedi, he saw the Queen's starship lift off. He also saw the boarding ramp was still extended.

Maul leaped over the Jedi, blocking his path to the rising ship, as their lightsabers continued to weave and smash into each other. The ship had just moved above their position when the Jedi leaped straight up and landed on the extended ramp, his lightsaber still blazing.

Maul watched the ship rise away from the desert, taking the Jedi with it. He deactivated his lightsaber and continued to stand where his feet were planted. Within seconds, the ascending ship vanished in the sky.

Maul tasted sand in his mouth. And blood. He continued to watch the sky as he felt almost overwhelmed by his humiliation. He had never felt such shame before. The shame was darker than any darkness he had ever known.

He found the darkness pleasing.

Maul had no reason to remain on Tatooine. He recovered his speeder bike and rode back to the *Scimitar.*

He transmitted a report, notifying his Master that the Jedi had escaped with Queen Amidala, and that he would be returning directly to Coruscant. He did not mention his run-in with the Togorian pirates in his report, nor his less significant encounter with the Sand People, because he knew his Master would be displeased. His Master would not be interested in explanations. His Master would only accuse him of allowing himself to be snared by the pirates and distracted by the Sand People.

As the Sith Infiltrator lifted away from Tatooine, Maul continued to contemplate how Sidious would respond if he learned about his apprentice's misadventures. If Maul admitted he had sustained a leg wound, his Master would regard him as weak. But because his leg wound was already almost healed, he questioned whether it was even necessary to inform his Master about it.

Concealing details from his Master was impossible. Sidious always knew everything about Maul's thoughts and actions. However, Maul knew his Master would not wish to be distracted by information that had nothing to do with conquering Naboo and destroying the Jedi. A wounded leg was beyond trivial. If he and his Master were to proceed, they would focus on moving forward.

The Sith Infiltrator left Tatooine's orbit and launched into hyperspace.

CHAPTER SIXTEEN

Arriving at Coruscant, Maul guided the *Scimitar* to the dark hemisphere, where night had fallen, angling past illuminated skyscrapers to the spire that housed Sidious's secret headquarters. He docked the Infiltrator in a landing bay, checked to make sure the landing bay was secure, and then went to meet with his Master.

He found Sidious's hooded figure seated in the middle of the otherwise empty meditation room. The door slid closed behind Maul. Sidious said, "Report."

"Queen Amidala and the Jedi *were* on Tatooine, Master. A Jedi and a young boy were running for the Queen's starship when I came upon them in the desert. The Jedi and I dueled. I nearly had him. But the boy reached the ship, the ship lifted off, and the Jedi leaped to it. I failed to stop them, Master."

Because of his Master's cowl, Maul could not see his

Master's eyes, but he watched the lower half of Sidious's face, staying alert for any slight twitch at the mouth or change in skin tone that would indicate his Master was angry. But his Master's expression remained neutral as he said, "You feel you would have defeated this Jedi?"

"Yes, Master. I felt him tire. I can defeat him."

"Was he bearded?"

Maul nodded.

"Good. That is Qui-Gon Jinn. He is the stronger of the two. His Padawan is Obi-Wan Kenobi."

Sidious sounded satisfied, which puzzled Maul. He had imagined Sidious would be furious with him for failing to stop the Jedi and the Queen. But then it suddenly occurred to Maul . . . *The Jedi will deliver the Queen to Coruscant, because the foolish Queen will think the Senate can help her.* Maul realized he could have another opportunity to please his Master. But before he could announce his deduction, his Master said, "Queen Amidala believes the Galactic Senate will support her. She has already arrived on Coruscant. She is staying in the Senatorial quarters."

Maul stiffened. "And the Jedi?"

"They are on Coruscant as well."

Maul's hand shifted to the hilt of his lightsaber. He felt a burning that began in his chest and spread outward. "Let me kill them, Master."

"Not here," Sidious said. "Not on Coruscant. I have another plan."

And then Maul sensed Sidious was preoccupied by other thoughts. He seemed oblivious to Maul's presence. Maul left the meditation room and went to his own quarters.

As soon as he was alone, he wondered whether his Master was actually furious and was now only delaying punishment. *Is he aware of my battle with the pirates? Of my foolish decision to follow the bantha tracks? Did he sense my leg wound?* Maul would not be surprised if his Master was just waiting to punish him like never before. He felt ashamed.

But then he thought of his Master's teachings. *Think of the now. Think of the future. Do not meditate on the past.*

Maul knew what he must do. He would use his shame, turn it inward to feed the darkness and hatred that flowed through his veins. He would direct his fury at his enemy, the Jedi named Qui-Gon Jinn.

In the past, Maul had never cared about the names of the people he'd killed. To him, enemies were nothing more than targets. But now he said Qui-Gon Jinn's name aloud. He clenched his teeth and repeated the name, then began chanting it like a curse.

I will destroy you, Qui-Gon Jinn. I will see the shock in your eyes when I run you through, Qui-Gon Jinn.

I will stand over your dead body in triumph, Qui-Gon Jinn.

Because of you, I have failed my Master.

You will pay.

Hours passed. Maul's comlink chirped. His Master was summoning him to the strategy room. Maul went. He found his Master shrugging out of the robe he wore in his guise as Palpatine, and realized his Master had returned from the Senate building.

"Queen Amidala will attempt to bring the Senate to her cause," Sidious said with pleasure. "She will ask them to outlaw the Trade Federation blockade of Naboo." He chortled happily.

Maul had never seen his Master in such a jovial mood. He thought, *My mistakes don't matter. Unless he is distracted by current events and will turn on me later . . .*

"I anticipate the Queen will return to Naboo," Sidious continued. "No doubt the Jedi will accompany her. Foolish girl." He smiled at Maul. "Come. Let us contact the Neimoidians and share the good news."

Sidious pulled on his dark robe, lifted its hood up over his head, stood before the communications console, and activated the holocomm. Maul stayed out of sight in the alcove behind Sidious's seat and watched as holograms of Nute Gunray and Rune Haako materialized in the air. Many light-years away, in Theed Royal Palace on the planet Naboo, Nute looked anxious as he said, "Yes, Lord Sidious?"

"The Queen will soon be on her way to you. I regret she is of no further use to us. Destroy her when she arrives."

Nute nodded. "Yes, my lord."

"Is the planet secure?"

"We have taken over the last pockets of primitive life-forms. We are in complete control of the planet now."

"Good," Sidious said. "I will see to it that in the Senate, things stay as they are. I am sending my apprentice, Darth Maul, to join you."

"Yes, my lord."

Sidious broke the connection and the holograms disappeared. Still facing the comm console, he laughed. "Soon the Neimoidians will no longer be useful to us. What a fine day that will be." He turned to face Maul. "Make sure the Neimoidians take care of Queen Amidala. You yourself must destroy the Jedi. Do not fail me again."

Maul bowed to his Master, then left quickly for the Sith Infiltrator.

When the *Scimitar* exited hyperspace in the Naboo system, Maul saw a single Droid Control Ship, the only remnant of the Trade Federation's blockade, in Naboo's orbit. Although the Neimoidians were expecting his arrival, Maul had activated the *Scimitar*'s cloaking technology to guarantee they would not be aware of his ship approaching the planet. He thought it would be best if he presented himself to Nute Gunray unannounced.

Naboo was a small world, covered by grassy plains, verdant mountains, and clear, unpolluted seas and lakes. As Maul descended through the atmosphere, he saw a flock of large, graceful birds soaring away from a waterfall that plunged over the edge of a steep cliff. Maul imagined what Naboo would be like if it were reduced to a lifeless, smoldering rock. He grinned at the thought.

He guided the *Scimitar* to the capital city of Theed. The city's architecture consisted primarily of elegantly designed domed structures, most of which appeared quite old but also well maintained. The largest structure was Theed Royal Palace, an interconnected cluster of domed spires that rose from a high cliff. As Maul landed his ship, he thought of Queen Amidala growing up in such rich, comfortable surroundings, with her handmaidens and assorted servants seeing to her every need.

Pampered weaklings.

From Maul's perspective, death could not come soon enough for the people of Naboo.

The Neimoidians had seized Theed Royal Palace as their own headquarters, and had settled into its lavish rooms as if they had owned it for years. Maul found Nute Gunray in Queen Amidala's private bedroom. He was lying sound asleep on a plush couch, a coverlet of soft shimmersilk draped over his body. Maul yanked away the coverlet and delivered a swift, hard kick to Nute's side.

Waking in a panic, Nute exclaimed, "Are they invading?!" And then he saw Darth Maul looming over him.

Maul glared with open disgust at the Neimoidian leader. "Get out. These are now my quarters."

Nute scrambled to his feet. He was taller than Maul, but Maul looked at him as if he were an insignificant bug. Nute tried to take the shimmersilk coverlet with him, but Maul snatched it and tore it in half. Maul said, "Send someone to remove the traces of your presence here."

Eager to distance himself from Maul, Nute shuffled quickly out of the bedroom. Maul looked around at the Queen's furnishings and laughed. He had no desire to sleep in such an extravagant room, but he had enjoyed terrifying Nute.

Leaving the bedroom, Maul thoroughly inspected the palace. Everywhere he looked, from the floor-to-ceiling windows to the grand hallways and staircases, he saw evidence of fine craftsmanship. He reconsidered the bedroom. Although he had been raised to associate luxury with weakness, he found satisfaction in the idea that there was nothing to stop him from claiming the palace as his own. There were no rules for how and where the Sith Lords should live *after* they achieved their goals, and Maul doubted that his Master expected him to rule from a small room with bare walls. He wondered if he had been too quick to envision laying waste to the entire planet. He could imagine worse fates than ruling from the opulent palace. And the Naboo plains and forests were rich with wild beasts ready for slaughter.

He made his way to the throne room. There he found Nute, seated on the throne, talking with Rune Haako. The Neimoidians looked up with alarm as Maul approached. Maul took pleasure in watching Nute cling desperately to the throne's broad arms, as if Maul might yank it out from underneath him. Maul said, "Status report."

Unable to meet Maul's gaze, Nute blinked his large eyes and said, "Things are . . . er, going well."

"Most of the Naboo people have been captured," Rune chimed in. "We have them in camps. A few have eluded us, but we shall crush them soon. As for Queen Amidala, every Trade Federation troop in the area is on alert, watching for her ship. We expect her to land in the city's central plaza, and that she will attempt to negotiate with us while using the Jedi as her shields. She will not slip through any of our safeguards."

Maul scowled. "Unless she is already here."

The Neimoidians glanced at each other and cried out at the same time, "Impossible!"

"I suggest we inspect the security around the plaza."

Nute and Rune babbled their approval. They shuffled

after Maul as he led them outside to the wide plaza. Maul imagined that the plaza was usually crowded with citizens, musicians, and merchants and the air was filled with conversation and singing birds. But now the only sound was the distant, clanking footfalls of droid troops. Maul enjoyed the desolation. However, he was not deceived by the overall quiet. Looking up at the cloudless sky, he thought, *A storm is coming. A death storm. Jedi will die.*

Rune pointed to a detachment of Federation battle droids that was marching across the opposite end of the plaza. He said, "They are timed to cover the plaza every fifteen minutes."

"Make it every five," Maul said as he scanned the surrounding buildings.

"But Lord Maul," Rune said uneasily, "what of the few citizens who have so far resisted us? Shouldn't we keep the troops spread out?"

Maul fixed his yellow eyes on Rune. "Do you think," Maul said, "the Queen will dawdle when she arrives, and simply wait for you to pick her up? *Think*, cretin. Where do you think she'll be heading?"

"Five-minute patrols!" Nute barked into his comlink. "Cover the plaza every five minutes!"

Maul gestured to the balconies that overlooked the plaza. "There should be surveillance at all times. Infrared sensors to alert the patrols."

"It shall be done," Rune said.

Nute's comlink signaled. He glanced at it anxiously.

"I suggest you answer that," Maul said, "or I'll throw you over a waterfall."

Nute pressed a button on his comlink and said, "Report."

The voice of a battle droid command officer responded flatly, "The Queen's starship has been found in the Naboo swamps, Viceroy."

Nute looked stunned. "Have you captured her?"

"The ship is empty, Viceroy," the officer replied. "There is no sign of the Queen's party. They have disappeared."

Nute and Rune glanced at each other. Rune's mouth was agape. Neither dared to face Maul. Still clutching the comlink, Nute said, voice trembling, "Send out patrols. Search for her."

Maul grabbed the comlink and switched it off. Through clenched teeth, he hissed at Nute, "Everything is under control, you say? You'll pay for this. Now we must contact Lord Sidious."

Nute nodded obediently as his mottled face turned a more sickly shade of green.

Maul led the two Neimoidians back to the palace's throne room. Nute seated himself quickly on the throne. Maul stood near Nute while Rune activated the holocomm, sending a transmission to Sidious. A moment later, a hologram of Maul's hooded Master flickered to life. Sidious said, "Yes, Viceroy?"

"Lord Sidious." Nute cleared his throat. "The Queen and the Jedi . . . they are on Naboo, but did not arrive where we expected."

Sidious frowned slightly, then said, "Go on."

"We've sent out patrols," Nute continued. "We already located their starship in the swamp. It won't be long, my lord."

"This is an unexpected move for her," Sidious said. "It's too aggressive." His hologram shifted. Even though Sidious's eyes were lost in shadow, Maul knew that his Master's gaze was now on him. "Lord Maul, be mindful. Let them make the first move."

"Yes, my Master."

While the Neimoidians scurried about the palace, Maul stood in a dark chamber near the throne room and meditated. He visualized the fight he knew would come, the inevitable duel with Qui-Gon Jinn. On Tatooine, he knew he had been wearing down the Jedi Knight. He had sensed that Qui-Gon Jinn fought without fear, but also without hate.

He will know fear. And I will make him hate me.

Maul heard someone running toward him. Annoyed by the interruption, he turned to face Nute Gunray. Nute cried out, "She is assembling an army!"

CHAPTER SEVENTEEN

"According to our patrols," Rune Haako said, "Queen Amidala contacted the Gungans, the primitives in the swamp."

Maul had not anticipated that the Queen would join forces with the Gungans, Naboo's amphibious natives. He turned to face Nute Gunray. "You said the primitives had all been rounded up."

"They went into hiding!" Nute exclaimed. "They know the terrain better than we do. . . ." Seeing Maul's angered glare, Nute went silent.

Rune said, "The Gungans are not a concern. They are no match for our forces. The Trade Federation droid army and weapons are invincible."

Maul could only guess what Queen Amidala thought she might accomplish. All her starfighters had been confiscated. Her volunteer pilots and officers were being held in camps. Desperate for help, she had turned to her planet's lesser life-forms, amphibious humanoids. Still, she had the Jedi on her side. Unable to determine what the Queen was planning, Maul said, "I must contact my Master."

"We should return to the throne room," Rune Haako said, gesturing to a four-legged Neimoidian mechno-holoprojector he had brought for Nute Gunray's convenience.

"We'll walk," Maul said as he went to the holoprojector and activated it. Less than a minute later, Sidious's hologram appeared, his gaze directed at Maul, Nute, and Rune, who followed the ambulatory device as it crawled through a palace corridor on its sharply tapered metal feet.

"The Queen has an army, my Master," Maul said. "She has allied with Naboo's Gungan population. They must be planning to strike against the Trade Federation's superior forces." Maul grimaced. "I feel there is more to this, my Master. The two Jedi may be using the Queen for their own purposes."

"The Jedi cannot become involved," Sidious said with authority, his hologram bobbing gently back and forth along with the movement of the walking holoprojector. "They can only protect the Queen. Even Qui-Gon Jinn will not break that covenant."

Maul had not considered the fact that the Jedi, by tradition and the rules of their Order, did not fight in wars. His Master never overlooked any details.

"Our young Queen surprises me," Sidious continued. "She is more foolish than I thought."

Nute said, "We are sending all troops to meet this army assembling near the swamp. It appears to be made up of primitives."

"This will work to our advantage," Sidious responded. Maul noticed that his Master actually sounded pleased.

The holoprojector came to a stop in the corridor. Maul, Nute, and Rune stopped beside it, their eyes fixed on Sidious's hologram. Rune said eagerly, "I have your approval to proceed, then, my lord?"

"Wipe them out," Sidious replied without hesitation. "All of them." Sidious's hologram flickered and vanished.

Maul, Nute, and Rune proceeded to the throne room. A large viewscreen was built into one wall, and displayed a view of the palace's outdoor plaza. Looking up at the viewscreen, the Neimoidians were startled to see the Jedi Knight and his apprentice cutting down battle droids who had been guarding the palace. The Jedi were accompanied by Naboo soldiers and pilots. Some soldiers were on foot, and others arrived in armored landspeeders that carried blaster cannons.

Rune whispered, "How did they get into the city?"

"I don't know," Nute said, shaking his head as he watched the Naboo soldiers fire Federation tanks. "I thought the battle was going to take place far from here." Eyes wide with fear, he added, "This is too close."

"I told you there was more to this," Maul said. "The Jedi *are* involved. They have come to Theed for a reason, Viceroy. They have a plan of their own for defeating us."

Looking even more alarmed, Nute said, "A plan?"

"One that will fail, I assure you." Maul glared at the images on the viewscreen. "I have waited a long time for this. I have trained for it endlessly. The Jedi will regret their decision to return here." His hand flexed near his lightsaber. "Wait here until I return." He walked past the Neimoidians, heading for a tall doorway.

"Where are you going?" Nute demanded frantically.

"Where do you think I'm going, Viceroy?" Maul answered without breaking his stride. "I'm going to the main hangar to rid you of the Jedi once and for all."

The Queen's pilots managed to liberate more than a dozen Naboo starfighters from the Theed hangar before Maul's arrival. Maul saw the sleek, gleaming starfighters climb into the sky and suspected they were heading for the Trade Federation's Droid Control Ship. Because the control ship carried more than one thousand droid starfighters, Maul doubted the Queen's pilots would survive more than a few minutes. *Fools.*

He entered the air base and made his way to the hangar's entrance, which was sealed by blast-proof durasteel double doors. Lowering his gaze to the floor, he reached out with his senses. He detected movement on the other side of the doors. He knew the Jedi were approaching, walking straight toward his position.

The double doors slid open. Maul lifted his gaze. He faced Queen Amidala, who was with a group of armed Naboo guards and two handmaidens. Seeing Maul, the group had come to a dead stop. Maul spotted the two Jedi behind the guards and locked his eyes on Qui-Gon Jinn.

"We'll handle this," Qui-Gon Jinn said as he and Obi-Wan Kenobi moved forward, side by side, edging past the guards.

"We'll take the long way," Queen Amidala said as she rushed with her remaining allies toward a side passage.

Keeping his eyes on the Jedi, Maul lifted his hood back, revealing his horned head. He shrugged off his cloak and let it fall to the floor. The two Jedi did the same with their robes.

The Queen, her guards, and the handmaidens were still running for a nearby exit when three Trade Federation destroyer droids wheeled fast from around a corner and into the hangar. The droids stopped quickly, then rapidly unfurled their tripod legs and built-in blaster cannons, activated their deflector shields, and opened fire in the Queen's direction.

While the Queen and her retinue took cover and fired their blasters at the droids, Maul drew his lightsaber and activated one red blade. Gripping the lightsaber in his left hand, he extended his arm forward and activated the second blade. The Jedi activated their lightsabers, and Maul noticed Qui-Gon Jinn's blade flashed a fraction of a second after Obi-Wan's.

The old Jedi's getting slow.

Maul made a jabbing motion at Obi-Wan. Obi-Wan leaped at Maul. Their lightsabers clashed as Obi-Wan flipped over Maul's head and landed behind him. Keeping his eyes on Qui-Gon, Maul angled his lightsaber to block Obi-Wan's blade from behind, then ducked fast to evade Qui-Gon's sweeping blade.

Maul advanced toward Qui-Gon and spun, deflecting blows from both Jedi as the fight shifted across the hangar deck. Rapidly spinning his lightsaber, he anticipated their moves with ease. Having expected a greater challenge from Qui-Gon and Obi-Wan, he felt even more disgusted by them. But if the Jedi held no surprises in combat, Maul knew he had his Master to thank for that. If not for his Master, he never would have been a match for two Jedi at the same time.

Over the crashing noise of lightsabers, the destroyer droids' cannons, and the Naboo guards' blasters, Maul heard a starfighter's laser cannon firing across the hangar. He did not need the Force to be peripherally aware that the shots came from one remaining Naboo starfighter, which had just lifted off the deck and was now angling for the destroyer droids. He kept up his assault on the Jedi while the starfighter fired again and again, knocking out the destroyer droids' shields before shattering them completely. A moment later, the Queen and her group fled through a doorway, and then the Naboo starfighter soared out of the hangar.

Maul was not worried about the Queen. He would deal with her later. But for the moment, he was busy.

He kicked Qui-Gon in the chest so hard that he knocked the Jedi off his feet. He flipped away from Obi-Wan, flinging his body through the air to land before a doorway that led to Theed City's power generator. With one hand gripping his lightsaber, he reached out with the Force and seized a large piece of debris from one of the ruined destroyer droids, then launched it at the door's opening mechanism. The mechanism exploded in sparks and the door began to slide open.

Qui-Gon was already up and he rushed toward Maul, but Obi-Wan reached him first. Maul spun his lightsaber, deflecting his opponents' strikes as he backed through the open doorway. He launched a high kick that connected with Obi-Wan's jaw. As Obi-Wan fell back and rolled across the floor, Maul backed up, luring Qui-Gon toward the power generator. Obi-Wan got up fast and sprinted to rejoin the fight.

That's it. Come to me.

Qui-Gon swung. Maul parried and swung back fast, clipping Qui-Gon's blade and then Obi-Wan's. The double-bladed lightsaber was a blur. Maul backed onto an inspection platform that was suspended high over the generator's deep shaft, and kicked off, backflipping to one of the many catwalks that spanned different levels in the shaft. Both Jedi leaped after him, and the fight proceeded along the catwalk.

Maul leered at the Jedi as he edged around a towering acceleration shaft that glowed brightly with plasma used to energize Theed City. With his lightsaber in constant motion, he kicked Obi-Wan straight off the catwalk. Before he could determine whether Obi-Wan had plummeted to his death, Qui-Gon struck and surprised Maul with a backhanded blow to the head that sent Maul over the catwalk's edge.

Maul did not cry out. He knew the shaft's central catwalk lay below him. He kept his lightsaber activated and held its pommel close to his chest as he landed hard on his back on the catwalk. The impact would have broken an ordinary man's back, but Maul was not by any means ordinary. He did feel pain, but as ever, the pain only fueled his rage.

He was still lying on his back as he saw Qui-Gon leaping from above. The Jedi landed close to him, and Maul had to move fast to block the Jedi's blade. Then Maul was up again, moving backward along the central catwalk. In the distance, beyond Qui-Gon's back, Maul sighted Obi-Wan clinging to the edge of a lower catwalk. Maul realized he didn't want Obi-Wan to fall, because that would deprive him of the pleasure of killing the young Jedi.

Maul leered again at Qui-Gon. *You think you're driving me back. You have no idea that I'm in control. You don't know where I'm taking you.*

The central catwalk terminated at the entrance of a security hallway that led to the generator's core. The hallway was protected by six consecutive laser doors that opened and locked shut in response to potentially lethal power outputs that occurred intermittently during the generator's plasma-activation process. As Maul lured Qui-Gon toward the hallway, he saw Obi-Wan leap up onto the central catwalk.

You'll both be dead soon.

Maul sensed the laser doors opening behind him. Qui-Gon was unrelenting in his ongoing attack, but Maul parried every blow. Qui-Gon swung at Maul's legs, but the blade swept under his feet as Maul jumped backward. Maul continued moving back, leading Qui-Gon into the hallway. They passed the first four security barriers before the doors activated and shut.

Transparent red curtains of pure energy, the doors would kill any life-form on contact. Maul was suddenly sealed in the passage between the fifth and sixth doors, and Qui-Gon between the fourth and fifth. Gazing past Qui-Gon, Maul saw Obi-Wan trapped between the first and second doors.

Facing Maul, Qui-Gon deactivated his lightsaber and dropped to one knee. Maul jabbed at the laser door that separated him from the Jedi, and succeeded only in producing a noisy flash. Maul deactivated his own weapon and watched the Jedi warily. He watched Qui-Gon take a deep breath and close his eyes.

He's . . . meditating?!

Keeping his eyes on the kneeling Jedi, Maul paced back and forth within his confined area of the hallway. He was baffled by the Jedi's mentality, the urge to meditate at such a moment, the desire to remain calm. The effort was so pointless. Glancing through the doors behind Qui-Gon, Maul saw that the worried-looking Obi-Wan had deactivated his own lightsaber. With his arms extended at his sides, Obi-Wan looked like a hopeless clod. Maul grinned.

They don't know the power of the dark side. But they will . . . when I slay them.

Minutes passed. And then the laser doors opened.

Maul and Qui-Gon activated their lightsabers at the same time. Qui-Gon sprang forward, Maul moved backward, and the fight resumed. Behind Qui-Gon, Obi-Wan raced up through the security hallway, but he had to stop fast when the sixth laser door activated, cutting him off from Qui-Gon.

Warding off Qui-Gon's attack with each backward step, Maul maneuvered around the circular mouth of the generator's core, a virtually fathomless pit. Maul sensed

Qui-Gon was fighting without hatred, just as he sensed Obi-Wan's helplessness from behind the transparent laser door. He spun his lightsaber to deflect a rapid series of strikes from Qui-Gon's blade, then brought his own lightsaber up fast and slammed the side of its pommel against Qui-Gon's face, stunning the Jedi. And then, with a flick of his wrist, he drove one of his red blades straight through Qui-Gon's chest.

"No!"

The echoing shout came from Obi-Wan, who was still trapped behind the sixth laser door. Maul yanked the lightsaber free from Qui-Gon's torso and the Jedi collapsed beside the core.

Turning his back to Qui-Gon, Maul fixed his gaze on Obi-Wan. He deactivated his lightsaber and began pacing before the laser door, watching Obi-Wan as he waited for the door to open. He bared his teeth hungrily.

You're next.

When the door opened, Obi-Wan's lightsaber was blazing and so was Maul's. The young Jedi practically flew toward Maul. Their lightsabers smashed into each other. Maul spun and turned, flipping his lightsaber and forcing Obi-Wan to move that much faster with his inferior single-bladed weapon. Maul noticed that Obi-Wan was fighting more offensively than Qui-Gon, but it didn't matter. The boy would suffer the same fate as —

Obi-Wan's lightsaber came up fast and swept through the pommel of Maul's weapon. One half of

Maul's lightsaber shattered, leaving his left hand clutching what amounted to a still-functional single blade. Before he could react, Obi-Wan kicked him in the chest and he was sent sprawling onto his back near the edge of the core.

Obi-Wan leaped over Maul and tried to drive his lightsaber through Maul's prone body, but Maul blocked the strike and flung himself up from the floor. Obi-Wan landed behind Maul, but Maul turned and blocked another series of strikes before he kicked Obi-Wan in the jaw.

The Jedi moved with the kick, letting it carry him into a backflip. Landing on his feet, he struck back at Maul, driving them both away from the core. Maul flipped to the side and then used the power of the Force to shove Obi-Wan backward. Obi-Wan lost his grip on his lightsaber as he hit the floor. The lightsaber was still bouncing across the floor as he fell into the core.

Obi-Wan's lightsaber came to a stop. Maul grinned as he walked toward the weapon and then kicked it into the core. He leaned over the edge of the core to watch the lightsaber fall down the apparently bottomless hole. The lightsaber fell past Obi-Wan, who had managed to grab hold of a nub that jutted out from the core's upper wall, about two meters below the floor level.

Maul glared at Obi-Wan. He wondered how long the Jedi could cling to the nub. He knew Obi-Wan's hands and arms would get tired eventually. Growing impatient, Maul swung his pared-down lightsaber against the metal edge of the core's upper rim, sending sparks flying out over Obi-Wan's head. Maul noted that his blade did not damage the metal and realized it was impervious to energy weapons. He wondered if the metal could be crafted into body armor.

And then he noticed Obi-Wan was not looking up at him. The Jedi was staring at something along the core's upper wall. Or was he looking at something beyond the wall? Baffled by what the Jedi might be attempting, Maul scrunched his face angrily.

Obi-Wan flew up out of the core. Maul had forgotten about Qui-Gon Jinn's lightsaber, which flew up from the floor near the fallen Jedi's body and landed in the waiting hand of the still-airborne Obi-Wan.

Maul rapidly transferred his lightsaber from his right hand to his left. Obi-Wan activated Qui-Gon's lightsaber as he soared overhead and landed behind Maul. Maul spun fast, but not fast enough to stop Obi-Wan from swinging Qui-Gon's blade through his midsection.

Maul grunted involuntarily as every nerve in his body went into shock. His vision blurred and he blinked his eyes, trying to regain his focus. He wanted to fight back. He wanted to slay Obi-Wan, but his body would not obey him. Obi-Wan slid out of his range of vision, and then Maul saw the chamber's ceiling. He realized he was falling backward into the core.

No.

And as he fell, the upper half of his body separated from the lower.

No.

As his remains tumbled down the generator shaft, he kept his eyes open and fought to remain conscious. But then his head struck the shaft's wall, and everything went dark.

No!

His mind screamed. Despite everything he had learned about death and duty from his Master, Maul knew he was not yet ready to die. Not after so many years of training, and with so much more to accomplish. Not so long as he still had so much hatred within him.

Obi-Wan ruined me!

He willed himself to see. A moment later, his vision returned. The shaft's walls were a disorienting blur. Across the shaft he sighted his own black-clad legs, scissoring lifelessly at the air as they fell. He struggled to right his torso so he could see downward.

Can't die!

He fell past an oval shadow, and then a similar shadow raced by, along with a whooshing sound.

Air vents.

Maul hoped that there was at least one more vent below, that it would be large enough to accommodate his diminished body. He extended his arms, and his left hand's fingertips suddenly burned with friction as they brushed against the cylindrical wall.

Must live!

Hoping, wishing, praying for one more air vent . . .

Must kill Obi-Wan!

. . . he reached out with the Force.

CHAPTER EIGHTEEN

"Far above . . . far above . . . we don't know where we'll fall," muttered the creature as he used a broken bit of blackened bone to scratch a drawing onto the wall of his cavernous dwelling, his bare back warmed by the small fire he'd built. "Far above . . . what once was great is rendered small." The drawing consisted of a pair of small silhouettes, a man's upper body separated from his lower body, each half apparently descending between two vertical lines that indicated a deep chute.

The creature sighed. "Nowhere to go but down."

More than a decade had passed since the skirmish that had become known as the Battle of Naboo. The creature that had once been Darth Maul moved on his spiderlike droid legs through a tunnel on the planet Lotho Minor. He still didn't know how long he'd been in the tunnel, or how or when he'd arrived on such a dismal world. He still remembered nothing about his life before, when he lived aboveground. All he had left were his anger and his hunger.

"Falling, falling, falling." He looked at his other drawings of small figures on the wall. Some figures were being tortured, others killed. Many were fighting with burning sticks. Some sticks were blue. Some were red. The creature liked the red sticks.

No, not sticks. Sticks are wrong. Something else that cuts and burns like . . .

He heard something move in the upper levels, a slithering sound that he recognized as coming from the one who called himself Morley. Morley was a snakelike scavenger who should have kept his distance. *Stupid Morley.*

And then he heard footsteps. Someone was walking with Morley.

Someone very big. On two legs.

Lowering the bone he'd been using as a drawing stick, he kept to the shadows as he scurried up a wall, careful not to make a sound. Despite his damaged memories, he knew every crevice and foothold in the tunnels.

As he shifted his metal legs up toward the ceiling, he looked down and saw Morley's shadowy form slink into the dark chamber. Near Morley, another dark form shifted, a hulking humanoid. A small point of light radiated and moved across the area of the big man's chest.

Something glowing, something burns . . .

"He's going to get you!" Morley cried.

The big man spun around and moved away from Morley. Morley shouted, "He's going to eat you alive!"

The creature clinging to the ceiling did not know whether Morley was threatening him or encouraging him to make a feast of the big man. The creature didn't care. He descended fast and pounced on Morley.

"No!" Morley screamed. "Not me! Please, not me!"

The creature squeezed Morley's writhing body. He liked the sounds of Morley's screams and desperate gasps for breath, but not as much as he enjoyed the loud snapping of bones as he broke Morley's spine.

Now for the big man.

The creature spotted something glowing in the darkness, recognized it as the point of light he'd seen on the other intruder's chest. He lurched forward on his metal legs and was about to spring when the man ignited a long red stick.

Not a stick.

A red blade made of pure energy. It was familiar. . . . *Mine!*

The creature *knew* he had once owned the weapon, or one very much like it. He glared at the intruder, saw that the point of light against his chest was a small amulet that hung from a chain around his neck. The man's head was illuminated by the glowing red blade. His strong face was tattooed with jagged patterns, and horns extended from his skull.

A reflection?!

For unknown reasons, the creature thought of a boy floating outside a window.

Me? No! Not me!

Confused and outraged, the creature shrieked and launched himself at the intruder, slamming him against the wall. He grabbed for the weapon's handle but the intruder knocked him back. His six metal legs clattered as he tumbled across the floor, but he rolled up onto his tapered feet and lashed out again, punching and kicking. His fingers struck armor and powerful muscles. He barely noticed that the intruder was only trying to ward him off with the red blade, not strike him down.

He pried at the central grip, trying to yank the weapon from the intruder's grasp. He did not assume that the weapon housed separate components for each blade, his shattered mind not even comprehending the incredible technology. He just knew that it was familiar and deadly, and that he wanted it.

The weapon snapped in two, leaving the intruder holding one red blade and the creature with the other. And then they were fighting, the two blades clashing in the darkness. Their fight carried them through the cave, but then the intruder grunted and fell back.

"You, Darth Maul," the intruder said, "are who I've been searching for."

Darth Maul?

"I thought you were dead. You are my kin."

Memories flickered in the creature's mind . . . in *Maul's* mind. He growled. "No!"

"We are brothers."

Maul shook his head. "You don't know," Maul snapped. "You don't know anything!"

The intruder placed his hand over his chest. "I know I am your blood."

Maul glared at the intruder. *I don't know you!* He tried to read the stranger's expression. *Sorry for me? Disgusted?* Maul's blood began to boil. The stranger was nothing to him, not even a threat. Sneering, he cast aside the weapon and retreated into the cave.

He clambered over junk and shoved aside rotting carcasses, making his way back to the fire he'd built. It was still burning. He crouched on the filthy floor, stared at the drawings on the walls, and began chanting, "Never never never never never . . ."

The hulking stranger followed Maul to the fire. Looking around, the stranger said with dismay, "This is where you live?"

Without looking at the stranger, Maul nodded in response. He picked up a nearby bone and began gnawing on it.

The stranger noticed the weird and violent drawings that decorated the walls. "How long have you lived here?"

Maul nipped at the bone, his eyes rolling back and

forth madly as he replied, "Years and years and years and years."

"You are a powerful Sith," the stranger said solemnly. "The whole galaxy shook before your power. Do you remember?"

The whole galaxy?! Maul leered. "Always remember, always remember."

The stranger eyed the robotic apparatus beneath Maul's rib cage and said, "Your legs?"

"That scum took it," Maul said.

The stranger seemed pleased by Maul's answer. "The Jedi . . . you remember." Taking a cautious step toward Maul, the stranger said, "I've brought a gift for you."

"For me?" Maul said with disbelief. "Food?"

"No. Something to regain your memory." He removed the glowing talisman from his neck and handed it to Maul.

Maul clutched at the talisman. Rocking back and forth on his robot legs, he began chanting.

The stranger leaned closer to Maul. "Brother, what are you saying?"

But Maul wasn't listening. His focus was on the talisman, which glowed increasingly brighter in his hand. And then his mind was flooded by fragmented memories.

My childhood . . . my training . . . my Master!

In his mind, he saw a young man.

Scum!

The man was a Jedi.

Jedi scum! What's his name?

He knew the man's name was Obi-Wan Kenobi.

Maul's eyes went wide. And then he collapsed.

EPILOGUE

The hulking man claimed his name was Savage Opress. Like Maul, he was a Zabrak. According to Opress, Talzin had transformed him into a monstrous warrior, endowed him with dark side powers, and given him the amulet and sent him in search of Maul. Maul had no recollection of the amulet, the talisman Talzin had brushed against his bloodied arm years earlier. He didn't remember anyone named Talzin.

When Opress's starship left the planet Lotho Minor, Maul was with him. Opress had plotted a course for Dathomir. He explained that they would find Talzin on Dathomir, that Talzin would help Maul. Maul didn't know why Talzin would help him, but he did know that he needed help.

Because now he knew the identity of the person who had transformed him into a monster. He knew the man was a Jedi named Obi-Wan Kenobi. If Opress and Talzin could help Maul, they might help him find Kenobi. But

Maul also knew he was in bad shape, that what he could really use was a new set of legs.

And then he would make Kenobi pay.

He looked at Opress, who was seated behind the controls of the starship that was carrying them to the hyperspace jump point that would take them to Dathomir. Maul was not certain that Opress was his ally, let alone his brother. But Maul was willing to take a chance.

Maybe he's a reflection . . . maybe he's the boy outside the window.

Maul could only imagine what the future held, or whether he could trust the man who was bringing him to Dathomir. He hoped Opress was indeed his friend.

Everyone else could burn.

ACKNOWLEDGMENTS

Star Wars: The Wrath of Darth Maul reveals many new details about Darth Maul's life but also draws dialogue and situations from previously published books, including the screenplay for *Star Wars*: Episode I *The Phantom Menace* by George Lucas; the movie novelization of *Star Wars*: Episode I *The Phantom Menace* by Terry Brooks; and most notably *Star Wars*: Episode I *Journal—Darth Maul* by Jude Watson, which provided a wealth of information about Maul's childhood and training. I borrowed from Watson's book liberally and with great respect. The story also incorporates details from the television series *Star Wars: The Clone Wars* episode "Brothers," scripted by Katie Lucas.

I'm extremely grateful to writer James Luceno, who generously gave me some great ideas so *The Wrath of Darth Maul* would mesh with his novel *Darth Plagueis*, and also provided an early draft of his short story "Restraint," from which I also borrowed liberally; I encourage readers to read "Restraint" for a more expansive account of Maul's exploits on the planet Orsis. Thanks also to former Scholastic editor Annmarie Nye for enlisting me to write this book; to editor Frank Parisi and Lucas Books executive editor Jonathan Rinzler for their valued input; and to Lucasfilm's Leland Chee for helping us *Star Wars* writers maintain continuity. Thanks to Greg Mitchell for reminding me about the *Dusty Duck*. And thanks to my daughter Violet for reading an advance version of this book's early chapters and reassuring me I could make at least one person feel sorry for Darth Maul.

Books by Elinor Lipman

The Family

The

FAMILY MAN

Elinor Lipman

HOUGHTON MIFFLIN HARCOURT

BOSTON · NEW YORK

2009

For information about permission to reproduce selections
from this book, write to Permissions, Houghton Mifflin
Harcourt Publishing Company, 215 Park Avenue South,
New York, New York 10003.

www.hmhbooks.com

Library of Congress Cataloging-in-Publication Data
Lipman, Elinor.
The family man / Elinor Lipman.
p. cm.
ISBN 978-0-618-64466-7
1. Gay lawyers — Fiction. 2. Stepdaughters — Fiction.
3. Fathers and daughters — Fiction. 4. Upper West Side
(New York, N.Y.) — Fiction. 5. Domestic fiction. I. Title.
PS3562.I577F36 2009
813'.54 — dc22   2008046222

Book design by Melissa Lotfy

Printed in the United States of America

DOC 10 9 8 7 6 5 4 3 2

A portion of this book appeared, in slightly
different form, in the *Southern Review.*

This book is for

MAMEVE MEDWED

STACY SCHIFF

ANITA SHREVE

The Family Man

1

I Hate You Still

ENRY ARCHER DID not attend his ex-wife's husband's funeral, but he did send a note of condolence. The former Denise Archer wrote back immediately and urgently: Would he believe, after twenty-four reasonably happy years, that life as she knew it had been snatched out from under her? Her postscript said, "Your number's unlisted. Call me," and there it was, a bridge he'd never planned to cross.

His quiet greeting, "It's Henry Archer, Denise," provoked an audible sob. She quickly clarified that it wasn't bereavement he was hearing in her voice, but relief, a sense she'd been thrown a lifeline.

"Me?" he asked.

Could he stand hearing the whole sordid story? Had he known that Glenn Krouch had two sons from another marriage? Because they were getting everything, every last thing except the clothes, the furs, the jewelry, and one signed Picasso, which was only a pencil sketch. Was he sitting down? Because some famously heartless lawyer had set *twenty-five* years of marriage as the watershed anniversary after which the prenuptial agreement would deem her long-suffering enough to be a true wife (voice crescendos) *and not some piece of shit!* It was, in the opinion of two lawyers (husbands of friends, not their area of expertise, should she get a third or fourth opinion?), a hideously airtight legal document. And now these stepsons were taking the will so *literally,* as if twenty-four faithful years didn't render a pre-nup null, void, and vicious. How many times had she asked Glenn if he'd updated his will, meaning, *Am I in it?* To which he'd always said, *Yes, of course.*

The "of course" amounted to a monthly allowance under the thumb of older son and executor, Glenn Junior. Horrible! And so much for Glenn Senior's famous love for Thalia! Henry remembered Thalia, didn't he? Another indignity: Thalia's portion was in trust until she was thirty-five. How condescending and sexist was *that*? Had she mentioned that these sons, not even thirty-five themselves, were not only Glenn's favorite children but his business partners as well? And who but she, their reviled stepmother, had arranged every detail of the black-tie party celebrating the addition of "& Sons" to all signage and had invited the boys' mother *and* seated her at the head table?

She'd helped raise these stepsons since they were eight and ten, buying bunk beds and electronics for their alternate weekends, enduring camp visiting days and humid swim meets. In some families, the ice might have melted; young Glenn and Tommy could have developed warm filial feelings toward her as years went by and the marriage appeared to make their father happy. But apparently nothing mended a mother's broken heart like sending the second wife to the poorhouse.

If only she'd known . . . well, she had known. She'd signed the hideous document, thinking divorce was the only thing she had to fear. Besides, who thought Glenn with his good stress tests and low blood pressure would die at seventy? The boys got the business, its buildings and outbuildings, and the unkindest, most ridiculous bequest of all: Denise's marital home, the five-bedroom apartment on Park Avenue! Could Henry even imagine what it was worth now? Her friends said the noninheritance was antediluvian, like a Jane Austen movie or a *Masterpiece Theatre* miniseries where the male heirs get to throw the mother and daughter to the wolves.

Infuriating and unfair! One would think that she, the second wife, was single-handedly the home wrecker, no fault of Daddy's, because of course he had made restitution with cars, then condos, then partnerships. Who could hold a grudge this long? If only she'd had a job that had contributed to her own upkeep and toward the mortgage payments. *Were* there mortgage payments? She wished she'd been paying better attention to that, too. Admittedly, ten rooms were too many for a woman living alone. But wasn't downsizing a widow's prerogative? Three real estate agents from one office, all clucking their condolences as they took measurements, had spent hours counting closets and flushing toilets, exactly two weeks and one day after Glenn's funeral. And yes, the sons did offer something like an extension: Denise could stay as long as she paid the common charges and the taxes, which, conveniently for her new overlords, exceeded her monthly allowance.

"I wish you'd been there," Denise told her ex-husband.

"Where?"

"At the wake! If my friends hadn't seen it with their own two eyes, they'd never believe that Nanette crashed the receiving line, wearing a black suit that screamed *I'm the widow, too.* Yes, I hugged her and yes, we looked like one big happy family in mourning, but I was numb. I didn't mean it! I was on widow autopilot."

"Maybe," Henry ventured, "Nanette was there to support her children."

"All I know is that the minute I turned my back, that self-appointed chief of protocol, Glenn Krouch Junior, pulled his mother into the receiving line. I don't think I've ever felt so utterly alone."

"Thalia wasn't there?" Henry asked.

"Thalia was there. Thalia chose to stand at the other end of the line."

"Because?"

"Who knows why daughters do these things? I can't keep track of my maternal shortcomings. She and I . . . well, never mind. Needless to say, we weren't speaking before that and we're not speaking now."

"I'm sorry. One would think, especially on that day —"

"I should have had a child with Glenn, a flesh-and-blood Krouch. And when I think that I viewed his vasectomy as one of the original selling points —"

"Selling points in favor of your extramarital affair?" asked Henry. "How soon did that come up? The night you met?"

"Oh, hon," said Denise. "Is that always going to be a sore subject? Even though you've made peace with your sexual orientation?"

I hate you still, he thought.

How odd to be his ex-wife's confidant. Henry has done nothing to advance a rapprochement, but Denise has called him daily to rant further about greedy stepsons and the breadline. Her chumminess and her invitations suggest that he is a safe companion for a widow, that a gay ex is something of a status symbol, that her betrayal is not only ancient history, but has been absolved

4

by his subsequent sexual homecoming. When Denise pauses for breath, he asks about Thalia — location, job, marital status, content of their last communication, and particularly what Thalia understands of the short-term father named Henry Archer who didn't fight for her in court. Invariably Denise, the new woman who has declared herself a work in progress, changes the subject back to Denise.

2

A Widow with a Child

H E EXPECTS TO BE astonished by the lavishness and
size of the Krouch home, but he is not. Its color scheme
is a range from oatmeal to sand. The upholstery is
nubby, and the variegated gold carpeting is wall-to-wall. Luckily,
Denise had announced while her key was still in the lock, "You
won't be impressed. Glenn liked his furniture pushed against the
walls and coffee tables in front of every couch. I finally gave up."
An odor of cigar smoke has lingered, and oversized ashtrays dec-
orate every surface. Henry crosses the room to inspect the photos sitting on a ceiling-high étagère made entirely of Lucite. The
dominant photograph is a wedding portrait of Denise and Glenn,
he in a dark suit and she in a pink ensemble that manages to look
bridal. "It was just before a judge in a private room at Lutèce." She
sighs. "We ate there on every anniversary until it closed. What a
shock *that* was."

He would have smiled at Denise's misplaced mourning if

he weren't staring intently at a graduation photo, quite surely of Thalia, and then candid shots of her in action: helmeted on a horse, helmeted on skis, in a headlock between two laughing young men. "That's her, all right," he says. "That's the girl I used to know."

Or is it? The resemblance to the baby Thalia is imperfect, not a time-lapse morph by a police artist. Yes, she is brown-eyed and brown-haired, dimpled still, baby cheeks now defined by excellent cheekbones. The photos convey a fun-loving and friendly girl, but why, he wonders, do they suggest something more immediate, something observed firsthand? He tries to concentrate: Where has he seen this face? "Trying to place her," he murmurs.

Denise, wiping her finger along a dusty frame, stares as if he has said something odd and symptomatic of lost brain cells. "Henry? It's Thalia. You know that. My daughter."

"I mean — I know her now."

"She's got one of those faces," says Denise. "I often think I see her in a crowd, but then I find myself tapping the shoulder of some other brown-haired girl with a pleasant expression."

"No," he says. "It's more than that. I see her regularly. I know I do. I just can't put my finger on the context."

"Are you saying that you two are in touch?"

He shakes his head no and closes his eyes.

Denise rattles off impatiently, "In the park? On the subway? In a restaurant? Maybe you're neighbors. She moves a lot. I can't always keep up with her changes of address."

An image is creeping closer, and he is relieved: It is neither compromising nor threatening. It is one of good humor and good service. And now he knows, absolutely: She is the unfailingly friendly girl behind the half door who hangs up his jacket and offers the coral smock before Giovanni cuts his hair. She is the coat-check girl with the big brandy snifter at her elbow in

7

which he places one dollar as he collects his outerwear and she tells him that this is a very good cut for him.

Denise is dusting like a novice, using a tissue from her purse. "Do you have it yet?" she asks.

It's too soon, and he can't be sure what an ambitious mother would do with this knowledge. "Not quite," he lies.

Because his next haircut isn't for another ten days, he makes an appointment for a procedure he's never wanted: a manicure. "I'll take your first opening," he tells the receptionist. One hour from now, she tells him. Can he make noon? He says he can.

"Special occasion?" she asks.

He says yes, then not really, distracted by another question on his mind: Shall he confirm the name of the coat-check girl, ask if she's working today and at what hour she goes to lunch? Fearing that such unwelcome interest would be within seconds shouted across the room to Thalia, he says, "Till then," and nothing more.

How could he not have noticed the resemblance between baby Thalia and this woman now reaching across the partition to take his navy blue blazer? How had he failed to spot the same shiny brown hair framing the heart-shaped face captured twenty-five years ago in photos that have never left his mantel? He says, "I'm only having a manicure today. Do you think I need a coverall?"

She scratches her chin and narrows her eyes as if his question requires deep concentration. "It depends on who you get and what color polish you choose," she says, then laughs. She asks, rather miraculously, he thinks — that she would start a conversation on this signature day — "This isn't your first manicure, is it?"

"Yes," he replies, adding, "I'm Henry Archer," but without a paternal or confessional timbre, nothing that says, *That name should ring a very profound bell in your head because I was your father for a while.*

"Want me to hold your newspaper?" she asks.

"Will you be here when I'm done? Because I know I'll forget to ask for it if someone else is covering for you."

"I'll be here," she says.

He decides that the moment is right: He doesn't care about a manicure. If what he brings up gets complicated or emotional, he'll reschedule. "Is your name, by chance, Thalia?" he begins.

She is not even close to being astonished. She does not seem to feel that it is a missing person's case solved, but merely a long-standing client trying to recall her name. "That's me," she says. "It's Greek. One of the three Graces."

When he doesn't answer, she adds, "Also, one of the nine Muses."

He is never tongue-tied, so what is wrong with him? A thunderbolt from Zeus might as well have smote him because he loves this Thalia instantly.

Throughout his manicure — how foolish he feels to be seen having his nails buffed and cuticles discussed — he ponders how to reveal himself to be the John Henry Archer whose fatherhood dissolved with a divorce. He hates deception and is not good at it. But is Thalia's workplace the proper setting to announce a fact that would most certainly startle her? As he sits even more foolishly, fingers splayed under a contraption with lights and a whirring fan, he decides what to do: He will buy a card with a blank interior at the nearest Duane Reade, write the truth, seal it, return to the salon, and leave it in Thalia's wide-mouthed brandy snifter. He will say, as he exchanges his token for his blazer, "I'll be right back," implying that he is off in search of change for a twenty.

9

Fifteen minutes later he is shrugging into his blazer when Thalia says, "Not so fast; I want to see those new, improved hands." Sheepishly, he holds out his fingers and thumbs. Thalia says, "Very nice. Think you'll make it a regular thing?"

He is unable to give the simple yes or no the inquiry would require. He says, "Let me get some change. I'll be right back. Will you be here?"

"You don't have to get change on *my* account," she says.

"I know," he says. "But I'd like to."

"May I point out that change is available on-site, at a little invention we have called a cash register?"

He smiles. "In that case . . ." but doesn't walk away. "I know this is coming completely out of the blue, but may I have a few minutes to speak with you in private?"

"About what?"

"About a personal matter." He remembers one of the tactics he had rehearsed on the subway: Invoke, if necessary, his attorney-hood. He continues. "Personal only in that it does involve a family matter."

"Is this a coffee-break-length talk or lunch? Because I can do either." She checks her watch. "I usually go from one to one forty-five."

"Lunch, please," he says.

How is it possible that Thalia Wales Archer Krouch, child of divorce, child of Denise, estranged daughter, and coat-check girl, can appear so well adjusted, so content? She sits across from him at an Italian bistro on West 57th Street, where he encourages her to order the three-course lunch.

"Will I need a glass of wine?" she asks.

"Please. I'll have one, too."

"House red," she says to the waiter.

"Which is what?" asks Henry.

"It's fine," says Thalia. "I'm sure it's good here."

"Chianti Classico," says the waiter.

"Fine," says Thalia. And when Henry doesn't object she says, "Two glasses, please."

The waiter leaves them with menus and now it is time. Henry says, "Thalia? That personal matter? It involves me. I could say that I am an old friend of the family who knew you as a child, but let me say this, which might do the job on its own: My full name is John Henry Archer."

Thalia reaches for the bread, dips a piece into a saucer of olive oil, then asks calmly, focaccia poised in midair, "The John Henry Archer who used to be married to my mother?"

There it is, the huge and homely fact, the one that testifies to his inadequacies and lifts the curtain on decades of paternal regrets. He says, "Yes. I was married to your mother for two years, technically three when the divorce came through."

Thalia asks easily, "Did you know at the time that you were gay?"

Isn't this generation wonderful? he marvels. He says, "*Unacknowledged* might be the best word to describe what I was."

"But it was a real marriage?"

"It was."

"And I was how old?"

"Three." And then, unexpectedly, his voice fails him. Here before him is that same little girl. True, she is cross-examining him; but she is calm, judicious, accepting. His mind floats outside the frame, views the tableau, and thinks, *the reunion of my dreams.* "Three then four," he manages, "and then she left and took you with her."

The waiter arrives with the wine. With hardly a glance, Thalia signals, *Leave it. Come back later.*

"I'm sorry," Henry says. "I didn't know I would get this emotional."

Thalia pats the closer of his two hands, the one that is clenched around the stem of his wineglass. He blurts out, "I didn't do enough. I could have done more. I had my rights."

"As a stepfather?" she asks. "For a year or two? I don't know why you're beating yourself up over this. I mean, did you love her?"

Her? he thinks. *Not her. You!* He manages to say, "It was time for me to get married, or so everyone thought. Your mother was rather obviously put in my path —"

"By?"

"A colleague, well-meaning. His fiancée was from the funeral director's family that conducted Denise's first husband's burial service. They sat us together at their wedding reception, at what was designated the singles tables except everyone else there was engaged. Quite awkward. But after a few glasses of champagne, the joke of the night was that we'd be next. As it turned out we were. She liked me well enough, and I was very good with you." He adds, sounding apologetic, "I found the idea of a widow with a child very appealing."

"And now? Do you hate her?"

"I did when she left. The *way* she left."

"But not anymore?"

The waiter is back, pen poised over order pad. Thalia asks Henry if he wants to share. He doesn't, but he recognizes that this might be a symbolic gesture. He says, "Yes, let's. You pick one and I'll pick one and how about an antipasto?"

"Calamari?" she counters.

"Absolutely."

For her entrée she picks the dish he believes should have been retired with the fall menu — pumpkin ravioli — but he says yes, he likes that very much. What would she think would be a good complement to that? Without hesitation she says, "No, your turn. As long as it's not the tripe."

"Do you eat veal?"

"Definitely."

"Shall we have the one with the capers and lemon juice?"

"Love that," says Thalia.

He pays some needless attention to the cloth napkin on his lap before announcing, "Your mother and I have been in touch since the death of her husband."

Thalia, after a pause that he senses is his to fill, adds, "Glenn. My father of long duration."

"Of course. I'm sorry. I should have expressed my condolences the minute we met."

"Did she send you to talk to me?"

"Absolutely not. She doesn't even know that I know you from the salon. I made the connection myself after seeing photos of you in her apartment."

When the waiter sets a glistening heap of calamari between them, Henry waits and watches. He doesn't see Denise in her, except for the eyes. But the echoes of the baby Thalia seem so obvious now, so unmissable. The rest must come from his predecessor, the doomed biological father who fell off a mountain in Peru, who had been tall, long-legged, known to successive husbands as a photograph in the nursery: hands on his hips and a tolerant grin that seemed to say, *Okay, I'm posing. Take your photo and let me get on with my adventures.*

Thalia picks up her fork, puts it down, and says, "Okay. I confess. I've known about you for a long time. Well, a long-ish time."

"That's not possible," he says.

"It's very possible! I'm in my little cage under the stairs and over there is the reception desk, and I hear you walk in and say,

'Henry Archer . . . I have a one o'clock with Giovanni . . .' So I look up your address on the computer and I do a little Googling, and I figure out that you are *that* Henry Archer. Besides, you look the same."

"The same as what?"

Thalia says, "This is going to embarrass you."

"Maybe not."

"I know already, after ten minutes, that it will. But here it is: Denise always claimed you were the handsomest of her many husbands, with photos to prove it. Even with red-eye, you had the bluest eyes."

Thalia has guessed correctly: He is not good at fielding compliments. He says only, "My hair used to be dark. And not this short."

"Hmmm. Twenty-four years go by. Hair turns gray. I didn't need a salon colorist to solve that mystery."

"Still, you had no desire to introduce yourself?"

"What would I have said?"

"Just, 'I'm Thalia.' I would have known immediately what that meant."

"But I didn't know how you'd react. What if I'd said, 'Here's your smock and — by the way? — I'm Thalia Krouch. Didn't you use to be married to my mother?' You might have run out the door, never to return."

He says no, he hopes not, then asks how long ago she Googled him.

"Just two or three months ago. Maybe four. Not that long."

"A long time to keep something like that to yourself."

"Not that hard. Not for me, anyway."

"Because we've hardly exchanged any words?"

"No," said Thalia. "What I meant was not very hard to play a total stranger . . . because I'm an actress."

Henry wants to appear enthusiastic, but he is a seasoned New Yorker who translates "actress" as workshops taken and head-shots posed for against the odds.

"I was waiting for an opening," she continues. "If you had introduced yourself or asked my name . . ." She adds, after a pause, "Or asked me a question about myself."

"Do you remember me at all?" he asks. "*Any*thing?"

Thalia says, "I have memories I never quite knew what to do with: Did we ever take a carriage ride around the park on a really cold day?"

"We did! Christmas Day. You were four and a half."

"And was there a cat somewhere in the picture? Or a kitten?"

"Almost. I took you to the Humane Society and you picked out a kitten — neglecting to clear that with your mother first. Very bad preemptive move on my part."

Thalia finally sticks a fork into a calamari ring and pronounces it the best ever. "Did you imagine what the next step would be after you announced that we're long-lost step-relatives?" she asks.

He isn't sure from her tone whether the door is opening or shutting. He says, "I imagined that I would ask you questions about the intervening years, and vice versa, in the manner of two people getting to know each other."

"Okay," says Thalia. "You first."

Out of politeness, he asks about her acting.

"One commercial and one movie," she says.

Her answer fashions a whole new view of Thalia. "A movie! How wonderful! That means you aren't just hoping to break into acting, but you're on your way!"

"Not quite," she says. "Do you know what a stand-in does?"

Henry chews, swallows, asks with fork poised over the next piece, "I'm guessing it's something like an understudy?"

"It's a person who substitutes for the actor *before* filming, for things like lighting. Once in a while, depending on the director, you read some lines."

"Have you stood in for anyone I might know?"

"I was a stand-in for the mean secretary, the one with seniority, in *The Devil Wears Prada*, but only when the real stand-in went home sick. And I was a clacker in another scene, which is what they called the editorial assistants running around in high heels. Unfortunately, no sign of me in the final cut."

"Still," says Henry. "A foot in the door and a very real credit on your C.V."

"And you're a lawyer, right? At least I know you went to law school. Vanderbilt, correct?"

"Once upon a time I practiced law. I quit after Thanksgiving. Retired. Quite early, unrelated to my lack of affection for the law. And I'll tell you why: My father keeled over of a heart attack at fifty-five, and I thought I should get out in time to enjoy life in case I inherited his arteries."

"And do you?" she asks. "Enjoy life?"

"In my own quiet way, I think I do."

"How are *your* arteries?"

"Good. As much as my cholesterol count testifies."

"As you know, Glenn also died prematurely, a massive heart attack, and his cholesterol was good."

"I'm being followed, just in case." He smiles. "I only have fried calamari on special occasions."

"Do you live alone?"

"I do."

"Are you in a relationship?"

"You first. It's bound to be more interesting."

Thalia says, "That'll be easy: There's no one."

"Even in the wings? On the horizon? Recently decamped?"

"I'm between boyfriends. Which is fine. I try not to date actors or hairdressers. What about you?"

"No one."

"Even in the wings? Recently decamped?"

"Recently deceased," he says quietly.

"A longtime companion?"

"Very."

"Please tell me it wasn't AIDS."

"It wasn't AIDS. It wasn't even a male companion."

"A woman? As in girlfriend?"

"A very dear woman friend, Celeste. Cancer. 'Companion' in the sense she was my movie date, my dinner date. We liked the same theaters and the same desserts, and neither of us put that much stock in reviews so we saw almost everything. We'd go to an early screening and grab a bite afterward. Sure enough some dame — her word — would waltz into Trattoria Dell'Arte with a grotesque hat or sequined ruby slippers, and Celeste would lower her eyes and make one of her trademark cynical remarks, and I'd practically need a Heimlich."

"Was she a lawyer, too?"

"She was a teacher, kindergarten, public school. She threw herself into it and the kids loved her. She'd wear crazy stuff to school — shoes with bows like Minnie Mouse or big polka dots, pop beads. You're too young to remember pop beads. But she collected things just for their effect on five-year-olds. You know how little girls are — you were like this — anything fancy or glittery or pink is a work of art."

Smiling, Thalia says, "Go on."

"Every once in a while, a girl or boy, grown up now, would come up to her and say, 'Miss McGonagle? I think you were my kindergarten teacher.' And she'd always pull something out of her hat, some memory that was absolutely spot-on. As soon as they were out of earshot, she'd say, 'Don't be impressed. For my entire career I recycled the same unit on sinking and floating.'"

Thalia says, "That does it. Now I want to go into teaching and change my name to Miss McGonagle and have grown-up students deliver testimonials . . . But I guess I meant go on about me — details my mother would have to refer me to a nanny for."

Henry, so very happy to relate the Thalia lore he's bottled up, says, "I remember the oddest things. You loved olives. You snacked on them like they were — what do toddlers usually snack on? — raisins. And you liked strawberry ice cream better than those more complicated flavors, but you'd spit out the bits of actual strawberries."

"Still do."

"You wouldn't go down the slide in the park. And when you finally worked up the courage, you went on your stomach, head-first, and banged into a little boy who didn't get out of the way fast enough. Wham. An hour later you had a black eye. And your favorite thing, at least in the coloring book genre, was dot-to-dot. When you were three, I was buying the ones that were recommended for ages five to seven."

"Such a girl genius," she murmurs.

"I know all parents think that, but in so many areas —"

Thalia leans forward. "It must have been a shock to find me passing out smocks in a hair salon."

"No!" he says. "Don't say that. I couldn't be happier. If Celeste were here, she'd be dancing on the table."

"Because . . . ?"

"Because she loved children and she knew about you, knew I wanted to fix this. And even though I wouldn't call it her dying wish, she'd open her eyes during that last week and say, 'She's probably right under your nose. Make some phone calls, for chrissakes.'"

Thalia's eyes — and should this alarm or thrill him? — are now red-rimmed.

"I'm sorry," he says. "Let's change the subject to something less lugubrious."

"Not at all," says Thalia.

"I only meant to say that she was a marvelous friend."

Thalia leans in. "I bet she thought you were marvelous, too." She pronounces it "*mah*-velus" and she is teasing him. Is she an aristocrat directed by the Marx Brothers, or is she vintage Billy Crystal on *Saturday Night Live*? He doesn't care. Her timing and delivery are excellent, and within the tease lies a compliment. He is smiling again and hungry. Thalia can act!

3

You Sound Dubious

HE ASKS, PREFACING the question with "You mustn't feel obliged," would Thalia care to make lunch a weekly commitment?

He watches carefully for a telltale hesitation, and his heart contracts when he hears, "Sometimes I skip lunch if I'm leaving early because of an audition —"

"I understand," he says. "Of course."

"Hey! Don't fold. I was about to say, 'Great! Love to.' You'll give me your contact info so if I hear about an audition, I won't stand you up."

He adores her all over again—such decency and good humor! "Did you enjoy your meal enough to make this our regular place?" he asks.

Thalia blinks hard. "Did I enjoy my meal? Did you ever see anyone enjoy her food as much as I just did?"

"Would you like to order something for later?" he asks.

She groans, but gratefully, delightfully.

"Shall we make this our regular spot?" he asks again. Thalia looks at her watch, says, "Yikes," then immediately adds, "Oh, so what? I'll explain the very dramatic, life-altering nature of my lunch." She leans in to ask, "How insensitive is it of me to propose we meet next time at Trattoria Dell'Arte?"

"Insensitive?"

"You know — in case it's kind of sacred."

"Celeste, you mean?"

"Exactly."

"That would be no problem," says Henry.

"Your next haircut is on the second," she says. "Should we make it then so you don't have to make an extra trip?"

"Perfect," he says. "On the second. Trattoria Dell'Arte."

She is on her feet now, knotting a long orange scarf that looks homemade and intentionally potholed, then tapping his numbers into her cell phone as fast as he dictates. "And next time you won't be tempted to bring along any estranged relatives of mine, right?"

"No, I promise. Just me."

"So no mediating?"

"I swear. And why would I include her when she's had you to herself for twenty-some-odd years?"

She smiles. "Because you don't hold grudges?" She doesn't wait for an answer but asks if he'll at least let her pay the tip.

"You run. I've kept you too long. I'm fine here," he says, waving his hand over the table to mean *Of course this is — and always will be — my treat.*

She leans over and kisses one cheek. "Awfully glad to officially re-meet you," she says.

It is worse now when he's alone. He is every man he hates on *Prime Time, 48 Hours,* and *CNN Reports* — the absent father who surfaces decades after the hard work has been done and the tuition paid. Look what he's missed: twenty-four years of Thalia. He had rights. It didn't have to be the surgical separation that it was. But to a relatively unschooled bachelor father, the biweekly lunches and teas were ordeals: Thalia cried when she had to leave her mother and her turncoat homophobic nanny, whimpered at restaurants while the surrounding patrons glared. With no one's goodwill — not Denise's or her new husband's nor the little girl's herself — the outings grew further and further apart until they stopped.

Now what will he say when Thalia inevitably asks what made him disappear? *Too bitter and too angry with your adulterous mother to be a man, especially with the courts hinting that I was something less than that?* Your stepfather wanted to adopt you and the affidavits all made the same argument: that the inconsistent presence of a man, a virtual stranger with an unconventional lifestyle, was confusing to the minor child.

Precisely because he doesn't like to lie and is a very poor dissembler, he avoids Denise. "Sorry I missed you again," he tells her answering machine, returning her calls at an hour he thinks she will be out. Denise doesn't take the hint and keeps trying to enlist him for her morning walk. He tries "cold coming on" and "waiting for the boiler service guy." After more than a week of white lies, he is out of excuses. He agrees to accompany her — in fact, in one hour. Since their détente, she has been overconfident and unceremonious, and he realizes that she has placed him under her girlfriend banner. The phone rings twenty seconds after he hangs up, and it is she again. He doesn't answer, quite sure that she wants to know if he's figured out why Thalia looks so familiar. But she's not calling about that; instead she's complimenting their new, comfortable, remarkably honest friendship. "And since

I know you're standing there listening, I'll end with, How did I ever let all these years go by without mending fences?"

He resists the impulse to lunge at the phone while she's on the line and purge some of the old bile. *Don't be so coy. I always hated that in you. And furthermore, just because I agree to take a walk doesn't mean we've mended fences.*

But he doesn't pick up. He erases her words after replaying only their first sprightly syllables. He will be a neutral party for some greater good, the one ahead that he hasn't quite imagined yet.

As soon as she spots him, Denise yells across Fifth Avenue, "I've decided to get a job." When he reaches her side, she tells him she's been researching careers online. Did he know there was a whole world of jobs out there that she thinks she'd be very good at? At the top of her list, well, not exactly a career but a one-pronged plan of action: to get her real estate license so that she can sell her apartment herself—how hard can that be?—and divide the gigantic commission with the listing broker. She can take courses at the New York Real Estate Institute; she likes the look of the place, likes its slogan, Profit Through Knowledge, and likes its location on the north side of Macy's. What does he think of that?

They walk east, then turn south on Madison, her daily route. "It's not a job you can jump into," he tells her. "It's an attractive field, and it would be overrun if it didn't involve several big hurdles."

She slows down as they pass a shop window filled with cashmere and stops fully in the next doorway to gaze at the bejeweled shoes on display. "I used to shop here," she says. "I'd try on pair after pair and wouldn't even ask the price."

"Are we walking or shopping?" he calls back to her.

She sighs and follows. "I know it's not a job I can jump into. I

23

know it involves courses and exams and a license. Is that so beyond my reach? Because you certainly sound dubious."

"Because you're counting on that license to sell your own apartment, and one doesn't get a real estate license overnight."

Denise is shaking her head vigorously. "I can stall the evil stepsons. I'll plead widow's mourning period or lead paint removal or chronic fatigue syndrome. They're in no hurry, believe me, with the market out of whack."

On every block she nods to fellow walkers, all of whom, he is quite sure, are noticing and evaluating the new widow's companion. "What else are you thinking about as a career path?" he asks.

"You know," she confides, and slips her arm through his as they pass two muzzled German shepherds on leashes, "don't laugh. But I think it would be fun to be one of those greeters in a nice restaurant."

"Do you mean a hostess?"

"What I'm picturing is one of those cozy restaurants where the owner's wife greets you at the door, welcomes you warmly, and hands the menus to a waiter who then leads you to your table. You and I both know that in this city there are plenty of restaurateurs who don't have wives."

He says, "You know, of course, that managers and owners hire — if they can get away with it — the youngest, most attractive, most buxom woman who applies for the job."

"That doesn't intimidate me! I'm thinking of a place with an older clientele. A bistro, probably French. Probably in my own neighborhood." She waves to a passerby, a tiny elderly woman swaddled in a fur coat. "She's ninety if she's a day," Denise whispers. "So's the coat."

How petty she is, he thinks, and therefore scolds, "It isn't like having guests in your house who arrive at seven-thirty and leave by ten. You'd be on your feet for an entire shift. I think after one night it would lose its luster."

"Why are you taking a tone with me? I know that jobs involve work and not flitting in and out like a volunteer."

"Good."

She points to a coffee shop across the street and asks if they should reward themselves with a cappuccino.

"Reward ourselves for what?"

"Walking this far in the cold. And you walked across the park, so you're even more deserving."

He says, "Let's keep going. It makes more sense to have that on the way back."

"You've gotten bossier in addition to being more patronizing," she says rather cheerfully. She speeds up and begins pumping her elbows in a power-walk impersonation. "C'mon," she says. "It burns more calories." She stops for a Don't Walk signal at the corner of East 64th. "What would be your idea of a Denise-compatible job?" she asks him. "And don't say bank teller or nanny or dog walker or taxi driver."

He says, "I can just see you behind the wheel of a gypsy cab."

She leads him across Madison, heading east. "I pick up my lunch on Lex," she explains.

"Have you acquired any hobbies?" he asks. "Hopefully one that could convert into a paying job."

"I wish *docent* paid. I'd spend a different afternoon in each museum. Another thought I had was *decorator*."

"For which you'd need a license. And experience." *And not ten beige rooms utterly devoid of personality.*

"I'm getting offended," she says. "I don't hear one single note of confidence in your voice. Is this how you'd talk to a son or daughter who was shopping around for a new career? Wouldn't you say,

'What are your strengths? Let's look in the classifieds. Let's give you one of those skills assessment tests'?"

Shouldn't the word *daughter* remind Denise of her own child? He doesn't bring Thalia up because the reunion is still too thrilling and too sacred to be uncorked. "Now, now," he says. "I'm playing devil's advocate."

"I'm sure all of these people heading for the nearest subway work in offices," Denise says with a sweep of her arm. Do they know something I don't know? And did they start off with more credentials than I have?"

"Can you touch-type?" he asks.

Denise stops and lets her jaw drop theatrically. "Can you see me as someone's secretary? Answering a phone? Taking shorthand? Emptying coffee grounds?"

"Then don't ask my advice! It's not an unreasonable idea. There are receptionist jobs that amount to being a greeter in an outer office. Always nicely dressed. Gracious. Keeping your shoes on under your desk."

"I'm mildly intrigued," she says.

"Then read the want ads. Make some phone calls. Charm some HR people."

"Is this wishful thinking? That I can dress up and sit at a beautiful desk in an atrium with a gorgeous arrangement of flowers — you've seen those giant, hotel-lobby-sized ones with birds of paradise and hydrangeas — and greet clients when they get off the elevator? Or that jobs like this exist at all nowadays? Don't companies want armed guards?"

"We used a headhunter who specialized in law-firm hires. I can look her up. There's bound to be firms who'd welcome someone with social skills and maturity —"

"Maturity! That's what I'm up against: age discrimination! You know where I'll end up? Waitressing at one of these places where they brag about their elderly help, and their nametags say how long they've worked there. I saw that in a Beverly Hills delicatessen once: 'Dottie, forty-five years.' 'Pauline, thirty-three years.' No, thank you."

"Would you consider sales?"

Denise recoils. She stomps right on Lexington and picks up speed.

"I was thinking of a place like Bergdorf's or Bendel's," he offers.

"Well, I certainly know my way around those places —"

"But?"

She stops, strikes a pose, imaginary cocktail in hand. "'Oh, what do I *do*, attractive single man whom I've just struck up a conversation with at a dinner party? I work at Saks. No, no, not *Goldman* Sachs. The other one, the flagship store on Fifth. I sell pocketbooks and occasionally fill in at costume jewelry. I wrap your purchases in tissue and then I run your credit card. Fulfilling? No. But I do get an employee discount. And what did I do before that? Nothing, actually. I had a grant from the husband foundation. How about you?'"

Henry smiles. Had he ever noticed a talent for showmanship in the young Denise? He doesn't think so. Certainly there were good looks, a flattering gaze, and small talk that bordered on the charming. He asks, "Were you this entertaining in the past?"

Denise grins. "I must have been. Because you know who inherited my sense of humor?"

He *does* know but doesn't answer.

"Thalia. She's funny in the way I'm funny: not joke telling, but just — what would you call it? — putting a story across."

This would be the time to ask if Thalia is putting that ability to good use, but he is saved by the sudden appearance of particularly big and beautiful artichoke hearts attached to their stems marinating in a café window. Denise gasps. "I must have one of those," she says. "That'll be my dinner, with a cold glass of something crisp and white."

"That's not enough for dinner," says Henry.

"Then my lunch," says Denise, "which I'll eat the minute I get home."

He follows her inside and overrides her when she tells the man behind the takeout counter, "One of those artichokes in the window."

"We'll take six," says Henry. "Four for her and two for me." His billfold is already in his hand. Denise is protesting but not strenuously.

"He feels sorry for me," she tells the man behind the counter. "My husband died and took all the money with him."

The man smiles uncertainly. After all, who would say such a thing if it weren't a joke?

"I'm the ex," Henry volunteers, then wonders what's gotten into him.

4

Bygones

BECAUSE HE'S BEEN seeing Sheri Abrams, PhD, for decades, the reference to Denise Krouch requires no biographical footnote. Henry's divorce was the very catapult that landed him in this black Eames chair twenty-four years before, opposite the then newly minted clinical psychologist, chosen purely on the basis of Upper West Side geography. Her leafy office is untended and book lined, radiator clanging, tribal kilims on two walls, a four-minute walk from West 75th Street. He brings lattes for himself and Sheri — first-name basis from the beginning — and a gourmet peanut butter biscuit for her standard poodle, the third identical dusty black dog in his tenure. Their sessions have evolved into conversational sparring between opinionated friends. Sheri — and this is why he'd never consider psychoanalysis — talks back, advises, and editorializes. They discuss movies, plays, op-ed pieces, and the openings and closings of restaurants on the West Side. She discharges Henry every few seasons, pronouncing him over the hump and better adjusted than he knows. Yes, she always replies wearily; yes, we could meet for coffee or lunch, but after that, naturally, I'd have to refer you to another therapist. Accordingly, he is careful not to chat when they find themselves waiting in the same lines at Zabar's. After a few months, with or without a setback, he feels that something is missing. Most recently, it was Celeste's diagnosis, and now, on the heels of that loss, this: His longtime nemesis is filling his voice mail with messages. And her lovely, bighearted daughter! Could he even explain to Sheri without embarrassing himself what one lunch has meant to him?

"When did you and Denise start talking again?" Sheri asks, frowning.

"About six weeks ago. I sent her a note of condolence when her husband died."

"Which husband? I've lost count."

"Her third."

"Magnanimous of you."

"I wrote a note, nothing profound, the usual *sorry for your loss*. She wrote back sounding a little desperate. So I called."

She says evenly, "I see. You picked up the phone and called your ex-wife."

"Yes, I did." He pops the plastic lid off his latte and says quietly, "I was curious."

"Curiosity is good," she says with so little conviction that he laughs.

She asks what is so amusing, and he mimics her "curiosity is good" with a more pronounced strangulation of the syllables.

"So we're letting bygones be bygones? Or is this some kind of Trojan horse that gets you across the border into the enemy land?"

"I thought you'd applaud this as — I don't know — diplomacy. Progress."

"Is this about Celeste?"

He doesn't think so but says, "You could be right. It did seem like an odd coincidence — Denise losing Glenn and me losing Celeste —"

"Six, seven months apart? Not an earth-shattering coincidence."

"You're holding my grudge," says Henry. "Wouldn't that qualify as reverse transference?"

"No such thing," she snaps.

"You're forgetting the service that Denise provided, the one you drilled into me, that if she hadn't abandoned me —"

"And kidnapped your child."

"— and kidnapped my child, I might still be hiding in the closet; i.e., Denise did me a favor, broadly speaking."

"That clean?" she asks. "Denise as knight in shining armor?"

"She's been humbled. Which seems to be bringing out the best in her."

"Humbled because her husband died?"

"No. Humbled because of a prenuptial agreement."

"She's broke?"

"Not by most people's standards." He smiles. "Go ahead — ask."

"What do you think I want to ask?"

"You're *dying* to know: Did she come to me for money?"

"Never crossed my mind."

"For the record" — and he raises his voice as if dictating directly to the clipboard in her lap — "she did not come to me for money. Besides, I contacted her first."

"Which I don't necessarily see as a good thing," she counters.

"You will soon."

31

She looks up with a start, as does the deaf black poodle at her feet. "Thalia?" she asks.

"Thalia," he confirms.

Ten years before, in late spring, his abandonment and surrender of Thalia had been all he wanted to discuss. At an emergency session Sheri stated, "You know what triggered this, don't you?"

He had said of course, the math: Thalia was five when the divorce was final, so she had just turned eighteen in June, and therefore must be graduating from high school, imminently.

"Not that," said his therapist. "Think again. What have you seen lately?"

"Seen? The inside of my office. Briefs. Second-year law students interviewing for jobs."

"I won't waste our time," she had said. "The reason we're back to Thalia after all these years is that scene where Billy Bigelow's ghost puts his arm around his daughter at her high school graduation and she feels his presence and holds her head up higher. Am I right?"

She was right. He'd seen the revival of *Carousel* in previews and had devoted a good portion of their next session to the talents of Audra McDonald. "But," he countered, "aren't you supposed to point out that Billy Bigelow triggered some very deep feelings, which most mental health professionals wouldn't dismiss out of hand?"

And now he has dug out the letter assigned but never sent and, in fact, never turned in to Sheri Abrams, harsh vettor of exploratory epistles. In it he had introduced himself as the man who had married the widowed Denise Ellis Wales, mother of Thalia Alexis Wales, whom he'd subsequently adopted and ~~cherished loved~~ provided for, all too briefly. The first paragraph was a curriculum vitae, the second a legal thicket, and the third a cri de coeur. He'd loved her as his own true daughter, the only child he'd ever known. He'd been young and selfish when he relinquished his rights and now ~~he was alone~~ he'd seen the error of his ways. If he could turn back the clock he'd tear up Glenn Krouch's adoption petition and fight it in the courts. Parentheses followed, citing case law. It was a first draft, on yellow legal notepaper, ending with anemic congratulations on finishing high school. He studies the stillborn postscripts: "~~I hope you'll accept the enclosed gift certificate If you ever needed anyone to talk to Would you kindly apprise me of your college plans?~~" which had given way to a more democratic, "Perhaps at this juncture you are going on to college or starting a job. I'd love to know what your plans are." And finally, the sentence that was code for *I am a man of means and perhaps someone you'd like to know:* "I live in a townhouse on West 75th Street. I've never remarried nor have I had any other ~~issue~~ children."

It was the lone piece of paper in a manila folder marked "Thalia, Correspondence." Would it be a terrible idea to bring this draft to lunch on the second, testimony to his long-standing good intentions? He'd explain why he wrote it, and he'd be honest: His therapist believed in homework. This was an old assignment, prompted by a rough patch he'd gone through a decade ago concurrent with her high school graduation and the prospect that she might be independent, reachable, curious.

Would excavating a never-sent letter strike Thalia as creepy? Could he lighten the mood by quoting his therapist implicating *Carousel?* Yes, because an actress would appreciate the fact that his graduation fixation was inspired by Rodgers and Hammerstein? No, because the word *therapist* might raise a red flag?

These questions, aired before Sheri Abrams, prompt her to note, "It isn't like you to weigh every word."

"I've always done that. Lawyers can't just stand before the bench and prattle."

33

"You were never a litigator," she snaps.

He leans forward in his chair. "Let's settle this now. Am I going to meet resistance every time I bring up my daughter?"

"What is our goal here?" she asks, staring over her half glasses. "Are weekly lunches going to be enough? Then dinners? Then dinners with orchestra seats? And soon enough, in no particular order, a roof over her head and a codicil to your will?"

He inhales sharply. He hasn't dared look past lunch at Trattoria Dell'Arte in two weeks, but "roof over her head" strikes Henry as a first-rate goal for a delinquent father with a vacant maisonette.

5

On Advice of Counsel

IS TRUST ATTORNEY READS the codicil, removes his glasses, buzzes for a pot of Earl Grey, and finally asks, "This isn't one of those foolish midlife things that besotted men do, is it?"

"Foolish besotted *heteros*, maybe. And, George, don't be vulgar. I'm her father."

"All I'm saying is, what's the rush? Unless you're not telling me something, healthwise."

"I'm fine," Henry says. "Although that's what Glenn Krouch thought, too. Fine one day, on life support the next —"

"Not before remembering her in his will, I understand."

"In trust! She won't see that money for years. It's beyond insulting, as if she were an irresponsible child."

"I still think you should give this some time. You're in the honeymoon phase. You don't know if her arms-wide-open embrace is sincere. Or durable."

"Here's something that might surprise you, George. I wouldn't care! I adopted her once, and I didn't fight for her. On advice of counsel, I might add. I'm putting her back where she belongs, and I'm perfectly capable of adding a codicil without the blessing of my suspicious lawyer."

"This isn't me talking exclusively as your lawyer, and you know it."

He does know it. George was the partner who issued the cease-and-desist order twenty-five years earlier: Office mates were to refrain from setting Henry up with their wives' girlfriends and attractive associates, and why didn't they open their eyes and stop putting him on the spot, for chrissakes?

"I'm not under her spell," he says. "This is not the result of Thalia ingratiating herself. She's known for months that I was her mother's ex but never said a word."

"Therefore how could someone in such a passive role be a gold digger?"

"Correct."

"Acting talent notwithstanding."

"Acting talent still undetermined," murmurs Henry.

"Can I meet her?"

"Under what guise?"

"No guise! Former partner who knew her as a baby."

"Did you?"

George squints at a framed photo of a Christmas tree rising behind his four sons in seasonal sweaters. "Didn't we have an office party once with a Santa?"

"No, we did not."

"Then I must have seen a photo of her. Didn't you have one on your desk?"

"Many. Which are back on my mantel."

George takes his notary seal from its leatherette sheath, slips it around the codicil, but stops short of embossing it. Henry says, "It's not a pound of flesh, Georgie. It's only property."

"Must've been *some* lunch," his lawyer says.

Giovanni has never been one to chat while styling hair. Even after these many years, he comments only on cut, potential color (Giovanni believes that Henry's gray hair could so beautifully be blond in concert with his blue eyes), and the salon's ever-expanding line of products. But today Henry worries that in-house gossip may have traveled upstairs to this station. He owes Giovanni a firsthand explanation. "I don't know if you've heard anything," he begins.

Giovanni's scissors stop. He waits, meeting Henry's eyes in the mirror.

"About Thalia, your coat-check girl? I know this will strike you as absurd for several reasons, but I used to be married to her mother."

"Yes, we know," Giovanni says mildly.

"We? Other people, too?"

Giovanni shrugs.

"Did Thalia herself tell you?"

"Sure. Many weeks ago. I cut her hair."

"Did she tell everyone?"

Giovanni's scissors stop again mid-snip. "I think no. I think only me."

"Because you and Thalia are friends outside of work?"

"Sure," says Giovanni.

Sure? Is that what a father wants to hear? Nonchalance from a skinny, ill-shaven, tattooed hairdresser? He hears himself ask, "How old are you?"

Giovanni smiles. "She's twenty-nine and I'm thirty-eight. Not terrible, do you think?"

"Not terrible, no," Henry lies. Because Giovanni is running electric clippers over the tops of his ears, he waits a minute before asking, "In terms of corporate structure, would you be Thalia's boss?"

"I am no one's boss. Gerard is my boss and that is all I know." He takes a can from a drawer, sprinkles talc on a sable brush. "Let me clean you up. Isn't this nice? You'll smell like cloves for your lunch date." He tickles Henry's forehead and nose with the brush, unsnaps the nylon cape, holds up the hand mirror for a back view, and says, "Always a pleasure. I look forward to seeing you next time."

As intended, those words remind Henry to pull out Giovanni's tip. But something is impinging on his generosity today. Before Giovanni returns from the laundry chute, Henry, to his own surprise, lightens the thank you by two crisp bills.

The maitre d' at Trattoria Dell'Arte kisses Henry on both cheeks and squeezes Thalia's hand. "Have we had the pleasure?" he asks.

"I work around the corner. Salon Gerard?"

"That's only her day job," corrects Henry. "This is Thalia Krouch, the actress."

"Go on," says Thalia. "Tell him the rest."

Does she mean career or relationship amplification? Thalia points back and forth between them: *you, me, us.*

"What she wants me to tell you is: I used to be married to her mother."

"My stepfather! For real. Until my mother ran off with Mr. Krouch."

The host yelps, "I love her! I love this stepdaughter!" He turns to the waiter at his elbow, says, "Twenty-four," and then to Henry, "My favorite booth. Enjoy. And welcome back."

Seated, Thalia shrugs out of her jacket and assumes a brand-new posture, fingers interlaced on the table, interrogation style. "Why do I stay in this job, Mr. Archer?" she asks, unprompted. "That's easy: It's so brainless that any one of my friends can sub for me at the last minute if I have an audition." She opens her menu, says, "I love the antipasto bar. And don't worry. I'm not working my way up to beauty school."

"These friends," he begins. "Are they actors, too?"

"The ones who can fill in for me are. No, wait. Arielle is a grad student. And Amanda is a temp."

"Do you have roommates?"

Thalia groans.

"A bad one?"

"How do I say this? An undergraduate who's smitten."

Henry says, "Do elaborate."

"A junior at NYU. His parents came through with a couch and a TV, so I made an exception to the youngster rule. He's perfectly nice."

"By smitten do you mean — ?"

"A crush. Partly my fault."

Henry waits.

Thalia says, "Okay. One kiss. Well, a couple more than that, but confined to one night after watching a particularly stirring episode of *Sex and the City* guest-starring David Duchovny. So it's my own fault."

Ordinarily, this would be exactly the kind of gossipy report tinged with sexual bravado he thoroughly enjoys, but not from Thalia.

"Would you rather not hear such things?" she asks.

"It's fine," he says. "I'm cool."

Thalia laughs. "So I see."

39

"What's this roommate's name?"

"Alex."

"Have you discussed this with Alex and reached some kind of understanding?"

"Had to, on the spot, because he assumed we were moving directly from couch to futon. I had to give that little speech about how irresponsible it was of me, and don't get me wrong, you are an excellent kisser, but actual sex would be disastrous for roommate relations."

"Futon," Henry repeats. "Is that what he sleeps on?"

"Actually it's what *I* sleep on."

"In a bedroom?"

"Sort of. It's three rooms so we use two as bedrooms."

"And one bath, I imagine?"

"Don't faint. The bathtub is in the kitchen. No, really, it's fine. We work it out. We have a painted Chinese screen on three sides of the tub and an honor system. Besides, he never has classes till noon so he's always asleep when I bathe before work."

"Is a bathtub in a kitchen up to code?"

"Doubt it. But it's cheap, and actually quite charming if you don't mind a few bums on the stoop. Kidding! No one calls them bums anymore. No stoop, either, just a noodle joint on the ground floor. Not great, but open till two A.M. And I'm a stone's throw from Little Italy, Nolita, the Bowery, SoHo, the Lower East Side, and every subway line known to man. That was the rental agent's big selling point, that I'd be in the epicenter of Manhattan."

"Where exactly is your place?"

"Chinatown, Mott Street. A fourth-floor walkup. Which I don't mind at all. It's very New York. You've seen those movies in which tenants are trudging up the stairs after a hard day's work or pushing a drunk date past a cranky non-English-speaking neighbor? That's me, sans elevator, sans doorman."

40

It is the first time she's alluded to a grander former life. Henry wonders, Would George consider this reference to be an outstretched hand? *Subsidize my rent so I can move back uptown?* "Very admirable," he says.

Thalia says no, it isn't, not at all. And now, with what can only be described as acute acting talent, she tells him that she has a safety net. "I like living there. I could afford a doorman building in the Village if that's what I wanted . . . I don't know if you know that Glenn Krouch left me money. A lot. He owned a very successful box factory."

Henry says, "I did know that."

Thalia adds, "My brothers run it now. And as you can imagine, online shopping has sent the sale of corrugated boxes through the roof. Now would Mr. Archer care to share the twelve-item antipasti?"

Could she have uttered anything less gold-diggeresque or more perfect? He can't wait to tell George: Thalia lied to me so I wouldn't worry about her dead-end job and her nineteenth-century plumbing.

"My situation, my life — it's all good. Really. Good for me and good for my art."

He feels a stinging behind his eyes but manages to subdue it. From his inside breast pocket he brings forth a small leather appointment book and its companion pencil. "Sometimes I cook," he says.

6

You Might As Well Say Yes

NOW THAT DENISE rings Henry every morning after
breakfast, he points out that it's exactly the telephone
relationship she had with her mother while they were
married.

She says, "I'm flattered that you remember."

Henry says, "You wouldn't be so flattered if you knew the context. I found it highly annoying."

The newly, seemingly impervious Denise laughs. "All my husbands would agree. Have I mentioned my mother lately? She's
eighty-two and has all her marbles. I have a stepfather, too, a
cousin of a cousin's in-law, not Greek American but Greek. In
Greece! Eleni's come full circle, straining yogurt in the village her
parents ran from. She's quite the conversation starter, apparently,
with her boob job and her Sub-Zero."

Henry, who is finishing the Monday *New York Times* cross-
word puzzle as Denise prattles, stops mid-clue. "Since when?"

"The boob job? It was her seventy-fifth-birthday present to herself. And would you believe she was engaged in three months, thanks to the Internet? The photo she uploaded starts at her waist."

"Remarkable," Henry says.

"I'll e-mail you their wedding portrait. They didn't meet until she went over for the wedding — very nineteenth century. Except for the Internet part, it was your basic arranged marriage. The fiancé neglected to mention that he was a head shorter. Well, not really: He comes up to her ear. But she doesn't mind. She sounds very happy. He's only seventy-something and unexpectedly — to use her favorite word — virile."

Henry doesn't need much in the way of aural cues to respond to the word *virile*. A euphemistic reference to geriatric sex will suffice. He needs a boyfriend. And just as he is thinking about what excuse will get him off the phone fastest, Denise asks, "Henry? Speaking of relationships, are you seeing anyone?"

"Not at the moment."

"Would you like to?"

When he doesn't answer, Denise says, "You know perfectly well why I'm asking. I have friends, dozens of them! All gay and many unattached."

"I don't think so," he says.

"Don't think what? That my friends are gay, or that you'd care to make their acquaintance?"

"Don't think there are 'dozens,' especially if you mean my age. We're a near-extinct group —"

"Then I'll trick you. I'll invite you to a dinner party and surround you with a roomful of candidates."

Henry says, "I'd better get going. Thanks for the warning. I'll be sure to decline the invitation."

"But it won't be a blind date. I'll call it something else: my

43

birthday, for example. That's soon enough. I'll move you around the table so you get to experience everyone."

Henry tries, "A dinner party can cost a fortune."

"A cocktail party, then. Wine and hummus."

"I can't." He adds weakly, "I wasn't being truthful before. I am seeing someone."

"Who?"

"Someone I met . . . we're volunteers for the same charity."

"Which one?"

"The Innocence Project," he says. The words tumble out easily; he's been meaning to look into pro-bono work.

"No you're not! I'd have seen the signs. You'd look less pinched. And you'd be giving fewer sidelong glances to countermen."

"It's ridiculous, being set up by my ex-wife —"

"It's not ridiculous. It's an outlet for me. As you know, I'm in mourning *and* in crisis. You might as well say yes. It's going to happen whether I get the green light from you or not."

Henry does want to meet someone, but not a buddy of a garrulous ex-wife who will extract detailed morning-after reports from all parties. "It wouldn't be comfortable for me," he says.

"Nonsense. I'd be very low-key about it. I'd make it seem accidental."

"Which implies that you'd be chaperoning."

"I'm getting bored with this conversation," says Denise. "I'm just going to spring something on you when you least expect it."

She doesn't say goodbye yet. It seems she has ordered a free-range chicken from Fresh Direct. How about if she brings it to his place and cooks him dinner? Not to worry: She's turned into something of a chef ever since Glenn signed her up for a week-long course on a farm in Tuscany that pressed its own olive oil. Has he been reading about the benefits of a Mediterranean diet?

This is the plus and the minus of Denise and why he can easily keep his own counsel: She monopolizes all conversations. The uneasy topic of Thalia does not come up as long as Denise is free-associating. Is he being deceitful? He reminds himself that as Mrs. Archer she kept large and rather malignant secrets from him. A burgeoning friendship with a neglected and estranged daughter, he decides, need not be called to her attention. He says yes to dinner because he doesn't have plans, and even at 9:45 A.M. he can almost smell the rosemary perfuming his kitchen.

It is Denise's first visit to his townhouse, and she asks for a tour while the roaster is resting under aluminum foil. She is an appreciative visitor, complimenting his rugs, his variegated parquet, his wainscoting, his lithographs. He narrates: This was the original molding, the original ceiling fixture; this came from a flea market in Arundel, Maine, this from an auction house in Philly. Picture these four walls papered in khaki grass cloth! That's what I was up against. And this marble fireplace unearthed during renovations!

Too late, as they round the corner into his living room, he remembers that photos of baby Thalia are prominently displayed on his mantel.

"Where'd these come from?" Denise asks.

"They were always here," he lies.

"Now that I see your shrine, I feel bad," she says.

Just like that: The central tragedy of his life, and its perpetrator finally suffers a pang. "Bad because you let your husband cut me out of Thalia's life? How does that strike you now? As reprehensible? So many lost years, every birthday, every milestone?"

"Horrible," Denise says. "Unforgivable. Although I have to say, I don't remember you putting up much of a fight." She puts her arm through his and pats his hand. "You know what we should do? Let's call her. Now that I see this adorable little face I'm not even sure what our most recent squabble was about except that it addressed my maternal shortcomings. Where's your phone? I'll promise her that I'll reform. Or at least try. She's very forgiving. Maybe she's cooled off."

Henry appreciates the testimonial to Thalia's forbearing nature but rejects Denise's offer to concoct a united family. He wants and deserves Thalia to himself.

"That sounds like a very long conversation," he says. "A shorter phone call might be to one of those bachelor friends of yours. Who's at the top of your list?"

Denise's face registers *new mission in life*. Successfully sidetracked, she rushes for her purse and her phone.

"Can we eat first?" Henry calls after her. He hears not one but two identical messages being left on answering machines, first to a Jeffrey, then to a Todd: "You remember that my ex turned out to be gay?" she chirps. "Well, guess what? He's unattached. Call me."

How did I ever marry her? Henry wonders. And simultaneously, *Jeffrey? Todd?*

7

Where Are My Manners?

I T IS 9:45 P.M. and Henry is watching *Jane Eyre* in his pajamas when Thalia calls, asking if she may drop by.

"When were you thinking?"

"Is now okay? I'm four blocks away."

He dresses quickly and as casually as his wardrobe allows, just
in time to answer the doorbell. On the top step, Thalia is trying
not to shiver in a too-thin yellow wool coat. Next to her, running
his hands appraisingly along the stone mythical animals decorating either side of the door, is a tall, gaunt, unsmiling stranger.
"I'd like you to meet Larry—" Thalia begins, but doesn't amplify
once she steps inside. "Wow! I had no idea! Now I have to re-
adjust my whole mental picture of Henry at home."

Henry reaches around Thalia to offer his hand to the stranger.
"Please come in. I'm Henry Archer."

The stranger shakes Henry's hand but says only, "I know."

Thalia is staring up at the elaborately carved and domed foyer ceiling. "It's not that I expected you'd live in a fourth-floor walkup, but, yikes. I mean, you could tell me I was in Gracie Mansion and I'd believe it."

"How many square feet?" asks the guest.

"No idea," Henry lies.

"Sorry — Henry, did I mention this is Larry Dumont, famous actor?"

"Actually I'm Leif now," the visitor corrects. "*L-E-I-F*."

"Noted," says Henry.

"We had dinner over on Amsterdam," Thalia says.

Before Henry can ask for their coats, Leif embarks on a self-tour. His first stop is the oil painting over the living room fireplace. He studies it — a bouquet of dying flowers dunked blossom side down into a clear vase — then declares, "At first I think *Dutch still life*. But then I think, no, modern. With a narrative: Her lover betrayed her and tried to win her back with flowers, but she was too enraged to accept a peace offering."

Henry glances at Thalia, who returns a wonderfully screwy look that says, *Don't ask me.*

"Is this something you'd be willing to sell?" Leif asks.

"Sell?" Henry repeats.

Leif doesn't wait for an answer. He's moved on to Henry's wall of shelves and is gyrating his favorite snow globe. "You have good taste," he says. "And I like the way you intersperse antiques between the books."

"Leif just moved into a new apartment," Thalia explains.

"Here in New York?"

"In Tribeca, a sublet: three thousand square feet with city views and a screening room."

Henry winks at Thalia and says, "Where are my manners? Can I get either of you a glass of wine? Coffee? Tea?"

"Single-malt Scotch?" Leif asks.

"I'll check. On the rocks?"

"Neat," says Leif.

Thalia announces she's going to find the powder room but instead follows Henry into the kitchen.

"Who *is* this man?" Henry whispers.

"I'm kicking him out after one drink. Can I tell you then?"

Henry, at the open refrigerator, asks, "White okay? Sancerre? Or I can run downstairs for a nice red."

"White's good," says Thalia. She motions to the hall outside the kitchen. "Let me go flush a toilet so it doesn't look like we were back here talking about him."

"First door on the right, under the stairs. Tell your friend I'll be out with his Scotch in a minute."

"Hope he's not stealing anything," she says.

Leif's tour has taken him to the library, where Henry finds his guests seated side by side on his tufted leather sofa. "So how do you two know each other?" he asks.

"We had the same acting teacher," Thalia says. "About five years apart."

"Six," says Leif. He asks Henry how he came into possession of coasters that say *A Raisin in the Sun,* and are they suede?

"At auction. A fundraiser for Broadway Cares. Originally the sets were cast gifts on opening night."

"I love that play," Thalia says.

"Take them," says Henry. "Really. I'd love you to have them."

"Absolutely not. I'll visit them here. Besides, I don't have a coffee table to put them on." She takes her glass and Leif's from the tray Henry has set down. "And don't give me that look."

"Which look?"

"The one that says, 'I'll wrap them up and surprise you for your next birthday. And a coffee table to go under them.'"

49

"Making up for lost time," Henry says.

"Are you looking to get rid of them?" asks Leif.

"No, he is *not*," Thalia answers. "He's being generous and, if I may be so bold, paternal."

"I used to be married to Thalia's mother," Henry explains. "For a short time, a very long time ago. Denise was a widow with a child when we married. Thalia's biological father died in a climbing accident."

"He was dashing and brilliant, I understand," says Thalia. "I, of course, take after him in every possible way."

"How do you know that?" Leif asks.

Thalia puts down her glass, closes her eyes, and moves her hands in circles over the coffee table. "We talk. When he doesn't show, I try the Ouija board."

Henry smiles. "She's very entertaining, my ex-stepdaughter, don't you think?"

"I don't know yet," says Leif. "We just met today."

There is a prolonged silence as all three sip their drinks. Finally Henry asks, "Would I have seen any of your work, Leif?"

"*Land of Louie*, probably," says Leif. "Unfortunately, I was typecast by that role."

"It was a sitcom," Thalia says. "He wasn't Louie. He played the creepy upstairs neighbor —"

"Boo Trumbley. For the entire run: five seasons. I assume you have cable?"

Henry nods.

"It's in syndication on TVLand. Channel eighty-five here."

"I'll be sure to catch an episode," says Henry. "Or many."

"You won't like it," says Leif. "Not that I'm disowning it. Every door I've passed through since then was opened by Boo Trumbley."

Leif is looking more and more to Henry like an undesirable

50

upstairs neighbor. His forehead is high and bony, and he doesn't appear to blink.

"Leif now produces and stars in horror films," explains Thalia. Henry raises his glass. "What fun," he says.

"They're not fun," says Leif. "They're terrifying — which I say proudly."

"I love Hitchcock," says Henry. "I once rented a car when I was in California and drove to Bodega Bay just to see where *The Birds* was filmed. The schoolhouse is still there. I turned one of my photos into my Christmas card."

Leif says, "Hitchcock didn't make horror films. He made thrillers."

"Of course," says Henry. "And I'm sure you're sick of every person waxing lyrical about Hitchcock as soon as you state your genre."

Leif's professional annoyance has made him down his Scotch in a few gulps. Henry asks if he'd like a refill, an offer Thalia thwarts with, "Leif has meetings in the morning. You and I should probably get started on that legal stuff you were going to help me with."

Leif stands up to his full gangly height. Henry shakes the enormous hand and manages to say that it was very nice of him to drop by.

"Thalia will fill you in," Leif says.

Henry makes her a perfect cheese omelet, which he serves at his rose granite kitchen island. "I'll back up," she says. "Last week I was approached by the former teacher of mine —"

"Teacher when you were how old?" he asks sharply.

"No, no. Not that. No restraining order needed. This was after college. An improv workshop, Sally Eames-Harlan —"

"From the acting Harlans?" he asks.

"Married into them, now hyphenated. You listening?"

"Sorry. Go on."

"She called me about another ex-student of hers, one of her more illustrious alums." Thalia pauses. "Who turned out to be Leif. So far, not bad, right?"

"We'll see," says Henry.

"Anyone who's ever taken a class with Sally has heard about Larry Dumont, who wasn't — to put it mildly — just another pretty face in Hollywood. So we're on the phone and she's going on and on, and I was tuning her out because I was at work, and I thought it was just the Leif report. And then I hear, 'This is where you come in.' I said, 'Me?' Sally says, 'His people would like to meet with you.' I immediately think, audition. 'For what part?' I ask. Sally says, 'Serious girlfriend.' 'But in what?' 'Life,' she says. 'He needs a serious relationship that can go public. I thought of you immediately.' Now I'm paying attention. I ask, 'Don't you mean, Would I like to go out on a *date* with Leif?' And she says no. This is a campaign designed by a publicist to repackage him as someone who's attractive enough to be a regular character actor and not a monster —"

"She said that?"

"Not in so many words."

"Because," Henry says, "there's only one reason a successful actor needs a publicist to manufacture a romance —"

"Nope, not gay. It was the first thing I asked Sally, who got a little huffy about how she'd never help a gay man find a beard, blah blah blah — followed by her first-person testimony to his straightness." Thalia takes her first bite of the omelet and pronounces it delicious.

"Why doesn't this Sally sign on? Wouldn't that be a better story — acting teacher takes up with her irresistible star pupil?"

"Nope, wrong profile: She's twice his age and married. They're looking for someone he can propose to within a matter of weeks."

Henry says, "Are we actually having a conversation about your becoming engaged to a total stranger?"

"A *fake* engagement! An acting job! If he doesn't announce that extra step, it's just Boo Trumbley dating a nobody. The thinking is that an engagement gets you into 'Milestones' at the back of *People*. Besides, you've met him. It would take an actor of great skill such as *moi* to carry this off."

Henry says, "Eat. It's getting cold." Then: "It strikes me as very sad—that this is what acting has come to. And it also strikes me as very sad that a man has to buy his way into a woman's affections."

"It strikes you as very sad as in 'Don't do it,' or it strikes you as very sad as in 'Yes, do help the poor fellow out'?"

Henry says as calmly as he can, "Whichever answer makes you say no."

Thalia taps the tines of her fork lightly on his hand. "You're being a purist. Wouldn't you get even a little thrill out of opening your newspaper and seeing a blind item that said, 'What human gargoyle and his girlfriend were seen photo-op shopping at the diamond ring counter of a famous jewelry store on Fifth Avenue?'"

Henry says, "They don't have blind items in the *New York Times*."

Thalia slips off the stool, helps herself to a handsome transparent peppermill, returns. "I'm going to say yes because it could be very good for me. I'd get a salary, a housing allowance, and an entire year of health insurance. Sally claims there are hidden depths and appeal there, or some such. All I have to do is be seen at clubs with Leif and pretend to be in love. *Which* I consider a professional challenge."

"And if your public finds out that you're taking money to be romanced, and it's all a hoax? Doesn't that make you a punch line? Not to mention a paid escort?"

"I need to do this," she says quietly. "It's not the money. It's the exposure. You don't put 'stand-in' on your resumé. If it weren't for one commercial and my union card, I'd be officially an actor-wannabe." She opens a cupboard, finds a glass, fills it with water, and returns to her chair. "It seems to me a win-win situation: I get to play a leading lady. I get a platinum American Express card to beef up my wardrobe. No sex. We'll put that in writing. After six months, he dumps me. I keep the ring. I sell it and donate the proceeds rather conspicuously to Oprah's school for poor girls in South Africa, no doubt earning myself a guest spot on her show."

Henry doesn't mean to smile or be intrigued, but he is thinking of Celeste, who lived for gossip and blind items, who unapologetically devoured the supermarket tabloids he brought to the ICU. "Is any of this on paper yet?" he asks.

"Not yet. I say yes, and then his people talk to my people. Or as the case may be, my person."

She is smiling at him with such an impishly angelic grin that some primal Sunday school impulse makes him think, *Celeste arranged all of this.* Immediately he shakes that off; he is not given to beliefs about dead friends or deities watching over him. But he does settle on another notion, halfway between reason and magic: *This is why I have been restored to fatherhood.*

8

The Guest Room

N o, THALIA DOES *NOT* think her mother needs to be consulted. Would she care if Denise learned from a newspaper that Thalia Krouch is being seen around town with horror luminary Leif Dumont? Have she and her mother ever seen eye to eye on the topic of men anyway? Why invite another fight?

"She didn't approve of certain boyfriends?" Henry asks.

"No, that was me doing the disapproving. But never mind. Long, ugly story that I'll tell you someday when I can stomach it." Thalia may be a little drunk on several refills of Sancerre, but who could blame her? It is delicious, chilled to perfection in a green marble ice bucket at her elbow. She gestures expansively around the kitchen. "Did I live here when you were married to my mom?"

Henry says, "Not when we were married. But you visited here. Afterward."

"Denise visited after running out on you? Should I read something into that?"

"Such as?"

"That it wasn't as clean a break as everyone thought?"

Henry says, "It was a very clean break. An amputation. Denise wasn't the visitor. You were. For a while, anyway, every other weekend . . ."

"Like a custody arrangement?"

"Like a custody arrangement. Until Glenn adopted you."

"Did I have sleepovers?"

"Unsuccessfully. The first few times you cried for so long that your mother had to come get you. After that, your nanny came along."

"Which nanny?"

"The horrible British one. I have her name somewhere. I hope she's out of business."

"I think Dad fired her when I entered kindergarten."

"Good! She was too strict, too British. I even remember her hands — big and red and chapped. I hated watching her give you a bath — she scrubbed your poor little scalp as if she were delousing you — and then dumped a pitcher of water over your head! When I said anything critical, she'd pluck you out of the water and walk away in a huff. Thank goodness you don't remember."

"Did my mother have an opinion about any of this?"

"Your mother's attitude was, we were the amateurs and Nanny was the pro. *Nanny.* No wonder I don't remember her name. Such an affectation."

Why *hadn't* he done something? Besides the baths and the attitude, he'd objected to the nursery food, which was steamed, plain, presumably tasteless. Who would ever call plain yogurt "pudding"? Shouldn't a little girl be trying Chinese food, quiche, lasagna, maple syrup on her French toast? Denise — and truth-

56

fully he'd recognized this twenty-five years ago — was not the mother he'd want for a baby they might have had together.

Thalia asks if the visits stopped just because she was so miserable on the sleepovers.

"No. They stopped because Glenn Krouch's lawyers didn't think this house was a proper environment for you to be exposed to."

Thalia harrumphs. "Not proper, meaning gay?"

Henry says, "It didn't help that I had a live-in boyfriend at the time."

"Who?"

"Roger. Short-lived, but unfortunately the root of my custody problem."

"*He* was the root? Or my parents turned him into the root?"

"He was, as it turned out, nothing. And once Krouch adopted you, what was I? The ex-father without any rights."

Thalia says, "It's so sweet that you use the term *ex-father* without the *step*."

This is the time then. Henry says, "I haven't been completely honest with you about my tenure as your stepfather. There's more to it than —"

"Wait! Let me guess: When you met my mother, Roger was already in the picture, but there were social and professional pressures on you — how old were you? Thirty? — to find a hostess slash wife and settle down?"

"No. Much more mundane than that. Well, not mundane to me, but in the sense of legal documents —"

Thalia jumps in again. "You and my mother were never legally married! The nanny knew it and that's why she didn't take any orders from you."

"We *were* legally married. Absolutely. And here's what I'm leading up to: At the end of the wedding ceremony, the judge announced to the guests that it was his privilege to proclaim flower girl Thalia Wales, officially on this day, Thalia Archer."

Thalia, uncharacteristically, looks stumped.

"No one ever told you that I legally adopted you?"

Thalia closes her eyes. "Wait. I have to let this sink in: You. Adopted. Me. This means what in relationship to . . . the Many Fathers of Thalia?"

"Nothing cataclysmic. Just that I was legally your father for two years during the marriage, and for another twenty-two months until Glenn Krouch prevailed."

Thalia studies him for a few long seconds. "What's that look? You just curled up in a ball when you told me that."

He shakes his head. "Guilt," he finally says. "Cowardice."

"Even though it was my mother who ran off with another man and took me with her? What were you supposed to do? Show up the next day and take me to the circus?"

Sensing that Thalia is either irreversibly in his corner or immune to startling personal revelations, he confesses all: "I didn't fight in court. I let you go. I signed the adoption papers because it was the easiest thing to do. You saw me less and less, so of course each time was more difficult. I signed those damned papers and I never saw you again." He says, "Okay. Maybe I did. I used to watch you skate at Wollman Rink. From a safe distance. I knew you had lessons on Sunday morning in the fall and winter."

"This is getting a little heartbreaking," says Thalia. "Not to mention cinematic: Youngish man, divorced, loses custody and sneaks over to Central Park to watch his little girl, through binoculars. Cue the Viennese waltzes. Was I always dressed in an adorable skating outfit trimmed in ermine, or was that Judy Garland in *Meet Me in Saint Louis*?"

Should he laugh? Would Sheri Abrams ask him to probe deeper until he got to . . . what? Issues behind his low self-regard and regrettable non-battle over custody? He hates that word: *is-sues*. "Is that an ish with you?" Celeste used to ask with a jab to his ribs. "Should I have dumped all this on you tonight, on the heels of Leif Dumont?" he asks.

"It's fine. In fact it's better, considering what's ahead. If by any chance I'm in the spotlight, and *Entertainment Tonight* starts looking for dirt —"

"Such as, father number two was gay and lost custody because of it?"

Thalia pours the last drop of wine into her glass. "And you know what I'd say to that? I'd say, 'I'm very lucky that my only surviving father is gay. It's a gift, just when I needed a nice, stable, parental relationship.' And please note the irony of it coming full circle: What once made you a bad father in the eyes of the court now makes you the perfect ex-father. Wouldn't it be harder if you were straight and single and I was eating lunch with you and dropping over and seeking your advice, and I had to worry about sexual tension?"

"This is true," says Henry.

"You've read those creepy father-daughter love story memoirs, right?"

"Read reviews of one or two."

"I *have* had a lot of fathers," Thalia muses. "And they haven't had such good luck. I'm the Henry the Eighth of daughters."

"Or Denise is the Henry the Eighth of wives."

Thalia smiles. "Let's hate her together. It'll be fun."

Henry says, "I find you remarkably . . . resilient."

"I thought you were going to say, 'remarkably mean to your recently widowed mother —'"

"Whom you might consider telling about Leif Dumont before she reads about your engagement in *People*."

"No, thank you. Mrs. Krouch and I are taking a break."

Another confession is called for: that he has kept his reunion with Thalia private. He says, "I haven't exactly told her that you and I are back in touch."

"Totally understandable," says Thalia.

"It's selfishness on my part."

Thalia says, "Poor Henry. He's selfish. He's a wuss. He's wracked with guilt. I think it's my job to raise your self-esteem."

"To which my therapist would say, 'Ha! Good luck with that.'"

She puts her glass down and begins making lines and loops with an index finger on the granite. After a few invisible tracings, she asks Henry if he has a pen handy. He does. Now she writes words on a paper napkin, shielding them from his view. "How's this?" she asks. "Stage name only. I wouldn't change it legally."

She has written "Thalia Archer" in block letters and then in cursive, each signature less legible, as if practicing an autograph-worthy scrawl.

Henry says the first vaguely official thing that comes to mind: "You were registered for kindergarten as Thalia Archer."

"It's a little Kate Hepburnish, don't you think?" — and answers her own question with a throaty, high-spirited "Thalia Ahcha!"

"But" — and here in victory Henry is being chivalrous — "you've been *Krouch* for so long. Are you worried that you might feel a loss of identity?"

"Henry! I'm selling my soul anyway! Why not lose my identity? I've given *Krouch* a nice long tenure."

Up till now, he has been careful and respectful, lest his anti–Glenn Krouch animus backfire so soon after the man's sudden death. But something has liberated him. "Krouch," he repeats. "I can't say it ever had a ring to it."

"A *homophobic* ring, maybe," says Thalia.

• • •

Their faux argument proceeds this way: cab versus subway for her return to Mott Street. She says "almost midnight" is not late, and besides, 11:35 P.M. is not midnight. He asks how far the subway stop is from her front door, and she says, "Four, five minutes . . . depending on how many panhandlers I engage with."

He asks if she has a part-time doorman, a live-in super, . . . anything? And she says, "Oh, Henry. I love your worldview." She gets down from the stool, stretches in a few different directions, and says, "I should let you get to bed."

"There's another option," says Henry. "I keep new toothbrushes on hand, and I can loan you pajamas that have never been worn."

Thalia says, "Dental floss? Retainer? Birth control pills?"

"Dental floss."

She strokes her chin as if there were a perplexing offer on the table. "I was half kidding. I'd love to stay. We modern girls carry our pharmaceuticals with us."

"Should you call your roommate so he won't worry?" he asks.

"I'll text him," she says. "Not that I want to set a precedent."

He leads her up the front stairway, not intending a full-fledged tour, but Thalia stops in the doorway of the master bedroom to admire what she calls its sleek good looks. She wanders in. He immediately apologizes for its size — the result of reconfiguring three second-story chambers into one bedroom, dressing room, and a bathroom that could accommodate two grand pianos.

She asks the color of the walls and he says, "I'm a little embarrassed to know the answer off the top of my head but I do: It's Coastal Fog."

"Do you just love it?" she enthuses. "I'd never leave. All you need is room service."

He tells her that once there was no turning back, he worried the suite was ostentatious and the whole property less salable.

"Can't wait to see the guest room."

He leads her to the end of the hall, to the only room untouched by renovations, a small space under the eaves that is white and crisp except for its faded antique quilt. "It's very sweet," says Thalia. "Even a little girly." She walks over to the bureau after spotting the three tarnished pieces — comb, brush, hand mirror — all alone on an eyelet bureau scarf. "Whose monograms?" she asks.

"My mother's."

"*W*? But not an *A*?"

"*W.R.* for Williebelle Randall, her maiden name."

"Is she still with us?"

"Afraid not. It'll be three years in May."

"Did I ever meet her?"

"At the wedding."

"Was she actually named Williebelle?"

"Awful, isn't it? Sounds like she grew up in Dogpatch. For some reason, she wore it well."

"And this was her room?"

He points with his chin: rocking chair, quilt, afghan.

"Was she living here when I used to visit?"

"No, much later. She lived with me for her last two years."

"Did she die in this actual bed?"

"No. She died at Columbia-Presbyterian in a lilac satin bed jacket. Pneumonia. She was ninety-one."

"Good genes," says Thalia.

"Not entirely. I must have mentioned since I'm mildly obsessed with the fact that my father had a fatal heart attack at fifty-five."

She points to the closet.

"Be my guest," says Henry.

She opens it and yelps, "Holy shit!"

"I know. It's shameful. I haven't thrown one thing away."

"Are you kidding? I think I just died and went to hand-me-down heaven." She is sliding hangers back and forth in sale-rack rapture. "So you'll have to excuse me so I can start trying things on. Is there a guest bathroom?"

"Of course, of course. New toothbrushes in the medicine cabinet. Towels in the linen closet. I'll leave the PJs on the edge of the tub."

She has brought forth a navy blue dress that looks old-ladyish to Henry, and severe, but Thalia is swaying, an arm holding it against her waist in dancehall fashion. "Are you thinking what I'm thinking?" she asks.

Henry says, "I'm afraid not."

"I'm thinking that if I could borrow some of these —"

"Of course! Of course! You'd be doing me a favor."

She tosses the first dress onto the bed and brings forth one he actually remembers his mother wearing in Wilmington: black-and-white check, with buttons that have little rhinestone navels. "This one has to be from the nineteen fifties," says Thalia. "It's a shirtwaist. And ohmigod, it has a silk flower still pinned on it! This is too fabulous. Everything is."

"You'll probably want to take it to a dressmaker for . . . what would be the right term? Updating?"

"No! There's so many. I'll find the right ones. But turn around. Don't look."

He faces the hallway and hears the rustling of clothes coming off and clothes going on. "Not yet," she says. Then in half a minute, "Okay, *now.*"

She is wearing the navy dress. It's shinier — raw silk? — than he'd seen at first. It manages to be both too big in the bust and too short in the sleeves. Thalia twirls, and the skirt billows. She cuffs her hand around one wrist. "And can't you see it with a big wide bracelet? And very high strappy shoes? Burgundy patent? Don't you love it?" she demands. "Isn't it amazing?"

"It's all amazing," Henry says.

9

The Maisonette

THALIA COMES DOWN to breakfast in another Willie-belle frock, this one of a translucent crinkly fabric, either yellow or yellowed with age, decorated with dainty sprays of violets. Clearly she's wearing it to make Henry laugh, over her jeans and turtleneck sweater. On her head: a short pink veil anchored with a furry bow, its netting decorated with pink velvet butterflies. Thalia says nothing but hums, "In your Easter bonnet."

Henry doesn't hear her until his espresso machine stops its grinding. Turning around, he jumps, then laughs.

"Good morning, darling host and costumer," Thalia says.

"That hat," he says. "What does it say about me that I remember it vividly, and as a child I thought it was the most beautiful thing in the world?"

Thalia kisses his cheek and says, "President of Future Homosexuals of America?"

How does she do it? he marvels. Has anyone else of his acquaintance ever possessed this talent for simultaneously shocking and disarming?

"Did I offend?" she asks breezily.

Henry selects a mug and an espresso cup from the cabinet above and holds both up for her consideration.

"A double, definitely. You didn't answer my question — is it okay to joke about your . . . personalhood?"

"From you, it's quite okay. In fact it's very nice when someone doesn't consider the topic unmentionable."

"Good! And it's out there? Friends? Relatives? Lawyers and judges?"

"Why?"

"Just asking to prevent future big-mouth faux pas." She accepts her mug of coffee and motions toward the espresso machine. "I'm watching how you do this so I know which buttons to push."

He points: This one under the green light gives you the coffee, and this one means refill the water tank. He asks if she'd like him to steam some milk and she says no, black. Did she drink a whole bottle of wine last night?

Henry says no, he helped. And wouldn't it be easier to drink her coffee minus the chin-length veil?

Thalia folds the netting up one turn into a goofy cuff. She takes a sip and says, "I'm sure it was meant to be worn at teas and . . . where else did your mother go where food was served? Bridge club?"

"How do you know these things?"

"Old movies, dahling: tea parties, bridge clubs, country clubs, June Allyson, and, of course, church."

"Willie did, in fact, play bridge and go to church."

"Where was this again?"

"Wilmington, Delaware." He taps his mug against hers. "Where I was a celebrity."

"No you weren't!"

"Minor, very: I was one of those New Year's babies, first child born in nineteen fifty-two in Wilmington. My mother and I made the front page."

Thalia asks, "What time?"

"What time was I *born*?"

"To win. Was it a squeaker?"

"Not at all. Two-oh-two A.M."

"Did your mother save the front page?"

Henry smiles. "You'd think so, wouldn't you? But I was the fourth boy." He counts off on his fingers. "They didn't mean to have four children, they were praying for a girl, and, most likely, the photo of my mother wasn't flattering."

"I'm noting the irony of this," says Thalia. "She didn't want a fourth child or a fourth boy, but who took care of her in her old age? Whose guest room did she more or less die in? Who was such a great comfort and host while his older brothers were — I'm guessing — too busy with their wives and offspring to take her in and preserve her wardrobe?"

"She did come around," says Henry. "I didn't mean to imply that I was unloved."

"And she was fine having a gay son?"

"She was fine having a *divorced* bachelor son. Still, she left her not-insubstantial engagement ring to my future wife, the posthumous one."

"So sweet," says Thalia. She rubs the sleeve of Williebelle's dress, then sniffs it. "Did she wear Chanel Number Five?"

"Nothing but."

"Sensory memory! Very good acting tool. Maybe it's why you

haven't given her stuff away: You wanted to be able to walk down the hall and open that closet and feel her presence."

"Possibly. Or maybe I didn't know who'd take it off my hands." Thalia says, "At your service. Trash bags will work, and when I come back, I'll bring a duffel."

Henry, from the open refrigerator, a butter dish in one hand and an egg carton in the other, says, "Or you could just move in."

The phone rings. Closer and unencumbered, Thalia picks up the handset and intones in Brooklynese, "Archer residence. Thalia Archer Krouch Archer speaking."

Why didn't he anticipate Denise's post-breakfast check-in? He closes the refrigerator with a backward kick of his foot and waits for Thalia's smile to collapse.

"May I ask who's calling . . . ?" Her eyebrows lift. "He's right here." She hands him the handset and relieves him of the egg carton, announcing, "A gentleman for you."

Henry hears an indifferent male voice announce, "I'm Denise's friend, Jeffrey . . . Denise Krouch's? She left me your name and number."

"It's not a great time to talk," Henry says, as Thalia signals, *Yes, it is.*

"Maybe there's been a misunderstanding," says Jeffrey.

Henry says, "Not at all. Let me call you back. Is this your home number on my caller ID?"

"Office. Denise gave you a heads-up, I assume?"

Henry repeats, "I'll call you back." He hangs up and asks Thalia if he can make her an omelet like last night's. Juice? Half a grapefruit? He's inherited Williebelle's grapefruit spoons.

"One sec. Did I hear my mother's name crackling over the wires?"

"You did."

"She's setting you up?"

"I knew she gave my name to two of her friends — a Jeffrey and another one whose name I forget."

"How did he sound?"

"Nice enough."

"Nice enough for what?"

Henry smiles. "Nice enough to ask Denise what he looks like."

Thalia sighs. "You boys: so concerned with externals."

"As opposed to you girls?"

"Henry! Have you forgotten that I'm practically marrying Herman Munster?" She finally plucks the hat off her head and tosses it, Frisbee-style, onto the farthest kitchen counter. "Speaking of my romantic partnership, I think we have to meet with Leif's people and sign the papers. Unless of course I *don't* sign the papers . . ."

"What would change your mind?" Henry asks. "Because if it's a matter of money or a more comfortable living situation, you know I'd want to help."

"It's not. But thank you. I only meant that Leif might not have found me to his liking."

"Not possible. Unless he's daft; unless he wakes up this morning and realizes that the whole scheme is undignified and demeaning."

"For him, you mean?"

"I know your position: It's an acting challenge. All publicity is good publicity."

"Do any of us feel a little sorry for Larry Dumont, so desperate to be seen as appealing that he trades his dignity for an artificial girlfriend?" She holds her cup out. "Your coffee's delicious. Any cereal? That's what I usually have."

Henry opens a cupboard and reads, "Raisin Bran, Cheerios, Total . . . nope. That one must be five years old."

"Cheerios, please."

68

He tucks the box under one arm and brings bowls and spoons to the island. Thalia asks, "What you said just before the phone rang? About me moving in? Were you serious? Or was it more like a stray thought?"

"Not a stray thought," he says. "Very much premeditated."

"Since . . . ?"

He doesn't say the first thing that presents itself — *Since I learned that you bathe in your kitchen* — but substitutes a weightier, historical answer: "I bought this house because I was a father who thought his daughter would be visiting me every other weekend and on future school vacations, and I wanted her to have a second home and not some bachelor flat with a sleep sofa. You know the rest of the story: The Krouches got you."

She says, absent her usual light tone, "But you must have kept track of how much time had passed. And after I turned eighteen, wasn't it okay to get in touch with me? Didn't you wonder what I was up to?"

Now, then, is the time to confide his *Carousel*-induced preoccupation. "It was all I talked about after I did the math and figured out when you'd graduate from high school and most likely leave the nest."

"But what stopped you?"

"Fear that you'd shut the door in my face, call your mother, call your father, call a lawyer, call nine-one-one."

"What about a letter? I'd have rushed to the nearest phone."

"I know that now."

She pours milk into her bowl and after a few spoonfuls asks, "What were you thinking?"

Her words add up to a reproach except that Thalia is chomping contentedly on her cereal.

"I wasn't thinking," Henry allows. "I was angry at your mother, your father, myself —"

"Not that," Thalia says. "I meant the moving-in part. Did you mean I'd get Williebelle's room, or were you thinking I'd move into the maisonette?"

Has he mentioned a maisonette to her? The previous owner called it an in-law apartment, a label that has kept it fallow and unrenovated ground.

"Leif spotted it; thought it was a separate apartment. He looked in the windows before we rang your doorbell. We weren't sure if you lived up here or down below. I couldn't help noticing it was empty."

"It's a separate apartment," he says. "Three rooms, untouched."

"And a full bath?"

"Of course."

"Don't you want to rent it out?"

Henry says, "I have no desire to be a landlord."

Thalia says, "That's fine. I can appreciate that."

"Wait," says Henry. "Did you mean you? Because you wouldn't be a tenant. You'd live here. You're family. I wouldn't be renting it out. Strike all of that. The jury will disregard any mention of me as landlord."

Thalia grins and jumps off her stool. "The jury would like a tour," she says.

10

A Piece of the Action

THALIA GETS a text message at work confirming that Leif has deemed her suitable for the mission ahead. She calls Henry, who asks, "That was his wording? 'Suitable'?" Thalia says, "No, it was more personal than that. Actually, pretty nice. Don't forget: This could be leaked to a news outlet, so message number one needed a romantic ring to it."

"Such as?"

"'Can't wait to see you again. L.D.'"

"Anything about the parties getting together?"

"That's why I called: Are you free to take a secret meeting after work today?"

"Secret, but with counsel?"

"Definitely with counsel. Counsel required, in fact: Waldorf-Astoria, six o'clock. Leif's arriving via some underground entrance they use for presidents. The unknowns can walk through the front door. We're supposed to pick up an envelope at the concierge desk that will tell us what room to go to. Very *Amazing Race.*"

Henry doesn't watch *The Amazing Race* but scribbles the words on a scratch pad.

Thalia asks if he could swing by the salon and they'd walk over together to discuss strategy. Giovanni is promising a quick blow-dry beforehand, so time is a little tight. Five forty-five?

Henry asks, "Does he know?"

Thalia says, "Not yet. I won't give my notice till I sign the contract."

Henry considers saying, "I inferred from Giovanni that you two have a relationship outside the salon" but then doesn't have to. Thalia says, "I hope you don't believe everything your beautician brags about."

Her hair is glossier and more asymmetric than usual, with new layers in new places. "Very nice," Henry says. "And very stylish, I'm sure." Her jacket, powder blue and pink plaid with golf-ball-sized buttons, can have come from only one source. Several bracelets fill the space between cuff and wrist. He says, "I think I'm getting an idea of what your look is. I think my mother used to wear gloves with that length sleeve."

She says, "I was so right: Nothing beats a gay father."

They are heading east on 57th, her arm hooked through his. "What remains to be discussed?" he asks.

"*Numero uno*, no sex. Mr. Munster and I can be seen holding hands and kissing, but that's only for public consumption."

"I couldn't agree more."

"Even if they say blah blah blah, there're so many shades of gray, and what if his hand slips and should cup a buttock when you're dancing? You'll explain that I'd be a paid escort if there are any sex acts involved, right?"

"Happy to."

"The monthly stipends should be in cash, don't you think? If it's by check, won't some bank employee know I'm being paid by Leif?"

"I'm sure they'll launder it. Unless they're incompetent, it wouldn't be from Leif's account or from his publicist's."

"And I absolutely have to tell Arielle and Amanda about the deal — can we ask for a couple of relatively discreet best-friend leaks, because I can't just get engaged overnight to someone I've never mentioned. They'll sign confidentiality agreements, too. In fact, I think they'd love that."

Henry asks, "Which does beg the question: Will the public buy it? Won't it appear awfully precipitous?"

Thalia says in mock dismay, "Henry, I think you're forgetting that I met Leif through Sally *years ago* and we've been seeing each other secretly for months. She had us both to dinner, a small group at her apartment on Jane Street, at which she served spaghetti with puttanesca sauce and three tropical flavors of gelato. Ages ago, as you may recall. So you see, it's been quite a long romance."

A stern female voice answers their knock with, "Door's open." Henry puts a hand on Thalia's forearm and whispers, "No. We're not room service. Let them get off their asses."

The same voice, more annoyed now, calls, "Who is it?"

Henry says, "Miss Krouch and her lawyer. We can come back if you're indisposed."

Footsteps approach. The door opens to reveal a woman in, Henry guesses, her last trimester of pregnancy, attired nonetheless in a three-piece black pinstriped suit. "We're all here now," she says as her eyes surveil the hallway.

Thalia and Henry enter the suite's living room, an old-fashioned

73

affair in shades of gold and yam. The fringed drapes are drawn. A second, younger woman, dressed in a short leather skirt and denim jacket, is seated on a sofa, her yellow hair spiked and her eyeglasses a leopard print. On the coffee table in front of her are legal folders and a bowl of red grapes. The two women stare at their visitors for a few seconds past necessary. Thalia approaches both and shakes their hands in the manner of someone who must take introductions upon herself in the face of lapsed etiquette. "This is my lawyer," she adds. "Henry Archer."

"Attorney Michele Schneider," says the pregnant one.

"I'm Mr. Dumont's publicist," says the blond. "Wendy Morelli. New York office of Estime."

"Is Leif joining us?" asks Thalia.

A toilet flushes — once, twice. Water runs. Wendy says, "He's a little under the weather. He had vindaloo last night."

Leif emerges from the bedroom dressed in jeans and a black T-shirt bearing his production company's logo, a mummy behind a movie camera. Most startlingly: He has shaved his head and pierced both earlobes, now displaying blueberry-sized diamonds. He says, "I'd shake your hand, but I don't know if I have a bug or if it's what I ate last night."

His lawyer asks, "Shall we get started?"

The mission, she summarizes, is this: Candidate will be seen publicly and socially with Leif. Their engagement will be announced six weeks from first tabloid — print or electronic — coverage and/or tersely acknowledged after engagement ring is sighted on the future Mrs. Dumont's hand. At a point to be determined, but not before the romance has spawned a sufficient number of news items, photographs, blind items, et cetera, and Estime is satisfied that his profile has been measurably enhanced, Mr. Dumont will break the engagement when a higher-profile Hollywood actress to be named later comes between them. From the outset, the candidate will neither confirm nor deny the status of the relationship verbally —

"Why not?" asks Henry.

"We've had some disasters with that," says the publicist.

"Acting talent aside, not everyone can think on her feet," adds Attorney Schneider.

Henry says, "I have to be honest: I'm not greatly in favor of this arrangement. I don't see how it advances my client's career."

"This is a *gig*," says the publicist. "This is not a career. The job description is, 'Be pretty, be arm candy for Leif, and don't sound stupid. Act like you're in love and he'll do his best to reciprocate in a way that repackages him as a desirable and attractive actor.' I think you fully understand that there are hundreds, maybe thousands, of women in Manhattan alone who would gladly fill the role."

Henry doesn't speak but directs his gaze to the unappetizing groom, who has folded himself into a club chair, barefoot.

"For the sake of argument, what would make the mission more attractive to your client?" asks the lawyer.

Thalia is helping herself to grapes, eyebrows signaling, *I can't wait to hear this.* Henry declares, "We want — in the notoriety sense — a piece of the action. It's reasonable to expect that your team has contacts with studios and that Thalia will come away with a very good role in a major feature film."

The lawyer says, "I don't even have to caucus on this one. The answer is no. We are not casting directors. I'm an attorney. She's a publicist. We can't possibly commit to that."

Henry says calmly, "Our goal is to raise Thalia's profile. She's a lame duck from the outset. We are asking that your firm represent Thalia when Leif breaks the engagement."

The publicist says, "I can't authorize anything like that. I have to talk to Dorian."

"Who is . . . ?"

"Our CEO."

"Estime is not a charitable institution," says the lawyer. "They don't do pro-bono work."

Henry says, "I'm sure Estime will want Thalia Archer on its client list after this plays out triumphantly in the tabloids." He nods to Thalia, *Follow me,* then tells Leif's people they can have their privacy. He and his client will talk outside.

From a safe distance at the end of the carpeted hallway, Thalia says, "Nice work in there. Very creative. Very . . . lawyerly. But I'd rather the deal didn't fall apart."

"It won't. Leif is in there saying to Wendy, 'Look, I've got you on retainer. I'm paying you a fortune. You'll make some phone calls for her when it's over, and put out a few press releases.' They want you and he wants you and you should relax."

Thalia says, "Okay. If you're sure."

"Quite sure. I saw him staring at you. And worst-case scenario: We take what's on the table."

Thalia finally smiles. "Love the bold, spontaneous Henry. Truly — it's like improv, and someone's yelled out 'ball-buster lawyer!'"

They walk back to the suite and knock. Leif himself answers, looking a little worried. Henry suspects he's been instructed to give nothing away. Henry and Thalia take their seats and stare at the opposing team.

The lawyer says, "We were able to reach Dorian." She frowns, waits.

"And?" says Henry.

"As you can imagine, she wasn't happy. She said, 'Let's open up the search. This is the opportunity of a lifetime for the right person.'"

Henry casts another appraising look at Leif, who is hunched against a wall and gnawing on an energy bar.

"I'm sure Dorian is right and you'd have a line out the door as if this were an actual casting call," Henry says.

"Leif?" says Thalia. "Do you want to jump in?"

Leif chews, swallows, and checks with the lawyer, who signals, *Permission granted.*

"I didn't speak to Dorian myself. They didn't put her on speakerphone in case you could hear out in the hall."

"But?"

"I told them that it didn't seem like such a big deal —"

"No need to rehash the entire conversation," interrupts the lawyer. "And of course there's the matter of client confidentiality."

Henry says, "Which I don't believe applies when it's the client himself speaking."

The lawyer nods to the publicist. "Eventually, after several phone calls back and forth, Dorian agreed that we'd be willing to help keep Thalia in the news."

"Meaning?" asks Henry.

The publicist snaps, "That's like asking for our trade secrets. She'll be our client. We'll do what it takes for a six-month period, post-Leif."

"Two years," says Henry.

The publicist, then the lawyer, and belatedly Leif excuse themselves to caucus in the bedroom.

Henry whispers, "It's all for effect. They know exactly what we want." He holds up an index finger and mouths *one.*

Thalia unbuttons her jacket. Underneath is something pink and lacy that Henry trusts isn't an undergarment. The Leif team reappears and takes its seats. "We reached Dorian," says the lawyer. "Our last best offer is, accordingly, one year, post-Leif, if the campaign is successful."

"Thalia?" asks Henry.

"I can live with that," she answers.

"When do we start?" asks Leif.

"One last thing," Henry says, "which I offer not for my client's benefit but for Leif's. I know this young woman. You might think it prudent to muzzle her and limit her responses to 'No comment' and sly smiles because you've dealt with a great many Hollywood starlets where the less said, the better. But you won't be getting your money's worth. You should let her speak. I don't know Mr. Dumont well enough to grade him on his repartee, but I know Thalia's will be a great asset. Even with what is, in effect, a gag order, he'll want her to step up to the mike, literally or figuratively."

With only that, Thalia stands up. ". . . When did I *know*? It sounds almost too ridiculous, too predestined. But when he rang my doorbell for our first date, he was wearing a tie with these swirly dancing stars against a blue background. I literally gasped and said, 'Who told you?' He didn't know what I was talking about, so I led him to my computer, and then he saw why I was so flabbergasted: His tie and my screen saver were Van Gogh's *Starry Night*. We just stood there for a minute trying to take it all in."

Thalia sits down and bestows on Leif a quiver of a smile that says *love of my life*.

The lawyer and publicist exchange glances as readable as a handshake. Henry maintains his game face.

Leif says, "But I don't have a tie like that."

Ancient History

D ENISE WONDERS ALOUD on Henry's answering machine where he's been hiding and why they haven't talked in nearly two weeks. "Call me!" she chirps. "Lots to tell you. And by the way, is Jeffrey correct in assuming that you've given him the brushoff?" Her financial miseries and stepson backlash often make Henry pick up his remote and watch the news on mute as she rails. Immune to the insult inherent in Henry's not returning her calls, her follow-up messages don't scold. Her tone remains warm and animated, as if he's out of town and will play back a message marathon upon his return.

One detail, delivered as he's leaving the house for the Waldorf-Astoria, does make him pause at the front door: Denise is confiding that she extended an olive branch to Nanette, Glenn's first wife. Thanks to Henry's example, really — peace in our time and all that.

Thus Henry's list of relationships kept secret from Denise

grows by one item. He knows Nanette in a way that is hardly worth mentioning: After Denise ran off with Glenn, his fellow injured party and cuckolded spouse called him. Hadn't both their marriages been ruined by absenteeism, Nanette home with flu symptoms and Henry stuck at work the night of the fateful dinner party? The hostess seated handsome solo Glenn next to adultery-prone Denise. Chemistry ensued.

The forsaken Mrs. Krouch called the office: Would Henry care to meet her for a drink some evening to toast their new freedom? She pronounced the last two words with such bitter sarcasm on his answering machine that he knew any time at all spent discussing their shared humiliation would be deeply unpleasant. He had his secretary deliver the brushoff, woman to woman, maternally and diplomatically: Mr. Archer isn't quite ready to toast his freedom but wishes you and your sons well. Perhaps another time.

Nanette waited until the respective divorces were final and tried again. She didn't want to step over any line . . . oh, okay, yes she did, but she had a lovely friend, single, recently divorced, no children, applying to law school most admirably at thirty-six years of age, and perhaps they could meet for coffee and advice. He could hear in Nanette's voice the wink that meant, "Of course I'm positioning this as career advice but you and I both know it's a blind date."

This time he wrote the note himself. "I would most certainly be happy to meet your friend for coffee and discuss a career in the law. I wouldn't want her to have any social expectations, if that isn't presumptuous, because I have since my divorce made peace with my homosexuality. I hope that neither that fact nor my bluntness will offend you."

Nanette called immediately. At first, she reported, there was — to be completely honest — a letdown. But almost immediately she said what all women in New York City say upon receiving this social clarification: What could be better? Gay men make the most delightful companions. Would he like to join her for, well, anything at all? And she of course had other delightful gay male friends he might like to meet, some of them members of the bar.

With ground rules established, they finally met. Nanette was not unattractive but she was colorless. She reported on her comings and goings — swimming laps, signed up for driving lessons — as if that alone constituted interesting conversation. But as she spoke, and as he dutifully appeared to be listening, he was thinking, *Never again.*

Now the taxi heading home from the Waldorf speeds up Park Avenue — a reminder of Denise's messages unreturned. His mediator instincts revived by negotiating with Estime, he asks the driver to pull over, which he does instantaneously with a swerve to the right and a screech of brakes. "If the party I'm calling is home, I might get out here," Henry explains. He dials Denise's landline, and she picks up on the second ring. "Thank goodness! I was starting to worry — although God knows there's a little irony in that."

Because the meter is running, Henry doesn't ask, "How so?" but, "I'm in a taxi, one block south of you on Park."

"Which means you're calling to say hello or you're about to ring my doorbell?"

"The latter. If it's not a bad time."

"Get out and come up," she commands.

"Have you eaten?"

"Pay first. Don't overtip. I'll tell the doorman to send you up. Nine B."

Denise is waiting in her open doorway, wearing a white terry-cloth robe with a Ritz-Carlton crest on its breast pocket.

"Tell me you didn't steal that," he says.

"I most certainly did not. Don't you notice those little cards in the pocket that say, 'This robe is available for purchase in our gift shop'?"

Henry hands her his overcoat and kisses her cheek. "I always wondered who buys a hotel bathrobe. Didn't it take up an entire suitcase?"

"Didn't have a suitcase on *that* check-in," she says. "And not to worry: I'm fully dressed underneath. My choice was either get into something decent or call down to the doorman. By the way, did Rudy give you a look like *She's dating already*?"

"The doorman? I didn't notice. Not that I'd recognize such a thing."

"A little paternal?" She demonstrates. "As in 'Mrs. K's husband has only been in the ground for *X* weeks, so why is she entertaining a male visitor?'"

Henry says gently, "Denise? Is it possible that underneath these jokes there's a wife mourning the loss of her husband of twenty-five years?"

"Twenty-four! A major difference in this case, believe me."

"Do you want to invite me to sit down somewhere?"

Eyes welling, she presses an index finger against her lips and shakes her head.

"No, you don't want to sit? Or no, you aren't in mourning?"

She shakes her head again.

"Too much? Too many emotions to sort out?"

She nods and fishes a tissue out of her bathrobe pocket. She blows her nose, then asks, "Do you still like mushrooms? Because I have a pizza on the way."

Oddly, for a grand apartment that boasts ten rooms, its kitchen is cramped. A high round bistro table and two soda-fountain stools take up the entire breakfast nook, leading Henry to wonder where the full set of children used to sit.

"I'm going to tell you something now," she confides, filling two wineglasses to the rim. "It's the story behind the story of what got me into several people's doghouses."

"If it's about us — I mean, about why or how you took up with Glenn —"

"Oh, please. Ancient history. This is about Glenn's funeral. Correction: *me* at Glenn's funeral." She dangles a mushroom stem above her plate, pats it back in place, and takes a cleansing breath. "I botched it. I stood up at the microphone and gave a eulogy that was supposed to be honest and helpful — or so I thought — in a way that would remind my fellow mourners that Glenn could be . . . well, not exactly an asshole — who isn't at times? But annoying. And who better than a wife to say, 'He was human. He had his idiosyncrasies and shortcomings'? Which, by the way, I was running through to make people smile through their tears. I was just trying to liven things up! Besides, all the speakers before me had covered every sterling quality he'd ever demonstrated or someday might potentially demonstrate."

Henry is making the most of one half of the small pizza and drinking red wine that tastes like grape juice. He asks, "And what was it that you said in your roast?"

Denise blots her mouth with a pizzeria-supplied napkin. "First, overall, it was a great event. He would have loved it. I stand by my comments. Sometimes, you just don't know how your message is going to get across."

"And your message was . . . ?"

"That he was human! I thought I'd give a little balance. Fortunately or unfortunately I haven't been to a lot of funerals, and the ones I've attended have just been religious ceremonies with one forgettable eulogy by the guy in charge."

"Had you been medicated?" asks Henry.

"One little Ativan!"

"Do you remember what you said?"

"Not word for word. But I remember the highlights."

"Please," he prompts.

"All small stuff! He was being described up here" — her hand rises as high in the air as she can reach — "and I wanted to bring it down to here" — she pokes herself on the Ritz-Carlton crest, presumably indicating *heart*. "I wish you'd been there so I could have an objective reading. Okay, here's a perfect example of something that should have been well received: Glenn was the only person I knew who ate an apple from the top down, like there was no core, like it was a cupcake."

"Interesting," says Henry.

"*And* observant *and* affectionate *and* in no way a value judgment!"

"Was that all?"

"No. The next part was for anyone who'd ever been here for a dinner party: He thought he could cook — he couldn't — but he'd put on a chef's apron and get out the knife sharpener, big production, swish, slash, back and forth, steel on steel. But he had no palate! He thought salt should be added at the table, so everything he served was bland. It was a family joke! It wasn't a criticism! And in the same vein, whatever needed slicing or dicing or chopping he'd do it right on the Corian without a cutting board. He'd peel an onion and then chop the hell out of it like the host of an infomercial." She turns around and points. "See, I finally installed butcher block and said, 'Here, go to town.' I thought that painted a picture of his passion and joie de vivre."

"Okay. Not elegiac. But so far nothing horrible."

"I guess I started to ramble. My delivery may have been a little too stream-of-consciousness. And, I don't know . . ."

"Too much speaking ill of the dead?"

"I wasn't," she wails. "I knew things that no one else knew about him. But here's what no one else got: Glenn would *not* have liked being described as a saint." She takes a swig of wine and grimaces. "Ugh. Did I tell you that the sons carted away Glenn's wine cellar? Anyway, he would have been the only one in the pews with a smile on his face. But you know how it is when you're flopping and the hole you're digging just gets deeper and deeper? *Very* hard to change course."

Henry tests his new license to call Denise on her self-delusion. "You must have said something more offensive than how he ate his way through an apple."

"If I did —" she begins brusquely, but then her expression softens. "If I did . . . okay, maybe I did. But isn't that some stage of grief? Anger? Festering resentments? Loss of judgment?"

"Go on," says Henry.

"I might have made a little fun of his thing for cars, that he couldn't just go through a car wash. It had to be brushless. He had to get them detailed. Which I know isn't funny, but it wasn't meant to be. It was a segue to something touching. And that was that he helped a guy who worked on his car by putting him in touch with a friend who was an immigration lawyer."

"And took care of the bill?"

"What bill?"

"The worker's? His lawyer's bill?"

Denise says, "No. Sorry. It was just meant to show that Glenn could appreciate someone else's legal problems, someone that would be beneath any other customer's radar screen. But he wasn't Santa Claus. The message was: He understood Spanish and he wasn't afraid to give an undocumented worker a friend's business card. And Henry — I was his wife. The spotlight was on me. What was I supposed to say? 'Twenty-four years ago we fell in love and cheated on our spouses and broke up two families'? 'He sometimes wore the same pair of socks two days running'? 'He didn't have erectile dysfunction'? I didn't want this to be about me."

Henry is irritated and still hungry, thinking about the half carton of pad thai in his refrigerator at home. Besides, what support can one offer to a widow who ruined her husband's funeral? Of course, there is for Henry a footnote to all things Krouch, if only he can broach it as the disinterested party he is pretending to be. "Is your eulogy the reason Thalia isn't speaking to you?" he ventures.

Denise raises her wineglass and through it he detects a sardonic glint. "Ask her yourself," she says.

May I Help You?

THIRTY YEARS of negotiating and lawyering have perfected Henry's poker face. He tests Denise's challenge with, "Ask her as what? A total stranger? After all these years? She'd be terrified."

"I thought maybe . . ." she begins, then shakes her head.

Henry walks his plate and wineglass to the sink. When he turns on the water, Denise says, "Leave it. Maria comes tomorrow morning. Sit."

He returns to the table but stands behind his chair. "Did you think I went looking for your daughter?" he asks.

"It wouldn't be out of character! You crossed this one big divide — us — so I wouldn't be shocked if you took a leap with Thalia. Part of me would love to see the three of us sitting around a table some night."

"Because . . . ?

"Because I think you're a peacemaker! Look what you've done

for us, two old foes. You're a lawyer. A diplomat. You'd never stand up at a funeral and turn everyone against you. And let me say this: I think Thalia would adore you." She leans in closer. "Just don't tell her who sent you."

This could be the graceful juncture for Henry to announce, "Truthfully, we have been reunited. I was waiting for the right time to tell you." But he doesn't. He's only human, he reminds himself. Cuckolded husbands have money in the bank, at least in the honesty account. This was between him, Thalia, and—less and less—Sheri Abrams, PhD. Even the most amicably divorced, scrupulous gay men can hold a surprising quantity of marital bitterness in their hearts. He does ask, "In terms of alienating a roomful of people, do you think that's what caused the rift with Thalia?"

"Not *caused* it. I think she'd say it was the straw that broke the camel's back."

He is tempted to spin the stranger angle further, to ask, "Is that how she talks? In aphorisms?" But he doesn't for fear his poker face will slip out of gear. He checks his watch rather ostentatiously. "Look what time it is already. I'm going to grab a cab and maybe catch a movie."

"Which movie?"

He names one, mayhem-filled, meant for teenage boys and meant to deter her.

"Alone?"

"No shame in that," he says. "And always easier to find a seat."

"If you wanted company, I could get dressed in five minutes and see something playing next door."

He doesn't want her company. He says with his newfound freedom to be less than tactful, "Actually, I lied. I wanted to make a graceful exit. No movie. I'm going home to catch up on some work."

"What work? I thought you were retired."

88

He answers solemnly: "I've taken on some pro-bono work that's pretty close to my heart."

Denise pats his wrist. Her eyes convey *heartbreaking gay cause*.

When Henry ducks out his front door, bathrobed and barefoot, to retrieve his *Times* the next morning, he hears a high-heeled clacking from below. He leans over the railing to see a leather-jacketed blond peering in the barred windows of his downstairs maisonette.

"May I help you?" he calls down.

She doesn't startle or even turn around. "I need a key," she answers.

"And you are who?"

The woman frowns, reaches into a very large, red, reptilian-skinned pocketbook, and brings forth a BlackBerry. After thumbing a few buttons she asks, "Are you John Henry Archer?"

"I am."

"And this is where Thayleeah — did I say that right? — Archer is going to live? And you're her lawyer or next of kin, or something like that?"

Dear God. He has tempted the fates with his instant embrace of fatherhood and look what he has wrought. "Is Thalia okay?" he asks, both hands gripping the cold railing.

The woman smiles. "I haven't met her yet, but I've heard she's fab-u-lous."

"Jesus," he says. "You scared me. I thought you were here to break some horrible news."

"Of course not! I'm here on business."

"Which one might deduce is breaking and entering."

The woman strides to the bottom of Henry's front steps. "I love you already! I love your spirit." She fishes out a hot pink business card. "This should explain things," she says.

Henry stays put. She looks up, disappointed, a commuter at rush hour encountering a dead escalator. She takes the stairs, card in the lead. *Anne-Marie Albano, media coaching, strategic planning, and crisis communications,* Henry reads. He hands it back. "And you go door to door?"

She frowns, consults a fax in her purse. "You *are* John Henry Archer, the lawyer?"

"I am."

"Then it's my understanding we have an appointment."

For the second day in a row, the dormant lawyerly pulse throbs in his temple. "First, Ms. Albano, if we have an appointment, I don't know about it. Second, I'm not one of those people who genuflect at the words *media coach.*"

Ms. Albano allows the kind of condescending smile one bestows on a belligerent idiot whose future cooperation is essential to a mission. "Let's start over," she says. She offers her right hand, shoulders straighter and head erect. "Anne-Marie Albano, consultant to Estime International. I do a lot of work with them. I was misinformed, and I apologize. Someone was supposed to set up an appointment. Is there any way you could spare some time now?"

"I can't," he says. "I have appointments all day. And you may have noticed that I'm wearing what my mother used to refer to as lounging clothes."

"One question, five seconds: Is there a back door? Or a door between your apartment and the one below?"

"Why?"

"Access!"

"Access for whom? Because this" — he elbows his front door — "is a private residence. Mine. With a security system. No one will be accessing these two residences except Miss Archer and me."

"I understand. Again, I'm very sorry."

"Apology accepted. Why don't you call and set up an appointment with me directly."

She nods once, briskly. "Is there a working landline downstairs?"

"No —"

"Will someone be home today between one and five?"

"Do you mean me?"

"Anyone. If not, I'll need a key."

He remembers anew the root cause of his contempt: Hollywood entitlement. When movie crews block off New York streets and impose crowd control on unsuspecting pedestrians, one is supposed to comply. He says, "I am not interested in being coached or packaged. I'm Thalia's legal adviser —"

"And her landlord! Look — there could be a dozen paps on your doorstep, if everything goes according to plan, by Monday morning. You might have to march right up to the cannon's mouth any minute."

"Paps?" he repeats.

"Paparazzi!" She leans over the railing to gaze down at the maisonette's entry. "I'm not the stylist," she says, "so I'm speaking off the cuff. But I think that this street and this house are going to be perfect. And with all the coffee shops this way and that, it's ideal for their waiting around."

Henry says, hand on the doorknob, "I have work to do. Good luck with the crisis management. My neighbors will appreciate your keeping the paps to a minimum."

She calls after him, "But paps are the whole point!"

He's forgotten his newspaper. One step back outside and he adds, "And these stone griffins? They're sculpture, not benches. I hope the press will respect my property."

Once inside, he spies on her from behind the library drapes. She is thumbing her BlackBerry. Because her expression is one of bewilderment rather than anger, Henry considers calling the 917 number on her card. But he doesn't. The other side has to understand that he is no fan of this arrangement and no pushover. Sunny and cooperative Thalia can be the good cop, but it's very much in her best interest for him to play the bad.

He resolves to be more compulsive about retrieving messages when he finds that Thalia tried to reach him the night before. "Hope it was okay to give Estime the address," her message says, restaurant noise in the background. "They want to check out West Seventy-fifth versus my block on Mott so they can decide which is better for my i-*mahj*—rags to riches or silver spoon in my mouth. You can call my cell. I'm with Leif, in public, in Chelsea. A dress rehearsal. He's in the bathroom. Again."

He calls her immediately but gets her voice mail. "They sent someone," he says. "I wasn't very cooperative. It's a little after nine. Are you working today?"

The second unclaimed message is from someone named Todd, who is merrily narrating, "The dreaded Denise gave me your number, but I'm calling anyway." The voice changes as if it's going off the record. "Were you two really married? I find that fascinating. She says you're a catch. Oh, sorry—that was crass. I didn't mean *catch*—I have better values than that. I meant *prince*. And if Denise says so, well, we all know what a foolproof judge of character *she* is. Oh, sorry. I forgot for a second that she's in mourning. If only one could edit one's messages." He ends with, "Yours truly, Todd Weinreb, and if I haven't offended you, here's my phone number . . ."

Henry waits until five to return the call. Todd is home. He, too, lives on the Upper West Side, does indeed like sushi, is free for dinner, and does have—despite wisecracks to the contrary—a soft spot for the appalling Denise.

13

Here It Is

TODD WILL SAY, "I wasn't even in sight of the restaurant, yet I looked up and there's this guy checking his watch — gray-haired, lawyerly, obviously nervous, obviously love-starved despite devastating good looks — so I say to the woman with the twin stroller who's standing between us, 'Excuse me. May I trade places with you? I think that handsome gentleman to your right is my blind date.'"

In fact, all that is exchanged on the corner of 86th and Broadway is a "Henry?" which evokes a "Todd?" followed by a handshake and a shared laugh over sound hunches.

"Delighted to meet you," says Henry.

The light changes. Todd will testify, in his future Technicolor version, that the mom with the stroller calls over her shoulder, "Have fun, you two."

They don't even make it to the sushi restaurant, but duck into a bar that is near-empty, its small round tables and little lamps suggesting a swing-era nightclub. They both order martinis, the house specialty: one cantaloupe and one peach.

What does Todd look like? Later Henry will describe him this way to Sheri Abrams, PhD: You know the short, redheaded boy in high school whose mother put creases in all his clothes? Clean-cut and very cute? Probably on the gymnastics team? Add thirty years and a few inches to the waist. *Et voilà.*

Denise is, of course, the men's first topic of conversation. Henry asks how they met, and Todd says, "I crashed a party she threw. No, I take that back. I went along to help the caterer, a friend; okay, maybe a boyfriend — that lasted a minute. But I was useless, all thumbs — ever try to pipe deviled egg filling out of a pastry bag? — so I took off my apron and joined the party. Eventually Denise noticed me and asked, 'Have we met?' I said, 'I came with the caterer, but he threw me out of the kitchen so I decided to console myself with a glass of your excellent champagne.' She didn't mind. In fact, she was very gracious. She introduced me to the guests of honor — her stepsons — as her new friend Todd and didn't miss a beat."

"I heard about that party," says Henry. "The boys had just been made partners."

"Tweedledee and Tweedledum. Ever have the pleasure?"

"Never."

"Not that I talked to either one of them, but my impression was: merchant princes who think they're Donald Trump Junior and Donald Trump Junior the Second. Ever meet the husband?"

"I did once. Socially." Henry raises his eyebrows above the rim of his glass. "Before I knew he was sleeping with my wife."

"Ouch. Sorry. But I have to say I didn't see what the attraction was, unless he cut a more dashing figure in his adulterous youth.

Quite the gasbag, too. He gave an endless self-congratulatory toast to his new partners that was all about the boom in the box business. I sneaked out before he finished."

Henry confides, "You know, I'm sure, that he left everything to those boys."

"I most certainly did *not* know!"

"There was a pre-nup. Which Denise signed, then promptly suppressed. As you can imagine, she was back in touch with me with a vengeance."

"Not for money!"

"For advice. And — please note the irony of this — a shoulder to cry on."

"What about the daughter?"

"What *about* the daughter?" Henry asks carefully.

"Diana? Athena? Something mythological, right?"

Henry says only, "It's Thalia, who was one of the Muses. So, yes, mythological."

Todd leans closer, squints diagnostically. "And how should I characterize that expression on your face?"

Don't be tempted, Henry thinks. *Don't start waxing euphoric and paternal.*

"You can trust me," says Todd. "I mean that." His grin is gone, replaced with a gaze so solemn that the next thing Henry says is, "Thalia and I are reunited. You probably don't know that I adopted her when I married Denise, then lost her in the divorce."

"I didn't even know about *you*, let alone which child came from which husband and who was lost in the process."

"I was husband number two. Denise's first husband died when Thalia was a baby."

"Which makes her how old now . . . ?"

"Twenty-nine." Henry smiles. "Which is all I can say unless I

95

have your promise that what I tell you won't be reported to her mother."

Todd raises his right hand. "I solemnly swear that whatever you say to me, right now, or next week, or a year, or ten years from now, will stay between the two of us." Another solemn gaze goes straight to Henry's bloodstream. Immediately, Todd says, "Sorry. Tell me about the daughter."

"Thalia. She's great. I didn't have to go looking for her because she works at the salon where I have my hair cut."

"Who recognized who?"

"I saw her picture at Denise's and recognized her."

"And what's the confidential part I must never tell Denise?"

Henry, though still holding on to news of the misguided Hollywood arrangement, feels free to say, "We've been reunited. So far, seamlessly. She seems to have come through the divorce, and through Denise, unscathed."

"And how did Thalia turn out?"

"Wonderfully."

"Actress, right?"

"Some TV. Making inroads."

"Beautiful?" Todd asks.

"More interesting than beautiful."

"Spoken like a true father," says Todd.

"Thank you," says Henry. "And just in case I forget to mention it, Denise doesn't know that Thalia and I have been reunited."

"Doesn't know and won't find out?"

Henry smiles. "I think I'm punishing her. She had an exclusive for twenty-five years, and it's my turn. It helps that mother and daughter aren't on speaking terms—"

"Since when?"

"I don't ask—"

"*I* could ask for you," Todd says happily.

Too much, too fast? Henry wonders. But no, he's wrong. Todd is joking. Todd is not overstepping the line between Thalia and the rest of the population that Henry is monitoring. Todd lowers his voice. "You weren't at Krouch's funeral, were you?"

"I wasn't. But I heard about it. Denise told me she rambled on about stupid stuff. Trivia. She couldn't get out of the hole she was digging."

"Did she tell you that the sons walked out? First one, then the other, wives trotting after them. Then one by one their stiff-necked friends."

"I didn't get the impression it was that bad."

"Bad? It was fabulous! Although I may not be the best judge of what's offensive at the funeral of someone I hardly knew."

"At what point did the sons walk out?"

"I believe," Todd says dryly, "that that particular point would have been . . . let me see . . . the vasectomy soliloquy."

"No," says Henry. "Not even Denise —"

"Yes! To the tune of: *He never told me until we were married that I couldn't have his child. Well, maybe I knew, but it didn't sink in until we were on our honeymoon. He had you two boys, the heir and the spare, and Thalia, you were his princess, DNA notwithstanding. My biggest regret* — read: grudge — *was that we didn't have a child together.* Subtext: to even the sides. And then we heard how the boys' away games ruled their weekends for at least a dozen years, further testimony to Glenn being father of the year, every damn year, all twenty-four of them. P.S. He had no interest whatsoever in reversing the vasectomy."

Henry, who has been shaking his head throughout, asks wearily, "Was she drunk?"

"If only!"

"Was this in a church?"

"A chapel in a funeral home. Do you think she'd have said anything different if it was Saint John the Divine?"

"No wonder she's been ostracized. No wonder she turned to me. I must be the only person she knows who missed this."

Todd says, "*Please* don't be saintly about this. Because if you're saying Denise isn't the most outrageous widow who ever gave a eulogy, I'm afraid I have to go home now."

Does Henry feel a pinch of loyalty or pity for the inappropriate Denise? No, he does not. He slides the check toward his side of the table and says, "I'll get this one."

Up the street, they secure the last two seats at the sushi bar, not ideal for conversation, but most agreeable for meaningful contact between adjacent shoulders.

"What do I *do*?" Todd volunteers before Henry asks. "That's always an awkward question."

Henry waits, hoping this isn't the moment when Todd's resumé reveals something unsavory and insurmountable, or a lifetime of dead-end auditions. "Awkward because . . . ?" Henry ventures.

"Because it usually stops the conversation dead."

"Out with it," Henry says. "Unless it's something I wouldn't want to testify to under oath."

"Here it is," says Todd. "The humble truth: I'm in retail. In table tops. At Gracious Home."

On one hand, Henry is relieved; on the other, a question relating to *Last year of education completed?* rears its snobbish head. "Which store?" he asks.

"Here," says Todd. "Broadway and Sixty-seventh. And, believe me, I know: It's not a career a mother brags about over a game of bridge."

"But you like it?"

"I do," says Todd. "I like my coworkers, and" — he smiles — "I get to make the Upper West Side's table tops a little more beautiful."

One of the two sushi chefs puts the finishing touch on an elaborate roll, looks up, and asks the men what they want.

"Are we hungry?" Todd asks Henry.

"Quite."

Todd points to a model vessel behind the chef. "I've always wanted to get the Samurai Sushi Boat. You game?"

The chef asks, "You like challenging?"

"Excuse me?" asks Henry.

"Challenging or beginner?"

Henry turns to Todd, who says, "Let's go for it."

"Challenging," says Henry. "And we'll get two more Kirins."

All tables are filled, and there is a line of patrons waiting to be seated. Anyone observing the two men would be surprised to learn that they'd only met this night. They are both whittling splinters off their chopsticks as they joke about the big boat that will — in both retellings — become the centerpiece anecdote of Our First Date.

14

Three Humble Rooms

THALIA MOVES INTO the maisonette with the help of two uninsured and unincorporated young men whom she found on Craigslist. From his lookout on the second floor, Henry hurries downstairs to meet the truck as its front wheels bump up onto his sidewalk. Thalia exits the truck's cab, looking a little more animated than a week of packing should induce and carrying a pint-sized Christmas cactus, which, she reports, has never bloomed.

For the next hour, Henry silently notes the transport of her sad little lot: a futon frame and its mattress, covered with a fitted sheet he recognizes as Marimekko, circa 1970. An unmoored door and the concrete blocks that hold it up; lumber and more concrete blocks that become a bookcase; a matching rattan love seat and chair with jungle-print cushions; a dozen boxes of college texts and paperback novels; two plastic hourglass-shaped stools in lime green that turn out to be night tables; a computer, a printer, and a naked headless mannequin.

This charmless junk depresses him. "Did your mother and Glenn ever visit your apartment?" he asks as he watches her unwrap what she is euphemistically calling china.

"Probably. Maybe not Mott Street, but the one before that. Why?"

Instead of answering truthfully — *How could they let you live an unfurnished life?* — he asks what he can do to help. Does she need tea towels or sponges? His cleaning woman put the shelf paper in. Does she like it? Gracious Home had other patterns, but he thought polka dots.

"I do. I love them." She is lining up mugs, all four of them. When he compliments a pale blue cup and saucer, Thalia says, "This was from my Angel Sister my freshman year in college. Do guys have Angel Sisters? Like secret Santas? She was a senior on my floor and one of those beautiful creatures that everyone worshiped from afar." She holds the cup up into the light of the hundred-watt ceiling bulb. "You can almost see through it. It wasn't new when she gave it to me. It was hers, and she must've wrapped this up in a hurry for the big Angel Sister reveal. But I liked that better, that demigoddess Jodi Kleinholz would keep a teacup and saucer in her dorm room — and then it was in mine."

The way she is talking about and gazing at her cup and saucer is breaking Henry's heart — this love of beautiful things narrowed to two pieces of bone china. He squelches his impulse to say, "Please come look through my cabinets. Please take what you want."

Thalia must see Henry's pained expression because she says, "They're giving me a decent housing allowance and I'm sure it would cover . . . stuff. The stylist threatened to take me shopping, but I don't want this place to look decorated. It's supposed to be the three humble rooms of a struggling actress."

"But if you like pretty things, and if you're not inviting the paparazzi inside . . . ?"

"I'm not. But they have their telephoto lenses and probably their night vision goggles. I've been warned never to walk around naked or even in my underwear in case . . . " She tilts her head toward the still-quiet street outside.

Just as Thalia pronounces *underwear* the movers enter the kitchen with a clipboard and a pen. "We need your signature," says the driver and apparent boss. Since they've arrived, Henry has noticed a surfeit of good manners: This boss has been instructing his sidekick to wipe his feet each time they cross the threshold and has run his palm along the walls like a man who understands wainscoting. Henry has also noticed that this team leader is quite good-looking — dark-haired, olive-skinned, hazel-eyed, untattooed, Strand Books T-shirt, hair well cut.

"It's just to say that your possessions arrived safely and nothing broke in transit," the man explains.

"I haven't unpacked everything yet," says Thalia, not altogether inhospitably, "so I can't really say that with any authority, can I?"

"Anything particular you're worried about?"

"Dishes and stuff," says Thalia, and gestures to the one unpacked box on the counter.

The man smiles. "How about if we unwrap the remaining valuables before I leave, and we'll see what damage we've wrought." He extends his hand — as if they haven't been in each other's company for three hours — and says, "I'm Philip."

"Then why is your friend calling you that other thing?" Thalia asks.

"Nickname," says Philip. "Dino. Left over from college."

"Meaning what?"

"Meaning nothing except it's short for Dinosaur."

"And why is that?" she asks.

Philip, uninvited, is unwrapping mismatched glasses that appear to have started their lives as jelly jars. "I got a late start. Worked construction. I was a couple of years older than the morons in my house."

His buddy is standing in the doorway, looking resigned in a way that makes Henry think that Philip's conversational overtures are not atypical.

Henry says to Thalia, as lightly as he can manage, "Don't forget this young man and his partner are paid by the hour."

Philip says, "That's true. But the clock stopped ten minutes ago. That's Sid. And this gentleman?"

"Henry," Thalia provides. "Landlord and guardian."

Henry nods, then turns his attention to the document on the clipboard.

"He's a lawyer," Thalia warns.

"Uh-oh," says Philip. Then, "Just kidding. It's boilerplate, off the Web. All it says is, 'We didn't break anything or destroy your property.'"

Henry reads, purses his lips, nods, and passes her the clipboard. She scrawls a signature, which Philip studies for a few seconds. "*Thalia*," he says. "That's an unusual name. Is it French?"

"Greek," says Thalia. "My mother's of Greek descent."

"I had one Greek grandparent," says Philip. My mother's mother. I grew up celebrating two Easters."

"Really? Me, too." They unwrap and inspect in silence, side by side at the counter, until Thalia asks, "So do most of your friends call you Philip or Dino?"

"Both. Either. Just when I think I've heard the end of it and I've been reincarnated as an adult, someone pops up from my past and I'm Dino again."

"Hey, *Philip*," says Sid. "We were due in Park Slope a half-hour ago."

Philip takes the clipboard, scribbles some numbers, tears off the top yellow sheet, and gives it to Thalia.

"Don't I need to write you a check?" she asks.

Henry doesn't hear the answer because vendor and customer have left the kitchen and are conferring by the front door. Sid does not follow. Henry asks him after a minute has passed, "Is there more business to conduct?"

"Nope."

"She's kind of spoken for," Henry says. "Maybe you could tell him that."

"Maybe she's tellin' him right now."

Henry says, "I'm sure you don't have to stay in the kitchen."

Sid slides his baseball cap back on his head and forward again. "Are you her father?"

"Stepfather," then thinks to add, "and I live upstairs."

"He's an okay guy. And smart. This is his day job."

"What does he do at night?"

"For work? He's a deejay."

"Oh," says Henry.

"The real thing."

Henry doesn't know what defines *real thing* in that field. His only frame of reference is the freelancing radio disc jockeys who were hired to spin forty-fives at dances in his youth.

"He's got a following," says Sid. "Mostly East Village. But it's growin'."

"Do you do that, too?"

Sid laughs. "No. I do *this*. Days, and small jobs at night that I can do by myself. I've got a kid."

"You really should get insurance," says Henry. "You could charge more and do bigger jobs."

He shakes his head. "Not my call."

From the outer room comes a cheerful, "All set, dude!"

Sid tips his Mets cap and heads for the front door.

All set with what? Henry doesn't like this development at all.

"It isn't me being prudish," he explains, raising his voice to be heard above the vacuum cleaner. Thalia is cleaning up the detritus of packing materials, and Henry is trailing behind. "It's just that I know the signs —"

"Of what?"

"Of potential complications."

"If . . . ?" she shouts.

"*If?* You can't mean that. Any minute now you're going to be publicly in love — nay, engaged — to Leif Dumont. You can't have a little thing on the side."

Thalia shuts off the vacuum and says, "Wow, cool," when the cord retracts with a loud swoosh.

"Maybe I'm wrong," Henry continues. "Maybe I was witness to nothing more than a gracious service person making pleasant conversation with his patron. Maybe you weren't aiding and abetting."

She points to the vacuum and asks, "Where does this go?"

"It's mine," he says. "I'll bring it back upstairs with me. You can borrow it anytime. Actually, Lidia will be giving this place the once-over Mondays and Thursdays."

"Thank you," says Thalia. "I'll reimburse you from my generous weekly housekeeping allowance."

"No, you won't."

Thalia links an arm through his and asks if his cappuccino machine is up and running.

"Absolutely! And I have paper cups and lids. I'll be right back."

"Don't be silly. I'll come with you."

On their way up the back stairway, Henry tells her that this passageway connected the servants' quarters to the main house. *Upstairs, Downstairs,* Upper West Side version. He turns at the top step and says, "I can't quite believe you're here. It's just hitting me that you actually live downstairs."

"It's so great," says Thalia. "It's like *Nancy Drew and the Hidden Staircase.*"

"Note the unlocked door," he says, "which will stay this way."

"I'll call first," she says.

After he's made their coffee, after he's led her to the library and he's lit the precise arrangement of logs and kindling in the fireplace, Henry says, "Again, it's not me being prudish or paternal. It's me being contractual with respect to your new friend."

"Leif?"

"Not Leif. The mover."

"Nope," she says. "Nothing to worry about."

"There wasn't an exchange of phone numbers?"

"Only because I checked the box that said he could use me as a reference."

"Is that wise?"

She sets her mug down on a *Raisin in the Sun* coaster after admiring it anew. "Okay. I'm not doing a good acting job here. Which might be a politer way of saying, I'm fibbing. But let me tell you why all of this is beside the point: Men don't follow up. You could tattoo your number on the palm of their hand and they still wouldn't call. They don't e-mail unless they've left a

DVD at your place and want you to mail it back to Netflix. Okay, they send a text message, but it's *What was the name of that bar you told me about in Williamsburg?* If you run into one of them on the street he'll say, 'Oh, hi . . . I was going to IM you. Maybe we can get together later this lifetime.'"

"This is very hard to believe," Henry says.

"Is it different for you? With your gang?"

Henry smiles. "We don't text message."

"Seriously, I did *not* mean to flirt back. But you might have noticed how attractive and charming he was for a straight guy."

"I might have," says Henry. "But here's the problem: Let's say he does call. You're not going to be able to say, 'I've signed up to be someone's girlfriend, but it's only a publicity stunt, so if you could keep that to yourself and call me in six months . . .'"

Henry recognizes something in her face that her acting ability isn't masking — a war between her wanting to confess and wanting to protect him from the confession.

"You already told him," he guesses.

"Kind of . . ."

"A stranger you'd known for five minutes?"

"It *looked* like five minutes. But there were many hours of meaningful social intercourse at the other end. Then the ride over here took a half-hour. You learn a lot about someone from the way he reacts in heavy traffic. And would I be moving into a relative stranger's in-law apartment if I didn't have faith in my excellent judgment?"

"I'm listening," says Henry. "Nervously."

"Okay. This was very contractual: I made him swear on his mother's life that he'd never repeat what I'd told him."

"Which was what, exactly?"

"Mainly: That I had an acting gig coming up. That it involved a guy. It wasn't what it seemed. And he couldn't tell a soul."

"But you just finished telling me that men are utterly undependable—"

"Which is why I had him sign a confidentiality agreement! And you're forgetting he walked into the kitchen as we were discussing how I shouldn't walk around naked in case the paparazzi were outside. Where's he supposed to put that piece of information?"

Henry blinks, and his eyes stay shut for several long seconds. "How, may I ask, did you consummate a confidentiality agreement?"

"On his copy of the contract, the blue page. One sentence in legalese about never uttering a word. He signed it, dated it, and we shook hands."

Henry knows he cannot scold, cannot reveal his disappointment in Thalia, his distrust in the human race in general, or truck-driving deejays in particular. He gets up, adds a log to the fire, and jabs it with a poker.

"Henry. Okay. I know: I leap into things. Take this whole Leif deal. Sally Eames-Harlan calls me one day, and twenty-four hours later I'm eating bucatini across from my intended. And how about this? You and me. The father-daughter thing. I'm taking your name and your advice and wearing your dead mother's clothes on the strength of what? Trust and my excellent instincts." She pats the couch. "Come. Drink your coffee. I know you'll like this part: I didn't give him my number. I gave him *this* one. You can play Screener Dad. Suspicious Sitcom Dad. Won't that be fun? I thought it would be just the safety net you'd wholeheartedly approve of."

Henry curls his lip. "Monumental fun," he says.

15

So Soon?

H E PLANS TO CONFESS all recent developments — paternal, romantic, tabloidesque — to Sheri Abrams, but when and in what order?

He is relieved of that decision when he and Thalia are shopping at Zabar's, country of coffee-bean origin under discussion, and he comes face to face with his therapist. Henry says, "Um. This is Thalia. Thalia, Sheri Abrams."

Sheri says stiffly, neutrally, "How do you do."

"Are we neighbors?" Thalia asks.

"Of a sort," Sheri answers.

"My therapist," says Henry.

"Does she know about . . . the arrangement?" Thalia asks Henry.

Henry shakes his head, a very small arc to signal, *No, and let's leave it at that.*

Thalia says, "Oops. Forget I ever said a word. I just assumed . . . your shrink . . ." She takes a giant, balletic step backward. "End of topic. Nice to meet you," and pantomimes a key locking her lips. Then, in a stage whisper: "It's just that I think he'd like to bounce the whole thing off someone besides me."

Sheri doesn't answer, but Henry reads in her stare both curiosity and protectiveness: Will this putative daughter ultimately disappoint?

He doesn't tell Thalia to knock it off, to stop wearing her conversational heart on her sleeve and accosting strangers on the street, because more often than not he adores Thalia's Celeste-like lack of self-consciousness. She is, he thinks, what he would have liked to have been at twenty-nine. At any age.

What big thing — so big that his stepdaughter brings it up at Zabar's — should Henry discuss on the couch? Sheri needs to know as soon as he crosses the threshold holding one latte less than usual the following week.

Which topic from his list of secrets shall he illuminate? Definitely not the legally protected Leif business, which Sheri Abrams would berate as shallow and exemplifying what's wrong with Hollywood, with the culture, with this country and century. Perhaps the fact that he's met a nice man and they've had two follow-up phone calls, one drop-in shopping trip to Gracious Home, and a date for the upcoming Thursday night. The answer that floats to the top is the least personal one: *Thalia has moved into my maisonette.* He pronounces that sentence, and the doctor sits up straighter. "So soon?"

"Only the time it took her to find a replacement roommate for her place in Chinatown."

"Minutes, by my count."

"They all do Craigslist now."

"Is your place furnished?" she asks.

Henry laughs. Sheri asks what about her question was humorous.

"It wasn't what I was expecting: more practical than psychiatric. Something my mother would have asked if I told her I was renting out the first floor."

Sheri, he knows, loves discussing his mother and his childhood as the unplanned and athletically disappointing fourth son. There were a few weeks during Williebelle's residency at West 75th Street when Sheri lobbied for family therapy. The one session he agreed to wasn't fruitful. Williebelle had never been in therapy, nor, apparently, had she absorbed much from cultural conditioning or TV as to what happens inside the four walls of a therapist's office. In advance Henry told his mother that the doctor would be asking them both questions about her adjustment to a new city and most likely about their relationship, all toward the goal of understanding Henry better. Williebelle swept in, complimented the exotic decor and what she called the "big old darlin' puppy." Once seated, she gave unsolicited testimonials to the city of New York: How she wished she'd moved here in her youth, or even in middle age. Or even five years ago when she was a zippy eighty-year-old. Bergdorf Goodman was her favorite store. And truth be told: She had discovered a secondhand designer consignment shop across the big park where some goods had their original tags still attached! Henry took her to plays but wouldn't tell her what the tickets cost.

"It sounds like a seamless adjustment," the doctor said.

Williebelle frowned. Well, there was one disappointment. All her life she'd heard about the Automat, and that was a letdown when she found out it had closed. But then again, Henry said that it had been all about the novelty and not the food.

Sheri had tried to bring the conversation back to Henry with,

"You certainly appear to be happy living with that son of yours. I sense that he occupies a special place in your heart."

"I don't play favorites," Williebelle had said primly. "My other sons are busy with wives and children, so it's easier for a mother to be close to a bachelor son, especially one with extra bedrooms."

Henry said, "Mom, Sheri is a psychologist. You don't have to use words like *bachelor* if you mean *gay*."

"He wasn't always gay," Williebelle had explained. "He was married for several years to a young widow."

"She knows the whole story and all the players in excruciating detail. That's when I started these visits, around the time of the divorce."

"To find his way," Sheri had amplified. "To make peace with his sexual orientation. To get support."

Mrs. Archer had said with a sigh, "Henry was an accident. I didn't mean to have a fourth child." She looked over at him fondly, adding a smile as if that truth had lost any power to smart. "I *might* have minded his becoming a homosexual if I didn't have other sons who *weren't* homosexuals. But I've got plenty of daughters-in-law and more than enough grandchildren. I'm closer to Henry, not just because I'm under his roof but because of his interests." She had turned to her son and said, "Would you mind if I said you were the daughter I never had?"

Henry did mind, but he didn't want to introduce grist for a maternal return visit. He had said, "For someone her age and background, I accept that as her way of saying we both read the arts section before the sports page."

"How does that make you feel — your mother saying you were an accident?" Sheri asked.

"Happy I made it," Henry had said. "Glad to be here."

"His brothers used to taunt him about that," Williebelle offered. "They'd say awful things like, 'You were an accident.'"

Henry smiled. His mother, in an adjacent chair, patted his nearest hand. "But I loved him to pieces the minute he came out. Did he ever tell you he was the first baby of the new year in the whole state? We were on the front page of the newspaper, and to this day people still remember it was one of my babies who won that award."

"He never told me that."

"He might not remember because he was only one day old when the picture came out. I was a little woozy myself. I didn't even mean to name him Henry, but it was my husband's father's name and we only had girls' names picked. Sometimes I wonder if that had something to do with the way he turned out, swimming around in there being called Claudia June. There was a gap — how many years, Henry? Five, six? — between him and his brothers. So he was my little companion. I knew he wasn't like other boys — well, not like *my* other boys. A mother knows these things."

"How is *your* mother?" Henry asked Sheri. "I'm sure mine would be interested in hearing how you two get along and about your siblings."

"Does she live nearby?" asked Williebelle.

And so forth, until the doctor's face registered what Henry had known all along, that this visit was unnecessary and pleasantly going nowhere.

"What's your new tenant doing for work?" Sheri Abrams asks him.

"Same."

"Checking coats at your salon?"

He says, "Actually, she's given two weeks' notice. After which, she's going to concentrate on her acting."

Is that a lie? He thinks not. He also thinks that life may be working out in such a way that weekly sessions with a therapist are beginning to intrude on his increasingly busy days. Would he be jinxing things to quit today? If he weren't spending an hour a week hooked up to the lie detector that is Sheri Abrams, he wouldn't have to feel quite so much a dissembler, a withholder, and a covert social operator. He says, "I'm thinking of taking a hiatus."

"Of what kind?"

"Therapeutic," he says. "You and I. I feel as if I'm torn in several different directions, all good. I'm busier than I've been in years."

He knows she won't cajole. He adds, "And this time, looking ahead, I might throw caution to the wind and say, 'Let's meet for dinner down the road.'"

Sheri says, "One thing I have to say: a twenty-nine-year-old whom you've only known for a few weeks, who is finding herself, who just lost her father — you see where this is going? — who has just found a most congenial and generous stand-in, may not be best-friend material. I'm guessing you two are in the honeymoon phase." She forces a tight smile. "But I'm sure you see all of this clearly."

Henry says, "I'm oddly happy. I think most therapists would be tickled to write those words on a client's chart."

"I am," she says. She taps her pen against her notes. "I'm also underlining the word *oddly*."

"I met someone," he says, a farewell gift painless to bequeath because the wall clock is telling him that they have to stop.

He returns home to find Denise sitting on his front stoop, wearing blue jeans studded with grommets and holding a cake box on her lap. "Anything you want to tell me?" she asks with a match-maker's triumphant smile.

"No. What's in the box?"

"Cupcakes. Two for you and one for me." She opens the box to display rather ordinary cupcakes, two yellow and one chocolate, not the high-fashion confections that are causing lines to form out the door of the specialist on Amsterdam Avenue.

He sits down next to her. "And let me guess: You were in the neighborhood, so it was easier to stop by than to pick up the phone?"

"Ha! Leaving Henry Archer a message is an invitation to be ignored."

He is about to say, "Don't take it personally. I don't like talking on the phone," when he remembers that Denise has a very high threshold for divorce- and infidelity-related punishment. "I'm not this way with everyone," he says. "I'm sure it has to do with old resentments."

"Of me?"

"Of you, of your late husband, of his lawyer the homophobe."

"I understand now," she says. "I really do. And over the years I was tempted to call you and ask if you wanted to get a drink or come to Thalia's birthday party or a graduation or a recital."

"Tempted? Until you remembered that I was an unfit parent?"

"But you didn't fight us! You folded! You just let Glenn steam-roll over you and snatch Thalia away. I thought that you'd send a birthday present. A birthday card, for chrissakes. I thought you'd appeal. But it was as if you'd died. You moved. You changed your phone number. My Christmas card came back. My valentines came back—"

"Valentines? Is this to be believed?"

"From Thalia. Well, I bought them and she signed them. When she was six, seven, eight; when kids send valentines to the whole class. And when they came back 'Address Unknown,' that proved to Glenn that he was right: You were not interested in Thalia or fatherhood."

Henry jumps to his feet. "I resent that! You had no idea what she meant to me. None. You were too busy seducing other women's husbands to notice how I felt about that child! And, Jesus, you had my right address, unless quote-unquote *Nanny* didn't share it with you."

Denise is clearly stunned to hear insults hurled by the famously even-tempered Henry Archer. She pouts for a spell, eyes narrowed, fingernails clicking, before yelling back, "Maybe you'd like to form a club with Nanette, Glenn's ex. She'd be thrilled to hear from you. You two could picket my apartment building. You could call yourselves 'The Enemy of My Enemy Is My Friend Club.'"

In three long strides Henry is on the brick path that leads to the maisonette's front door. "Now it's my turn," he says. "And you know why? Because it's the will of the child. Not yours, not her stepfather's, not a judge's, or the state of New York's."

"What are you talking about?"

"This" — he gestures grandly — "is an apartment. It is the ground floor of my house. Where I live. I could rent it out, but I don't. I don't want to interview tenants and I don't want to be a landlord. I keep it for family and for friends in need."

Denise has risen to her feet and her expression has turned beatific. "Henry," she breathes. "I don't know. I'd have to see it. It looks small. And I'm so used to having a doorman."

"Not you! You wouldn't put your scullery maid in here. It's three dark rooms with linoleum on the kitchen floor. Jesus. It's too ridiculous to contemplate. Let alone the idea that you'd be sharing a house with me."

She joins him at the front door. "Then what are you babbling about? 'The will of the child' and 'friends in need.' Have you taken in one of those nieces or nephews? Or adopted someone?"

"I'm talking about Thalia. Thalia moved in here. Your estranged daughter and I are sharing a house. How does that strike you? As the arrangement of someone demonstrating inadequate and actionable noninterest in his child?"

He is not himself. He has lost his temper, yelled on the street in plain sight of his neighbors and dog walkers, and all but stamped his foot. And now he will have to explain to Thalia that, in a moment of pique and retribution, he has told her mother news that wasn't his to leak. He quickly adds, "Don't contact her. I'm not looking to be an arbitrator or a peacemaker. It slipped out."

"It didn't slip out! You were taking aim. Right here, between the eyes." She squeezes between two ornamental yews and peers into the front window.

"Jesus," says Henry. "Get away from there."

"Is she home?"

"She's at work."

"Do you have a key?"

"I certainly do not," he lies. "Nor would I let you in if I did."

Denise says unconvincingly, "I only meant that I'd scribble a note."

"Saying what?"

"Something friendly. 'I'm sorry.' Or 'Please call.' Or 'You're all I've got.' Along those lines."

Henry reaches over and pinches an inch of sleeve to guide her away from the window. "Here's what I'm asking of you: Please just consider this, parent to parent, as confidential information. As my way of saying only that your daughter is well and has a roof over her head and a parental eye watching out for her. Let the rest happen organically."

"What does that mean?"

"Let her contact you when she's ready."

Denise's glance goes up the townhouse façade to higher stories and back down to street level. "How long has this been going on?"

"Since I found her."

"Did you hire a detective?"

Henry says, "That is so . . . you. So overdramatized. No, I did *not* hire a detective. I just used common sense."

"I ask because she doesn't have a real phone. It isn't like the old days when you could call Information."

Henry still doesn't like to discuss his unearthing of Thalia at Salon Gerard. His discomfort, he is quite sure, stems from shame over never asking the charming coat-check girl her name or engaging her in conversation or possibly ever meeting her glance.

"Did she call you?" Denise persists. "Which wouldn't surprise me. The only father she's ever known is dead —"

"Only father she's ever known? Is that what you said? Do you have no filter? No censor? Do you not understand that I was her father, and I'd still be her father if it weren't for the rupture that you and your late, litigious husband inflicted?"

"Okay," says Denise. "I'll be your punching bag. I'm everyone's punching bag. My big mouth gets me in trouble every time I open it. So what are you saying? Leave the premises? Never darken my doorway and take your stupid cupcakes with you? Because really what I'm guilty of is bad judgment. You're right. No filter. Guilty as charged. But I don't think that in a world filled with terrorists and beheaders and child predators that my crimes are really so unforgivable."

Henry knows this. He knows that Denise's newly widowed heart is more or less in the right place. This is why he is keeping Thalia to himself — because Denise in her own annoying and logorrheic fashion is a decent enough, forgivable mother, especially in her remorseful and reduced circumstances.

She points to the box she left on the steps. "Don't you find it a little scary that I arrived here with three cupcakes? As if I knew on some extrasensory level that I was buying one for each of us? And now that I think of it, Thalia would go straight for the one with pink frosting."

He says, "I'd like some time alone with her. I'm getting to know her. Her moving in here was one big leap of faith for both of us. I'm not going to be her mother. I'm like a long-lost uncle who wishes her well and wants to help in any way he can. I think you owe me that much."

The rims of Denise's eyes are red and she is fishing in her pocket for a tissue. Henry knows he is supposed to feel sympathy and ask what's wrong. He lets her sniffle for another minute before asking, "Did I do this?"

"Yes, you did. And I'd like to point out: You were never like this."

"Like what?"

"Mean. And what's the right word? I want to say *selfish*, but maybe it's something closer to *what's good for Henry is what's good for the Krouches,* who — I'd like to point out — he hasn't seen in a quarter of a century, and now he's asking for custody."

Henry smiles. He repeats the word *custody.* He opens the box and peels the paper off the sole chocolate cupcake, without asking Denise if he's appropriating the one she wanted for herself.

16

The Human Condition

⟨◎⟩

A T THE UNGODLY hour of 11:45 P.M. Philip phones the number Thalia has supplied. His call wakes Henry, triggering a jolt of parental panic. "Archer here," he barks. There is music in the background and confusion in the caller's voice: *Wrong number? Trying to reach Thalia. Krouch?*

"It's Henry Archer, from the apartment above."

"Right, right. I remember. Is she there?"

He repeats, "I'm upstairs. You called my number."

"Sorry, you're breaking up. Let me move." Henry hears Philip fielding greetings from passersby as the music recedes, and then the sounds of traffic. "There. Better. You were saying?"

"I'm Thalia's upstairs . . . stepfather. She gave you my number in lieu of hers because of that matter requiring confidentiality."

Except for horns and sirens, there is silence at the other end.

"She has no phone downstairs," he tries. "Not a landline, anyway."

"Fine. I totally get it."

Now Henry has mishandled his job and whatever social nuance he was supposed to convey. "She only has one number, her mobile, and in another week it could be awkward," he tries.

Philip says, "Way too complicated, man. But thanks."

Henry dresses quickly in the shirt and trousers he'd worn earlier and makes his way downstairs, cell phone in his hand, down the passageway newly lit by a hundred-watt bulb, and listens at Thalia's kitchen door. When he hears David Letterman, then applause, then the band striking up, he activates what is now newly designated Speed Dial One.

"Henry?" Thalia answers just as he's about to give up. "Sorry. Couldn't find the phone."

"Sorry to intrude, but your moving man just called."

"Philip?"

"A few minutes ago. There was music in the background, so he must have been at work."

"Wait. I'm hearing you in stereo. Are you downstairs?"

Before he can answer, the door opens to reveal Thalia in an oversized bathrobe, faded periwinkle, so woolly and unglamorous that he laughs. Behind her the kitchen is more cheerful by electric light than what the northern alleyway exposure affords by day. A new potted plant, its leaves the shape of elephant ears, sits on the scarred circle of wood that is her kitchen table.

"Tea?" she asks.

He says no, couldn't impose; bad manners to drop in, and very bad precedent.

"Please shut up," she says cheerfully. "Earl Grey or tutti-frutti?"

"Earl Grey. If you're sure." He points to the plant. "Have I seen that before?"

She plucks the card from its plastic perch and hands it to him.

He reads aloud, "'Wishing you good luck and good times in your new home. In lieu of flowers, Leifs. Love, L.D.'"

"Get it?" Thalia asks. "Leifs? Leaves? Is that even a *pun*?"

"Paper trail," says Henry. "I think you can expect daily deliveries."

"Sad," she says.

As he watches her fill the kettle and set out mugs, he thinks: *Look at me in this domestic tableau, sitting on a bridge chair, chatting with a bathrobed, ponytailed daughter in a manner most fathers would take for granted.*

"Well?" she asks from the stove. "I'm listening."

"Paper trail. If reporters start snooping about when this whole thing started —"

"Not that. The moving man. Let's have it."

How to begin? "I have no doubt his call was in regard to seeing you again —"

"But?"

"He was somewhat disconcerted at reaching me instead of you."

"But you explained, right?"

"I alluded to the upcoming job —"

"As in 'Call back in six months'?"

"It was a very brief conversation, and I'd been snoozing —"

"How did you leave it? That I'd call him?"

She is holding up a mug and a teacup for his consideration. Henry points to the mug, which has ceramic feet and gesticulating arms. "If I were to be completely honest and lawyerly," he ventures, "I might ask at this juncture: Do you really want to get involved with someone new right now, especially someone who'd have to fly beneath the radar?"

"The bonus guy's *always* under the radar," Thalia says.

How much is polite to solicit and how much is not? Before he conjures the right line of inquiry, Thalia volunteers, "Okay, first:

Relationships in multiples are all now history, so don't get nervous. Although it's really adorable that you are."

"How multiple?" asks Henry.

"No records broken: At the same time I was seeing Giovanni — *sort* of seeing — I was also with someone else."

"Someone at the salon?"

"Henry! How many straight hairdressers does one salon have? No, someone else. Remember? Alex? My roommate?"

"The undergraduate?"

"Exactly."

"You once said that you put the kibosh on that."

"Kibosh," she repeats. "I love that word. Do you know what language it is?"

"Not changing the subject, are we?"

Thalia asks, "How do I explain this? I wasn't dating two guys at once because you can't call what we do dating. We go out — to bars, to movies, to clubs. You get popcorn or nachos or a new friend on Facebook, but you don't get dinner and you don't get a boyfriend." She leaves the kitchen and returns with a fat hardcover dictionary, already open to a page displaying thumbnail photos of Khomeini and Khrushchev. "'Kibosh,'" she reads. "'Origin unknown.'"

The kettle hisses, then whistles. She returns to the stove and pours water into two mugs, narrating, "Always, *always* pour water over the tea bag. I learned this at my nanny's knee, her being British, of course, and Earl Grey–obsessed. If you do it the other way around, it doesn't infuse properly. Sugar? Honey? Anything?"

"No, thank you. Just sit."

She brings the mugs to the table, goes back for napkins, and when she returns asks, "Weren't we talking about Philip?"

"Alex," he says.

"Right. Alex. He was sure I was resisting because I'm eight years older, so he was devoting a lot of time to making his case for the younger man. He's very sweet. But this move came at a good time."

"But he's, essentially, at peace with the way it ended?"

"He'll get over it. I told him we'd meet in Madison Square Park at the Shake Shack on July Fourth in ten years. If neither one of us is in a relationship, we'll go to a hotel."

Henry laughs. "I thought you were going to say something delicate and romantic like, 'If neither of us is in a relationship, we'll go to City Hall and tie the knot.'"

"He's twenty. I was thinking *consolation prize hookup*. Besides, it won't happen."

"Because . . . ?"

She dips her tea bag up and down a few times. "Well, I'll be thirty-nine in ten years. I'd like to think I'll be off the market by then." After a longer pause she asks, "So you think we really pissed Philip off?"

Henry says kindly, "Given the task ahead, I wouldn't pursue it."

Thalia says, "I'm not a kid. I've been at this for a long time. And it's not about his rather obvious outward charms. We talked a lot."

"You're putting a lot of stock in one morning's worth of loading and unloading."

"This is really all about the human condition: You're with one person and you're attracted to another. And sometimes you sense that it's not just some little tingle in your extremities but something bigger. Is a person — me, for example — supposed to ignore a possible big thing because I've accepted a six-month gig playing the phony fiancée? I think I can handle both."

"Okay. I'm not arguing with any of that. But I do have to ask:

You decided this was worth the potential trouble from a few hours of watching a man lug your stuff into a moving van?"

"And drive it uptown. And lug it into its new home. A rather hot man, you might have noticed."

"Okay. Will concede hot."

"I'm actually putting a lot of stock in — you'll excuse the expression — love at first sight; well, something at first sight. I'm sure you've experienced that."

Todd comes to mind, and their handshake on Broadway. He knows he'll get to that but for now says, "I know something about love at first sight. Have we discussed that: your mother's taking up with Glenn Krouch after one dinner party . . . what's that? Four courses? Two hours?"

"You and *I* have discussed it. My mother always prettied up how they met." She rubs a leaf of her new plant, sticks the tip of her index finger into its pot, and pronounces it root-bound and too wet. "Interesting that you still talk about it in that way," she says.

"Which way?"

"Like you'd still be married to her if Glenn Krouch hadn't shown up."

"It's the principle," says Henry. "Some things are unforgivable, a violation of a trust that you entered into in good faith, even if the marriage was a bad idea in the first place."

Thalia leans closer and stares diagnostically.

"What?"

"I'm seeing something," she says. "Something new. Something that doesn't jibe with *unforgivable.* You're looking a little — ¿cómo se dice? — happy."

"I might be a little happy. Don't want to jinx anything . . ."

"Out with it! It'll be fun. Look at us. Having tea at" — she glances around the clockless kitchen — "late into the night. It's

125

like we're living in a dorm, in the best sense, I mean. In fact, this bathrobe is from that era."

"Okay," says Henry. "I might be feeling optimistic, socially speaking."

"I knew it! Who is he?"

"A blind date, believe it or not."

"Set up by . . . ?"

He puts his mug down and says, "I don't see any reason to lie about this: He's an acquaintance of your mother's."

Thalia says, "Why would I mind that? She owes you, big-time. Do I know him?"

"Todd Weinreb."

"Well, good for her. A good deed at last. Is he fabulous?"

"There's only been one date and another upcoming, this Thursday. Plus a few conversations."

"Cute, I bet."

"Quite."

"Did you Google him?"

"No need. In the sense that he's not someone about whom articles would have been written."

Thalia says, "Fine. Absolutely. No need."

"He works at Gracious Home."

This is why he loves Thalia: Her response is backlit by an enthusiasm that even great acting talent couldn't manufacture. "Gracious Home! Which department?"

"Table tops," says Henry.

"Did he pick out my shelf paper?"

"He helped."

"Can I meet him? Is it too soon? I know it is, but it would be fabulous if we can sneak in a meeting before the Leif thing hits. Be honest. Say no. I'll completely understand."

Henry says, "Normally, it would be too soon. But given what's ahead —"

"Where and when? I could give you two a half-hour alone before I barge in."

"Not necessary. You and I can walk over together, or cab together. We haven't picked the restaurant yet. And I should check with Todd first."

"You know what this makes me think? That he must be great."

"Based on . . . ?"

"Based on your knowing you can drag me along on a second date. I think that shows he has excellent family values."

He smiles. "Hard to say at this juncture."

"One possible hitch: Let's say I reach Philip, and Thursday's the best night for us to get together."

Now he must tell her what he hasn't fully confessed or aptly characterized: his mismanagement of the future boyfriend. He winces, then reports, "Philip didn't take kindly to your giving him my phone number in lieu of yours."

Thalia gets up from the table and opens a kitchen drawer, already a mess of papers and takeout menus. "My files," she explains.

"I tried to correct that impression," Henry continues. "But after all, what could I promise? That you'd go out on a date, or arrange a clandestine meeting in a parking garage? I didn't have that authority."

More searching produces a business card, black with silver engraving, which she slips into her bathrobe pocket.

"Is that his card?"

"His club." She pats the pocket. "Of course you are welcome to finish your tea, but I'm going to jump into the shower and head out."

"It's almost twelve-thirty. Don't you have work tomorrow?"

Thalia laughs. "I do. I'll pack fresh underwear." She pauses to say, "I'm teasing you! Stop worrying."

"How will you get there? Not by subway this time of night? Take a taxi. My treat." He reaches back into the pocket where his wallet would be if he hadn't left it upstairs.

"Don't be silly. I have money." She smiles. "Petty cash for moving extras. *Merci*, Estime International."

"Irony noted," says Henry.

She is pulling the rubber band out of her hair and tousling the new layers. "So you'll check with Todd about Thursday night?"

"First thing tomorrow."

"Great. I can't wait. More tea? I forgot to ask if you take lemon. Not that I have one."

"I'm all set," says Henry.

As soon as she's out of the kitchen, her baritone Henry impersonation reaches him: "Todd, I'd like you to meet my daughter, the hussy. She'll join us for dinner before she goes clubbing. No, not *every* night. But she's sowing her wild oats before her soul gets sold to the devil next week."

He chuckles, then calls back, "Okay. Point taken." Suddenly he is thinking of Celeste, how much she would have enjoyed the one-woman show that is Thalia. He rinses their two mugs and leaves through the kitchen door, up the secret staircase, and into bed. Due to baseline paternal worries about third rails, alcohol, drugs, unprotected sex, and breaches of contract, he takes a pill.

17

Thank You for Joining the Boys Tonight

A T GRACIOUS HOME, Henry watches as Todd waits on a tall young woman in workout clothes whose navel is exposed and whose emerald-cut diamond engagement ring is colossal. From her backpack she brings forth a tablecloth depicting scenes that might be Colonial Williamsburg or Plimoth Plantation. Todd, at the register, asks her where she acquired this piece of homespun Americana.

"At one of my bridal showers."

"From anyone you'd ever invite to dinner?"

"My fiancé's mother."

"You poor child," clucks Todd.

"She's okay," says the future bride unhappily. She slides the tablecloth across to Todd. "It's a family heirloom."

"Are you thinking table runners to disguise it?"

"I was just thinking napkins. I have a gift certificate."

Frowning, Todd runs his right hand across the surface. "This kind of thing usually came with matching napkins."

"It did. I have seven. She said the others were either lost or stained."

"Seven's plenty! You're just having the in-laws, right?"

"I think I have to use it for Thanksgiving." She points to the artwork: Indians. Corn. Stockades. "So I'll need a total of ten. Eleven if my sister brings someone."

"You know what I'd do, hon? See what you get for wedding presents and what you still need, then come back with your gift certificate and ask for me, Todd. As for filling in with napkins? I'd go kitschy, paper, Thanksgiving-themed, and I'd find some really awful retro salt and pepper shakers on eBay, turkeys or Pilgrims. You've got time. And next year? Tell this mother-in-law that the dry cleaner lost the tablecloth. Believe me, she hates it, too. She couldn't wait for her son to get engaged so she could dump it on his unsuspecting bride."

From the sidelines, Henry adds, "Besides, she should have Thanksgiving at *her* house next year."

"You're right," says the customer. "I'm not doing it two years in a row. I hate Thanksgiving."

Todd folds the tablecloth into an expert rectangle, wraps it in tissue paper, and slips it into a Gracious Home bag. "It'll be fine," he says. "Big platters covering the settlers. A gravy boat, a center-piece. Now give me a hug. When's the wedding?"

"June ninth."

"Lots of luck. You'll be a gorgeous bride." He takes an appraising step backward. "Vera?"

"Vera," she confirms.

"And tell your intended that I said he's a lucky guy, unless he's the jealous type. In which case, tell him I was *not* flirting."

130

She says she *will* tell Patrick, but won't hug due to still being sweaty from her Pilates. Halfway up the escalator she blows several kisses.

"I didn't want to get you in trouble, socializing at work," Henry tells Todd.

"Are you kidding? Me? Mr. Retail? Mr. Sell-Ice-to-the-Eskimos?"

"Low to no pressure, I noticed."

"That's my secret: If they see you're not pushy, they trust you. And if they want something we don't have, I tell them who carries their miserable little item." He smiles his best retail smile and says, "And what may I help you with this morning, sir?"

Henry and Thalia walk together down Columbus to West 64th at an hour and a location designed to overlap neatly with the end of Todd's workday. Trying not to hover or interrogate, Henry hasn't seen Thalia since her post-midnight departure for the East Village three nights earlier. He's pleased that she has dressed up tonight — a long skirt, hippie-ish, and a lavender twinset that was Williebelle's. It is, she tells him, in recognition of her second-to-last night of anonymity and fashion freedom.

"Saturday night," he confirms. "Do you know the particulars?"

"Absolutely: Dinner first. Very fancy. Per Se. Then we go clubbing. We dance. We fall in love. We get noticed. All plants, of course. There's no turning back or getting sick or chickening out because it's already in the pipeline."

"In its own way, it's fascinating," says Henry. "For me, a crash course in celebrity journalism."

"Me, too," says Thalia.

"Not a word to Todd, though. Do we agree?"

They walk a half block in silence before Thalia says, "I'm not big on impulse control."

"So I've noticed."

"Philip, you mean?"

"Is that anything we have to worry about? In terms of nondisclosure?"

She smiles. "I'd say no."

"Did you speak to him at his club?"

"I went. I stood back. I waved." She demonstrates, just barely a raised palm. "He knew what it meant that I came."

"But you didn't exchange any words?"

"As in 'talk'? Actually not. But that was fine. It was" — she makes a complete stop to study a gauzy, ruffled dress of pale yellow in a shop window — "what you might call a meaningful exchange of smiles." She walks to the far edge of the window. "Can you see the buttons on the back? They're red! Isn't that great? Would you have thought *red* on a yellow dress?"

"Never in a million years," says Henry.

"Am I stereotyping? Because I wouldn't have asked a straight guy a question about buttons."

"If you are, I don't mind." They continue south, Henry mindful of the nineteenth-century father-and-daughterliness of their stroll. He hopes onlookers are noticing, further hopes he will run into acquaintances, setting in motion introductions. He adds, "Buttons, color, fashions — all very safe topics with Todd. In fact I can picture him soliloquizing about crimson buttons. Or maybe that's the wrong word. Maybe I mean extemporizing. In very entertaining fashion."

"*Cannot* wait," says Thalia.

Todd is ten minutes late, apologizing and confiding that he ran home to shower and change for this most important night.

He kisses Thalia on the knuckles and Henry on the lips, then straightens up to blink theatrically and ask, "Where the hell are we?"

Thalia laughs. Henry says, "The cheese cave. I asked for it when I made the reservation."

"It's a relationship test," Todd confides to Thalia. "Extreme *fromage.*"

Henry says, "Too much?"

"Actually," says Todd, "I might love it here." He pulls out the chair next to Henry's, spreads his napkin across his knees, then surveys the walls. "It's like a cheese version of the candy house in *Hansel and Gretel.* Don't you just want to reach over and break off a piece of Wisconsin cheddar?" Immediately he turns back and says, "So, Thalia! Thank you for joining the boys tonight."

"It was my idea. He was worried it was too soon to inflict his daughter on you."

Todd bites his lower lip. "I *am* quite reserved. And bashful. Henry probably told you that."

"Apparently," says Henry, "there's a chemical in cheese that brings out his uninhibited side."

Thalia looks at Henry. "Well, well, well," she says.

"What?"

"Apparently someone else is less reserved around . . . someone else."

Todd says, "I'm taking that to mean he's not always talk-show-host material. I'm also taking it as a compliment."

A waiter enters the room, clasps his hands operatically, and delivers the cheese cave orientation. As soon as he's set the menus before them, Thalia says, "It's not that Henry isn't entertaining. It's just that his other sterling qualities are more obvious."

"Such as?" Todd asks.

She counts on her fingers. "He's very kind, very open-minded, very generous. He's an excellent audience — which is high on my list. Very hospitable. Very thoughtful."

"Enough," says Henry. "I'm here. No need for the testimonials."

"I think you should let this flow uninterrupted," says Todd, with a full swivel in Thalia's direction. "Is that a vintage twinset?"

"It is. Yet new to my collection."

"Let's get some wine and let's make some decisions," Henry says.

Todd winks at Thalia and opens his menu. "Hmmm. This sounds delicious, doesn't it: cheese *du jour à la cave odeureuse.*"

"Where?" says Thalia.

"He made that up," Henry tells her.

"Are you funny at work?" she asks Todd.

"I would be if place mats and napkin rings lent themselves to jokes."

"They do," says Henry.

Todd passes the breadbasket to Thalia, noting that Gracious Home carries this very line of damask in which the rolls are swathed. "Henry happened to observe me in action: A woman brought in an heirloom shmatte tablecloth, and I had a little fun with her. Which can only happen if you've read the customer right. It's a waste of my time to make jokes with a stiff."

"I know exactly what you mean," says Thalia. "And don't you find that you recognize almost immediately — from a look, a twinkle in their eye — how far you can take it? My high school drama coach used to say, 'It's not just acting. It's reacting,' because some of the kids would say their lines and just stand there expressionless until it was their turn again." Immediately she demonstrates the slackest, most high-schoolesque glazed eye a director would ever call for. "That's when I leave it at hello, goodbye, and thank you."

"When Henry told me you're an actress, I was thrilled," says Todd.

"Did he tell you about my day job? Well, my day job until today, anyway. Coat-check lass at Salon Gerard? On West Fifty-seventh?"

"Not laid off, I hope?"

Thalia looks up from her menu, a silent consultation with Henry. "Not laid off," she says firmly.

"With something else lined up?"

When neither Thalia nor Henry answers and they appear to be sending signals across the table, Todd says, "It's okay. I get it. No shame in that."

"In what?" Thalia asks.

"Stepdad underwriting sabbatical? Isn't that what I'm reading?"

Henry sees Thalia's eager, confessional face and shakes his head.

"C'mon," says Thalia. "It'll be fun to tell him."

Henry knows she is right. What they have to report is Hollywood chatter of a very high order. But he is her lawyer and Todd is a near-stranger —

Thalia says, "I know you're torn. I'll take full responsibility. You weren't present when I spilled the beans, okay? How's that?"

"Not good if you're lying under oath."

"I'm dying here," says Todd, just as the waiter returns and recites the night's featured dishes. They order in one fell swoop: three Cosmos, three of the special salads, two halibuts, one organic chicken breast, a California white, the six-selection cheese course, and a chocolate soufflé that requires advance notice.

As soon as they are alone again, Todd raises his right hand. "If this were a bookstore, or a synagogue, or my born-again coworker Sharon's apartment, I'd have my left hand on a Bible." He asks if

Henry would like to have a word with Thalia in private, because he'll be happy to visit the men's room. Will a few minutes be enough time?

"Thank you," Henry says.

But Thalia says, "I don't think that's necessary, do you? He's sworn not to tell a living soul."

"The courts take these agreements very seriously, Thalia." He turns to Todd. "Thalia has signed a confidentiality agreement, which, I've noticed, she is compelled to violate once a day. Nothing that we say here can be repeated, ever. It would mean not only the end of the agreement, but of her career."

"So-called career," says Thalia.

"I think I *will* excuse myself," Todd says.

Henry says that might be very helpful. Todd leaves the cave, but not before flashing a V sign back toward Thalia. Henry waits, takes a sip of water, checks the door. "What's the hurry?" he pleads. "There's so much time! If Todd should see a headline or a photo he can ask me what's going on and I can say, 'It's not what it appears. Ask me again in six months.'"

Thalia touches Henry's closest hand. "You're worried about the relationship not lasting, but I'm not. He's a keeper." And with a flourish to an invisible master of ceremonies she says grandly, "Please bring him back in."

Todd is ecstatic. He says it'll be like presidential letters, unopened until ten or fifty years after his death. What about clothes for this gig? What about her apartment? Is anyone styling it? What an opportunity! And down the road? Any chance that this Leif Dumont could grow on Thalia? Because that would be the real fairy-tale romance. You're hired, purely business, and you fall in love!

"Starring Julia Roberts and Richard Gere, thank you," says Thalia.

"Not possible?"

Henry says, "He's a very odd duck. There's nothing obviously appealing about him."

Thalia says, "He was sick the day we had the meeting at the Waldorf."

"Intelligent?" Todd asks.

"Hard to tell," says Thalia. "Too strange —"

"And socially awkward," Henry adds. "Even Aspergian."

"How's he going to fare in the limelight?" Todd asks.

Henry says, "That's where Thalia comes in."

Thalia strikes a pose that is all head, shoulders, and red carpet.

"Wardrobe?" Todd asks.

"On its way, they tell me."

"And her grandmother's hand-me-downs," says Henry.

Thalia says, "Henry? I forget: Did Williebelle know me?"

"She met you. Certainly. And of course she was at the wedding."

"I was the flower girl," Thalia tells Todd.

"Is there a video?" he asks.

Henry shakes his head. "Denise was widowed. It didn't seem . . . seemly."

Thalia hoots, "Ha! 'Seemly.' Who thought that? Not the bride, I bet."

Todd says, "Can we get back to Leif Dumont? What has he done, and why would the paparazzi care where he's clubbing and with whom?"

"*Scar Tissue?*" Thalia offers. "*Frantic? Torso Motel?*"

"Produced, directed, and starred in," Henry explains.

"*Land of Louie* launched him, sort of," adds Thalia. "The TV show? He played the upstairs neighbor that everyone ran away from."

"Hence the PR problem," says Henry.

"I assume money is changing hands for this romantic under-taking?" Todd asks.

"*Mais oui,*" says Thalia. "And my lawyer here negotiated a few nice perks that have to do with career expansion after Leif pub-licly breaks my heart."

The waiter enters the cave with three Cosmos on a tray, a stun-ning spiral of lime zest decorating each glass. "This could really be quite delicious," says Todd.

Don't Look So Worried

E STIME INTERNATIONAL'S grooming team arrives at West 75th at 5:00 P.M. on Saturday. Henry and Todd are upstairs in the little den off the library, drinking mint juleps in honor of the Kentucky Derby, an hour away on NBC. They are fully aware that a hairdresser and a manicurist are making house calls below, because both, arriving separately, rang Henry's doorbell in search of client Thalia Archer. Todd is itching to consult; at the very least shouldn't they call downstairs and see if Thalia needs second and third opinions on any aspect of her toilette? Finally Henry puts the Derby preliminaries on pause and calls downstairs. Thalia's voice has the stilted quality of someone whose hair is being styled against her will. She says, "I do have company. But if Todd wanted to shoot downstairs for a quick hello — and you, too — I can definitely take a break. Bring some alcohol."

Todd is signaling, *Let me.* Henry hands him the phone. "Is everything okay?" he asks, then listens, pacing. "Okay. I know you can't talk in front of her. I'm on my way." He clicks the phone shut and says, "Let's go. Beauty nine-one-one."

"We called *her.*"

"Need I say more: bangs." His fingers chop along his forehead.

"Doesn't she have bangs already?"

"She has layers. Someone is asking for bangs, right to the eyebrow. C'mon. You'll play the lawyer card if necessary — creative control or client approval or whatever." He leads the way, into the foyer and toward the front door, but Henry says, "No, this way. We don't have to go outside. There's a stairway from the kitchen."

Halfway down the passage, Todd stops and touches the wall behind the handrail. "Excuse me, but I'm noting there are chunks of granite and, if I'm not mistaken, dirt. Are we right up against the foundation? Don't these rocks sweat in the summer?"

"Truthfully, I don't know what they do in the summer. It's only been since Thalia moved in that I've used this stairway."

"Better lighting, please," says Todd, pointing at the single bare bulb. "I don't want you to fall and break your neck." He gives the shoulders in front of him a brief, protective squeeze. Henry stands still, takes it in, manages only, "Thank you. I'll be careful."

They find Thalia draped in a plastic cape on a kitchen chair in the middle of the room, hair wet and unattended. A sinewy woman in a tank top frowns by the kitchen sink, arms crossed, a comb in one hand and a scissors in the other. An Asian woman in a lab coat is studiously filing the nails of Thalia's left hand.

"Hello, my people," Thalia says. "Here we have Dawn and . . . ?"

"Yumi," says the manicurist.

Todd says hello, thanks for coming, and what is the thinking behind bangs?

Dawn says, "My *thinking*? That she needs them." She strides over to her client and pushes wisps of hair off Thalia's forehead, none too gently. "Would you agree that it's splotchy?"

Henry asks, "Where?"

Todd, with a mild shrug, asks, "Who's doing makeup?"

"I am," says Thalia. "And don't look so worried. They gave in on that one."

"Do you have concealer?" he asks.

"I have a stick. And powder. I can fix it. Nobody's ever noticed I had a splotchy forehead." She smiles mysteriously, a signal Henry is beginning to recognize as a leap into improv. "Especially Trevor, in that ivory tower of his. I could show up as a blond tonight, or with a mouth full of braces, and he wouldn't notice."

"So you've shared with Dawn what tonight is about?" Henry asks carefully.

Thalia says, "I haven't had a chance." She turns to Yumi. "Trevor is my law school professor. I've worked for him as a TA all semester. He's taking me out to dinner tonight as a thank-you. And it's now or never. I graduate in two weeks. He's taking a job in Alaska. If he doesn't declare his love tonight, it's over." She sighs. "And here's another reason to nix the bangs: He's thirty years older. I don't want to remind him of the age difference."

"And don't his twin daughters, the teenagers, have bangs?" Todd asks.

"He's married?" Dawn asks.

"Of course not," says Thalia. "He's a widower."

"More to the point," says Henry, "her last haircut was lovely. I wouldn't monkey with it too much."

"And Trevor knows me this way—plain, simple, recognizable."

Dawn picks up a lock of Thalia's beautifully highlighted hair, with a smirk that says, *Plain and simple, my ass.* She plugs in an extension cord, then a hair dryer, and brings forth an enormous cylindrical brush from her suitcase of wares. Yumi retreats to the kitchen table. The men watch as Dawn dries and styles in silence, her expression a frozen neutral.

"Nice and shiny," says Henry.

"It's the vodka," says Thalia. "Back when Dawn was speaking to me, she told me her secret: vodka in the shampoo." Without consulting a mirror, she runs her fingers through the front locks, reversing their direction.

"I like that you gave her more loft," says Todd. "Which is just right for a night on the town. Just that extra little oomph she needed."

"Not to mention under very primitive conditions," Henry adds.

"A trainee could have done it," Dawn snarls. "A beauty school dropout. What I do is cut. I don't even style. I certainly don't blow-dry."

"La-dee-dah," Todd mumbles.

"Sometimes, Dawn, a client just needs a shampoo and a blow-dry between cuts," Thalia tells her. "It's not a character test."

"Where do you work?" Todd asks. "I'd be curious to know."

Dawn maintains her haughty silence as she packs up her tools. Last to be reclaimed is Thalia's plastic cape, which the hairdresser de-Velcros, pulls off, and folds aggressively. "Good luck to all of you," Dawn grants with the last snap of her metal travel case. The manicurist resumes her work as the front door slams. With her head bowed over the application of a base coat, Yumi finally speaks. "She always be like that: diva."

What to wear? Henry and Todd missed the delivery earlier in the day of what Thalia is calling costumes, chosen by a personal shopper who'd been told only dress size, height, coloring, event, destination, and exaggerated celebrity status.

The portable rack dominates the small living room, and its garment bags look undisturbed. "Hate them all," Thalia tells her advisers.

"Let's not be hasty," says Todd.

Henry takes a seat on the rattan love seat. "Are they returnable?" he asks.

"I assume so, since the note said to keep the tags on whatever I don't want."

Todd begins his evaluation, inspecting labels, rubbing fabric, frowning at hems, beading, fiber content, and seam allowances. Eventually, he segregates a half-dozen candidates at one end of the rack.

"May I see the note from the store?" Henry asks.

"Not from the store," Thalia says, fishing in the wire wastebasket under her makeshift desk. She hands Henry a letter on Estime letterhead. Attached is a business card he knows: *Anne-Marie Albano, media coaching, strategic planning, and crisis communications.* The note says only, "I think I got a sense of your look. Hope something here appeals. Please don't remove the tags of anything you'll be returning. Have fun! P.S. Leif <u>loves</u> red."

Todd gets to work and a minute later is holding two hangers in each hand, all displaying red dresses, all of them shiny and short.

"Those are reasonable," says Henry. "Aren't they?"

"Not my look *at all.*"

Henry and Todd exchange glances, which then travel to Thalia, dressed in dark green cargo pants and a long-sleeved jersey that looks like thermal underwear.

"Uh-uh," she says. "No you don't. I know that look. 'Poor Thalia. Poor Cinderella. Let's dress her up and send her to the ball.'"

Todd says, "Sorry, but you're wrong. We both understand that you are more than capable of gussying yourself up and making a dramatic appearance tonight. I just think that you should try a few on before rejecting them all." He holds up one tag. "Four thousand dollars. Sometimes that can turn into a very nice look."

"And if I may," Henry adds, "these clothes may have been negotiated in return for product placement. Estime probably approached a few designers and promised you'd be photographed in their goods."

"No one told me," says Thalia. "Certainly not" — and she takes back the letter — "Anne-Marie Albano. I see this, a new wardrobe, as purely voluntary. I'm not wearing anything I don't like or feel good in. Besides, it's a date with Leif Dumont. He's never seen me in anything but jeans or a Williebelle."

Henry asks, "What does Ms. Albano mean when she says in the note, 'I think I got a sense of your look'? Does she mean from a headshot?"

"Oh," says Thalia. "Actually, I met her. She came over and went through my closet."

"Like one of those consultants who organize your apartment and tell you what to keep and what to throw out?" Todd asks. "I always thought I'd be excellent at that."

"No. It was more specific: What did I own that said *rising star and love interest*?"

"Not an unreasonable criterion," says Henry. He points to the rack of runners-up. "Maybe that black one. It's theirs, but at the same time it's not outlandish."

Todd is still holding the four red dresses up for inspection. Thalia chooses one red candidate and the black dress. "I suppose you want to see me in them," she grumbles.

When the bedroom door closes behind her, Henry says, "I've never seen her nervous. And certainly never moody."

"It's a huge undertaking," says Todd. "Embarking on something that could turn your life upside down. I think we're witnessing a little revolt."

"On top of which —" Henry begins, then hesitates. "There is an unforeseen complication."

Todd says, "Let me venture a guess: She has a boyfriend, a real one, and she's worried that she'll lose him if she goes through with this."

"Not quite. She met a guy a week ago, which she's characterized as love at first sight."

"Who is he?"

"A deejay. His day job is with a moving company. He moved her here."

Todd raises his eyebrows, a silent social probe.

"We don't discuss those things. But I'm guessing no; they haven't even had a proper date."

"Is she going to sneak off and meet this guy —"

"Philip."

"Meet Philip for secret assignations? Is that why you didn't want her to tell me about the faux engagement? Because she already told one potential loose cannon?"

"She actually had him sign a makeshift nondisclosure form. He knows she's off the market for six months, and he should disregard whatever he sees in the tabloids."

"What are you two whispering about?" Thalia calls.

Todd says, "Come out and we'll tell you."

She glides into view, in knee socks, pelvis forward, mocking a model's gait. Below a petulant runway stare is the red dress, its neckline plunging, exposing a utilitarian beige bra.

"Not quite," says Todd.

"Next," says Henry, wincing.

"Can't. This is it. The black one didn't fit. I couldn't even zip it."

145

Todd is on his feet, reassessing the candidates, measuring a fabric's stretch and give. "Did they even *take* your measurements?" he asks.

Thalia sends Henry a wry look, exactly what's needed by one who's been feeling unhelpful and dispensable. It says, *He's your boyfriend. I'll dress in crimson. I'm doing this for you.*

19

We Won't Get in the Way

TODD SAYS THIS IS CRAZY. Cra-zy! Thalia needs to be better prepared, better equipped, less forgiving toward her pre-Leif wardrobe. Isn't that what the up-front lump sum was earmarked for? Of course he wants to help, but in a less nerve-racking manner, please. Yes, he has his talents, but a needle and thread are not among them. Red dress number two would have been great with a few tucks in the waist and without that inane ruffle posing as a sleeve.

"What would you suggest?" Thalia asks, bent over her knees, applying near-invisible pearlescence to her toenails.

"Shoes! It's insane to be shopping an hour before your date is due!"

"Now I have them," Thalia says calmly. "And I think these will go with pretty much everything."

"They're silver," says Todd. "They are not going to go with everything."

"Needle and thread aside," Henry tells him, "I think you *are* cut out for beauty nine-one-one."

"Poor Henry," Thalia says. "Is any of this interesting?"

"He's seeing me at my worst," says Todd, "so now I have that to worry about."

"Doubtful," says Thalia. "He's looking all googly-eyed." She screws the cap on the bottle and hands it to Todd. "Okay. We're almost there. Mind if I kick you out now?"

Henry says, "Of course not. Hope we weren't underfoot. All I'll say is have a wonderful time. Or at least a wonderful meal. Definitely order the tasting menu. It's supposed to be astonishing. Call me tomorrow?"

"Why do we have to leave?" Todd asks. "We won't get in the way, but we'll be right there if she needs anything —"

"Such as?" asks Henry.

"A quick press?" says Todd. "That last two inches of zipper?"

"We don't want to be underfoot," Henry tries again.

"Yes, we do! This is business, and we're her people."

Thalia says, "All true, but a girl needs to dart between her bathroom and bedroom in her underwear. How's this: You'll come back at seven forty-five, as long as there's no second-guessing the fashions."

"Deal," says Todd.

"And no tweaking Leif's outfit, either."

"Note how she underestimates me," Todd says.

They return promptly at 7:44 to hear music blaring from the living room speakers and Thalia singing along in the bathroom.

"We're here," Henry calls.

"Man on the floor," Todd adds.

They try again when the CD pauses between songs. Thalia

calls back, "Okay. I'm coming out, so don't get emotional, okay? And Todd? Really; I need you to be very Zen about this."

"I make no promises," he calls back.

It is abundantly clear when she comes into view that her grooming and fashion disclaimers were a matinee performance. She is wearing one of the original red dresses, diaphanous over something tight and silky and strapless. Her hair shines, Henry thinks, as if it were polyurethaned, yet free and soft. She points to her eyes, outlined, lids glittery, eyelashes attenuated. "Too whorish?" she asks.

"Compared to what?" Todd asks. "A gym teacher? An Orthodox *rebbetzin*? Don't be ridiculous."

The new shoes are silver straps of spaghetti, and her earrings are waterfalls of diamonds. Both men gasp. "Is the lipstick too dark?" she asks.

"It's perfect," says Henry. "A perfect match. Is that what you were going for?"

"I am stunned," Todd says. "I bought the act. I believed with my whole heart that you'd come out of that bathroom with your hair in a ponytail and what? What would be horrible? A sequined shell over culottes? And look what walks out! Thalia Archer, goddess."

Thalia fingers the dangling diamonds. "They're real. On loan, of course. I don't even want to know what they cost."

Henry says, "I think he meant the whole picture. You look beautiful."

"What about a wrap?" asks Todd.

"This one, for good luck," she says, and leads them into the living room where a Williebelle sweater, bejeweled and white, is draped on the back of her ancient desk chair. "One little stain on the cuff, not noticeable."

"Let me see that —" Todd begins, just as the doorbell rings.

"I'll get it," says Henry.

It is not Leif on the threshold, but a uniformed driver. "Car for Miss Archer," he announces.

"Is Mr. Dumont in the car?" Henry asks.

The driver says, "He's making a phone call."

"Please tell him Miss Archer is waiting to receive him." Henry closes the door.

"We really don't have to go through those motions yet," says Thalia.

"Call me old-fashioned, but there are basic good manners, and one doesn't honk the horn from the curb."

"So to speak," says Thalia.

"Your old man was brought up right," Todd tells Thalia. "And all the mothers of his dates loved him for it."

"Let's not stand here like a firing squad," says Thalia.

The doorbell rings again. Thalia answers, and to Henry's chagrin he hears a flat, joyless, "Wow. You look hot."

"Can you come in for a minute?" she asks.

Leif steps into the room. He is wearing a tuxedo jacket over a black T-shirt bearing his company logo in iron-on magenta iridescence, black jeans, black boots — all of which attest to a parallel fashion conference at the other end. The two-day growth of stubble appears carefully cultivated and his earlobes look infected. Thalia says, "Of course you know Henry. And this is his friend Todd."

Leif says "Hullo" twice and nothing more.

"Feeling okay about all of this?" Thalia asks him.

"All of what?"

Her answer is an eloquent twirl of her wrist: *you, me, this counterfeit date.*

"Doesn't she look beautiful?" Todd tries.

Leif's complexion and scalp go red.

"Let the record show an affirmative response," says Thalia.

"Thalia tells us you're going to Per Se," says Henry. "Have you been there before?"

"No. Someone else picked it."

"Someone with good taste and *pull*," Todd says.

"I'm starved," says Thalia. "All I had all day was tea and Oreos."

"I wish I'd known that," says Henry.

"He'd have roasted you a leg of lamb," says Todd.

"Shall we go?" asks Thalia.

"It might rain later," says Henry.

"The driver has a big umbrella with my logo on it," says Leif, pointing to the mummy on his chest.

"All set," says Thalia. She kisses Henry, then Todd, who whispers, "Reapply the gloss after every course."

"And definitely do the wine pairings," says Henry.

Leif says, "They told me to do that. And Thalia's getting the Kobe beef because that's what they told the papers in advance."

"Interesting what they think the public wants to know," says Henry.

"Bye, my people," Thalia says. "You go do something fun, too."

"We'll close up here," says Henry. "Do you have your key?"

Thalia snaps open her silver-spangled evening purse and says, "Check."

Leif nods stiffly to each. Clearly for their benefit, Thalia follows him to the door with unbent knees and robotic arms — Mrs. Frankenstein heading out for a night on the town.

Street Sense wins the Derby, which they replay and watch again. Todd wonders aloud if the winning horse knows he crossed the finish line first and feels some equine version of jubilation.

"He must — all the hoopla, the hugging and kissing. The blanket of roses. I wasn't raised around horses, but they're supposed to have emotions. Did you read *Seabiscuit*?"

Todd says, "Loved the movie. And what do I remember most? When he rejected the goat who was supposed to be his best buddy and tossed him out of the barn. I wanted Seabiscuit to have a companion, even if the rest of the world wanted him to settle down with a nice mare."

On the screen the delirious owner is hugging Street Sense's trainer. It seems as good a juncture as any for Henry to slip his arm around Todd's shoulder. "It happened in real life, too," says Henry, "by which I mean in the book, just with a little less drama. Biscuit picks the goat up with his teeth and drops him over the door to his stall."

Todd covers the hand resting on his shoulder. "Look at us: two shy boys at the movies."

Henry points the remote and mutes the color commentary. The cable box reads 8:40. "They're well into it," he says. "I wonder how it's going."

"He seemed startled," Todd says. "What do you think that was about?"

"The way she looked, like a million bucks. He'd only seen her in rags."

"He turned purple!"

"I think it's safe to say he's never been out with a girl like Thalia."

"Or any girl."

"Debunked that," says Henry. "According to Thalia, he had a bona fide affair with the acting teacher who set this whole thing in motion."

"A woman?"

"Definitely. Sally, hyphenated name. She confessed when Thalia asked the question, 'Am I being hired as a beard?'"

"It's not that I picked up a vibe. It was just that he looked a little panicked when he saw the two of us."

"It wasn't us. It was the shock of seeing Thalia looking magnificent. And there we were, taking notes, figuratively, witness to the fact that he can't get a girl on his own. Most humiliating, I'm sure."

Todd answers in a lifeless monotone, "Hullo, sir. Hullo, other sir. Thalia, you look hot."

"I know: awful. Imagine being his mother or father. It must be a little heartbreaking to have a child turn out so unappealing."

"You are a dear man," Todd says. "If I had any disposable income to speak of, I'd march you over to Per Se myself."

Henry shuts off the television. "There are other options," he says.

"Of course! I wasn't hinting. Pizza's fine. Or that noodle joint on Columbus."

"What I meant," says Henry, "was other options. And *then* dinner."

"Finally," says Todd.

Each has read in *Time Out New York* that there's a place serving great burgers in the West Seventies, but neither remembers which block. Todd narrates as they walk west, checking posted menus outside the neighborhood's seedier taverns, "If they were shooting a romantic comedy about us, this is where we'd see a montage of us engaging in fun-filled couple things: Rollerblading in the park, waiting in line for a foreign film, walking a herd of dogs and getting tangled up in the leashes."

"Signifying . . . ?"

153

"The awkward phase is over. No more *Will they or won't they?* Everything's good. We'll thank our matchmaker in the credits."

"'With grateful thanks to Denise Krouch, who matched us up on the basis of *this one's gay and so's this one.*'"

"Let's call her," says Todd. "C'mon. Let's see if she wants to meet us for a burger. Maybe she knows the name of the joint we're looking for."

"On the *west* side of Manhattan? Not a chance." He stops them at the next curb to avoid a delivery man on a bike who is ignoring the red light. Henry says, "Now that she knows I found Thalia — she's calling it 'getting custody,' by the way — it would be one long third degree. She'd be relentless, and I'm a bad liar. If she asked where Thalia was tonight, I'd have to make up a story."

"Couldn't you just say, 'The subject of Thalia is off-limits'? That way you're not lying. You're just setting ground rules."

"Maybe another time, but not tonight," says Henry. "*Especially* not tonight."

"Have I mentioned that she ends every message with 'Say hi to Henry for me'? And don't you find it sweet that in her own Denisean way she's happy for us?"

"She's happy for *herself*. She wants full credit and a standing ovation, which I find a little patronizing, actually."

Todd has stopped in the middle of the block and is no longer smiling.

Henry does not have to ask, *Is something wrong?* "If anyone else had introduced us I'd be sending orchids," he says.

"Good," says Todd. "I feel better. Thank you. This is where I'd kiss you if you were a guy who tolerated public displays of affection."

Henry smiles. "That's the other guy, the one playing me in the movie."

"A tour de force," says Todd. "I think he's going to win a Golden Globe."

They move on, agreeing that a peek at the new *Zagat* might help. En route to a magazine kiosk, Henry says quietly, "I quit therapy last week after twenty-five years. And a day later I kicked Denise off my property. Some of us think that's progress."

"Believe me, I get it. It's hard to thank that little goat for anything. But you're holding all the cards: Not only are you and Thalia reunited, but you're a team. She's crazy about you, you know."

"We are a team, aren't we?" Henry says.

"So let's review: Spent entire life with her mother? Not speaking and estranged. Missed several decades with allegedly unfit father? Bosom buddies and trusted allies. You win! I think your ex-therapist would agree that Denise is no threat to you or to —"

Their cell phones ring almost simultaneously. Both men check the caller ID, and both take a sharp breath. It is Krouch, D calling for Todd, and Krouch, T calling for Henry.

20

Closets Galore

TODD IGNORES DENISE'S CALL, as Henry answers Thalia's with a terse, "What's wrong?"

"Not a thing. I'm calling with an update for my team."

"From?"

"A toilet stall."

"You sound funny."

"I'm relining my lips. Almost finished. Is that better?"

"Everything okay so far?"

"Not horrible. We're talking. He seems to have memorized a short list of conversation starters."

Henry pauses to brief Todd. "She says so far, so good. She's calling from the ladies' room."

Thalia says, "I'd better get back out there, but here's the headline: Leif suggests that after a month or two we should announce I'm pregnant."

"Over my dead body," says Henry.

"What?" Todd asks. "What did she say?"

"I hope you told him in no uncertain terms —"

"I said, 'Oh, really? And then what — I wear a prosthesis? Or do I disappear for a few months and resurface holding a lifelike baby doll named Leif Junior?' Puh-leez. I told him I never signed on for that, and better luck with the next girlfriend — smiling the whole time, of course."

"What's he's trying to pull?" Todd demands. "Is everything okay?"

"I didn't call to upset you," says Thalia. "I thought this was funny, or at least good gossip. I'd better get back before he thinks I crawled out the window."

"You know what I'd tell him? The truth. That you found his request alarming and a breach of contract, and you felt it was necessary to call your lawyer, who is appalled at the mere suggestion of a pregnancy."

"No way," cries Todd. "I'm appalled, too. A pregnancy. What's next? A sex tape?"

"Pregnancy *rumor*," corrects Thalia. "Big difference."

"I don't care how many starlets are having out-of-wedlock babies. It takes some nerve to propose that on a first date."

"Guys! It was just floated out there. I dealt with it. It might even have been a joke — hard to tell with him. Are you two having fun?"

Henry switches ears, collects himself. "We are. We watched the Derby, and now we're off in search of dinner."

"Leif's allergic to mushroom spores," says Thalia. "He told the maitre d' before we were even shown to our table. And then, of course, he confided same to our waiter, who was very gracious and reassuring."

Henry hears new female voices. Thalia is no longer alone. "Let's review," she instructs Henry. "They can watch the whole movie, but then right to bed, lights out, no reading, no dilly-dallying. And tomorrow? Mommy will make Belgian waffles for breakfast with her new waffle iron."

"She's bored to death," Henry tells Todd.

They walk seven blocks to Chirping Chicken, where they order two deluxe burgers and one order of onion rings.

When they're seated, plastic cutlery and skimpy napkins in place, matching peach iced teas in hand, Todd says, "Why do I sense you're not an habitué of joints recommended under 'Cheap Eats'?"

"It's fine. I like it here. And if it's good, I'll get a half chicken delivered some night. Sweet potato fries sound delicious. I was tempted."

Todd asks, minus his usual gusto, "Would a whole roast chicken at my house some Friday night hold any interest?"

"Friday night? As in Shabbat dinner? You do that?"

"Not wholeheartedly."

Henry leans in, squints diagnostically. "I'd say yes, I'd love to — except for the look I'm getting."

Todd points to his own face. "*This* look? Dread and terror?"

"Based on . . . ?"

Todd mouths, "My mother."

"I'm good with mothers," says Henry.

Todd shakes his head.

"Not a good idea? Because she's difficult? Unfriendly? Inhospitable?"

"Very hospitable. Not difficult."

"So we're talking about dread over your cooking? Or something ridiculous like whether I'll like your apartment?"

"If only," says Todd.

"Stupid me. I just got it," says Henry. "Is it because I'm not Jewish?"

Todd says, "No, dear boy. It's because the introduction would go something like, 'Mom, this is Henry. He's my special friend. I may have failed to specify in the past that I am what your friends refer to as a *faygeleh*.'"

Henry whispers, "You're telling me you haven't come out to your mother?"

Todd winces, bites one knuckle for dramatic effect. "Not in so many words."

"She knows. Trust me. Moms know. When you finally sit her down and tell her you've been gay your whole life she'll say, 'I always assumed so, but you never seemed to want to talk about it.'"

"Here's a confession: I think to myself, *Tell her, you coward. You traitor.* And then a little voice inside me says, 'She's eighty years old and she has high blood pressure. She's not going to live forever. Why make trouble now?'"

"C'mon. She lives in New York. She must have dozens of friends who have gay children. She might surprise you. She might say, 'Did you think I was so square or such a bigot that you couldn't tell me?' Or — the big one — 'that I wouldn't love you anymore?'"

"Then why hasn't she asked me? She's had several decades to say, 'Todd? Is there anything you want to tell me about your sexual orientation? I'll be fine with whatever it is.'"

"Because she's waiting for you to bring it up. She figures if you wanted to talk about it, you'd have done it a long time ago. Trust me. I bet if you told her you were bringing someone home for dinner and I walked in, she'd be very accepting. Possibly even relieved."

"Because that's how it worked out with Williebelle? You just rang the doorbell and said, 'Mom? That marriage, and that wife? It didn't work so great for me, and now I need you to stop giving my telephone number to women you meet in the laundry room and at the bus stop, because I am not attracted to that gender'?"

"Not quite."

"Because, as you claim, all mothers figure it out on their own?"

"No. My brothers figured it out, and one of them, at a Thanksgiving dinner I didn't attend, interrupted her musings about my nice friend Celeste with, 'Cut the crap, Mom. Henry's gay.'"

"And you know what *my* mother would have said to that? 'No, he isn't. Not my Todd. He had girlfriends in high school. And all through college he went steady with Binnie Chamish's daughter.'"

Henry smiles. "We all dated Binnie Chamish's daughter. You still need to say, 'There's an elephant in the room that we've never acknowledged.' And you'll take it from there." Problem on its way to being solved, he asks, "Where does she live?"

"Oh, that," says Todd. "Mortifying revelation number two."

Henry's first thought is, *Here it comes,* the inevitable deal breaker, the periscope lowered into Todd's as-yet-unrevealed moral abyss — his mother's in a welfare hotel, in a shelter, in a putrid nursing home —

"I live with her," Todd says pitifully. "There. Now you know everything."

On balance, the news is a relief: A lawyer knows that good sons don't grow on trees. "Williebelle lived with me for the last two years of her life," Henry reminds him. "And I certainly have no regrets about that."

"Huge difference: You brought her up from Delaware when she was elderly and alone and you gave her a room and made her last years happy and comfortable. Mine cooks and cleans and does my laundry. Then irons it."

"May I ask how large is this apartment that you share?"

"It's big! I was living in a studio in Murray Hill while she was rattling around in a classic six on West End Ave., maid's room off the kitchen, closets galore—rent-controlled! A nickel a month, it seemed like. I swallowed my pride and moved back home when my dad died ten, no, eleven years ago."

A goateed man and a woman with ropy red hair to her waist take the table next to them. She is hugely pregnant. Todd interrupts his narrative to smile and say, "Any day now?" Dinner banter ensues—First time here? First baby?—nothing that draws Henry in, but still he watches, recognizing that his life has taken a turn for the gregarious. He waits a polite interval before prompting Todd, "You were telling me about the apartment."

"Excuse us," Todd tells his new friends. "I was just confessing that I lived with my mother. At my age, I have a lot of explaining to do."

"She might as well live with *her* mother," says the man. "They talk on the phone ten times a day."

"Fuck you," the woman says pleasantly.

"I think that might be our order," Henry says, directing Todd's attention to the counter.

"I see cheese. Those are cheeseburgers. Sit tight. They'll call us."

"The Chirp can be a little slow," says the woman.

"I think Henry here needs to continue our conversation, but best of luck to you," Todd tells her.

"You, too."

Henry murmurs, "Maybe they could move their chairs over, and we could be godparents to the baby."

"My fault," says Todd. "Sorry. Where were we?"

"Your mother. What's the worst that would happen? She wouldn't love you anymore? She'd kick you out and disown you?"

"She'd still love me."

"But?"

"But I've already disappointed her. I don't have a career she can brag about, or a family, or Little League trophies, or season tickets to anything that would impress her friends. 'What does my only child do? He helps people match table linens to their flatware. Oh, and I just found out — he has a boyfriend. He'll never give me grandchildren, which was the only thing I wanted out of this life.'"

"Are we perhaps exaggerating?" Henry asks. "Are we understudying at the Thalia Krouch School of Dramatic Arts?" He checks his watch. "What time does Mom go to bed?"

"Why?"

"We can get the burgers to go, pick up some flowers on the way, and get it over with."

"As in: 'Mom? This is my special friend, Henry. We're going to listen to music in my room.' That should do it. That was enough to make her deduce that I had girlfriends at Stuyvesant."

"No. You'll say, 'Mom, This is my boyfriend, Henry. I'm dating him. He makes me happy. I hope you can be happy for us, and I hope you won't employ the word *faggy* at this juncture, or ever again.'"

"*Faygeleh*," corrects Todd. He is inhaling and exhaling noisily, drawing the attention of their new acquaintances. "He wants to meet my mother now," Todd explains. "I mean, like drop in unannounced."

"I'm not saying we wouldn't call first," says Henry. "And we can role-play on the way over."

"And you're afraid she won't like this lovely gentleman?" asks the woman.

"It's not him. It's me. She thinks I'm straight."

"No, she doesn't," says the woman.

"We're not married," says her companion. "Try telling *that* to a mother."

"See?" says Henry.

21

Ma

FROM THE ELEVATOR they step into a rose-hued hallway. Every few yards, wet paint warnings are taped to moldings.

"Benjamin Moore's Rhubarb," Todd says, then stops, sniffs, evaluates. "I don't think they used the oil-based."

"You're stalling," says Henry.

"You try it! You take a baseball bat and whack a hornet's nest that has been coexisting peaceably under the eaves of your house. See how you like it."

Henry gives Todd's neck a friendly shake. "C'mon. You know you've wanted to have this conversation for decades."

Their destination is 3GG, three doors away. Upon arrival, Todd takes no action except to close his eyes.

"Do we ring the doorbell?" Henry asks.

Todd takes a ring of keys from his pocket and opens the door.

Three careful steps into the apartment he calls, "Ma? You up? I'm back."

A little woman, five feet tall and shaped like a Jersey tomato, comes into view. She is wiping her hands on a striped dishtowel and smiling uncertainly. "You must be Henry," she says. She is wearing a quilted bathrobe, mauve and opalescent, which still has its gift-box creases.

"It is, and he made me call," Todd says dolefully. "Lillian Weinreb, Henry Archer."

"I'm the mother," she answers, and takes the hand Henry offers.

"I guess we should sit down," says Todd.

"What can I get you?" asks Lillian.

"Vodka on the rocks," says Todd. "But I'll get it. Henry?"

"Is a cup of tea too much trouble?"

"What a goody-goody," says Todd.

"Put some Congo bars on a plate, hon." Lillian leads Henry into a parlor that appears to be half Todd and half Mom. Its walls are a deep earth brown with stark white trim; the furniture is ice blue sateen. Henry sees Gracious Home in the periwinkle mohair throw and the phalanx of candles on the mantel. An oil painting of a mother, father, and sailor-suited boy hangs above an immaculate white-brick fireplace.

"Your family?" Henry asks, pointing.

"The summer before Todd started school." She motions toward the sofa. Henry sits down, back straight, hands folded in his lap. He notices her slippers, elf wear, toes crescenting upward, embroidered with forget-me-nots. "Toddy! Bring a tray table," she yells.

"You're not his doctor, are you?" she asks Henry.

"Did you say *doctor*?"

164

She leans forward. "When your son calls and says he has something important he wants to discuss with you and he's bringing a friend, your imagination can go a little crazy. You think the worst."

Henry offers reassurance at the same time that he is thinking, *Maybe Todd does know his mother; maybe her "worst" is a son bringing home a boyfriend.*

"Because if Todd felt a lump somewhere, he wouldn't tell me. He'd go to the doctor during his lunch hour, and he'd keep everything to himself until he was in intensive care. That's the kind of thing a mother thinks about when the phone rings after nine o'clock."

"It isn't my place to reassure you, but —"

Todd enters the room with two mugs, his drink, and a plate of cookies on a tray. "I got you a ginger tea, Ma."

She accepts the mug and asks, "Is it your health?"

"Is what my health?"

"The thing you need to talk to me about."

Todd sits down next to Henry on the sofa and says, "No, it's not my health."

"Are you sure? Because I think you'd hide it from me. You might figure I'd go first so why burden me with bad news."

"Ma, I'm fine. I'm healthy as a horse. My blood pressure is ninety over sixty. My good cholesterol is in the eighties."

Lillian's lower jaw is quivering. "Are you sure?"

"Positive. Call Dr. Gordon."

Henry nods his encouragement.

"Thank God!" She fans her face and manages a smile. "So now, tell me anything. I won't care. See how health puts everything in perspective?"

Todd says, "Okay. Jumping right in . . . First let me say that I can't really explain why it's taken this long —"

"I can tell you why," Lillian says calmly. "You thought I'd be worried day and night because of the AIDS epidemic."

"Jesus," says Todd. "Ma, didn't we skip a major chunk of this conversation?"

Henry says, "She connected the dots in her own head. Now you have to reassure her."

"I don't have AIDS, Ma."

"You *think* you don't, or you got yourself tested?"

"Ma — no AIDS, no HIV."

Lillian puts her mug down on the ottoman at her feet, covers her face with her hands, and releases a wail.

"See?" says Todd. "Did I need this?"

"I think you have it wrong," says Henry. "I think those are tears of relief."

Todd says, "I forgot the tray table." He leaves the room and comes back with a box of tissues. "Ma? Is Henry right? Are you crying because you're relieved?"

"I've been sick with worry!" Lillian moans. "Sick. It was eating me up inside."

"Did I seem HIV-positive to you?"

"All I knew was that you've had fevers and colds. And bronchitis when you missed a week of work."

"Like five years ago."

"He had to have a chest x-ray," Lillian explains. "And he seemed tired to me."

Henry turns to Todd. "I'm sure it's not purely rational or scientific on your mother's part." Then to Lillian, "Do you believe Todd when he tells you he's fine?"

She nods bravely, then asks, "And you're fine as well? You're not one of those people swallowing fifty pills a day?"

"I'm fine. Thank you for asking."

She picks up the plate of Congo bars and offers it across the ottoman. "Homemade," she says. "No nuts."

All three take a cookie. "Delicious," Henry says.

"I use Splenda, but I don't think you can tell."

"Undetectable," says Henry.

Lillian takes a nibble, then puts the cookie back on the edge of the plate, a sanitary distance from the others. "I feel the need to say that I am a modern woman. And as much as I hate to pick a fight in front of your friend, I have to say it's humiliating to be viewed as the kind of parent who wouldn't love a homosexual son."

"That was never an issue, Ma."

Lillian repeats, "I'm a modern woman. And I was a modern woman before my time."

"I know that."

"Did you think I wasn't intelligent enough? Or did you think I was a secret religious zealot?"

"Ma, c'mon. It wasn't you. It was me. I was a shmuck, okay? And now everything's on the table."

"I'm not a prude and I'm a Democrat."

"I know that —"

"I was a woman ahead of my times. I went to Boston University."

"I know —"

"At a time when my parents wanted me to live at home and commute to Queens College on the subway."

"I know."

"No, you don't. You're just agreeing with me. You didn't know me in my youth." She hesitates and then says, "I could have been more forthcoming with you."

"What does that mean?"

She takes her cookie back. "I dabbled."

"What do you mean 'dabbled'?" Todd asks.

Lillian brushes invisible crumbs off her lap. "Sexually."

"You did not!" Todd says. And to Henry, "She's just trying to be one of the boys."

"Ask Fredalynn Cohn," says Lillian. "Call her if you don't believe me."

"When was this?"

"When do you think? In college."

"I thought you met Dad in college."

Lillian shoots Henry a worldly and indulgent smile. "I did. My senior year."

"I'm supposed to believe you were a lesbian before that?"

"I didn't say that. I said I dabbled. Nowadays you'd say I was experimenting."

"Did Dad know?"

Lillian shakes her head primly.

"Because it was just a one-time fluky thing?"

"Because your father and I didn't sit around discussing what we did with other people before we met."

"Ma! You just met Henry two minutes ago."

"Don't be a prude," Lillian scolds.

"May I ask what path Fredalynn took?" Henry asks.

"Same as me! She met a man over the summer, a waiter in the Catskills, a college student, Syracuse on the GI Bill, and came back her senior year pinned. No kids. They got divorced and she married his brother."

"Interesting," says Henry.

"How come you never told me this before?" Todd asks.

Lillian arches her eyebrows with as much irony as one round face can project. "By 'this' do you mean my private life? You're asking why my private life wasn't an open book in this house? Is that not the pot calling the kettle black?"

"You could've asked me about my private life. I would've told you the truth."

"That's not what the literature says. The literature says the child will tell you when he or she is ready, and the best thing the parents can do is just keep demonstrating their love and support."

Henry says, "Wouldn't it be wonderful if all parents read the literature?"

"There was a father in the mix, don't forget," says Todd. "A father who had only one child and Little League dreams."

"My husband wasn't cut from the same cloth as I am," Lillian explains. "If he were still alive, I might understand keeping this all a big secret. For *decades*."

"I came to you tonight," protests Todd. "Don't I get credit for that?"

Henry raps his knuckles ineffectually on the side of his mug. "You know what I'd say now if this were a mediation session? I'd say, 'We're on the same page. You accept him and love him, and he knows he was wrong to keep such a major fact of life secret. The clock is running, so let's move on.'"

"Are you a judge?" Lillian asks.

"A lawyer."

"And how long have you known Todd?"

"Three weeks."

"Three great weeks," says Todd. "So don't worry."

"And how did you meet?"

"A mutual friend gave him my phone number," says Henry.

"His ex-wife."

Lillian says, "Todd went through a phase like that, too. I could have made that mistake — pushed him into marriage. He dated plenty of girls, and I was guilty of saying things like, 'You know, Todd, after a year of steady dating, the polite thing would be to give her a ring. And don't forget Bubbie's diamond ring is in the vault waiting for you to pop the question.'"

Henry says, "Is there a gay man in Manhattan who doesn't have his grandmother's diamond ring appreciating in a bank vault?"

"We should sell it," says Todd.

"I already did," says Lillian.

"Was that hard for you?" Henry asks.

"Hard?" she replies. "You know what it was? Not the ring. It's the other stuff. What mother doesn't picture walking her son down the aisle and gaining a daughter? And then of course the missing grandchildren. I always thought I'd be a champion grandmother."

"I know, Ma."

"I'm not saying that to make you feel bad. I'm just being honest. That's what the literature says you have to get over, the death of the conventional dream."

"That's okay," says Todd. "That's good. You can say anything you want."

Henry has a thought, a topic yet unbroached that might appeal to a grandparent manqué. He hands his mug to Todd and stands. "This has been lovely, a wonderful night for all concerned, myself included. And I'd love to stay. But I promised my daughter I'd be there when she gets home tonight." He checks his watch. "Which could be any minute now."

"A daughter?" Lillian asks. "How old?"

"Twenty-nine."

"Married?"

Todd says, "No, but she's very popular. We think there's no question she'll marry someone of the opposite sex someday."

"Only one child?" Lillian asks.

"Just one: Thalia."

"She's fabulous," says Todd.

"And she lives with you, or is just visiting for the weekend?"

"She lives downstairs. I have a townhouse on West Seventy-fifth, and she lives in my maisonette."

A lawyer, a daughter, a townhouse. "You'll come back soon?" Lillian asks.

22

You Seem Good

THERE IS NO PRESS loitering outside Henry's house, and Thalia's apartment is dark. The streetlamp allows him to see a long white florist's box leaning against her door. Shall he call her? No: too anxious, too custodial. But once inside his own door, conjuring the unknown quantity that is Leif—the sheer size of him and the sociopathy of his movies—Henry rings her cell.

"Can you talk?" he asks, as music thumps in the background.

"Sort of," she yells.

"I mean is Leif right there?"

"Leif? No. He didn't want to come."

"Come where?"

"To Trance. It's a club."

Henry knows it's a club, Philip's club. "So he just dropped you off and went home?"

"I can't hear you," she yells, then volunteers, "Philip gets off at two."

He thinks of what a mother might ask an unmarried daughter in this uncommitted city: *Are you chasing this boy? Shouldn't you let him make the first, second, and third moves?* Instead he says, "You know best. I'm here. Come for breakfast."

"Don't worry, you," she says.

He runs a deep bath, turns on the Jacuzzi jets, sinks in. Yo-Yo Ma and Emanuel Ax are playing Beethoven through the newly installed bathroom speakers. He closes his eyes and smiles. When was the last time he entertained a thought close to *Life is good*? Immediately, this unaccustomed peace concerns him. He searches his mind for anxieties that will protect and balance his good fortune. There's always Thalia's psychosexual judgment, which might not be as sound as it could be. There's Denise to worry about . . . no, *worry* is too strong; Denise is a potential burden and pain in the ass. But then again, without her reentry there would be no Thalia at a parental crossroads. And most assuredly no Todd.

He runs more hot water. What about the promises he made to himself with respect to good deeds in early retirement? He should get going on the pro-bono work, on volunteering, on finding a legal clinic where the indigent need help with their tax returns. He leaves the tub and returns with the legal thriller he was reading in lonelier days. He'll buy smoked salmon when Zabar's opens, or find some frozen Belgian waffles he'll dress up with berries and whipped cream. Once again he thinks of Celeste. All of this would please her. Odd how an unusual number of blessings have rained down on him since he lost Celeste. Immediately, he chastises himself for the quasi-religious thought of fairy dust sprinkled by the dead. He thinks of Leif's box of flowers, unattended, and feels a twinge of pity for someone less fortunate than himself.

His landline rings at 9:00 A.M., and it's Todd asking jovially, "Do you want the good news or the bad news first — and relatively speaking, the bad news isn't half-bad."

"You choose."

"The good news is patently obvious: Lillian adores you. She adores me — no change there, except now she can sleep at night. There's the worry that you'll drop me for someone who has a swankier job, but she's not going to dwell on that. She's dying to see your house and meet Thalia, but I'm not supposed to tell you that. Of course I didn't say a word about Leif and the engagement plot. How did it go, by the way?"

"I don't know. We spoke for thirty seconds from the club where her deejay friend works."

"With or without Leif?"

"He was invited but declined. Not his scene. I'm sure she figures it's something like a last fling before the publicity blitz begins."

"Did she come home?"

"Can't say. I know her friend wasn't getting off work until two."

"Welcome to your new life — wondering if the kid made it home safely."

Henry says, "Not unwelcome, my new life."

"What's a decent hour to call down there?"

Henry laughs. "Now who's worrying about her safe return?"

Todd says, "You give me too much credit. It's the tittle-tattle I'm after." He reminds Henry that he hasn't heard the bad news yet, so here it is: Denise wants to throw them a cocktail party.

"Because?"

"Because she's thrilled that her matchmaking succeeded, and it would be a reason to reach out to some friends who aren't speaking to her."

"Did you tell her that widows should wait a year before they throw parties?"

"I didn't. But I did say, 'I don't think that's necessary. We can just have a quiet little get-together'—don't shoot me—'just the three of us.' That was my guilty conscience doing the inviting. If you don't want to come, that's fine. Although she did say she refuses to lose you as a friend after all those years of being estranged."

Henry says, "Or maybe we're in a contest for Thalia, and Denise wants to keep an eye on the competition."

"It could be both—she wants to win *and* she needs a friend. She said you were the nicest man she ever married."

"How kind of her to notice," says Henry.

Of course he would run into Sheri Abrams at the smoked fish counter at Zabar's. Without being asked, he volunteers that everything is great. The person he's seeing is named Todd. "You'd like him. I've met his mother."

Because Sheri appears unmoved, he elaborates. "And with Thalia living in my house, I recognize that I'm acting like a father. I have to think about things like, *Did she get home last night?*" Her blank reaction puzzles him, until he sees that his ex-shrink is sharing a shopping basket with a tweed-jacketed man who has the very fine white hair and pink scalp of the Mayflowered.

Henry offers his hand and states his name. The man looks to Sheri for what can only be permission to speak. She says, a warning, "Henry and I have a professional relationship."

"Not to worry," Henry says. "I'm an ex-patient now."

"It's always a tricky situation," says the man.

"How's that?"

"We share office space."

"You've seen his name next to the buzzer a million times: Axel Rice, marriage and family counseling." She traces the air between herself and her companion. "But this is a new development."

"And shopping for smoked fish together is tricky *how*?" Henry asks.

"I used to be married to another tenant," says Dr. Rice.

"Who not only has her dermatology practice in the building, but lives there," Sheri adds.

Henry can't help smiling. "And didn't I date her in high school?"

Sheri doesn't laugh. "You seem good," she allows. "Really good."

"I'm in love," he tells her.

There is still no word from downstairs by noon. He's set the table, read the entire Sunday *Times*, rewrapped and re-refrigerated the two varieties of smoked salmon. At 12:30 Thalia calls upstairs, groggily. "Let me jump in the shower, then I'll come up. Am I keeping you from anything?"

"Nope. I bought bagels at H and H this morning."

"Ten minutes," she says.

Just before one she lets herself in through the kitchen door, wrapped in the faded periwinkle robe, hair wet, her feet half into untied running shoes. She hands Henry the florist's box. "*Pour vous.* I only have one vase, and it's currently in use. Give these to your sweetheart."

"Or his mom."

"I sense progress," she says as she slumps onto the nearest stool. "Do tell."

"You first. Sesame, poppy, or sourdough?"

"Just coffee to start."

176

Over the hissing and frothing of milk he hears, "Checking coats wasn't such a terrible day job, was it? I was a relatively happy person when you met me, right?"

Henry asks, "That bad? Those talking points you mentioned?"

"At first. Then imagine this: Leif. Flirting." Thalia shudders, a full-body theatrical spasm. "His advisers must have told him to act seductive in public. Which Leif interpreted to mean, 'Give the waiter reason to run back to the kitchen and repeat what you blurt out over the *amuse-bouche*.'" She compliments the artistry of his smoked salmon arrangement. A magenta baby orchid tops the little haystack of thinly sliced red onion.

"Now I give you Leif's leading-man impression," she continues. She pushes her wet hair away from her face, twists and tightens it to suggest baldness, then says in a monotone, "'I found the panties you were looking for this morning, Thalia. They were buried under the covers, at the end of my bed.'"

"*What?*" Henry squeals.

Thalia continues lifelessly, "'They were my favorites. Pink. Can I keep them?'"

Henry says, "Even I could do better than that."

"I couldn't resist. I had to say, 'The pink transparent ones with the butterflies embroidered on the crotch?'"

He delivers a cup and goes back to fix his own. "How did that go over?"

"I swear the waiter gulped. He said, 'This is from our chef, a mini sashimi of fluke with pickled radish.' Leif asked if it contained mushrooms, then returned to the script. He said, 'I've cleaned out a drawer for you at my place.' So I felt compelled to say, 'No. Put them in the refrigerator. They're edible.'"

"This, too, in front of the waiter?"

"Of course! That was the point." She smiles over the rim of her coffee cup. "Most rewarding."

Henry says, "I never liked this arrangement. We should have asked for a trial period. Or at least dialogue approval. Wouldn't you think a trained actor would know how to carry on a conversation?"

Thalia is peering into the bag of bagels. "Too many years of playing monsters — and monsters without lines, don't forget."

Henry repeats, "Sesame, poppy, or sourdough? Let me do the cutting." Her cell phone vibrates on the granite, two low growls. "It's him," she says.

Her side of the conversation is short, businesslike. "My place," she says. She looks up at the microwave clock. "Two thirty's a little better. Do you have anything like a tape recorder . . . ? Okay, bring that. Ciao."

"Philip?" Henry asks.

"Leif."

"Leif," Henry repeats. "In that case, you may want to take the flowers back. And also in that case, I'm completely stumped."

Thalia is discarding the fleshy inside of her bagel and dropping capers into the gullies. "It's my idea: Obviously Leif needs help, big-time — coaching, tutoring, rehearsing. We'll start with the dialogue. If necessary, I'll tap Sally Eames-Harlan —"

Henry is shaking his head.

"No? No Sally, or no tutoring?"

"No tutoring by you. Let Estime contract with Sally if he's so unpresentable and insufferable."

"Because it's extracurricular on my part? Not in my job description?"

Henry returns his bagel sandwich to his plate. "No. Because it's kinder in the long run to stick with the game plan."

"Because . . ."

"I think you know. Todd and I are quite sure that Leif already has a crush on you, or will develop one shortly. He could easily misconstrue these rehearsals as your wanting to spend more time with him."

Now Thalia is shaking her head strenuously and flapping her free hand. When she's swallowed her substantial first bite, she says, "No, wait. I left something out."

"He's gay," says Henry.

"Please. Has there ever been such an unattractive gay man? Wrong. The reason why I can testify that Leif does not and will not have a crush on me is this: He's in love. Deeply, madly, eternally."

"With whom?"

"I'm not supposed to say. Estime didn't want me to know, but when I told him I had a boyfriend — I know, a little premature, but a good move — he told me he had a serious girlfriend at home. I believe he even used the term *secret love*."

"And why is this a secret if the whole mission is to make the world think he's the object of someone's affection?"

"My question exactly."

"And what did he say?"

"He said it has to be a secret for a while because it might be viewed as creepy. Or worse."

"Meaning the woman is creepy? He showed you a photo?"

"No, creepy as in — don't freak — the woman is a girl and she's still in high school."

That does it. Henry's fears now have a name, and he is filing a motion on Monday.

Thalia says, "Please note I said *creepy* rather than *criminal*."

"What year in high school?"

Thalia winces. "Junior. But here's the silver lining: He managed to fall in love with the president of the Beverly Hills High School's Abstinence Club."

"I'm speechless," says Henry. "I don't know where to start. A teenage girl returns his affections? Is he deluded? Is she? Do they go on dates? And why, if it's all so kosher, does he need an elaborate series of faux engagements?"

"That part, the campaign, is separate. He needs to get his name or his mug out there to create an image of him as a normal guy. Then we do the math: He dates me for six months, then a hotter chick for six more. That equals one year, at which time — *voilà* — Caitlin will be legal."

"And she's going to wait for him on the sidelines while all this promotional nonsense plays out?"

"Leif said they have a secret pact, a pledge, a contract, whatever, and a year isn't so long. He did seem a little worried about being so far away. But I pointed out, even if she cheats on him, it'll be with a member of the Abstinence Club."

Henry is out of his seat, jabbing buttons on his cappuccino machine. "I still don't like it. And I don't like the thought of you alone with him downstairs, teaching him how to be a better flirt. You could be an accessory to a crime."

"First of all, I'm a big girl. Second of all, he swears she's a virgin. And third, aren't we a little happy for him? Isn't it a relief, cosmically speaking, that such a specimen could find true love in this cruel and superficial world?"

"We'll see," Henry grumbles. "I doubt it."

"It's all very wholesome. They met at a cheerleader competition. He was a celebrity judge and Caitlin watched *Land of Louie* in syndication."

"Does she have parents? Do you have her last name?"

"Eat your bagel," says Thalia.

23

Who Jumps to Such a Conclusion?

HENRY IS TOO POLITE to turn his back on Denise indefinitely. This morning's voice mail — initially ignored from the treadmill across the room — begins with, "Guess who has a job? But that's all I'm telling. Don't call me for the details." A laugh. "How's that for reverse psychology?"

He makes it to the phone just in time. "Job?" he asks.

"You're there! Yes, a job — I'm in real estate! With Stribling."

"How is that possible?"

"You mean, how am I employed in real estate without any experience other than going to open houses for the fun of it?"

"Precisely."

"You know how these things happen — serendipity! Being in the market myself — well, if you can call my pitiful price range the market — I was meeting with an agent and she was apologizing for being late, distracted, phone interruptions, all of that. She said her assistant hadn't shown up for a week. I said, 'That's outrageous. I would never do that. I'd fire anyone who didn't show up for a week . . . Are you hiring?' That was a Tuesday. I started Wednesday. I love it. I'm getting much better on the computer, and I'm learning very practical skills."

"Such as?"

"I make coffee for the visiting clients. And chai. Do you know what that is? We use instant. I make appointments, I change appointments, I clip our ads from the classifieds. I call the newspapers and yell if there are typographical errors, which I now call typos."

"Are you getting benefits?" Henry asks.

"Don't be a wet blanket! You're supposed to say, 'Congratulations! I knew you'd land on your feet.' No, there aren't any *benefit*-benefits, but I'm learning a lot, and if I combine my paycheck with my monthly allowance, and I sell my jewelry, I'll get by."

The last door Henry wanted to open is the one marked "legal adviser." But the phrase "I'll get by" prompts him to ask if she's consulted a matrimonial lawyer or just the attorneys in her social circle.

"I thought you'd never ask!"

"I'm a corporate lawyer, Denise. Pre-nups aren't my bailiwick."

"But you must have the right kind of lawyer in your firm. Who did your will?"

When Henry merely grunts, "George," and nothing more, she asks, "Are you still mad at me? I get bonus points for Todd, right? If my worst enemy fixed me up with a man I liked, and it developed into a relationship, all would be forgiven."

Henry says, "I should have thanked you before this. You did a good thing."

"He's crazy about you! And Thalia—everyone's favorite human being. How is your stepdaughter-slash-new tenant?"

Henry has prepared for this question. He says, "She's fine,

working on her craft. Going to auditions. All those things that actress-hopefuls do."

"Do you think I should call and tell her about my job?"

"Up to you."

"I'm looking for a little guidance here, something in your voice that says she misses me. She feels sorry for me. She misses Glenn. She wants to get past whatever unforgivable thing she thinks I did. Do you know if she's going to be home tonight?"

"I don't know. She's out a lot. Happily, she has many irons in the fire."

"What kind of irons?"

"Work. Gigs."

"Does she have a boyfriend?"

Should he say *no* or should he say *several*? He is saved from fashioning an answer because her toast pops up. She says, "I'll call her today and I'm sure one of us will give you a report."

The phone rings within minutes. Denise, who must have just sat down with her toast and *Daily News,* shrieks in Henry's ear, "Ohmigod! Oh. My. God!"

"What's wrong? Are you okay?"

"You won't believe it! It's Thalia! I was leafing through it and I swear it's her. I almost had a heart attack."

"What page?" Henry asks.

"What page? Is that all you want to know? It's the gossip reporters, the married ones, Rush and Molloy, their page, with a big picture."

"Can you read me what it says?"

"It says, 'Horror helmer Leif Dumont haunting Gotham.'"

"What else?"

"It says under the picture, 'Boo, from nineties sitcom *Land of Louie,* above, with companion, makes a swift exit from chef Thomas Keller's Per Se.'"

"'Companion'? Not her name?"

"No name. She's getting into a limo ahead of him, and she's wearing a very low-cut dress, *very* low for her. If it isn't Thalia she has a bosomy twin."

"It *is* Thalia," he says. "I'm just surprised her name's not there."

"This guy, this Leif, looks like death warmed over. He's old and bald. Or maybe he's not bald. Or old. Maybe it's shaved. He doesn't look like her type at all. Why is she suddenly out on a date with someone who can afford to eat at Per Se?"

"He's an actor," Henry says. "She knows him through work. And he's not old. He's under forty."

"What kind of work? Are they on a project together?"

"Something like that."

He thinks he hears — please may he be wrong — Denise sniffling. "Are you crying over a silly photo?" he asks.

"I'm not crying over a silly photo. I'm crying over what it says to the world."

"Which is what? That she's dating a character actor?"

Denise spits out, "'Dating'! Look at her. The red dress, the big hair, the fuck-me shoes! Does the term *escort* not spring to mind?"

"You're hysterical," says Henry. "Your daughter is not an escort. I happen to know that this was a blind date and she's doing him a favor."

"A favor? A blind date? If I were going to run an escort service I'd *name* it 'Blind Date'! That's not what a mother wants to hear. If it's a real blind date, who fixed them up?"

"Sally Eames-Harlan," he says coolly.

"Why do you know so much? Does Thalia call you up and report on who she's met and where she's going? Because you're sounding as if you knew her picture was going to be in the paper."

"How does anyone know that?"

"Because who calmly asks, 'What page?' when someone hears his stepdaughter's picture is in the *Daily News*? You weren't thinking *gossip column*. You were thinking *police log* because you know what these gigs are. And why besides sloppy reporting isn't her name in there? Because she refused to give it. Don't you know the way the world works?"

"I'm dignifying none of this. You're insulting her and you're insulting me to suggest I'd sanction this, as if my gay moral fiber wouldn't even know right from wrong."

"Oh, please. I'm only saying find out something, anything, that proves this is a real blind date and not a trick."

Desperate to end the conversation, Henry barks, "Fine. I'll speak to her."

"And you'll get back to me? Because you're not so great at returning phone calls."

"Because we weren't on speaking terms for a while."

"And even though I pissed you off again, you'll still take a look at my pre-nup?"

"I'm sure there's nothing —"

"Can I bring it by? Or should we meet for lunch? Or I could cook dinner for you tonight. Veal saltimbocca. I never cook anymore. Or if that's too much too soon, you and Todd could take me out for a drink to celebrate my new career."

"I don't know. I have to recover from this. Maybe a drink next week. I'll check with Todd to see if and when he's free."

"And you'll get back to me? Was that the rest of the sentence? See how real estate is teaching me to be assertive?"

He walks to the nearest newsstand and buys three copies of the *Daily News*. There indeed on page twenty-two is Leif, convincingly projecting *C'mon, guys. Can't we celebs enjoy a little privacy?*

As for Thalia, it is true: Photographed from above, bending forward to enter the limo, she is revealing an expanse of skin that misrepresents both her outfit and her principles. Does she know? Should he call?

When he turns the corner to his own block, he sees her ahead, dressed in powder pink running clothes, sitting on his front steps. "When you weren't home, I was hoping you had a sleepover," she calls to him.

"Sorry — just a trip to the newsstand." Seconds later he is at her side, the tabloids in a fat roll under his arm.

"What's with that?" she asks.

He peels off one of the copies and hands it to her. "Page twenty-two."

"*Moi?*"

He nods, one firm, joyless nod. Thalia flips the pages. "Oh, gawd. I'm all boobs. The goddamn photographer must have had his lens down my dress."

"At first I was upset, too," Henry says. "But on my second viewing, I realized that the eye of the reader is naturally drawn to this" — he points to the sequined mummy peeking out between Leif's lapels. "My larger concern, given the mission, is that you're identified only as Leif's companion."

"Thank the lord!" She rips the page out and crumples it. "All that styling and primping for one hideous photo. Not a good start," she says. "Let's hope no one recognizes me."

When he doesn't respond, Thalia says, "I detect a meaningful silence. Who saw this and tipped you off?"

A better liar might say "Todd" or "anyone" or "no one." But Henry answers truthfully, "Your mother."

"Unacceptable!" Todd cries. "Leif should fire that *farshtinkener* public relations firm. The whole point of this . . . what does one call it? — charade! — is to get Thalia's name and face out there. Thalia. Archer. Actress. How hard is that? Who'd you call?"

It is Todd's lunch hour. They are sitting on a bench in Central Park, each holding half of a bulging pastrami sandwich.

"Two schools of thought here," Henry answers, carefully drawing a squiggle of mustard across his bread. "One is that Thalia was cheated because she wasn't identified, and the other, advanced by the subject herself, is that she's lucky she *wasn't* named."

"Did anyone call in a correction?" Todd persists.

"She doesn't want a correction."

"I don't get it. This is a nice juicy piece of gossip: 'We now know who was seen leaving Per Se with actor/director/producer Leif Dumont: actress Thalia Archer, whose credits include *The Devil Wears Prada.*' Look, it's right here: gatecrasher at daily news dot com. It's practically an invitation."

"Can't. I checked the contract. It assigns all publicity initiatives to Estime International."

"This is so not a publicity initiative! This is a citizen journalist who happened by the Time Warner Center as Leif Dumont was ducking into a limo with fan fave Thalia Archer. Besides, I don't think there's anything wrong with the photo. Granted, you can't see much of her face. And I know this fact may astonish you, but breasts sell newspapers." He opens his half of the sandwich, says, "Nice and lean. Good work." Then, "You know who's gonna love this and hate it at the same time?"

"Your mother?"

"Your ex! I bet she picks up the phone and calls Thalia, and poof, they're talking again."

"Not even close," says Henry.

With his mouth full, Todd gestures, *C'mon, out with it.*

Henry recites, "Because of the word *companion*, because of the cleavage, because her date appeared to be an unattractive old guy throwing money around, because of the low-cut dress and cheap shoes, and mostly because Thalia's life and work are a mystery to her, our friend Denise has concluded that her only child is a woman of the night."

Todd's eyes widen above the sandwich, his mouth full. He speed-chews, then swallows with a theatrical gulp. "To which you replied . . . ?"

"Is there any question what I said? I yelled, 'What is wrong with you that you'd think that your wonderful, smart, accomplished, talented daughter is, what? A paid escort culled from the Yellow Pages? This was a blind date with a fellow actor. Who jumps to such a conclusion about one's own daughter?'"

"A nut case! And mark my word, when her fetching daughter continues to be seen with" — he checks the headline — "'horror helmer Leif Dumont,' Denise will keep digging and squawking. I wouldn't put it past her to go to the press herself. Or call in the vice squad."

"So now what? Do I keep this to myself? Do I warn Thalia that her mother is advancing a slanderous theory?"

"The latter, definitely: Warn her. If I know Thalia, she'll find the whole cockamamie theory entertaining. And who knows? It could lead to a phone call, which could lead to a lunch, which could lead to Thalia confiding in Denise about signing a contract with Leif, which could lead to the end of the mother-daughter rift. Peace could be as close as one more teeny little breach of the confidentiality clause."

Henry says, "I don't want Denise on the team. Denise is not to be trusted. Whatever inane thoughts pass through her brain end up in a diatribe. Or a eulogy, for chrissakes. And I haven't even given you her whole critique."

Todd says, "I have exactly ten minutes before I have to be back at work, so start now."

Henry eats his last bite of sandwich so he can count on his fingers. "She thought the hair was too big. The dress wasn't Thalia. And before, when I said she called the silver sandals cheap? That was me being euphemistic because you helped pick them out. The actual descriptor was 'fuck-me shoes.'"

Todd sputters, "What's a girl supposed to be wearing with red chiffon? Spectator pumps? Did Fashion Plate Krouch say anything about the dress? Because it could *not* have been a better choice. And where did she get 'old guy'? Did you tell her that Leif Dumont is young enough to be her son?"

How lovely to have a thin-skinned champion in his corner. "I shall immediately," Henry says.

24

I Can't Stay Long

DENISE, IN A BLACK PANTSUIT and exceedingly high, pointy pumps, delivers a legal-size envelope the next morning. Henry doesn't explicitly invite her in, but because he is holding a mug of coffee she chirps, "Would love to, but I'm no longer a lady of leisure. Work starts in thirty-five minutes."

"It's a five-minute cab ride across the park," he points out.

She reaches into an outside pouch of her huge black pocketbook and flashes a MetroCard. "Bus," she says. "It goes straight across Seventy-second, if you get on the right one."

"The M seventy-two." He smiles. "You may want to write that down." He reaches for the envelope. "And this is for me? The pre-nup?"

"With a cover letter. I didn't know who it was going to, so I just wrote, 'Dear Attorney.'"

"George Quirke. I think you remember George. From the firm?"

Denise, who has started her descent, stops, looks up. "The Quirke who handled our divorce?"

"Correct. Good man. Knows everything there is to know about pre-nups."

"Is he the only divorce attorney in your old firm?"

"Yes," Henry lies.

"I didn't mean he was a bad lawyer. I just meant is he still mad at me for what I did to you?"

MetroCard in hand, a brown lunch bag visible from the purse he recognizes as a knockoff, Denise appears atypically sympathetic this morning. He says, "George is the consummate professional. He holds no grudges." Opening the door wider, he says, "How about if I give it a quick read now? You have time. I'll put you in a taxi."

She offers her hand as if they were partners at the edge of a dance floor. "I was telling my boss about your place," she says.

Two steps over the threshold, she looks up. "How would you describe your ceiling? Domed? Vaulted? And these— Did you know that sconces go with the property unless the seller specifies that they're not included? This chandelier, too."

He gestures toward the kitchen. "Coffee while I read?"

Denise checks her watch. "Is it one of those French press ordeals?"

"No. Ten seconds. I just push a button."

Denise follows him toward the back of the house, high heels clicking sharply enough to cause him concern for his parquet floor. At the kitchen door he freezes. Sitting on the counter, guarding the coffeemaker, in drawstring gym pants and a Coney Island Lager T-shirt, is Thalia.

He has not seen this Thalia before: the cold and contemptuous one. "How long have you been here?" he asks.

Pointing to her mug, she says, "When this was full. Three minutes ago? Four? And then I decided to stay and eavesdrop."

"It's nice to see you," says Denise. "Finally."

Thalia executes a slow, bovine blink, but says nothing.

"I can't stay long," says her mother. "I have a job. Part-time."

"Doing what?"

Denise opens her pocketbook and finds a silver case from which she extracts a business card. "Here. This is my boss."

"Real estate," Henry says. "Your mother calls herself a gal Friday."

Thalia takes the card. "Interesting. Girl Friday. Is that anything like my job?"

"Job?" says Denise. "Really? Henry didn't mention a word!"

"Gee, I could have sworn you were fully briefed. I'm a paid escort, remember? Streetwalker. Harlot. Call girl. Trollop. Isn't that what a mother deduces when her daughter's picture shows up in the *Daily News* wearing a party dress?"

Denise stares, first at Thalia, then at Henry. "I assume I have you to thank for passing along that little slip of the tongue?"

"Don't worry," Thalia says. "I'll use this, believe me. I can already see my friends laughing, ha-*hah!*" — an imaginary cigarette holder in play — "when I tell them my mother saw my picture in the paper and deduced — what else would a supportive mother deduce? — that I was turning tricks. I can't wait. Another Denise anecdote for my repertoire."

Denise swings her bulging pocketbook in Thalia's direction, a safe enough distance to miss, but close enough to make both Thalia and Henry duck. "I lost my husband!" Denise cries. "I can't be responsible for every little thing that slips out of my mouth. I didn't mean it. I was thinking out loud. In fact, I'd already forgotten it until you brought it up. I can't do or say anything right, can I?"

Thalia turns to Henry. "That would be a reference to Daddy's funeral. Would you like to hear about that?"

"I did hear some of it," he says.

"I told you all of it!" Denise cries.

"And then Todd filled me in."

Denise asks, "Todd was there? Did he sign the guest book?"

"Who cares if he signed the guest book?" says Thalia. "What does that have to do with anything?"

"I only meant —" Denise cuts herself off and asks primly, "May I have that cup of coffee to go? Black is fine." She adds, hitching her pocketbook into place, "I travel by bus now, and they run on a schedule."

"In that case," says Thalia, "bye."

"Bye?" Denise asks.

"Or take a seat. Tell Henry what happened at the funeral. He's fair and righteous. Maybe I'm wrong, and what you did wasn't so evil. Maybe Henry will set me straight, in which case I'll apologize for marginalizing my grieving mother."

Denise turns to ask rather elegantly, "Henry? Are you busy? Would you like to walk me to work?"

"You're wearing stilettos," he says.

"Tell him," Thalia persists. "Or I will."

Denise heads for the coffee machine. "I'll do it myself. Which button do I push?"

Thalia reaches around her and hits the button that starts the grinding of the beans. Henry slips a mug under the spout. Denise slumps, both hands bracing herself against the edge of the counter.

"Are you all right?" Henry asks.

She turns around. "Was this a trap?"

Henry says, "I didn't even know you were dropping by, Denise. Nor did I know Thalia was in the kitchen. That's hardly how one sets a trap."

"So she just lets herself in and makes herself at home?"

Thalia says, "That's correct. I walk in like I own the place." She points to the kitchen door. "That's our secret passageway. We dug it ourselves through solid rock. I come up — what would you say, Henry? Four, five, six, ten times a day?"

"She doesn't have a coffeemaker," says Henry.

"His is excellent," says Thalia.

Denise points to the refrigerator. "Do you have half-and-half?"

"Denise," Henry tries. "I think it would be very good if we cleared the air. Maybe there's been a misunderstanding. Maybe Thalia's upset about something that you said in jest. Or that just slipped out, like the escort service."

"Ha!" says Thalia. "Not this time. This isn't some passing thought. This was the full Denise, center stage, foot in mouth. Tell him. Tell him about the uninvited guest who essentially took over the whole event."

"There's nothing to tell." She turns to Henry. "I thought it would look very peculiar if Eddie wasn't one of the pallbearers. I thought *that* would raise suspicion. I had no idea everybody knew."

"Knew what?" Henry asks. "And who's Eddie?"

"Glenn's first business partner."

"Eddie Pelletier, asshole. Her not-so-secret paramour."

"That is so unfair! He and Glenn were in sales together at 3M," Denise explains. "Then they set up their own business. All very amicable. So much so that when the partnership broke up, and they left the lawyer's office after signing the papers, they went out for a steak."

"Can you *not* tell a linear story?" Thalia asks.

Denise repeats, "My crime was asking Eddie to be a pallbearer. He also got up to speak."

"We all knew!" says Thalia. "I did, and the boys did. And you can bet my father knew —"

"All your father knew was that Eddie started calling me when he was going through his own divorce."

Thalia harrumphs.

"For advice!"

"Like every two minutes, at top volume. He's an idiot. And it was still going on when Dad dropped dead of — quite possibly — a broken heart."

"Your father —" Denise begins. She bites her lip. "Your father died of a massive heart attack, Thalia. And since not one word was ever spoken between the two of us that would lead me to believe that he suspected anything, I have to disagree with you."

"Did you really ask your boyfriend to be a pallbearer?" Henry asks.

"And a speaker!" Thalia cries. "You should have heard him. Not just singing Dad's praises, but weeping. 'Glenn and I this. Glenn and I that.' I would have thrown a rotten tomato if I'd had one."

Denise says, "I repeat: To have left him out would be like holding up a sign that said, *Your suspicions are confirmed*. And why, if everyone knew, didn't someone come forward when Glenn was still alive and say, 'We know what's going on. Cut it out. We're all on to you'?"

Thalia turns to Henry. "I did."

"But that was before anything happened! It was just a warning — we see what's going on — but all it was then was a mental and emotional fling."

"Yet you plunged in?" Henry asks.

Denise raises her chin an inch higher. "No, we did not."

"Oh, please," says Thalia. "You did, too. You think that the names of hotels don't come up on caller ID?"

Henry asks, "How long did this fling last?"

"What difference does that make?" Denise asks.

"I'm curious. I ask as someone whose marriage ended after one dinner-party flirtation: If Glenn had lived, were you going to leave him?"

"Moot point, obviously," Denise snaps.

"Why the hell is that moot?" Thalia asks.

"Why? Because I'm a widow. If I were going to leave Glenn for Eddie, I'd be with him now, wouldn't I?"

"You probably *are* with him. But now it's secret until—what would Denise Wales Archer Krouch consider a proper waiting period? Six months? Six days?"

"Eddie Pelletier was a mistake. Okay? I'm paying for it now. I think he was harboring some deep-down resentment about how well the corrugated box side of the business did—he took the twine and label divisions—and he was using me to hurt Glenn. Or his wife, who took him back, I should add."

"Lucky her," mutters Thalia.

"I'd like to say one thing in his defense vis-à-vis the memorial service, and I say this as someone who hates him, too. People walked out in protest while I was giving my remarks. Eddie was not on the program, but then he saw the mass exodus and didn't want the funeral to end on such a hostile note. He and only he walked up to the podium, led me down the steps, then went back up there to deliver the closing remarks."

Thalia says, "If you really believe that Eddie Pelletier wasn't making a fool of Daddy and himself and you and all of us, then there's nothing more to say." She crosses to the sink and sloshes first her mug, then Henry's breakfast dishes, in soapy water.

"Ever?" her mother asks. "Thalia?"

Thalia shuts off the water but doesn't turn around.

Henry opens a drawer, removes a dishtowel — a favorite, blue and white, French jacquard — and drapes it over Thalia's left shoulder. "I'll see your mother out," he says, patting it into place.

Dutifully, he faxes the pre-nup to George, along with Denise's cover letter, which states, "Dear Attorney: This is not the original document. That one was burned in our fireplace on our first (paper) anniversary and I have Polaroids to prove it. Shortly after my husband's death, his two sons dropped the bomb that the pre-nup was still in effect because the burning was only a symbolic gesture, alcohol-induced. They claimed that it was the same as if the document had been lost in a house fire. In other words, no dice. A fire doesn't make it null and void if three other copies are still floating around, one for each lawyer and one in the safe at work (Krouch & Sons Cartons, Inc.) where their father was constantly reminding them he kept his personal papers in case anything happened to him. We were married for 23 years and 10 months at the time of my husband's sudden death on a Stairmaster at 70 years of age."

Within minutes, and too soon for him to have read beyond the cover letter, George calls to announce, "This has the makings of a wonderful lawsuit."

25

The Perp

A T LAST, PAPARAZZI! Two men with long professional lenses are waiting outside Thalia's apartment. Henry, on lookout, would like to know where they're from and the degree, if any, to which this is genuine reporting. It's too late to call Estime in New York, and perhaps too much of a nonevent to call the parent company's answering service to ask, "Are they yours?"

What is protocol here? Thalia is out with Leif. Tonight's date is a late dinner at a restaurant behind an unmarked door in the Meatpacking District. After that, clubbing. Leif's driver has a list of hot spots, admission guaranteed. No, they won't be going to Philip's club, Thalia told him, then asked with an airy smile, "Would I do such a thing?"

One photographer spots Henry looking out the window and aims his lens at him, with a grin that says, *Only kidding; not interested in you, old man.* Henry would like to point out that they're violating his privacy, but he's quite sure that their presence has been bought and paid for by Estime. He calls Todd's cell and gets his voice mail. "Paparazzi, here," he announces.

Todd calls back, can't talk. "You're bored. Ignore them. Go see a movie."

"I'm not bored."

"How ironic," says Todd. "Because *I* am, and I'm at work."

"Should I tell them that she won't be home for hours?"

"And bake them a cake, too, while you're at it. Listen, hon — keep your distance. If you have to go out, brush right past them, unseeing, like you're under a gag order. Like you work in the West Wing."

"I think not," says Henry.

Todd has teased him: Get a stethoscope, why don't you, and listen at Thalia's door. Or why not just go all the way and bug the maisonette? He always answers that it isn't nosiness that keeps him attuned to the basement, but acute hearing. Where there used to be the silence of an empty three rooms, there is now his preternaturally socially active twenty-nine-year-old daughter. At 11:35 P.M., when he snaps off the news and goes down to the kitchen for a frozen yogurt bar, he hears music, loud music, rock 'n' roll music, much too early for Thalia to have returned from formal date number two with Leif. Listening at the door, he hears another sound: the clothes dryer, located in the unfinished, communal part of the basement. An opportunity! He won't pretend he's throwing in a wash — she knows Lidia does that — but he'll say, "I heard the dryer going. I wondered why you were home so early. How did it go?"

But it is not Thalia thumping out a beat on his appliances. It is a bare-chested young man in crossword-puzzle boxer shorts — not Philip; not anyone Henry has ever met. He's heard of this, the Goldilocks syndrome of breaking and entering, whereby the intruder raids the refrigerator or tries on clothes. It is too late for Henry to retreat unseen. "May I ask who you are and what you're doing here?" he asks, not as sternly as the situation might warrant if the young man were fully clothed, or looked less like a prep school lacrosse player.

The stranger, to Henry's relief, startles as if *Henry* were the trespasser. "I'm Alex — Thalia's friend. Sorry! I'm doing laundry."

"I can see that."

"I'm her roommate. Or was. At her last place."

"What address?"

"Mott Street! Four B. I'm still there. My place is getting exterminated, so she said I could stay here." The washing machine bleats. Alex says, "I'm done except for maybe one more dryer cycle. You live upstairs?"

"Correct. I own the building."

Alex extends his hand but Henry doesn't shake it. "I think you should get dressed," he says.

"All my stuff's in there. Sorry. I didn't expect to be running into anyone. Thalia said she was the only one who used these machines. You're the dad, right?"

Henry does not think it's proper for him to be carrying on a conversation with yet another handsome young man in Thalia's circle, especially such a well-toned one wearing threadbare boxers. He says, "I came down to investigate because I heard the dryer and I knew it couldn't be Thalia."

"We're just friends. I didn't take my clothes off until she left." Alex lifts the lid of the washer and stares into it. After a pause he says, "She sees me more as a little brother. I'm okay with that. I'll take platonic over nothing."

If he didn't know Thalia's crowded dance card, Henry might

cite May-December romances in the headlines and in the works of George Bernard Shaw, but he knows there is no room for encouragement. He asks, "So will you be leaving once your clothes are dry?"

Alex repeats in remedial fashion, "My place is being exterminated. It's toxic. It's not safe to breathe the air."

"I understand that. I meant, 'Will you be going out?' Which I ask because there are photographers outside. They're here because the man Thalia is dating is a producer, director, and movie star."

"Thalia told me. I had to look him up. Leif somebody, right? Used to be on a sitcom?"

"Leif Dumont. They're bound to ask you who you are and where Thalia is and what time she's coming home."

He grins. "Cool."

"What I meant is, they might think you live here. With Thalia."

"Can't I just tell them the truth? I'm crashing here because my place is being exterminated and we used to be roommates?"

"I don't know. This isn't my forte. The culture of gossip columns has escaped me completely until now."

Alex opens the dryer, feels its contents, frowns, pulls out a pair of jeans — still damp, judging by his expression — and explains as he pulls them on, "Here's how it works: D-list celebs want scandal. They act bad on purpose so it gets into the gossip columns and the blogs."

"Your point being?"

"My point being: I walk out of her apartment. I look a little — sorry, man — happy, satisfied, but deer in the headlights. I run. They put two and two together. They snap my picture. She becomes a blind item. Bingo: more interest in Thalia because she's cheating on her boyfriend!"

"If you really think you have to go out at this hour —"

"It's like, what? Midnight? There's nothing to do here. She doesn't even have cable. If they stop me, I can just tell the truth. I'm a friend. My place is toxic. She's got a futon. It is what it is."

"Do you have a shirt to wear?"

Alex opens the dryer door. He takes out a black T-shirt, feels it, puts it back. "Ten more minutes," he says.

"And Thalia definitely knows you're here?"

"Honest. She let me in. I saw her before she went out."

Henry can't help himself. He asks what she was wearing. Alex appears stumped. "Jeans, definitely." Then he pantomimes: things on top. "A blouse? Maybe two together. Like a see-through thing over a black thing?"

"Layers?" Henry asks.

"Yeah, layers. She looked pretty." He pushes a button on the dryer. "Mind if I do the whites when I come back?"

"From where?"

"Pizza? Beer? Know a place around here where they sell it by the slice?"

"This is New York. Pizza comes to you. No need to leave the house."

Alex grins. "That's what *my* dad would say: 'You're in New York City. Why go out and risk your life when everything's delivered? And what about homework, Alexander? Don't you have papers to write?' He wouldn't care that I had my last final two weeks ago."

"We're all pretty much alike," Henry agrees.

More excitement of the variety he doesn't need. He wakes to find Thalia and a fully clothed Alex eating cereal in his kitchen just after 8:00 A.M. Thalia is dressed in what must be last night's jeans and gauzy layers, and her hair is up in a slipshod ponytail.

"I have news to report, plus I didn't have any milk," she explains. "You met Alex last night, right?"

Alex wags a finger from the hand that is shaking more Cheerios into his bowl.

Henry says, "I would've thought you'd be asleep at this hour."

"Didn't go to bed."

"What's the news?"

"You might want to sit down," says Thalia.

Henry tilts his head in the direction of Alex.

Thalia says meaningfully, "Alex knows I'm dating Leif, and that we're in sort of a discovery phase, but it might be serious." She widens her eyes: *How was that for delivery and discretion?*

Henry musters his best faux father-of-the-bride inflection. "Are you about to tell me that Leif popped the question last night?"

"Not even close," Alex answers.

Thalia says, "I regret to say that Leif was arrested last night."

Henry feels a surge of grapevine adrenaline. "For what?"

"Are you ready? Fare evasion."

Spoken through a mouthful of Blueberry Morning, those syllables don't add up to an offense that Henry recognizes. He asks her to repeat the charge.

"Fare evasion! He jumped a turnstile. If they catch you, they arrest you — like immediately."

"Are we talking about a *subway* turnstile?"

"Do you believe it? In Times Square, no less. Cops everywhere."

"What an idiot," says Alex.

"Why the hell did he jump the turnstile and what was he doing on the subway in the first place?"

Thalia says, "I believe there is a twofold answer: He wasn't carrying any money, and he was trying to impress me. In flip-flops, no less. Alex, give Henry your seat, please."

"He did this in front of police officers?"

"MTA guys, but the police were there in ten seconds. And it doesn't help when you miss the train and you're standing around waiting for the next one like a shmuck."

"What the hell were you doing on the subway in the first place?"

"Leif sent Rico, the driver, home at midnight. He has a new baby. Which was actually very sweet of him. And he thought that taking the subway was kind of a date-y, young-and-in-love thing to do. He didn't have any money, but I said it was fine because I had my MetroCard —"

"You know what that is, when you wait around after you break the law? Suicide by cop," says Alex.

"They killed him?"

Thalia says, "Not that I know of; last seen being led away and arguing. I did not accompany the perp."

"What an asshole," says Alex, who is now sitting on a counter and peeling a banana.

"Would you mind if I had a moment or two alone with Thalia?" Henry asks.

Alex says sure, no problem. Okay to take an apple, too?

Henry waits until he hears Thalia's kitchen door closing. "Do you think the arrest was staged?" he asks.

"If it was, he's a better actor than I've been giving him credit for."

"Did he call a lawyer?"

"We'll find out!" she says cheerfully. She reaches into her back pocket and brings forth her cell. "Let's see . . . nope, haven't heard from him. Maybe he's still in the slammer."

"Doubt it. He was probably put in a holding cell, then night court. Lots of waiting in between."

"Too early to call," she says.

"I couldn't care less if he's asleep! He gets arrested on your second date! I'm checking the contract to see if there's any language covering this situation."

Thalia thumbs two buttons and puts the phone to her ear. Her expression changes, and she puts down her spoon. "My stepfather wants to talk to you," she begins.

Henry motions, *No, no, not yet. Didn't mean that.*

Thalia says to Leif, "He's furious. He's thinking deal breaker." She listens, rolls her eyes, puts him on speakerphone. Henry hears, "I suggested community service, but when they saw I had no other warrants, I was released on my own recognizance."

"But now you have a rap sheet, right?" Thalia scolds. "For the rest of your life you're going to have to tell HR people that you were arrested for jumping a turnstile like a juvenile delinquent, except you were thirty-nine going on forty."

There is no response, until they hear a forlorn, "I had to walk home."

Thalia claps her phone shut and asks, "Was I awful?"

"I'm calling his lawyer this morning. I have her card somewhere. Michele somebody."

"She's on maternity leave."

"Someone has to be covering. I guarantee he made a call, and some lawyer got to night court in time to plead 'showing off for his girlfriend.'"

Thalia says, "Let me know what the lawyer says. I'm going to kick Alex out and get some sleep."

Henry asks, "What time did all of this go down, as they say?"

"A little after midnight."

"And then?"

She smiles. "Meaning, was I out gallivanting? Not really. I was invited out for a drink by some people who saw Leif led away in cuffs."

"Men people?"

"Tourists. Very nice. From Amsterdam. Two brothers. Spoke excellent English." She pats Henry's hand. "Now give Toddy a call and entertain him with the latest *scandale*. He'll be so happy."

"He'll be outraged. He's very devoted to you," Henry says.

Thalia reaches across the island to pinch Henry's cheek. "Translation: He's very devoted to *you*."

"He brought me home to meet his mother. Now she wants to meet you."

"His mother! How adorable. Did she love you?"

Henry's face reddens. "She's only met me once. I'm thinking of getting everyone together for a brunch on Sunday."

"Is he her only child?"

"Correct."

"So I could be something like a surrogate granddaughter-in-law. I can do that." She twists her wrist in the air. "I'm very versatile, wouldn't you agree?"

Unbelievably versatile, he thinks. *And popular: My daughter the crowd pleaser.* "Were the photographers still here when you got back?" he asks.

Thalia does *deep deliberation*, lips pursed and eyes narrowed. "Why, yes. I believe those two gentlemen I had sex with on the stoop were photographers. I made sure they got my name this time, and my best side." She fakes a yawn that grows into a stage-worthy stretch. "Ciao, darling. Must get my beauty rest now."

"In other words?"

"Stop your worrying," she says.

26

A Pledge to That Effect

H E CAME TO APOLOGIZE," Thalia tells Henry. "You could be a little more gracious. It's not like he can unring the bell."

Henry gets up from the leather couch where all three had been sitting abreast and stands before the fireplace. After rearranging a line of miniature Union soldiers, alternating the kneeling and the standing ones, he turns around. "We're nine days into this campaign, and what do you think you've accomplished?"

When Thalia opens her mouth, Henry says, "Let him."

Leif says, "The photos of me in the papers. That's been good."

"Good? Movie stills of you as a ghoul don't exactly say 'leading man,' do they? Isn't that the point? To stop typecasting you?"

"There's time," says Thalia.

"They're supposed to have a new headshot of me on file, but they seem to like the old ones better," Leif says.

"I don't think it's a matter of *like*," says Thalia. "I think it sells more newspapers to run a picture of you as a zombie ax murderer."

Leif runs the palm of his hand across the top of his head. "Do you think this was a mistake?"

"Whose idea was it?" Henry asks.

"The barber's. My hairline is receding" — he lowers his head to show the pattern — "and what's coming in is too gray."

"Too gray for what?" Henry asks.

"For a guy with my coloring, he thinks."

Thalia says, "In general, I think white guys shouldn't shave their heads. It ends up being too pale and drastic. How do you feel about it?"

"I think I look ugly," Leif says.

"Hair grows back," Henry says impatiently. "You can wear a baseball cap for a week, then reappear with a stubble."

Leif says, "I can't just get a baseball cap off the rack. My head's too big. I have to get them online. Bigdome dot com."

Thalia says, "I had no idea."

"I'm in the ninety-ninth percentile for head circumference," Leif says. He smiles proudly. "My mother always used to say it was because my skull was full of brains."

Thalia says, "If you don't like the gray hair that's coming in, there are really good colorists at my salon. And they'll do it upstairs so you're not on public display."

Henry says, "I don't know how many women you interviewed for this job, but I hope you realize that you won the lottery. Thalia seems to have some kind of missionary zeal to help you in the areas that need work."

"He means the stuff we practiced," says Thalia.

"We role-played," says Leif.

"He was Leif and I was me," says Thalia.

"I'd like to have a meeting with your people," says Henry. "Especially the new lawyer. Was she the one who represented you in night court?"

"He," says Leif. "The new lawyer's a guy."

"None of us was expecting this to take a turn for the criminal," says Henry.

"It was only a misdemeanor," Leif says.

"A criminal conviction nonetheless."

"Are you backing out?" Leif asks.

"No, he's not," says Thalia.

"I'm sorry about the turnstile," says Leif. "It just happened. It was an impulse, like when you walk by the Bing cherries in a supermarket and suddenly you've got a handful in your mouth." As he speaks, he is probing his inner thigh with the fingertips of his right hand.

"He pulled a groin muscle going over," Thalia explains.

Henry sizes up Seth Shapiro immediately—young, fresh from the gym, his dark hair gelled, a kiwi green tie—as starstruck and too young to be a partner. Clearly he is borrowing both a secretary and this office, with its bird's-eye maple paneling and its view of the Morgan Library. The nameplate on the desk says Alfred J. Ingle Jr., and a galaxy of framed photos show African American sons and daughters, capped and gowned. Henry, Leif, and Thalia sit in plaid wing chairs.

"How are we doing this morning?" young Mr. Shapiro asks, pen poised above a yellow legal pad. Thalia is wearing what can only be viewed as a costume, a coral gingham Williebelle frock with a square neckline and full skirt. It doesn't quite fit, Henry notes—roomy in the bust, and she's faked an alteration with safety pins.

Attorney Shapiro says, "I spoke with my colleague who drew up the contract, and she and I agree that our client's little excitement is very much in line with the goal of our campaign, which is, first and foremost, to raise Mr. Dumont's profile." To the right of the desk blotter are the relevant tabloids. He holds up the *Post* first and says proudly, "Page Six, no less: 'Boo Busted!'"

"It says 'Boo-*Who* Busted,'" says Leif. "I hated that."

"Poetic license. Not our province," snaps Shapiro, who moves on to the *Village Voice*'s "un-Fare!" and the *Daily News*'s "Two-Buck Duck."

Leif tells Henry, "That's because a subway ride costs two dollars."

"I taught him that," says Thalia.

"So why are we here this morning, other than the pleasure of meeting you and your client?" asks Attorney Shapiro. He smiles. Henry glances to his left to see if Thalia is smiling back. She is — eyes lowered, ingénue-demure.

Henry opens the briefcase at his feet and takes out a sheet of paper. "I think this answers your question."

Attorney Shapiro reads the paragraph, hands the paper back to Henry, and says, "No way."

"What does it say?" asks Leif.

"Essentially, that if you engage in any half-brained and/or il-legal activities in Thalia's company, you will pay her one million dollars in damages."

"I won't," says Leif.

"Won't what?" asks his attorney.

"I won't break any more laws."

Seth Shapiro stands, picks up his legal pad, and asks if his guests will excuse him and his client.

"Are we leaving?" Leif asks.

"We're caucusing. And not for long."

After the door closes behind them, Henry says, "He's admit-ted that he broke the law on an uncontrollable impulse. His next urge could be to steal someone's car with a baby in the back, and you're nabbed as an accessory."

She whispers, "Are we negotiating? I mean, are we trying for a *half*-million dollars in case of an arrest?"

Henry shakes his head no.

"You're serious?" She takes the piece of paper. "A million if he jumps another turnstile? Whose pocket does that come out of?"

"No one's, because it won't get to that point. He'll think damned hard before doing something stupid."

"Then why not just a pledge that says he won't *do* anything stupid or illegal?"

Henry puts his finger to his lips. "Let's see what the other side has to say."

Thalia asks if he wants to share a croissant. While she is en route to the sideboard, the men knock and reenter. Henry watches Seth Shapiro watching Thalia, who is taking her time rather prettily, head cocked in croissant contemplation.

"Thalia?" Henry prompts.

"I'm trying to figure out if there's an almond one in here without actually touching them," she answers.

"I can ask my secretary," offers Shapiro.

"Don't bother," says Thalia. She takes the topmost croissant, breaks it in half over a paper plate, doesn't announce its flavor. "It's fine." She smiles.

Is she flirting with opposing counsel? Henry wonders. And is this tall, dark, handsome, and unmistakably straight associate flirting back?

"Please sit down," Henry says. "Let's not drag this out any longer than necessary."

"Sorry!"

When she's back in her seat, petticoated skirt billowing in every direction, Attorney Shapiro folds his hands on the blotter.

"We propose — and this is beyond fair — that if my client is convicted of a felony *and* incarcerated, Miss Archer can be relieved of her contractual duties."

"A felony?" Henry says. "I'm hardly worried about *felonies*."

"We're not giving you misdemeanors, period. Your client could incite him to smoke a joint or jaywalk, and she'd have effectively written herself a check."

"Except that I wouldn't do that," says Thalia.

"I want her protected," says Henry. "I want a driver who doesn't disappear at midnight. I don't want any shenanigans committed in the name of publicity. I don't want her name dragged through the mud because your client sets a match to his shoe or marches naked down Fifth Avenue."

Thalia laughs.

"I said I was sorry, and that I wouldn't do it again," says Leif. "I'm not a crazy man. I have my own production company."

"And he'll sign a pledge to that effect," says Mr. Shapiro. "Today. Before he leaves."

Thalia taps Leif's arm. "What if you broke the law again, even if you didn't mean to? My attorney isn't going to be happy unless you promise something in return."

Leif closes his eyes and keeps them shut as he says, "Caitlin knows I went to jail. She has a zero-tolerance policy, but she's giving me one more chance. If I blow it, it's over."

"Who's Caitlin?" asks Shapiro.

"His off-the-record girlfriend," says Thalia. "The love of his life. They're waiting until she's eighteen to go public."

"Where does this leave my client?" asks Henry.

"Safe and sound," says Shapiro, "which I *know* was at the heart of your codicil."

Fuck you, Henry thinks.

"I'll draw up the agreement and messenger it over to you before five today."

Thalia opens her patent-leather clutch and takes out a card. *Cards?* Henry thinks. *When did this happen?*

She hands one across the desk to the smiling Seth Shapiro. "You'll need my address," she says.

27

Handsome Fellow

LILLIAN WEINREB PASSES a dictionary-sized Tupperware container across the threshold to her host. "It's not for brunch, but for you later," she says. "My baked apples."

"You weren't supposed to bring anything," Henry says, "but how wonderful."

"Todd guessed you like raisins."

"Of course! Come in. Thalia is overseeing the sausages. Chicken, of course. And turkey bacon. I know you're watching your cholesterol."

"This house," Lillian is saying. "This house! Todd — do we have floors like this under the wall-to-wall?"

"Not a chance," he says.

"Come meet Thalia," says Henry.

Thalia waves from the stove, her hand in a quilted potholder mitt. She has dressed for the brunch in an outfit Williebelle might have worn to a rodeo: khaki green culottes, topstitched in red, with a matching bolero jacket and cowboy boots.

"And this is Thalia," says Todd, "currently channeling a Girl Scout troop leader."

Thalia blows two kisses with the hand holding a pair of tongs. "Chained to the stove, but is this your adorable mother?"

"Lillian Weinreb — who, I proudly announce, walked here from West End Avenue at a pretty brisk pace."

"He's killing me," his mother says happily.

When the doorbell peals, they are four at the dining room table, three-quarters of the way through the meal. Henry says, "Let's ignore that."

Another buzz, then a knock, then a faint, "Yoo-hoo, Henry? Anybody home?"

"Unbelievable," says Thalia.

"Her mother," Todd explains.

Napkin in hand, Henry excuses himself. He opens the front door to find Denise's knuckles raised for another knock. "You're home! I've brought someone to meet you!"

"It's not the greatest time."

"Thirty seconds! I'm not staying. But look! Meet my new life!" Henry looks down. Huddled against Denise's legs is a tall, skinny, long-necked, shivering dog, unmistakably a greyhound. "I adopted him! Henry, meet Albert Einstein. Say hi to Henry, one of the good guys." And to Henry, "He hates men."

"Handsome fellow," Henry says.

"I'm supposed to be socializing him. He spent his first three years incarcerated at a dog track. But I think he may be a genius. He comes to work with me and when I'm on the phone and being harassed, he seems to sense it. I can tell by his body language. Right, boy?"

215

Henry repeats, "It's not a good time, Denise. I've got people over."

"How many?"

"Todd's mother is here, and Todd."

"And I'm guessing Thalia?"

"Correct."

"Who has always *always* wanted a dog! Why did I wait so long? But I won't intrude. I'll just slip by everyone on my way to your powder room. This is what I've learned: You can't just waltz into a coffee shop and pee if you've got a dog with you."

Henry gestures with a mildly aggrieved wave of his hand: *Then go. Do it.*

He finds himself holding the leash. Albert Einstein doesn't make eye contact and doesn't budge. Denise reaches into her raincoat pocket and takes out a small plastic bag. "Liver biscotti, I kid you not. This is a little trick I discovered: I can make him do something he doesn't want to do if I give him a treat."

"Brilliant," says Henry. "You should write a paper on that." He shortens the leash and gives a yank in the manner he's seen executed by authoritative dog walkers. Albert Einstein slinks forward, whimpering. Henry leads him to a spot outside the bathroom. "Sit. It's okay, boy. Denise? Say something so your dog knows you didn't disappear."

"I'm right here, Albie," she sings out. "That's Mommy peeing."

He returns to the dining room to find Todd's mother sniffling into a tissue.

"She didn't know I was taken away at four," says Thalia. "She feels terrible about the lost years. Well, actually, we've moved on from tears of sorrow to tears of joy, based on our being reunited. Is that an accurate summary?" she asks Lillian.

Lillian nods.

"Was that who we think it was?" Todd asks.

"Correct. Just happened to be in the neighborhood and wanted me to meet her new dog." On cue, Albert Einstein releases a plaintive whine from the hallway.

Thalia says, "Will everyone excuse me?"

"You're not leaving, are you?" asks Todd.

"Of course not. I want to see the dog."

"Can we all stay put?" says Henry. "Denise is just here for a minute, and letting herself out."

"Is this the woman you used to be married to?" asks Lillian. "The one we were just discussing?"

"They're friends now, sort of," says Todd.

"I brought it on myself," says Henry. "Her husband died recently, and I wrote her a note."

The toilet flushes and water runs. The table goes silent, waiting for the final sound effect of the front door closing. Instead, it is the sound of six feet padding in their direction and the appearance of Denise and Albert Einstein in the doorway. "Hello, Todd," she says coolly. "Hello, Thalia. I'm not joining you. I was walking my dog. Pardon my scrubs."

Todd says, "Lillian Weinreb, Denise Krouch —"

"The aforementioned mother," says Thalia.

Denise is glancing at the sideboard where a platter of scrambled eggs is warming. "Henry, I swear. Is that the Salton Hot Tray we got as a wedding gift? It's held up this long?"

Henry feels it is necessary — after all, what does Lillian know of him and his manners? — to ask Denise if she'd like some eggs.

"I know when I'm crashing a party," she says, "and besides, there's a little food issue with Albert Einstein."

"He's skinny as a rail," says Lillian.

"No! He's a great eater. It's just that he thinks all food in sight is his because when you're raised at a dog track you don't know there's such a thing as people food. If he can reach it, he'll eat it. I'm working on that." She turns to Einstein and commands, "Sit. This is not for you," as she pulls out an empty chair next to Thalia.

"It looks like I'll be getting you a plate," says Henry.

"I'll get it," says Thalia. "C'mon, boy. I'll get you some water."

"One of the blue cereal bowls," Henry instructs. "Not the china."

"For the dog, that is," adds Todd.

"Come, boy," says Thalia. "It's okay," then adds with a wry smile, "I'm your sister, Thalia. We should talk."

Albert Einstein lets Thalia lead him out of the dining room, but not without backward glances of anxiety and longing.

"Finally," Denise says, "true love. That's what makes all the work worth it. Would you believe he'd never climbed stairs before I got him? I had to teach him, one foot at a time. Which is why Henry's front steps make such a great destination."

"He's not drinking," Thalia yells from the kitchen. "Is there some trick?"

"He's waiting for you to drink first," Denise answers. "Just lean over and pretend you're lapping some up." To her tablemates she explains, "He's so not an alpha dog. The vet told me to do that."

"Quite an adjustment," Todd says.

"I was lonely," Denise says. "I wanted companionship." She shrugs. "I hesitated because I know it's a huge responsibility, especially now with my job." She waits.

"What do you do?" asks Lillian.

"I work at Stribling on Madison. They're letting me take him into work for the first few weeks because I explained to everyone that he's never been alone, ever—you know they're raised with hundreds of dogs around—and he could go berserk and jump out a window."

Todd says, "Ma, Denise is the one who engineered the match."

218

"Do you know Todd from Gracious Home?" Lillian asks Denise.

"From *my* gracious home. He attended a party I threw for my stepsons."

Thalia reenters the dining room, sets a place and a cup of coffee in front of her mother. "Was I at this party?" she asks.

"Of course you were!" her mother says. "It was to celebrate your stepbrothers being elevated to full partners. You came in rags, and we had words about your outfit."

"*Her* version of rags," says Thalia.

Todd says, "Details, please."

"I remember distinctly," says Denise. "The seams weren't finished. It looked like it was inside out. And frayed."

"I still have it. I'll show you. Made in Italy. Silk. Dark chocolate. She's prejudiced because I got it at Daffy's for twenty-nine ninety-nine."

"I can't do anything right," Denise tells Lillian. "Ask the judge and jury. It's one reason I got Albert Einstein: unconditional love." She takes her plate to the sideboard and serves herself a tablespoon of eggs, one sausage, and four berries from the fruit salad.

Albert Einstein returns, his neon green leash trailing along behind him. "It's okay," says Denise. "Show them how good I am at being a dog owner. Sit with Mummy."

Albert Einstein's big mouth opens to bare all of his teeth. "That's his smile," says Denise. "Isn't it amazing? Greyhounds smile!"

"He's in love," says Todd.

Denise spreads her napkin over her lap with a flourish. "He never leaves my side, and that includes sleeping with me. Nirvana, he thinks! But let's not go there. I shouldn't bring up my big empty widow's bed."

"How'd you come up with Albert Einstein for a name?" Thalia asks.

"His racing name was Kill Bill. I wanted something from the opposite end of the spectrum."

Thalia tells Lillian, "*Kill Bill* was the name of a movie, starring Uma Thurman, and — little-known fact — she cowrote it."

"My daughter's an actress," says Denise.

"Todd told me," says Lillian.

"And she's dating a fellow actor." Denise pauses. "Whose picture appears in gossip columns every day. It makes for interesting breakfast reading."

"Would I recognize the name of your actor?" asks Lillian.

"Leif Dumont," says Thalia. "Like Leif Erikson."

"An actor," says Lillian. "I find that so exciting. What am I saying? *Two* actors."

Denise is shaking her head.

"You don't find it exciting?"

"Something's fishy," says Denise. "When your daughter's romance is taking place on the pages of newspapers, it doesn't feel real. Why, for instance, isn't he here today?"

"We invited him, of course," says Henry.

"But he's out of town. He's shooting a movie in —" Thalia snaps her fingers. "What town did I tell you guys?"

"Gettysburg, Pennsylvania," says Todd.

"A Civil War epic," says Henry.

"Are you going to be in it?" asks Lillian.

"He asked me, but I said no. I'd always have to prove that I got the part on my own merit, and not because of the casting couch."

"A figure of speech," says Henry.

"Are there any roles for women in a Civil War movie?" asks Lillian.

"Scarlett, Melanie, Mrs. O'Hara," says Thalia.

"Suellen O'Hara," says Todd. "But weren't you up for the role of Clara Barton, Civil War nurse and founder of the American Red Cross?"

"So true," says Thalia.

"Who got it?" Lillian asks.

"I can't answer that. One of our understandings, Leif's and mine, is that we don't talk about his casting decisions."

"Very smart," says Todd.

"Although I did carry on a bit when he pulled that Clara Bunyon rug out from under me. She was always one of my childhood heroines."

"Barton," says Henry. "Rhymes with *carton*."

"Was that on purpose?" Denise asks.

"What?"

"Carton," Denise repeats. "As in Krouch and Sons Cartons?"

"Completely inadvertent," says Henry.

"Denise's late husband owned a box company," Todd explains.

"Widowhood." Denise sighs in the direction of Lillian, whose wedding and engagement rings also rest forlornly on the fourth finger of her right hand. "One day I was married with no end in sight, and the next day — gone. Everything, and I mean *everything*. Which reminds me, Henry — I haven't heard from your lawyer friend Mr. Quirke."

Henry says quietly, "I'll give him a prod."

Denise blots her mouth, then says, "Albie? Should we hit the road and let the party pick up where it left off?" Albert Einstein scrambles to his feet. "Very nice to meet you, Lillian. Todd, nice to see you. Thalia: Anytime you're ready. Henry, would you see me out?"

At the door Denise says, "I am a woman without a country. Except for you, I have no one to talk to. I would appreciate it if you could help me smooth things over with Thalia. 'Civil War epic!' I recognize bullshit when I hear it. And I recognize the game you're playing: *Let's gang up on Denise.*"

"Thalia is a grown woman, Denise. I can't tell her how to feel about her mother."

Denise takes a step closer and grips his shoulders. "I'm desperate," she whispers. "I can't even say for what — family, my old life, my rotten husband. But I need someone at my side."

Henry does not want Denise's hands on his shoulders or this close-up of her smudged eyes and rouged cheekbones. "It's going to be okay," he tries, backing up a step.

"How do you know?"

"Maybe. I'm not sure . . . If George could do a little something with the pre-nup? I'd have to talk to him first."

"Do something? Like what? A loophole?"

"Not a loophole," he says. "Look into case law. Possibly find a precedent where the burning of a document proves intent . . ."

Now it is worse: Denise lunges to wrap her arms around his neck and to place a wet kiss on his lips. Albert Einstein growls. "Denise —" Henry protests.

"Was that so terrible?" she asks.

28

The Boys

I N MORE THAN thirty years' residence in Manhattan, Henry
has never been to Long Island City, nor taken the number
7 train. Krouch & Sons Cartons is a factory on the corner
of two city blocks, whitewashed brick, three tired stories high,
nearly windowless. A side entrance next to the loading dock
turns out to be the unceremonial front door. Inside, there is
no reception area and no receptionist. Machines screech at, he
is sure, unsafe decibels. He knocks on the closed door that has
"Office" hand-lettered on its pebbly glass. A woman's voice calls,
"Come in. It's open." He enters a room frozen in 1958, its floor
swirly green vinyl tiles. An older woman with unnaturally black
hair is seated at what might be an army surplus desk; behind
her, family photos are mounted on a Scotch-tape-scarred wall.
"You're the guy who called, right? About a family matter?"

"Correct: Henry Archer."

"They're expecting you." She points — there and there, separate offices. "Stick your head in," she advises.

What would one expect in a second-generation box manufacturer, once described by Todd Weinreb, astute social observer, as "Tweedledee"? Behind three-story wire in-boxes, and possible samples of Krouch corrugation, is one son and his paperwork. He looks astonishingly like his father, at least from the photographic gleanings Henry has collected over the years. His blond hair is straight and combed over a balding crown. His eyes protrude in something of an amphibian manner. Henry thinks: *Time has passed him by — a young man stuck in his father's chair.* "You wanted to see me about what?" asks this Krouch.

"I'm Henry Archer. And you are which brother?"

"Glenn."

"And Tommy will be joining us?"

Glenn pushes a button on his desk phone, says, "The lawyer's here," and hangs up.

Henry asks — pointedly; an etiquette lesson — "Shall I take a seat?"

With his eyes back to whatever paperwork had his attention before his guest arrived, Glenn mumbles something vaguely affirmative.

Henry begins with what he believes is full disclosure. "I'm not sure if you're old enough to remember that I was the immediate past husband whom your stepmother divorced to marry your father."

Still not looking up, but with a twitch of a smile, Glenn says, "I'd express my regrets, except you probably got the better deal."

Despite his own distaste and old wounds, Henry takes umbrage. "Your stepmother is suffering the loss of the man she was married to for twenty-five years," he begins.

"Twenty-*four* years," says a voice from the doorway. Henry

turns around and has one overarching thought: that son number two got the looks, the height, the hair. "Tommy Krouch," says the new arrival, and shakes Henry's hand.

"Sit down," says his brother.

"Where?"

Glenn rattles a folding chair next to his desk. Its unformed carton slats slip to the floor. Tommy flips the chair around so he's straddling it back-end-to. "So why are we talking about Denise?" he asks Henry.

"You can't possibly be here as her lawyer," says Glenn. And then to his brother: "He used to be married to her."

"I'm not here as her lawyer. I'm here of my own volition, as a favor —"

"Not a big grudge holder, I sense," says Tommy.

"I thought you were coming all the way over here to talk about Thalia," says Glenn.

Henry hadn't thought of framing the situation as an orphans-in-the-storm housing dilemma, but now he says, "I've taken Thalia in. And I dearly hope I don't have to do the same for her mother."

"What are we talking about?" Glenn asks.

"You won't be surprised to hear: your father and stepmother's prenuptial agreement."

"Which Tommy and I are not parties to."

"Gentlemen," says Henry. "Don't insult my legal IQ. You're co-executors of the will. Except for that pre-nup, Denise would have everything. My guess is, you hold its twenty-five-year benchmark very dear."

"Actually," says Tommy, "we don't. Because that would be the equivalent of celebrating our father's premature death, wouldn't it?"

What has Henry been expecting? Not thoughtfulness or dignity. Why hadn't anyone told him that the boys might be decent

lads? Thus far he's interpreted their walkout at their father's funeral as intolerant hotheadedness. But now he's wondering:
Could it have been their attempt at restoring decorum? Henry
says, "Of course I wasn't implying that. I apologize. I only meant
on the narrow issue of the duration of the marriage —"

"It's not greed," says Tommy. "It really isn't. It's more like this:
We hate our stepmother. Period. Oh, and one other little thing?
At the time of our father's death, she was screwing around."

Henry pretends that nothing impeachable has registered. "I've
consulted a partner in our trust division whom I consider to be
an expert on prenuptial agreements." Henry pauses; is he imagining a soupçon of worry passing between the Krouches?

"Go on," says Glenn.

"Simply put: Your father burned the pre-nup on their first
wedding anniversary, documented by photographs."

"How do you take a picture of a burned document?" asks
Tommy. "I mean, even if there were a photo of every page being thrown into the flames, and close-ups, how do you prove it
wasn't just a stunt?"

"It is Denise's contention that he meant it. And in the Polaroids, he's the one holding the match."

"Where are you going with this?" asks Tommy.

"To court," says Henry.

"In your capacity as Dad's wife's ex-husband and quite obviously her very close friend?" asks Tommy.

"He means are you romantically involved with Denise again?"
asks Glenn.

"I am not," Henry says. "Nor would I be."

"Says you," barks Glenn.

"I'm gay," says Henry.

After an unhappy pause, Glenn says, "But you were married?"

Tommy says to his brother, "Like you don't know a dozen guys in that same boat — married but gay?"

"Not a dozen," says Glenn.

Henry senses a shift: Will Tommy's social sensitivity lead him onto a statesmanlike path? He says, "We are quite sure that if this question goes before a judge, he'll be persuaded, particularly after twenty-four years, that your father's intent in burning the pre-nup was, ipso facto, the destruction, elimination, revocation, you name the synonym, of the agreement. In which case, with the bang of a gavel, Denise inherits everything."

Glenn says, "I don't think so."

"What does she want?" asks Tommy.

Glenn says, "We're not asking what she wants without our lawyer present!"

"I'll answer, then, without being asked," says Henry. "She wants to keep her domicile of twenty-four years. And half."

"Half of what?" Glenn asks.

"Your father's estate."

"When hell freezes over! She was cheating on Dad when he died," says Glenn.

"Allegedly."

"Fuck 'allegedly'! She could've been screwing around for decades."

Henry says calmly, "Not that I'm stipulating to that, but the pre-nup covers the duration of the union, not the beneficiaries' suspicions."

"We have witnesses," says Glenn.

"No, you don't," says Henry.

"Thalia," says Tommy. "On a witness stand? How would you like to be up against that in full courtroom glory doing — who was that actress who stole the show in *My Cousin Vinnie*?"

What's this? Henry thinks. "Thalia is busy," he sputters. "She's not a party to this. She's already being pulled in several different directions."

"Like what?" asks Tommy. "Is she still working at that hair place on West Fifty-seventh?"

"As far as I know, she's not."

"I think we're done here," says Glenn.

"Denise can't touch the business," says Tommy. "Glenn and I *own* the business."

"Shut up, Tommy," says Glenn. "We're not saying anything. We have the pre-nup in the safe, unburned, uncanceled, unrevoked."

"Talk to your lawyers, gentlemen," says Henry.

How many admirers can one unavailable young woman juggle? Henry asks no one but himself as he waits for a 7 train to take him to any stop where he can hail a taxi. Has Thalia's overactive love life made him a bad judge of simple brotherly solicitude? Tommy, he reasons, was just the nicer stepbrother, closer in age to Thalia. He's seeing social outreach where there is none. Aren't both Krouch boys married to women who left the funeral by their sides, in protest? He'd quiz Thalia or Denise on that point — except for now he wants to keep his Long Island City mission off the record.

He calls Thalia from the back seat of a taxi, safely across the Queensborough Bridge. "Lunch anytime soon?" he asks. "I have a sudden craving for chicken tikka masala."

"Like, right now?"

"Earthen Oven? One hour?"

"I could almost do that."

"Where are you now?" he asks.

"Not home," she answers.

• • •

She slips into a seat opposite Henry and blows a kiss across the pappadams.

He asks, "Remember when we first met? This was our plan: weekly lunches. And now look at us." He opens his menu and smiles down at it. "You, me, and Williebelle."

"Ran home to change just for you," she says. "I believe this is what your mother would have called a housedress. The belt is mine."

Pleasantly, unaccusingly, Henry asks, "Still seeing Philip?"

Thalia hums, scanning the menu.

"Philip?" he prompts.

"He's okay. Why?"

"Just making conversation."

She looks up. "It's not a huge deal."

"But?"

"We had a little — what shall I call it? — misunderstanding. Now fixed."

Henry is never sure where his conversation ends and cross-examinations begin. He takes several casual and dilatory sips of water before asking, "About?"

"A photo he took of me. That I didn't appreciate."

She is speaking with remarkable equanimity, Henry thinks, *considering that an incendiary device has just exploded in my head.* He looks around, judging waiter proximity. "A compromising photo?" he whispers.

"Here's the thing: I was in fact naked but I had a sheet over me." She runs a finger across her clavicle. "All the way up to my armpits."

"Awake or asleep?"

"Asleep!"

"Did he ask your permission?"

"No, but really — I don't want you to worry. He snapped it with his phone so there aren't enough pixels to do much with."

Henry says, his voice barely restrained, "You are to tell him in no uncertain terms — or I will — that he is to erase that photo of you."

"I already did."

"*And?*"

"He said he'd never e-mail it, sell it, put it out there, whatever, so it came down to a matter of trust."

"Oh, please."

"He said it never would have occurred to him in a million years that taking my picture would be seen as morally reprehensible."

"Because he was born yesterday? Every time you turn on the news you hear about some contestant whose wet T-shirt came back to haunt her."

She motions to the bartender, who sends over a waiter. "Two chicken tikka masalas," Henry says. "And do we want beer?"

"At the very least," says Thalia. As soon as the menus are collected she says, "Shall we change the subject to something equally annoying?"

"Sure."

New patrons are being shown to the next table, two women with enough shopping bags to identify them as out-of-towners. Thalia lowers her voice. "Estime told Leif on Friday that no one's interested in Thalia Archer. He needs to find someone the public cares about."

"Just like that? 'No one's interested in Thalia Archer'? Whose fault is that? What are you supposed to do? Get arrested? What nerve. What arrogance!"

"They're giving it one more try. With cash."

"For whom?"

"Paparazzi — the ones you can buy off."

The waiter returns with two beers and two pilsner glasses. "We're fine," says Henry, nearly shooing him away.

Thalia says, "I figured you'd be happy about this."

Henry the parent is happy. Henry the lawyer asks, "Were they expecting instant results? Overnight limelight for a guy who's been under the radar his whole career?"

Thalia shrugs. "He says he stuck up for me. Might even have said 'fought' for me. Hard."

"Because he wants to do the right thing? Or because it would be excruciating for him to start over with a new faux girlfriend?"

"The latter, I suspect."

"Such a web of lies," says Henry. "I don't know how I ever let you say yes to this scheme."

"Because on paper it looked doable. And because I was deluded enough to think I could pull it off." She returns the smile of the newly seated neighboring diners, who, Henry realizes, are enjoying Williebelle's paisley housedress and its mother-of-pearl snaps. Thalia turns back to Henry. "Please don't make your *au contraire* speech now about what a talented and delightful person I am."

"I won't," he says unhappily.

She hands him one-half of the last pappadam. "Although, if you wanted to say something philosophical and parental that puts everything in perspective, this might be a good time."

Henry picks up his beer glass, thinks, puts it back down without taking a sip. "How's this: Sometimes I look down the road, and I wonder what toll it will take. I mean, will you tell your children that you pretended to be someone's girlfriend —"

"For money! For alleged fame and fortune. Because a man thought he was so unappealing he had to hire an agency to hire a girl to fall in love with him?"

"Not true?" asks Henry.

Thalia reaches down into her backpack and brings forth a folded piece of paper. "See what a nice world we live in," she says.

It is a printout from a website, a place he's never visited, The Superficial.com. Above a photo — finally, the two of them together, by name, allegedly being turned away from too-hot Bungalow 8. The headline above it declares, "Thalia Archer Has Terrible Taste."

29

The Long View

S AN ACT of good faith, Philip has purged his phone of the evidence after e-mailing it to Thalia, who forwards the photo to Henry. He calls Thalia immediately to say, "Now I know for sure I've been corrupted."

"I doubt *that*," says Thalia.

"It's true. I could see this perfectly lovely photo of you on some website with a clever headline such as 'Wake Up, Thalia Archer!' The implication would be, 'You're a smart and talented girl. What are you doing with Leif Dumont? You don't need him to make your way in the world. In fact, he's proving to be a millstone around your neck.' Is that something Gawker or TMZ might run?"

Thalia says, "Neither. I think I'd find that on Fatherly Advice dot com."

He loves *fatherly*; at the same time, he's embarrassed by his pop-culture clumsiness. "Never mind. Stupid thought. I guess I was supposed to say, 'Good for Philip. He's an honorable young man.'"

"He's right here. Do you want to tell him yourself?"

Henry says, "No, thank you. I'll let you get back to your company."

"Are you doing anything today?" she asks.

He isn't; he reminds her that the retirement consultants all say one shouldn't do much of anything for the first six months. But he'll take a walk and read. He and Todd are going to see an early movie and have a late dinner.

He changes into his new brown suede sneakers and has one proud foot out the front door before ducking back inside. Denise and her dog are carefully descending Thalia's steps, one paw at a time. He waits and listens. Should he make a run for it or stay put? He retreats to the kitchen and within seconds hears footsteps on the back stairway, followed by a sharp knock.

"You there? My mother's at my front door," Thalia calls. "Can we hide upstairs?"

He opens the door to find Philip at Thalia's side, wearing drawstring pajama–like pants and a T-shirt that says "Audioslave." She is, thankfully, in her pink sweats. "Sorry, man," says Philip. "No time to get dressed. I'm Philip. We met on moving day."

Henry says, "Come in. Does that woman ever call before she shows up on a doorstep?"

"I was going to ignore the knock," Thalia says, "but I could see the doorknob moving this way and that. Like a horror movie. I thought maybe I hadn't locked it and she was going to come charging in. So we bolted."

"Is she still down there?" Henry asks.

Thalia asks, "Which window is your lookout?"

Henry smiles and says, "I resent that," immediately followed by "Either one on the south wall of the parlor."

When she's left the kitchen, Philip asks, "This woman — was she Thalia's mother, or stepmother?"

"Mother. Still is, present tense. Her name is Denise. You probably know they're more or less, despite drop-in visits, estranged."

"Was there an argument? I mean, did they have a fight and no one wants to be the first to apologize? Or is it more all-encompassing?"

"You'll have to ask Thalia. I do know that Denise mortally offended everyone with thoughtless remarks at the funeral of her most recent husband."

Philip calls out rather jovially in the direction of the parlor, "Come back. I want to discuss what the big deal is. Life is short. You'll feel bad when she's dead. Just go talk to her."

Thalia's head appears, peeking around from the hallway. "Do you know something I don't know? Is Denise sick?"

"Denise is fine," says Henry. "Annoying as hell, but as far as I know healthy."

Philip says, "I'm not speaking from any insider knowledge. I'm just asking, What did she do that was so terrible that you can't have a conversation?"

Thalia says, "I'd need a couch."

"What's the worst thing?" asks Philip.

"The worst? Okay. How's this: terrible mother. I was baggage from the dead husband, and it didn't help that I looked like him. I was like a chaperone on a honeymoon, except that it went on and on. She was always trying to please Glenn, to show that she wasn't the wife who'd had two previous husbands. She wanted to erase her history, so how does a kid fit into that?"

Henry is thinking two things: I'm learning a lot. And look what an in-depth and openhearted conversation she is having with this young man.

"So? You're a grownup now," Philip says. "She was a lousy

mother. She wanted to prove he was the great love of her life — sorry, Henry — but it's not like she fed you bread and water and someone discovered you under a trapdoor ten years later."

Henry says, "Philip does certainly take the long view."

"Have you and your mom ever been in therapy together?" Philip continues.

"They sent me to a shrink when she ran off with Glenn and I was torn asunder from Henry."

"They did?" Henry asks.

"I don't remember any of it except there were puppets and M&M's."

"What about now?" Philip asks. "Would your mother agree to family therapy?"

"Are you speaking from experience?" Thalia asks. "Did you hate your mother, then find out you didn't, but it was too late? Something tragic like that?"

"Not me. A friend of mine was always on the outs with her mother — young, like fifty, healthy as a horse. And she was hit by a car — get this — on the way to the post office to mail a letter to my friend."

"What kind of letter?"

"A let's-get-over-this letter. A love letter, essentially. Imagine what that's like: You get a phone call from your father hearing that your mother died, and the next day you get a letter from her begging for a truce."

Thalia says, "That's a *Hallmark Hall of Fame* first act. You made that up."

"Okay, maybe part of it. She wasn't on the way to the post office. But she was in a car accident, and when this friend came home from work there were two messages on her machine: one to call the hospital, and the other from her mother, calling from her car, like a minute before the accident."

Thalia says to Henry, "Note the use of 'my friend.' Very discreet. Must be an old girlfriend?"

"Irrelevant," says Philip.

"Too late. She's gone, headed toward the park."

"I didn't mean now, today. I only meant soon. Ask her to lunch."

Thalia asks Henry, "Would you like to step in and tell Philip what lunches with Denise are like? Or maybe you agree with him; maybe you know that mothers do die and it's better to patch things up while everyone's still alive. You can be honest. I won't feel ganged-up on."

Henry weighs his obligation to *honest* in front of Philip the stranger/arbitrator. Finally he says, "Speaking selfishly, I'd be nervous."

"Why?" asks Philip.

"I know why," says Thalia. "He doesn't have to explain."

"A bitter divorce that cost you your only child?" Philip supplies.

Thalia moves from Philip's side to slip her arm around Henry's waist. "Only for a few decades," she says.

Henry would prefer feeding only Thalia but has politely made omelets for her (cheese) and her guest (jelly). Upon receipt of his breakfast, Philip turns the plate forty-five degrees this way and that in artistic appreciation and says, "This could be in an advertisement for the egg council."

"It's really the single thing I cook well," Henry says.

"Are you joining us?" Thalia asks.

Henry says he had oatmeal an hour before. He'll just wash the omelet pan and get on with his day.

"What *is* your day?" Philip asks. "What keeps you busy?"

"He's retired while still youthful," says Thalia.

"You putter around? The workbench-in-the-basement sort of thing?"

Henry says, "I do the legal equivalent of puttering around."

"And I'm the workbench," says Thalia. She asks Henry if he has any juice, but no, sit, she'll get it. "Philip?"

"What kind is it?" he asks.

"Orange," says Henry.

"He meant, 'Is it from concentrate?'" says Thalia. She slips off the stool, gets the juice, pours each a glass in what Henry sees is less than loving fashion.

Philip says, "I know you're the go-to guy for Thalia in terms of her contract with Dumont."

Henry, at the counter, studiously wraps up the cheese and washes the cheese grater.

"Henry?" Thalia tries. "Come sit down. I'll do that."

Philip says, "I think I know what your stepfather is thinking right now."

"Which is what?" asks Henry.

"If I were you I'd be thinking, 'Who *is* this guy? It seems like one minute ago he was a total stranger and hired hand, and now he's her confidant. What exactly is going on?'"

Henry doesn't like *confidant* and now, officially, doesn't like Philip. He will ask Thalia as soon as they are alone if this is typical Philip conversation and does she find it presumptuous. But for now, as ever, Henry remains the good host. He says, "Thalia from the beginning, from moving day, told me that you knew about the Leif arrangement."

"I understand celebrity," says Philip. "I see people in the club whom I'd characterize as near-desperate for attention, and I'm not just talking about attention from a guy or a girl. I mean they want their name in lights and their million hits on YouTube. They put up with all kinds of degrading treatment from bouncers and drunken playboys to be seen as someone who makes it past the velvet rope."

"Yet you choose to work in that environment?" asks Henry.

"My club isn't like those pseudo-exclusive places. We're relatively democratic. And you know what? In the end, that's what's really cool."

"We're all going down," says Thalia. "In the *Twilight Zone* version of us we'll end up in a world with no tabloids, no websites, no cameras, no clubs, no hooking up. We'll have to live quiet Amish lives in western Pennsylvania."

"If there was no hooking up, I believe we'd be Shakers," says Henry.

"You should come by some night," says Philip. "We take reservations and there's no bullshit about 'Don't see your name on the list, dude. Sorry.'"

"I'm probably not right for your clientele. And vice versa. But thank you."

Thalia, sponge in hand, wipes down the island and says, "I think it's time we let Henry get back to his routine."

Philip asks Henry, "How well do you know this Leif character? I mean, has he sat around your kitchen and engaged you like this?"

"Not specifically the kitchen. But he's been here for a drink."

Thalia adds, "I brought him home to meet Henry before I signed up. And then he came by to apologize after he was arrested."

"I've rented some of his movies," says Philip. "They're not bad for the genre, but I don't see any irony in them — not dramatic irony, not situational irony. Nothing really clever there."

"I haven't watched them," says Henry.

"I haven't either," says Thalia. "And don't want to. I read reviews on Netflix so I'd sound like a student of auteur Dumont if the subject comes up."

Philip says, "I don't know how much Thalia's told you about my views on this mock romance —"

"Nothing at all," says Henry.

"This might surprise you, given my own investment, but I think she has to stick with it."

Henry manages to repeat, "Given your own investment?"

"Emotional investment," Philip says. "I thought that was obvious."

Henry says, "This is the first conversation we've had since your moving truck pulled away. That makes it hard for an outsider to gauge your emotional investment."

This would be the time and place for Thalia to back Philip's claim or to deny it, but she says only, "Tell Henry why you think I have to stick with it."

"My major was Ethics, Society, and Law," says Philip. "I think she made a commitment — not just by signing a legal document, but by offering Leif something deeper."

"Oh, really?" says Henry.

"Friendship."

"The old-fashioned kind," adds Thalia.

"So your advice is that Thalia, at odds with what the contract asks for — essentially to fake a romance and an engagement — should stick it out despite the early humiliations, so Leif Dumont learns lessons about friendship?"

Philip says, "Thalia likes to act. In the role of Leif's friend, she is forced to be her true self."

Her true self! Henry prays that he can quote every word, every presumption, for later reporting to Todd. He glances at Thalia, hoping for a sign, for her signature wide-eyed comic double take. This isn't what he sees. Instead there is a look he's observed only during mother-daughter hostilities. It marks, he believes, the end of Philip.

30

I Get It Now

WHAT FINAL LEAP through what hoop must Thalia take to establish herself as attention-grabbing arm candy? Neither she nor her counsel is invited to the meeting at Estime where publicist Wendy Morelli and the West Coast brass on speakerphone contrive this: that Thalia will finally make some noise. She will publicly and loudly accuse a pretty girl — carefully screened, rehearsed, and paid — of blatantly flirting with Leif at the Box (strings pulled to secure admission). A fight will ensue. Slaps instigated by a jealous Thalia will be exchanged and Cosmopolitans pitched. Leif will break it up manfully, and Thalia will storm out. He will stay and try his thespian best to flirt with the interloper but after one round of drinks will tip the bartender a C-note and next be seen in the back seat of a limo kissing Thalia. Columnists will write about the catfight because Estime will promise serious gossip about celebrity clients whom the news outlets are actually interested in. Next day, the bribable paparazzi will cover a shopping trip to Tiffany & Co.

Wendy Morelli herself delivers the top-secret plan via e-mail. Thalia forwards the e-mail to Henry; a minute later, before he's responded to or even read it, she is knocking urgently on his bedroom door.

"You won't believe it! Are you decent?" she yells. "I e-mailed you. I printed it out. Are you alone?"

"Todd is here," Henry says. "What's wrong?"

"Are you *both* decent, then?"

"For God's sake, come in," Todd yells.

She half opens the door and peeks around. They are in bed, a sheet pulled up to their armpits. "Oh, big deal," she says.

Barefoot, she is wearing a Hunter College sweatshirt over pajama bottoms. "It's over," she says. "I'm free. Those assholes!" She brandishes the printout, belly-flops onto a free end of the bed, and reads the plan aloud, voice dripping with disdain.

"Astonishing," says Henry.

"No, it's not," says Todd. "It's the culture as we know it."

"First of all, an e-mail! Wouldn't you think I'd be the first person in on a meeting where it's decided I'm going to start a brawl?"

"With counsel," adds Henry.

"Like I'd do this? Like you can control a situation like this? Is anyone going to guarantee that I won't get jumped or pinned —"

"Or Tasered," says Todd.

Henry says, "I don't want to say I told you so, but this arrangement was never meant to be enjoyed or even endorsed. You signed on for an acting job. And now they're staging the finale."

"I thought you'd be wild," says Thalia. "I thought you'd want to get a restraining order!"

Henry laughs. "On what grounds?"

Thalia sputters, "For — I don't know — battery! Ludicrousness!"

242

"Has Leif weighed in on this?" Todd asks.

"I haven't heard from him, but you know Leif: He does what he's told."

Todd points out that Leif's role is hardly unattractive: two girls fighting over him. In his wildest dreams!

"Neither of you are as offended as I expected," says Thalia.

"We don't have to be offended if you're walking away," says Henry.

Thalia is staring at the e-mail. A different message seems to be appearing between the lines. She looks up. "I get it now," she says.

"What's to get?" says Todd. "It's all there, step by idiotic step."

"It's a fake plan! There's no cc to the lawyer or to Henry or to Leif. This is a trick. They came up with the most ridiculous idea anyone could think of so I'd walk."

Todd says, "I'm not so sure it's a fake. I think this is business as usual for a nobody trying to be a somebody."

"What's that look on your face?" Henry asks Thalia.

She sits up, points to her own cheekbone. "This look? As in, *Your mission, should you choose to accept it . . . ?*"

"Uh-oh," says Todd.

Thalia writes back to Estime and cc's Henry, "Sounds fine. What would you like me to wear? And do you need to measure my finger for the engagement ring?" An e-mail silence follows. "They're stumped," Thalia tells Henry. "I wasn't supposed to cooperate."

"Coffee?" he asks. "Come up. I bought Sumatra yesterday."

They take their mugs to the library and sink in unison into the leather couch, feet on the coffee table. "Have you talked to Leif since the plan was hatched?" Henry asks.

She picks up her cell, waves it as if it's a product to be pitched on the Home Shopping Network. "Listen carefully and observe.

I am going to call him now and tell him I am looking forward to our performance at the Box."

"Smoke him out, you mean?"

"Correct."

"Are you going to ask him if it's a trick to get you to jump ship?"

Smiling, she presses one number, waits, then nods to Henry. "Leif! It's Thalia. Just wondering if you heard about the plan?"

She listens, then says, "In an e-mail from your publicist. So here's my main concern: Think we'll get into the Box?"

Her smile is fading. She says, "Okay . . . yup. I should have figured that."

Henry whispers, "Ask him how he feels about it."

Thalia asks rather soberly, "How do you feel about doing this?" The rest of her responses are all brief and terse: No. I see. Today? What time?

She claps her phone shut and says, "He wants to talk to me in person. Alone."

Later she will act out, complete with baritone impersonations of Leif, what she characterizes as their watershed heart-to-heart. Side by side on her living room futon, he confided that it could have been worse; that ideas were batted around which he absolutely could never have agreed to and would have meant the end of Caitlin.

"Such as?"

"I'd rather not say."

"You wouldn't mention Caitlin if they didn't involve sex."

He had looked away, nodded at the radiator on the far wall.

"Intercourse?"

He'd said, eyes still averted, "On videotape."

When Thalia laughed, Leif had asked what was funny about that.

"It can't be on the level. It's in my contract, no sex, let alone sex on tape."

He'd turned his doleful gaze back toward Thalia. "They weren't planning to show you in the video. Just me."

"Meaning they'd hire a body double for me?"

"No. Not necessary."

"What's left then?"

"Close-ups. Wendy thinks they'd be good for my image."

"Meaning they'd only be showing Leif Dumont having sex? How is that good for your image? All that says is 'I videotaped myself having sex like you other perverts out there.'"

"Wendy thinks it would get people talking."

"Then she's an idiot! How much are you paying her to come up with ridiculous ideas like *make a sex tape*?"

"I'm very tall," he'd finally allowed.

"We know that."

"And sometimes, when a guy is tall . . ."

"Are we talking about the length of your penis?"

Leif had nodded gravely.

"And Wendy Morelli knows this how?"

"She asked me! Point-blank. She must have figured this could be a possibility in someone who is six feet four."

"And you, I'm sure, said it was none of her damn business."

"No," Leif had told her. "I figured it *was* business. She works for me. I wasn't bragging. I told her I had a nickname when I was in high school, back when guys showered together after gym."

"I'd love to know," Thalia had prompted.

He had clamped his lips together and shaken his head sorrowfully.

"Nightstick? Pogo Stick? Long Dong Silver?"

"Just Hose," he'd whispered.

When debriefed, Henry and Todd exclaim, "And that's it? You didn't ask for specifics?"

"How does a guy answer a question like that? Are you supposed to know your own stats, in feet and inches?"

"A follow-up question was absolutely imperative!" says Todd. "And since when are you a shrinking violet?"

"And weren't you raised by a mother who specializes in inappropriate conversation?" Henry asks.

"I did go as far as asking if Estime International got to see the goods as part of their intake procedure."

"Why would she ask to see the goods if he's vetoing her idea?" asks Henry.

"Maybe just curious. Maybe she was taking advantage because he's got that autistic thing going and it would be like asking the slow boy in the schoolyard to pull his pants down."

"For science. Like a nurse," says Todd. "Like a urologist."

"Like I did," says Thalia breezily.

They are clustered on the sidewalk outside their respective doors, but now Todd says, "Shall we take this inside?"

"No. I have an appointment — nails — so I'll be quick."

"Tell me you didn't ask him to pull his pants down," says Henry.

"Guys, please. I've seen plenty of penises. I was looking only for quick and clinical. I wasn't going to touch it. I asked like I was being shown a dessert cart." She points to Todd's zipper. "*Comme ça*, very coolly: 'So? Can I see it?'"

"Thalia!" says Henry.

"Did he oblige?" Todd asks.

"Of course not. I told him I was only kidding."

"Good," says Henry.

"What a prude," says Todd.

"Can we get back to the subject at hand?" says Henry.

"Todd and I have lost track of what that was," says Thalia.

"Is Leif endorsing the big bar scuffle?"

She is backing away, pointing to her watch. "Gotta run. I'm thinking it over. I'm thinking: performance art. I'm an actress. If a director asks me to slap someone and throw a drink in her face, I'd do it, wouldn't I? In fact, I'd consider it a juicy role."

"That's different," says Henry. "If that gets your picture into a newspaper, it's a still from the movie. And then there's the whole other follow-up plan, if you cooperate: The world will think you're engaged."

"You'll get presents," says Todd. "First you'll have to write fake thank-you notes, and eventually you'll have to shlep everything over to Mail Boxes Etc. to send them back."

"I'm hating this more by the minute," pleads Henry. "I say we stop it now. If we have to buy our way out of the contract, so be it."

Thalia says, "I still think it's a trick. And I'm also thinking 'Fair is foul and foul is fair . . .'"

"*Macbeth*," says Henry.

"I know," says Todd.

"Stay tuned," says Thalia.

31

The New Neutral

ENRY IS ON an escalator with Thalia, descending into Whole Foods, when his caller ID alerts him to a male Krouch on the line.

"I'd better take this," he tells her.

"Meet me in Salsa," she says. "Or Chips. Or page me. Is everything okay?"

"Could be good news," he says.

In the lobby, he is not happy to discover it is the less sympathetic Glenn Junior calling. Sorry, no, says Glenn; no second thoughts about wills and trusts. "No one can reach Denise," he grumbles. "The listing broker needs to get into the apartment, but all she gets is an outrageous outgoing message."

"Outrageous in what way?" Henry asks.

"It's a speech! No matter what time of the day or night you call, you get her diatribe. Have you heard it?"

248

"I have not. And you're calling because you think I have some sway over her outgoing messages?"

"Could you try?"

"No," says Henry.

"Call her landline," says Glenn. "*Then* talk to me."

From halfway down the escalator he spots Thalia, discussing avocados with a grizzled produce man. He thinks, *I don't do her justice, worrying about her open and possibly promiscuous arms. She talks to everyone. That's all it is: good old-fashioned charm. She should run for something.*

When he reaches her side she says, "This is Omar. He used to work in the Chelsea store, but his commute is shorter to this one. And his fiancée is a cashier, at number nineteen today. Omar, Henry."

"How do you do," says Henry.

He listens in his kitchen with a pencil poised over a scratch pad. "You've reached the home of Denise Krouch," he hears. "Thank you for calling. I'm probably at work now, or, if it's a weekend morning, at the cemetery. If this is in relation to the alleged sale of my apartment, please know that I am in no way a party to that. Any such viewings or open houses are being scheduled without my consent. I repeat: I am opposed to the sale of this apartment by Glenn Krouch Junior and Thomas Krouch, especially while legal matters are still pending. Proceed at your own risk, knowing that possession is ninety-nine percent of the law. No visitors outside the immediate family will be let up . . ." A pause follows; Henry senses that Denise is wondering, *What immediate family?* Her tone softens to merely businesslike. "If you're calling about anything else, I'll get back to you as soon as possible. Ciao. Thanks. And thank you for respecting my privacy."

What's all the fuss about? Henry wonders. He rather enjoyed the oration. Would Thalia find this decidedly Denisean rant at all entertaining? Probably not. He phones George at the firm and asks, "Would you mind? It's only a minute long. If you think she's going to get into more trouble for this, give me a call." He tells Todd's voice mail: "You won't believe your ears."

He decides to make her office his destination and will tell her he was motivated by those marinated artichokes he once purchased on Lex. He walks by the office, once, twice, then pretends to study the photos of properties in the window. Neither Denise nor Albert Einstein is visible inside. He hesitates to inquire, knowing from decades of office etiquette that part-time receptionists should not be receiving visitors. Finally a woman with an intelligent face behind her fashionably narrow glasses opens the door to ask, "Do you have any questions?"

Henry says, "Actually, I'm not in the market. I was looking for Denise Krouch."

The woman's face registers what Henry reads as perplexity over the identity of a part-time nobody. He adds, "She brings her dog, a greyhound, to work? I think she's here mornings."

"Please come in," says the woman. "You are . . . ?"

"Henry Archer. A friend. I haven't been able to reach her and I was getting worried."

She invites him to sit in one of the chairs opposite the reception desk. "Denise," she begins carefully, "did not come to work yesterday. Nor did she call in."

Henry nods, waits.

"We called her cell and then the apartment to no avail. Ordinarily we'd have left it at that, but her message sounded a little odd. Enough so that her boss went over."

Henry now understands where this is going and how bad it is: The boss found Denise, who never woke up —

"No! Sorry! I didn't realize how this was sounding. She was there, alive. The dog, too. In fact she yelled, 'Come in, the door's open.'" The woman pauses, then states as if the news couldn't be more disturbing, "Even from the hallway, Sheila knew it was paint."

"Pain?" he asks.

"Paint. She was painting the apartment."

"And that explains why she's not here today?"

"She was painting the walls black. Angrily, like a woman possessed. A flat finish."

"You fired her because of that?"

"She didn't show up for work, she didn't call, and she seemed, frankly, out of touch with reality."

Here I go again, Henry thinks, the default advocate and mediator. "I'm sure you know that she lost her husband a few short months ago and that her stepsons are putting the apartment on the market —"

"With Corcoran," the woman snaps.

"Walls can be repainted," he says. "Besides, how far could she have gotten with one brush and no ladder?"

"There's more: She told Sheila that she'd lost track of time and thought it was Sunday morning."

"Instead of Monday? And you think that constitutes cause? Because I don't see, as a lawyer, how painting her apartment matte black is an employer's concern."

The woman says, "Mr. Arthur, is it? Denise is not a licensed broker — not even close — but she does represent this office. More and more we'd be sending her out to turn on lights or arrange flowers or close a blind so that a property shows well. In other words, to exercise some aesthetic judgment. But let me say for the record, Denise was fired for nonperformance of duties. She failed to show up for work. You're right: Whatever color she chooses to deface the walls of her apartment with is none of our business." She stands, so he does, too. "I'm sorry. We liked having her around. Perhaps we can revisit this at some time in the future."

Henry says, "And that's your policy? One strike and you're out? You *should* be sorry." He spots a place mat with a doggy motif, a brown cartoon bone on white plastic, halfway under the front desk. Without asking, he seizes it.

The doorman says, "She doesn't want any visitors."

"I'm her lawyer," Henry tries.

"Can't help you."

"Can you tell her Henry's downstairs?"

When the doorman appears to be considering his request, Henry muses, "If anything happened to her, if she's fallen or if she's ill and unable to call for help, I wouldn't want to be representing the management of this building."

"She said no exceptions. And she's not dead, so I'm not buyin' that. She walked her dog this morning."

Henry slips two fingers into his shirt pocket and produces a strategically folded twenty-dollar bill. "I'm quite sure she'll answer the intercom," he says. "Also, I neglected to say that I'm Thalia's stepfather. Were you working here when she was living at home?"

"Name again?" the doorman asks, punching numbers from memory. Then: "Henry Archer here to see you, Mrs. Krouch." He listens, then says without eye contact, "Elevator to your right."

With the door between them, she asks if he's alone.

"Open up, Denise. Of course I am. Who else would I be with?"

"Glenn!"

"Glenn? Your late husband?" he asks delicately.

"No, not my husband! I haven't lost my marbles. Glenn his son! He's been calling here."

"And why would I have teamed up with Glenn Junior?"

"Don't bullshit me, Henry. I know you went to Long Island City."

"To *help* you. Not to team up with the sons. Just the opposite. Please open the door."

She does. She is wearing a flannel nightgown, an apparent veteran of too many permanent-press cycles. Her hair is flyaway and she wears no makeup, no lipstick, no foundation garments. Albert Einstein cowers at her feet, smears of black paint along his flanks.

"Are you all right?" he asks.

"They listed my home," she says. "I had to do something."

"May I come in?"

She takes a step back. The floor is covered with newspapers. "You won't like it," she warns.

He crosses the threshold and views the foyer. It isn't black, but darkest purple, a hideous sight. In better light Albert Einstein has purple streaks as well. "What made you think of this?" he asks as neutrally as if pointing to a paint chip under consideration.

"What else could I do? I wasn't going to take a pickax to the walls."

Henry walks up to a wall for closer inspection. He says, "You know, you did quite a good job."

"I know it! I was going to make a horrible mess of it on purpose and ruin the floors, too, but once I got going I had pride of workmanship. I've never painted a room before. You use a roller for the walls and they have this blue tape that keeps you from getting paint where you don't want it. Would you believe Home Depot opens at seven A.M. in this city?"

253

He peeks into the kitchen, still its original off-white. "Are you leaving some rooms as they are, or just haven't gotten to them yet?"

"I'm only doing what I need for maximum impact. I'm figuring a purple foyer and then a midnight blue hallway with black trim — what's worse than black and blue? I can barely stand it myself — and then I did the one viewable wall in the living room."

He peers down the hall. That one wall is a yellowish green that contributes to the hematoma theme. "You're right," he says. "It's disconcerting, to say the least. But let me play devil's advocate: Wouldn't a broker simply say to a potential buyer, 'Before we go inside, I have to warn you. The owner was acting out. Look past the paint, the colors, the bad taste. Just take in the bones of the apartment.' And doesn't a broker have the right to send a crew in here and make everything white or buff or greige or whatever's the new neutral?"

Denise says, "Only if my extremely loyal doormen let them in. They're on my side. And Christmas is only six months away. Want a drink?"

"Can we sit? Maybe in the kitchen."

Denise leads the way, hem raised daintily, newspaper sticking to her bare feet every few steps. "Do you think it's okay to use turpentine on Albert Einstein?" she asks. "I don't want the greyhound adoption people on my case."

"Did you use oil-based paint?"

"I don't know. I asked for whatever stuff would smell the least."

Henry goes to the sink, wets a sponge with warm water and a squirt of soap, and calls the dog, who shoots an anxious look at his mistress. "Try Kill Bill," says Denise. "Or Billy. I've been slipping back to that because he doesn't answer to Albert unless the topic is food."

Henry grips Albert by the collar and slides him across the linoleum to the sink. The yellow sponge takes on an inky tinge.

"Latex," says Henry.

"I love you," says Denise.

"So tell me why you're here," Sheri Abrams, PhD, asks, clipboard on her lap, gaze neutral.

"He thinks I'm losing my mind," says Denise. "And he could be right."

"Why do you think Denise is losing her mind?" Sheri asks Henry.

"I never said that. What I said was, 'I think you're depressed.' When someone doesn't show up for work and paints her apartment black, blue, purple, and chartreuse — in her nightgown — it could be a cry for help."

The doctor asks Denise how she feels about Henry's characterization.

"It's wrong! It wasn't a cry for help. It was a battle plan. It was one thing I could do to make the apartment a total turnoff. I wasn't going to blow it up like the crazy guy on East Sixty-second — remember him? Between Madison and Park? — to punish his ex because their divorce was forcing him to put his townhouse on the market."

"Go on," says Sheri.

"Henry only found out by accident because he went to my office and they told him I was fired."

"And not in great shape," Henry says quietly.

"Wait. Back up. Were you fired without cause?" Sheri asks.

"Totally! I was late and because I didn't answer my phone —"

"Tell her what your outgoing message said," Henry prompts.

"I don't remember word for word, but it was along the lines of 'This apartment is not for sale so if you're calling about that, take a hike.'"

"Potential buyers would be calling you? Isn't it in the hands of a broker?" asks Sheri.

"Two brokers!"

"Not an exclusive?" asks Sheri.

Henry slides lower in his chair.

Denise turns to him. "What? Why are you grimacing?"

Henry says, "The issue isn't whether the apartment has a broker, or the broker has an exclusive." He sends Sheri a look. "But it's not my job to keep us on track, is it?"

"First," says Denise, "we need to explain that when my third husband, Glenn, died, his children got everything. And guess how two boys divide a multimillion-dollar apartment straight down the middle? They sell it."

"I'm very sorry for your loss," says Sheri.

"So am I," says Denise. "And still in shock."

"How many months has it been?" asks the doctor.

"February. What's that? Four months. It feels like four *days*. Are you married?"

Henry says, "We don't ask our shrinks personal questions. You know that."

Sheri says, "I'd like to ask about your support system."

Denise says, "That's easy: my dog, who goes with me everywhere. He's new since Glenn died. I'd have brought him today, except . . ." And she gestures with what Henry knows is contemptuous acknowledgment of the ancient and unhandsome poodle at the doctor's feet. "He's so smart, and his EQ is so high that I named him Albert Einstein."

Sheri smiles, but not with the irony he thinks Denise's digression deserves. "I named my dog for the same reasons," Sheri tells Denise, reaching down to stroke the poodle's ears. "She's Simone, after Simone de Beauvoir."

Henry checks his watch. Only ten minutes have passed.

Sheri continues. "What about humans? Who among them do you turn to for support?"

Denise reaches over and takes Henry's hand. "Only my friend here. Plus my doormen."

Sheri says, "What about your daughter?"

"She's not speaking to me."

Henry extracts his hand from Denise's. Sheri says to Denise, "I meet you and I see someone who is outgoing, attractive, intelligent, all the things people want in a friend. So where are these connections misfiring? Could it be that you are expecting too much from friends? That they should be reaching out to you as a widow? Do you think, after a little more time passes, that you'd want to revisit these friendships and work a little harder?"

"Do you have children?" Denise asks. "Specifically, a daughter?"

"Don't ask her that stuff," Henry snaps.

"It's okay," says Sheri. "The answer is no. But I *am* a daughter. I know that a mother-daughter relationship requires work."

"What about an ex-husband?" asks Denise. "An ex-anything?"

"Denise!" Henry hisses.

"Let me finish, sweet pea. She should know that I'm twice widowed and you're in the middle of that marital sandwich, the meat and the cheese, a cushion between those two tragedies. You're all I've got, and I wish we'd sought counseling when we were still married."

Sheri asks, "Henry? What would you say to more meetings with Denise?"

"Your walls, Denise," he says sadly. "They're black and blue. That's why we're here."

Denise confides to Sheri, "He doesn't like to talk about our marriage or divorce: touchy subject. And complicated."

"Is that true, Henry?" Sheri asks.

"Am I in a fun house?" Henry asks. "Are we talking about marriage counseling — as if . . . what? Henry married Denise once, and they had their little issues, easily fixed, so maybe he'd do it again?"

"Of course not," Sheri says. "Please sit down."

"He paces when he's nervous," says Denise. "And I know why he's nervous: I kissed him like I meant it a few weeks back, and from time to time I tell him I love him. But that's just me. I'm very . . . what's the right word? Passionate. Besides, I know he's gay. I also know that's not a thing that comes and goes." She sends an air kiss in his direction. "I know you think I'm a pain in the ass. And I am! Maybe I am off my rocker and/or depressed and now jobless and soon homeless. But I think, underneath all of that, you're very fond of me."

Sheri Abrams, turncoat therapist, repeats, "Homeless? Literally?"

"Not yet," says Henry. "And maybe never. I'm doing what I can."

"My rock," says Denise.

My ball and chain, he thinks.

32

Every Time I Turn Around

TODD INSISTS he has to see it. *Has* to! His imagination fails him, accustomed as he is to muted, decorator-chosen palettes. So don't even make up an excuse, just, "Todd is dying to see what you did with the apartment."

"Does she ever go out?" Todd's mother asks. "Because she could have come to supper tonight. I could have called it a thank-you for fixing you up with Henry." She is at the stove, ladling too many meatballs onto platefuls of spaghetti. "If the occasion presents itself again, tell her she's very welcome and I use ground turkey instead of chuck."

"I'm trying to lay low," Henry says. "Too much Denise lately. Twenty-five years of relative peace and suddenly she's on my doorstep every time I turn around."

Todd says, "Want to know how nice Henry is? He took her to his shrink where she announced she had one friend in the whole world."

"John Henry Archer," says Henry.

Lillian brings a long loaf of bread wrapped in aluminum foil to the table and takes her seat. "What do you think she meant by 'friend'?" she asks.

"Buddy," says Henry. "Maybe confidant and free legal hotline."

"Co-parent, don't forget," says Todd.

"I noticed . . ." Lillian begins. "When she came to your brunch . . ." She stops, shakes her head.

"Ma, what?"

Lillian says, "Please help yourself to salad."

"Were you going to say that Denise was too chummy?" asks Henry. "Seemed too much at home?"

Lillian doesn't look up from the task of quartering a meatball. "It's understandable. You were married to her once."

"And you're worried he'd do that again?" Todd asks.

Henry, smiling, says, "I can promise you, if I were going to set up housekeeping with a nice widow, it wouldn't be Denise Krouch."

"Maybe that's not the most reassuring thing she ever heard," says Todd.

"You know what's lovely?" Henry asks. "That your mother has added me to her list of people and things to worry about."

Lillian takes a sip of red wine, Henry's hostess gift, before asking, "Are you going back to this therapist with Denise?"

"I promised her that if she'd see someone, I'd go along. The easiest thing was to call up my ex-shrink rather than start asking around for recommendations or explaining my whole life to a stranger. Don't forget the groundwork had been set through years of my talking about the divorce and what that wrought in terms of custody. But to answer your question, Denise is returning. I'm not."

"How's the daughter?" Lillian asks. "Still seeing that boy?"

"Which one?" Todd asks with a wink for Henry.

"The actor."

"We don't think it's going to last much longer," Todd says.

"It's complicated," says Henry. "Not a conventional romance. It's more of what you might consider a courtesy."

"You met her," says Todd. "You saw what a good sport she is. She's seeing him as — okay if I say it? — a favor."

Henry searches for words that will be code for *Don't make me violate the confidentiality agreement once again.* He tries, "You know how young people are. Why they see each other and *what* they see in each other is a mystery. In this case, especially, discretion is the better part of valor."

Lillian whispers, "Is he married?"

Todd says, "If only."

"You want her to be dating a married man?"

"I meant if only he were a married man, he wouldn't have needed . . ." Todd looks to Henry.

"A favor," says Henry.

"Is this another gay situation?" Lillian asks.

Todd says, "A very good guess, but no."

"She never got that part, did she? In his Civil War movie? Was that it? She wasn't in love with him but she thought it might help her career if she went out with a director? You can tell me. I know the way the world works, and I won't think any less of her."

"Or us," says Todd. "Her enablers." He puts his knife and fork down. "It's a flop. A grand scheme that never got off the ground."

"Stop beating around the bush," says Lillian. "What grand scheme?"

When Henry doesn't answer, Todd says, "C'mon. Thalia wouldn't mind."

"It's not Thalia who can sue me for breach of contract!"

"I won't tell a living soul," says Lillian.

"And she is, you have to admit, the queen of don't-ask-don't-tell," says Todd. "She didn't ask me a single personal question in forty-some-odd years."

Henry says wearily, "Thalia was contracted by a publicity firm to be Leif Dumont's arm candy, i.e., girlfriend. It was supposed to make the papers, big gossip item. Confirmed bachelor finds true love."

"That's it?" says Lillian. "That's the secret? I thought it was going to be some big scandal that someone could go to prison for."

Henry says, "Well, there's that, too. An underage girlfriend back in California —"

"Unconsummated, according to Thalia," says Todd.

"Is she disappointed?" Lillian asks. "Do you think she was hoping it might start as a business arrangement, but then turn into something more?"

"Thalia is philosophical," Henry says.

"She can be," says Todd. "We think there are many suitors waiting in the wings."

"What about her mother? I don't know her well enough to judge, but she strikes me as the kind of person who might want to throw a celebrity wedding so she could see herself on *The Insider*."

"For better or for worse," says Henry, "Denise took an instant dislike to Leif based on the most superficial reasons —"

"His looks," says Todd. "Whereas Henry delved below the surface to the man's undetectable personality."

"Either way, nothing fuels a daughter's interest like a parent's disapproval," says Henry.

"'Interest' is too strong," says Todd. "More like 'fueled Thalia's humanity.' It offends her that the papers call him names based on his appearance."

"Not a good-looking man?" Lillian asks.

"Not even a good-looking *monster*," says Todd.

"I'm surprised at you," says Lillian. "Daddy and I didn't raise you to judge people by their exteriors. He can't help the way he looks."

"Todd was being literal," Henry tells her. "Leif's work is mostly in horror films, which he'd like to break out of."

"Any I might have seen?"

Todd laughs.

"You don't know every movie I see," she says.

"Name one horror film you've seen."

"*Phantom of the Opera*. And what's the Alfred Hitchcock movie where the girl gets stabbed in the shower? Not *The Birds*. The other one."

"*Psycho*," says Henry.

"I saw that in the theater when it first came out. I may even have seen a sequel." She smiles a shaky smile. "I always loved Anthony Perkins." Her face changes. "When he died in real life, I was so upset."

"Translation," says Todd. "Gay. From AIDS. Very hard to maintain dinnertime joie de vivre when one's own son is in the same risk pool."

Lillian says, "No one's touched the garlic bread."

"I will," says Henry.

Lillian says quietly, "It won't be good reheated."

"I love Italian food," Henry says. "Every time I watched *The Sopranos* and they were eating at Artie's restaurant, I'd pick up the phone and order something close to whatever house specialty Artie was whipping up for Tony and Carmela."

Lillian says, "We don't get HBO." And after a pause. "His wife died on one of the planes that flew into the twin towers."

"Anthony Perkins's wife, she means," says Todd.

"I'd forgotten that," says Henry. "Almost incomprehensible."

"They had two boys," says Lillian.

Todd says, "This is the longest and possibly the only conversation we've had about Anthony Perkins at this table."

"I understand," says Henry. "We feel as if we know these actors. Then you find out he's sick, and you're upset, but keep it to yourself because you hadn't yet had that discussion with Todd."

"It's not rational," says Todd. "She knows I'm fine and you're fine."

"It's not that," Lillian says.

"Great," says Todd. "Let's have a guessing game. Whose turn is it to guess what's made my mother go silent. Anybody?"

"Nothing is wrong. I'm eating my dinner. If you need to inspect Denise's ruined apartment, and if Denise needs to see a therapist, there are plenty more important things in this world for me to worry about."

"Not Denise, then," says Todd. "Okay. Maybe nothing at all, just a long pause in the conversation so you could twirl your spaghetti into your soup spoon."

"I hope I didn't say anything to worry you, Lillian," says Henry.

Todd tilts his upper body toward his mother to ask, "Did you ever think I'd bring home such a mensch?"

Lillian puts both utensils down. "Do you know what my friends say, every single one, when I tell them about Henry? 'Don't get too attached! It's a recipe for heartbreak. You get attached to the person your kid's dating, and then they break up and you suffer more than they do.'"

"Who are these relationship experts?" Todd demands. "Aunt Mim, whose kids see her twice a year? Or your yenta bridge partners who only recently realized that *faygeleh* is politically incorrect? One of those geniuses?"

Lillian says quietly, "Some new friends. In PFLAG."

"PFLAG? No wonder," says Todd. "You're probably talking to the parents and friends of promiscuous gays and lesbians!"

"They're very nice," says Lillian. "I enjoy the meetings. And I really don't think anyone I've met has a promiscuous son or daughter, at least from our conversations."

Henry says, "Your friends don't want you to get hurt. Even in my very limited experience as Thalia's father, I can see myself getting attached to one of these beaus, and then what happens? They disappear from view overnight. It's like a death."

"Um, Henry?" Todd says. "Can you say something reassuring now?"

Henry reaches across the table and covers Lillian's hand with his. "What would reassure you, Lillian?"

"Maybe if I knew that you weren't seeing anyone else besides Todd . . ."

"I'm not."

"Because I know that with men it can be very hard to be monogamous. They're built different than women."

"Why all of a sudden?" asks Todd. "Besides the social education you're getting at PFLAG. Is something else going on?"

Lillian's chin quivers.

"Are you crying?" Henry asks.

"I think I know what this is," says Todd. He gets out of his chair, stands behind his mother, and massages her shoulders. Above her head he mouths *worried*, then pantomimes with his fist the opening and closing of myocardial valves.

"Your last checkup was good?" Henry asks her.

"Same old stuff: my pressure, my reflux, my weight, my cholesterol, the arthritis in my toes. No big thing."

Todd says, "So of course she's worried about who will raise me after she's gone."

"It's not funny to me," says Lillian. "I know you're a grown man. You can take care of yourself, and you'll stay here after I'm gone because your name's on the lease. It has nothing to do with who will raise you." She finds a crumpled tissue in an apron pocket and blows her nose. "It's about who will *love* you."

"Ma —"

"*I* will, Lillian," Henry says.

33

Not What Was Prescribed

WISH YOU COULD'VE been there, Thalia tells them, three abreast on a bench in Central Park, she and Henry sharing the salt and vinegar potato chips that came with Todd's turkey sandwich. It probably was, she tells them, the pinnacle of her improv career. Not so much the content, which was uneven —

"Stop torturing us," says Henry.

"I'm due back at work in twenty minutes, and that includes my travel time," says Todd.

Thalia adopts a tone suitable to a *Dragnet* voice-over. "Eleven fifty-nine P.M. We arrive at the Box. Leif and I, in fact, do get in."

"Wearing?" asks Todd.

"Not what was prescribed —"

"But not one of Nana's hand-me-downs?"

"No. Jeans and those boots you approve of. In fact, these very things." She lifts her feet and displays her impossibly pointed snakeskin toes.

"Proceed," says Todd.

"Okay. I see the other girl, the hired hand, approach Leif, according to plan. She's not a good actor, but then again, she wasn't chosen for her acting skills. Huge boobs, blond hair, fake eyelashes, glitter on cheeks, shoulders, cleavage; skirt up to her crotch — so ridiculous, so obvious, that I laughed. But mostly I was watching Leif. Completely fascinating — he just could *not* do it, could not perform as love object."

"So did you follow the script, or didn't you?" Henry asks.

Thalia nibbles prettily around the edges of a large potato chip until it's gone, then plucks a napkin from Todd's knee to blot her mouth.

"We're dying here," says Todd. "Tell us it all turned out fine, a triumph. Mission accomplished."

Thalia stands and faces Henry and Todd for the walk-through. "Okay. So this girl is all over Leif. I take out my phone" — she does — "and next thing I know I'm snapping pictures like I'm a fan, like won't my girlfriends back in Toledo be thrilled when they get these. I ask, 'What's your name?' She says, 'Heather Maze. Like *a*maze, without the *A*.' Now I realize that she thinks I'm the press and has apparently forgotten about Thalia the jealous girlfriend. So I ask, 'Who are you wearing?' which she doesn't get. I move on to, 'Are you a regular here?' She says, 'Um, well, no, but I'd like to be. It's awesome.' I ask, 'Are you an actress? Because you're so' — gag me — 'glamorous.' She says, 'I *am* an actress!' So I say, 'And who is this gentleman?' Now I've got a pencil poised as if I'm writing all this down — not really — it's lip liner and a bar napkin. Heather starts looking around, finally wondering what happened to the angry girlfriend who's going to throw the first punch. I ask her again, 'Who is this gentleman you're with?' She says, 'Um. Lee Dupont.' I say, 'Wow, a *Dupont*. From the chemical Duponts?' She says, 'I don't know. We just met.'"

"What's Leif doing while this is going on?" Henry asks.

"Nothing up to this point. But then, when I least expect it, he asks quite calmly, 'Thalia? What are you doing?' which clues Heather in. "'*Thalia?* You're Thalia?' Mispronounced, of course. So even though I hadn't exactly thought this through, word for word, I knew I had to say something meaningful. I *wanted* to say to the crowd, 'All of you got into the Box tonight. Does that make you happy? Popular? Better-looking and more important than your friends who didn't get past the velvet rope?'"

"You said that, or you didn't say that?" asks Henry.

She sits down again. "Did not say that. I mean, the place is big. It's loud. And what was my platform? Fellow club rat? It wasn't as if I was challenging them via satellite from a refugee camp. So I told Heather her job was over. She shouldn't demean herself, and she shouldn't confuse acting with real life." She takes another chip and with her mouth full mumbles, "Which is when I kissed Leif."

"What kind of kiss?" asks Henry.

"How many kinds are there?"

"A stage kiss?" Todd supplies.

"Maybe not," says Thalia.

The two men meditate on this. Finally Todd says, "It makes sense. Instead of starting a brawl, you were turning a sword into a plowshare."

"How did Leif react?" asks Henry. "And what did Heather do?"

"Well, Heather by now is all mixed up. She muscles me out of the way" — Thalia pantomimes a big chest moving in for the assault — "and now *she* kisses Leif. And I mean kisses."

"And is Leif standing there like a cigar-store Indian?" asks Todd.

"Leif did okay," she says.

"Meaning?"

"He actually looked the way a normal guy might look if two women were showering him with attention. And get this: He had his lips on her and his eyes on me. And you know what I saw?"

"No," they both answer.

"A look in his eye. Like he recognized the irony of the situation. As if he was saying, *Do you believe this is happening to us?*"

"Us?" Todd repeats. "He used that pronoun?"

"How could he use a pronoun? He was sending this telepathically."

"Which I notice you were receiving loud and clear," says Todd.

"How long did this public display go on?" asks Henry.

"Until I tapped her on the shoulder, very calmly, once, twice. Finally—and now her lips have slid south, somewhere around the Adam's apple—she mutters, 'What the fuck . . . ?' So I say, 'Heather? Why are you doing this? Do you need this job so badly that you'd put yourself in this situation, with people wondering if you're a floozy or a hooker or a pickpocket?'"

"No you didn't!" says Todd happily.

"I certainly did."

Henry says, "But she probably thought it was an honest day's work. Do you think it was right to humiliate her?"

Thalia pats Henry's knee as she says to Todd, "How very Henry of him to worry about Heather Maze, perfect stranger."

"What about phase two?" Henry asks.

"Remind me," says Thalia.

"You and Leif are photographed making up in the limo. Did any press show up?"

"Oh, that," says Thalia.

"No?" asks Todd.

"No. He was mad at me by this time. Livid."

"Probably because you didn't create the promised fracas," says Henry.

"You're missing a defining moment: I said Leif got *mad* at me. Leif the silent, the blocked, the inscrutable. He yanked me by the hand, out the door, and read me the riot act. Doesn't that sound like progress?"

"I don't get why it was a riot act," says Todd.

Thalia's lips move silently. Finally she says, "Along the lines of, I used him."

"How?" asks Todd.

"You've done nothing but help him!" says Henry. "Who could have been nicer throughout this whole fiasco?"

"I bet the kiss threw him off," says Todd.

"Something did."

"How was it left?" asks Todd.

"It wasn't. He put me in the limo, slammed the door behind me, and loped off into the night."

"With Heather?"

"Maybe she chased after him. I don't know. My driver took off."

"So this is it," Henry says. "It ends with a whimper instead of a bang."

Todd brushes crumbs off his knees and stands. "I have to run. Sharon is going to be eating her egg salad sandwich at the cash register if I don't get back. But here's my take: Leif is not livid. He's confused. He's still trying to figure out what happened." He compacts his lunch bag into a ball, tosses, misses the trash can, says, "I'll get it . . . Bye, sweetie. Hesh? See you tonight?"

They watch him cut over to the trash can, pick up not only his bag but two other stray wrappers, then head out of the park on a westward path.

"Do you think he's right?" asks Thalia. "About the kiss? Mixed messages?"

Henry asks, "Why *did* you kiss him? You must have known he was developing feelings for you. I can't imagine you were doing it purely as performance art."

Thalia doesn't answer, except for a repentant shrug. She walks over to a vending cart and returns with two bottles of water. "So what's on tap for this afternoon?" she asks.

"For me? The usual."

"Which is what on a beautiful spring day with no briefs to write or contracts to negotiate?"

"Nothing," says Henry.

"Me neither. We're bums." She smiles. "Hesh."

Henry says, "Yiddish, I think. It doesn't usually slip out in public."

A nursery school wagon carting a half-dozen toddlers approaches, pulled by two smiling young women, one in purple leg warmers and the other in red high-top sneakers. Thalia and Henry wave. The children stare. One teacher says, "Wave back, you silly chili beans!" and one or two do, perfunctorily.

"Only half of them were wearing sweaters," Henry notes after they've passed by.

"We are so bored," says Thalia.

Henry asks, "Want to walk over to Lincoln Square Theater and see what's playing?"

She shakes her head. "I'm sort of waiting for a call. Unless I'm supposed to be *making* a call."

"To Leif?"

"Either to yell or to apologize. I haven't decided yet."

"Up to you," says Henry. "Or just leave it."

"I've already texted him."

"Saying what?"

"No words. Just a question mark." She waits a few long beats before saying, "Maybe there's a little more to it than I've confessed."

"Such as?"

"You're not going to like it. I may have to sugar-coat it."

He suspects it's contractual, and already he doesn't like it. "Did you sign something without me going over it first? A non-comp agreement, or an extension?"

Thalia lifts her face to the sun, closes her eyes, and says, "Hmm. Extension. Let me see. Yes. That word could apply to what happened between me and Hose."

Henry waits for the next pair of pedestrians, bird watchers speaking German, to pass by before asking, "You slept with Leif?"

"These things happen," she says. "I think once the idea was planted in my brain about — you remember the penis discussion? — I became a little more, shall we say, attuned." She sits up again and asks, "Wanna walk?"

He says only yes, sensing that a good father doesn't ask a grown daughter for details about a sexual episode, especially an inadvertent one.

They head north, then turn onto West 75th. "Don't worry," she says. "We agreed that it was more or less accidental and spontaneous, and it shouldn't happen again."

When they reach his front door, Henry says that he's late putting annuals into the flower urns by the steps. He had postponed the planting, thinking paparazzi might kill his flowers with their cigarette butts. Thalia sits down on the stairway and pats a spot next to her. "Like that ever happened," she says.

He sits, her cell phone between them. "Has Leif told the little girlfriend?" he asks.

"I told him not to. I said, What's the big deal? Confessions are ultimately selfish. Who does it help to say, 'Remember the woman they hired to pose as my girlfriend? I fucked her. But don't worry! It was only sex. It meant nothing.'"

"You said that to him?" Henry asks.

"More or less . . . okay, less. All I said was, 'Don't blurt anything out in an IM to Caitlin.'"

"What does the Estime team know?" Henry asks.

"Nothing! Well, nothing about our little fling, but probably everything about my sermons at the Box."

Henry says, "I have to ask: Did Leif press you into having sex? Is there any chance it was the result of an action plan by Wendy Morelli?"

Thalia says no so quickly and firmly that Henry says, "Sorry. Just playing devil's advocate."

"I know I made a mess of this," she says. "Why did I think he was going to shrug it off?"

Henry doesn't know what to say next. He wishes Todd were here; Todd is so much better at this kind of thing.

"Maybe I'll go back to school," she says. "Isn't that what you do when you realize you can't keep saying 'actor' if your main job is checking coats?"

"This doesn't sound like you! You'll keep trying. There are headhunters and agents and managers. And you have a fallback."

"My trust fund? That doesn't kick in until I'm thirty-five. I lied about getting it now so you wouldn't worry so much about me living on tips."

"Not that fallback," Henry says. He puts his arm around her shoulders. Months have gone by and only now does he have his arm around Thalia in full view of neighbors and pedestrians on West 75th Street.

"You know what I think?" she says. "I think you're wishing some real-life guy will take me on that shopping trip to Tiffany's, and soon you'd be walking me down the aisle of Saint Nicholas. Will you admit to that?"

"No, I will not." He smiles. He points to the maisonette. "Because what if I got that wish, and your husband didn't want to live downstairs?"

"Are you kidding? *If* I ever get married it'll be to a starving artist or a slacker. In fact, your three and a half rooms will be the main reason he proposes."

Henry nods, then manages a "Good."

"You okay?" she asks. "Did I make you nervous? Don't be. I'm going to redo my resumé and get a job. I want to pay my own way."

Henry says, "I appreciate that. But at the same time, I hope you won't give up on your craft. I think you have talent. More than talent; you have that indefinable quality —"

Her phone vibrates, a growl from the stone step. Thalia, looking puzzled, doesn't answer immediately.

"Not Leif?" Henry asks.

She holds up the phone. "Krouch Carton," he reads.

275

34

The Waikiki

I T IS THE LESS gracious Krouch, Glenn Junior, barreling right to the point: He needs the lowdown from Thalia on Henry Archer. Is he trustworthy? Discreet? And what's in it for a gay ex-husband, this campaigning for Denise?

Thalia says, "I don't know what you're talking about. And by the way, nice of you to check in on me every millennium or so."

"Henry Archer? Your stepfather, right? You didn't know he came to see us about your mother?"

Thalia says — delivering up her best Katharine Hepburn — "How odd, yet how chivalrous! You can most certainly trust Henry. In fact, this upright citizen is sitting right next to me, on the veranda, not an inch away."

"Shit. Obviously you can't talk —" says Glenn.

"Yes, I can." Without waiting for an answer, Thalia says, unmuted, "Here. Talk to Glenn, my charming stepbrother."

Without preamble, and with her orange Razr phone to his ear,

Henry says, "I hope the reason you were calling my references is because there's been movement in your position."

Glenn says, "Hold on a sec." A corrugated box promotion fills the air until Glenn comes back to announce, most unconvincingly, "I decided to do what's right."

"Which means what?"

"We should talk. In person."

Henry says, "Tomorrow? I'll check with the firm to make sure there's a conference room available and I'll call you back to confirm."

"No," says Glenn. "I'll call you. I'm the executor. I don't want Tommy dragged into this. Bye."

Thalia takes her phone back and claps it shut. "It would appear to the casual observer," she says, "that you've met with at least one of my stepbrothers to discuss your ex-wife. When did this all come about?"

Henry says, "I went to Long Island City, once. For ten minutes, two weeks ago."

"So I've got Glenn Krouch Junior from that cast of characters calling me about Henry Archer, from this subset. And, silly me — I had no idea they'd ever met! You know what this reminds me of? It's like when a character from *Days of Our Lives* shows up on *All My Children*."

"It's not so far-fetched," says Henry. "Your mother turned to me for legal advice. I went to the factory to see if the sons would show her a little mercy."

"On which topic?"

"Money. Housing. I thought I'd begin with an appeal to their sense of fair play and generosity, if any."

He expects Thalia will say, "Ha!" but instead she says, "That might work with Tommy. Glenn, on the other hand, is an asshole."

"Yet he called," says Henry. "And he says he wants to do the right thing."

"Isn't life interesting?" says Thalia. "Just as I'm struggling with how to recognize what the right thing is, along comes an illustrated example in the unlikely form of Glenn Krouch Junior, torturer in his youth of small animals."

"Maybe he's genuinely concerned. Maybe he heard from the brokers that she's in a bad way —"

"Or maybe he's hearing from the ghosts of husbands past . . ." and adds, in an otherworldly voice, "'Glenn Junior, you must help Denise. Yes, it's Dad. Why do you doubt your own ears?'"

"I'm not getting my hopes up," says Henry. "Nothing ever gets accomplished in the first round of negotiations."

"Are you going to bring your client?"

"God no," says Henry.

Present in the law firm's smallest conference room are Glenn Krouch Jr. and a silver-haired, ponytailed man in a gray pin-striped suit and white sneakers, whose name, Eddie Pelletier, does not immediately register. "Mr. Pelletier is here in what capacity?" Henry asks Glenn.

"Blackmailer," grunts Glenn.

"He's kidding!" says Eddie. "I'm helping Denise, and so are you, right?" He reaches across the table to shake Henry's hand. "She said you were on her side, and you got this ball rolling."

Henry asks, "You're here on Denise's behalf . . . how?"

"He's fucking her!" says Glenn. "If she gets the apartment, he gets a roof over his head."

Eddie says, "That's uncalled for. I think we should keep this professional and, if possible, let bygones be bygones." He turns to Henry. "Here's what he's referring to: Denise and I, after some big hurdles, are making a go of it. I happen to know that the kids were offended that the friendship started before their dad passed, and I also happened to be married. I admit there was some to-ing and fro-ing in that department, but that's now settled. As for why this, now, today: My history with the family business puts me in a unique position to help Denise."

"How?" asks Henry.

"Extortionist," says Glenn.

"His dad and I were in business together at one time," Eddie says. "And even though the partnership broke up, the friendship didn't."

Henry puts his pen down on his yellow legal pad. "If it's about business, I need to know why I was called. And why is Mr. Krouch using terms like *blackmail* and *extortion*?"

"He's exaggerating!" says Eddie. "I used a little persuasion of the verbal kind, which is how people negotiate. I pointed out that life would be simpler and he'd feel like a better man if he wasn't turning his stepmother out on the street. It's all about him and his peace of mind. Ask Denise. She was listening on the other line."

Glenn says, "Don't look so innocent, Archer. Didn't you show up at my place of business and say, 'Give Denise what she wants or I'll take you to court'? Isn't that what you threatened?"

"I don't make threats," says Henry.

"Then what do you call it?"

"A statement of fact," says Henry.

"This guy, I can tell, doesn't make threats," Eddie adds. "Look at this place. Solid cherry table, and not just doughnuts and coffee, but fruit salad. This gives me a good feeling." Eddie grins. "How we doing, Glenn? Are we ready to call in Mr. Archer's secretary to draw up a settlement, and we'll sign it, and you'll never have to see me again?"

Glenn is staring appraisingly across the table at Eddie. "Is that my father's suit you're wearing?"

"Your stepmother gave away all of your father's clothes. I don't see how this could be his."

"Gentlemen," says Henry. "I still don't have a clear understanding of who wants what, or why I'm here."

"I told you over the phone," says Glenn. "I just decided to do the right thing."

Henry says, "I'm going to be blunt: Intimations of blackmail, combined with your previously stated hatred of your stepmother and your obvious disdain for Mr. Pelletier, do not add up to your doing the right thing out of sheer goodwill."

"Why does it have to add up?" Glenn asks. "Can't I just sign a piece of paper that gives her the apartment, and you get a gal to type it up?"

"Who's your father's trust attorney?" Henry asks.

"Look," says Glenn. "All I want is to get this over with. I don't need to pay my father's lawyer for time I spend answering a million questions about the whys and the wherefores."

"She just wants the apartment," says Eddie.

Henry frowns his best bargaining-table frown, the one that says *not good enough.*

"Here's the way I look at it," says Eddie. "It's not easy to evict a tenant who doesn't want to leave. So let's say that goes to court. The papers get wind of it. They write up stories about two rich brats — sorry, that's how they'd see it — who kick their widowed stepmother of twenty-four years into the gutter."

"Yuh. Like she needs an entire floor on Park Avenue," Glenn mutters.

Eddie leans forward and says, "Yuh, Glenny. Like you need a business on top of Krouch Cartons."

This, Henry can see, from the poisonous stare being returned across the table, is Eddie Pelletier's bargaining chip. "You have another business in addition to corrugated boxes?" asks Henry.

"Not in addition to the boxes. On *top*," says Eddie. "Literally. What time of the day did you get out to Long Island City?"

"Afternoon," says Henry.

Eddie smiles. "Broad daylight. That explains it."

Henry asks, "That explains what?"

"Let's call it the night shift. Upstairs. At the Waikiki."

"Which is . . . ?"

"What does it sound like?"

"A lounge?" asks Henry.

"You're close," says Eddie. "'Cause there's a lot of lounging going on up there."

Henry asks Glenn, "What is Mr. Pelletier alleging?"

"I'm not alleging anything! I know. I investigated. I *went* there."

"It's a spa," Glenn says. "Jesus. Big deal. Which Krouch and Sons Cartons, Inc., has nothing to do with."

"Spa!" Eddie says. "Know what a 'happy ending' is? Glenn can educate you and can probably give you a price list."

"If it's just tenantry —" Henry says.

Eddie says, "Yah, right. He sees no evil, hears no evil, never stays late, and never visits the tenants. Krouch and *Sins,* is more like it."

Henry turns to Eddie. "Are you or are you not blackmailing him? Because if you are, I'm obliged to tell you that you're committing an illegal act."

"No way am I blackmailing him."

"Did you threaten to go to the police if he didn't agree to your terms?"

"And say what? 'Fellas, I know there's three on every block, and you have to look the other way or else you'd be doing nothing else but busting massage parlors, but could you go write a ticket for the landlords of the Waikiki'? No, I didn't say that. What I said to Glenn was that a married guy shouldn't be spending so much time getting massaged by strangers or renting them rooms, and as the head of his church's parish council, he might not want to get caught with his pants down. Is that extortion? Or is that reminding him of the Ten Commandments?"

"Did your father know?" Henry asks Glenn.

Glenn says, "No comment."

"Tell him the rest," says Eddie. "Tell him what floor of Krouch Cartons your father was visiting when he suffered a fatal heart attack."

"You scumbag!" Glenn yells.

"How much of this does Denise know?" Henry asks.

"Nothing. We told her he died on a Stairmaster."

"What about Thalia?" asks Henry. "I don't mean the circumstances of his death. I mean as far as the business goes. Just reassure me that she's not benefiting in any way from the Waikiki. Or is she anything like a silent partner in Krouch and Sons? A board member? A stockholder?"

"No," says Glenn.

"Stockholder," says Eddie. "Ha! What's the symbol? Hand job?"

Henry picks up his pen again. "Is this an accurate summary of what got us here today: Mr. Pelletier is saying, effectively, if Denise loses her home, I could expose and embarrass you for immoral if not illegal activities?"

Glenn grunts affirmatively.

"I checked online," says Eddie. "It's not blackmail."

"And what is your personal stake in all of this?" Henry asks Eddie. "Because we seem to have an epidemic suddenly of people compelled to do the right thing."

Glenn says, "He gets to live rent free on Park Avenue instead of in a fifth-floor walkup in Hell's Kitchen."

"Clinton," says Eddie. "It's no longer called Hell's Kitchen. And I've got a view of the Hudson River."

"Was I misinformed when I was told that you and your wife, Mrs. Pelletier, are back together?" asks Henry.

Eddie says, "Look. I'm not such a terrible guy. I gave my marriage one last try and, okay, that came at a bad time for Denise. She hated me, but then she missed me. And let me say one more thing: the so-called masseuses?" He wiggles his index finger instructively in the direction of Henry's notepad. "Every one of them is an Oriental girl just off the boat. Which is why all of these places have names that sound like Chinese restaurants."

"Get him out of here," says Glenn. "I'm the executor. His job is done. Now it's between me and Denise."

Henry says, "Let's clear up one thing, so Mr. Pelletier doesn't have an urge in the future to phone your brother and play Sunday school teacher: You came alone because your brother has no knowledge of the shenanigans upstairs?"

Eddie says, "With 'Waikiki' flashing outside his window?"

"It doesn't flash," says Glenn. "And to answer your question: Tommy knows we rent eight hundred square feet to a spa. He doesn't use it, and he was out of town the week our father had his heart attack."

"Let's get a secretary in here," says Eddie.

Henry says, "I recommend that you call the real estate agent and tell her the apartment is off the market."

"Now?" asks Glenn.

"Now. On my phone."

"He means, no tricks," says Eddie.

Glenn takes Henry's cell phone and walks it to a distant chair, meant just for this, outgoing calls by the defeated and dispossessed.

"How about the monthly charges?" Eddie whispers. "Those'll set her back a fortune."

"Here's what Denise should do about those costs," says Henry. "She should sell this apartment for a fortune, buy a nice, pet-friendly two-bedroom, and live happily ever after on the difference."

"Big move," says Eddie. "And not exactly what she was fighting for."

"Are you employed?" Henry asks.

"I still have my side of the business. I dropped the twine, so I'm exclusively a label vendor, about ninety percent online."

"And not dependent on Denise for housing?"

"I'm not totally divorced yet," says Eddie. "And even if I was, it doesn't look good so soon after Glenn died."

"Denise, of course, being as sensitive to protocol as she is," Henry says.

"She likes you a lot," says Eddie. "In fact, I'd be jealous except that I know I don't have to be."

"Quite correct," says Henry.

He waits until he's home to call Denise. "Are you alone?" he asks.

"Just Albert Einstein, who — did I tell you? — is going to puppy kindergarten, even though he's twenty-one in human years."

"I meant, has your boyfriend returned yet?"

"Oh, hon," she says. "I guess you're up to date on everything."

"Has he filled you in on the meeting with your stepson?"

"He called the minute he got out of the subway. He said — and I was going to call you to confirm — that the spa above the factory is a brothel, and now Glenn knows that Eddie knows, and how embarrassed Glenn would be if his wife or mother or Saint Mary's of Manhasset ever found out."

"The apartment is yours," Henry says. "You'll be getting this in writing from George."

"It's so great! But do you think we should have pushed for more? If you were me, would you still take them to court over the rest of the estate? Then, as soon as I think that, I wonder, because of the pressure Eddie put on the boys, if we should just take the money and run."

"I'm not in the advice business any longer. There is no *we*. I don't like liars. I'm calling to say don't call me."

"Because of Eddie? Is that fair? He's not living here. And let's just say that ever happened? All you'd have to do is call ahead when you're coming over, and I'd send him to a movie."

"It's *not* going to happen. This is not the kind of friendship I want to maintain."

She yells, "You got Thalia! *My* daughter. Not yours. Mine. You've poisoned her against me. So have a nice life with all those adoring people I supplied you with. You win. I get a roof over my head and you get everything else."

"Denise —" he tries, but the line goes dead.

35

Something's Not Right

T HALIA E-MAILS HENRY to say that she dropped by
Salon Gerard, and would he believe they gave her old job
away — that stupid part-time minimum-wage *nothing*?
He opens the kitchen door and yells downstairs, "Are you
there? Want coffee? I have whipped cream in a can."

"Be right up," she says. "But let me warn you: I'm dressed for
success."

She enters the kitchen in an outfit as bland as he's ever seen
her in: a straight khaki skirt to the knee, a short-sleeved blouse
in pale pink, ironed, and Williebelle's double strand of costume
pearls.

"Job interview?" Henry asks.

"Temp agency."

From weeks of silent dwelling on the topic, he plunges into
his occupational wish list: Yale Drama School? Tisch? That actors' studio he likes to watch on Bravo with students in the au-

dience who don't look as if they're fresh out of college, either? What about *teaching* acting? To kids? Summer camps? At Elderhostel? Has she ever considered law school? She'd be so good before a jury. What about some kind of internship, maybe a cable news station, where a smart boss would catch on fast to the fact that she's smart, articulate —

"I'm thinking cleaning lady," she says. "If I took care of upstairs and downstairs, I'd at least be contributing to my upkeep."

"I see. And would I have to fire Lidia?"

"No," she says. "Of course not. Bad idea."

"Sit. A single or a double?" he asks, even though her favorite mug — John Travolta, in powder blue as Tony Manero — is already under the machine's spout. "I realize," he begins over the noise of beans grinding, "that the enlightened parent is supposed to say, 'If cleaning houses makes you happy, follow that dream.' But I know you're joking. I have great faith in your talent and therefore your future —"

"Too much faith! I'm almost thirty, and I can't even get my job back handing out rayon smocks. And yes, I'd love to go to the Yale School of Drama, but I'd never get in. And if I did, by some fluke, I'd be the oldest and possibly the least qualified —"

"Don't say that! You studied acting. We could compose a very respectable resumé —"

"Anyone can study acting. Is that what geniuses major in? Anyone who watches celebrity *Jeopardy* knows that they dumb down the questions those weeks."

He turns around, abandoning work on his own cup. "Where is this coming from? Please don't tell me that this fiasco with Estime has made you question yourself and your potential."

"I'm too old for potential. Look at my mother: I probably inherited her career genes." She holds the can of whipped cream at arm's length as it releases its last noisy froth into her mug.

"I have another," says Henry.

"I'm good." She takes her first sip. "Mom ever call you back?" she asks.

He hands her a teaspoon and napkin, then takes the second kitchen stool. "Is this from the daughter who never wants to see or talk to her again?"

"It's about you," says Thalia.

"How is it about me? Because when a person slams down the phone in the middle of my sentence, in fact a sentence that was about to turn conciliatory —"

"I know you! You don't like a grudge floating out there in the ionosphere, even if it's your cheating ex-wife."

"I'm a lawyer. I have hundreds of open grudges out there, defendants *and* plaintiffs."

"Doubt it."

He goes to the refrigerator for the new, unbidden can of whipped cream. When he returns he says, "She e-mails me. Regularly."

"Apologies?"

"Not in so many words. You know her: She has a blind spot for when she's being ignored. Or, by some members of her immediate family, being thrown to the wolves."

Thalia, between sips, says, "Utterly predictable."

"Which?"

"The mending fences. I knew this would happen, one big blended stepfamily, especially since you're not that great at banishing and abandoning."

Henry says, "I don't encourage her. My answers are quite terse. And I don't reply to every one."

"Ha," says Thalia.

"She always ends with something equivalent to 'How is Thalia?'"

"And you say what to that?"

"That's the part I don't reply to. Well, maybe every other time. Maybe just, 'She's well.'"

"Does she mention her boyfriend?"

"No."

"Just mine?"

Who is this "mine"? Henry wonders. Not Giovanni; not if he's filled the salon job with another pretty girl. The deejay? Not likely; he had his moments, but Thalia hasn't mentioned him or his club in weeks. After what he determines to be a nonchalant interval, he asks, "Did Leif ever answer your text messages?"

"So far, no."

Henry says, "Then I'm appalled."

"He's taking it all out on me: We flopped. He paid a ton of money for his big exposure, his reinvention, and what happened? *Nada.* A couple of insults on blogs and a few embarrassing photos."

"What the hell is wrong with him? Does he *not* know that if you have intimate relations with a woman and then don't call, regardless of what business failures complicate the relationship, it's rude and it's loutish?"

Thalia says, "Listen to the expert. I love it."

Henry says, "I learned a lot, secondhand, from Celeste. I was something of a repository for her romantic woes. Out in public, we were often mistaken for a mister and missus." He smiles so wistfully that Thalia asks, "What? What are you remembering?"

Henry says, with difficulty, "I shared this at her memorial service . . . Once, a waitress — it was a nothing place on Columbus, now closed — came over to our table and said, 'You two aren't married, are you? To each other?' And we said, 'No, why?' and she pointed to another waitress, who waved from the counter. 'We have a little bet going. I said you couldn't be married because you two talk to each other. For real. Constant conversation. Married people tend to bring a newspaper. Or stare out the window. Or fight.' So Celeste motions to the waitress, *Come closer*. Then she announces, 'You're very observant. He and I are having an affair. So if either of us comes in with our spouses, don't say a word. They're rich. We married them for their money. But *this* is the real thing.'" Henry shakes his head as if he's been babbling foolishly.

Thalia asks, "Hesh? Would it be news to you that Celeste was in love with you?"

"You never met her! She had no illusions about our friendship—"

Thalia puts her mug down to count on her fingers. "You were married once. She was single, heterosexual—have we established that?—and probably showing up at your front door with casseroles when Denise left, if it went back that far."

Henry says, "I don't remember any casseroles. She wasn't much of a cook. In fact, over the entire course of our friendship—"

Thalia interrupts to say, "Okay. Never mind. I love that you were blind to this."

Henry says only, "She was wonderful company."

Thalia says, "But now you have me. And Todd. Don't you think we're wonderful company? Or used to be, before my downward spiral?"

"There's no downward spiral. It's just a bump in the road. All actresses at one time or another work temp jobs and wait tables. It's honorable. And it makes for a better human interest story when you hit the big time. Rags to riches—people love that."

"Too late," she says. She pats the pockets of her skirt and brings forth a silent phone.

He asks if she is expecting a call.

"Not any more than usual."

"Not Leif? May I ask that?"

"You can ask, but he's so furious that he won't even answer a text message."

"Something's not right," says Henry. "Leif Dumont is not a lady-killer. This is a man who can't quite carry on a conversation, who is probably interpreting an order from Estime along the lines of 'That's over. She's out. Next!' to mean 'Don't contact Thalia, period.' My guess is that his head is spinning. He's hired this outfit for advice and guidance, and look where he is now: even less famous and a lot more confused."

"You know what I should have done? I should've spoken up before this got off the ground, when he first invited me on board. I could have asked, 'How much are you paying this outfit? Let's just try it. Let's go out on a couple of dates and I'll have my bartender friends e-mail Rush and Molloy, Gawker, all the places that ask for tips and sightings. Let's give the campaign a shot without Estime — just amateur hour. Just try it as Leif Dumont, horror helmer, and Thalia Krouch, wannabe actress/nobody.'"

"Please don't say that."

Thalia's left hand again moves to her neckline and rests on Williebelle's pearls. "Can't a person be a little depressed as she heads off to take a typing test?" She looks down at her feet. "Especially in brown pumps from Payless."

"I can fix this," Henry says. "I will. You signed a contract. Promises were made and terms were violated. I'm going to call Estime's lawyer as soon as I reread the file."

"Which terms exactly?" Thalia asks. "Because if you're going to sue based on the no-sex clause, Leif might argue that it was more or less consensual."

"More or less?"

"Okay: my idea."

"Nonetheless," says Henry. "May I rue the day I ever signed off on this?"

She turns to the job of squirting more whipped cream into her mug, a napkin held against her interview shirt front. "It made a *little* sense," she finally says. "Leif came along, a fellow actor, my teacher's ex-student if not old paramour, which was an interesting footnote. I heard the plan, essentially *Be my pal, pose as my girlfriend, no strings attached, we throw in an allowance.* I mean, how can you not feel sorry for a guy stooping to this? So there was my rescue fantasy: I'd take him under my wing, he'd succeed, and then, with an Estime team behind me, pitching my previously unnoticed talents — presto, the limelight."

"What happened to *your* Estime team? Your piece of the action?"

Thalia shakes her head. "Doesn't happen when the hired hand can't get her name in boldface type on Page Six. Or any page."

"Then I won't call Estime. I'll call Leif."

"To say what? 'Where are you? Are your intentions honorable?' Please don't. Because my guess is he's confessed his sins to Caitlin and he's on a plane trying to convince her that his heart is true despite a little slip-up in the abstinence department."

"Why does everyone confess everything to everybody these days?" Henry asks.

Leif is not on a plane heading west to make things right with Caitlin, but one flight down, knocking on the maisonette's front door. When she doesn't answer, he calls Thalia's cell, which she has switched from vibrate to a festive Caribbean ring. She stares at the name and its 310 area code. "It's him," she says.

"I'll give you some privacy," says Henry.

She shakes her head, *No, stay,* and answers with a brisk "Thalia Archer."

After a moment, and clearly for Henry's edification, she repeats, "You're at my door? Sorry. I'm not home. I'm meeting with my lawyer." She listens, twists her mouth this way and that. "Yes, actually, that does mean I'm upstairs. But I'd like Henry to be present. He has some serious concerns about, um . . . violated codicils."

Another pause. "Afterward," she answers, her voice no longer brittle. "Maybe we can go downstairs for that conversation."

She hangs up, excuses herself, and disappears into the powder room. When she emerges, her hair has been newly tousled and her cheeks are pinker, pinch marks evident. "You need some basic ladies' grooming aids," she says.

When the doorbell rings, Thalia says, "I'm actually nervous. How ridiculous is that?"

"I'll get it," says Henry. "You wait in the parlor."

He opens the door to find Leif in a suit, tie, no diamond studs in his earlobes, and a blue baseball cap that says "L.A." "Thalia's in the parlor," he says.

"I think I'm supposed to talk to you first."

Henry, though unprepared, realizes he's never before spoken with Leif alone and shouldn't squander the opportunity. "Quite right," he says. "This way," and leads him past the parlor, past a puzzled Thalia, into the library.

Leif has already taken off his cap. His hair is coming in, an uneven sprouting of lackluster brown going gray. He doesn't sit or speak. Henry motions to the couch and says, "I guess you're waiting for me to ask what happened."

"Which part?"

Henry says, "Let's start at the end and work backward."

"The club," says Leif.

"You stormed off. And that was the last contact you've had with Thalia. Is that correct?"

Leif says, "I didn't storm off. I put her into the limo and then I left, which is what you do when you get the message, big-time."

"She assumed you were furious."

Henry hasn't closed the door to either the library or the parlor. In seconds, Thalia materializes, sits down on the couch, folds her arms across her chest, and says, "Go on. I'm listening."

Henry watches Leif. His face and ears turn the red of past mortifications.

"Henry's asking about the night at the Box," Leif says.

"Your disappearing into the night. I heard."

"That's as far as we got."

"Do you not think that was rude? Not to mention loutish? Especially after accusing me of using you?"

Leif says, "I do. I also think, maybe, this was the conversation we were going to have downstairs."

Henry says, "I can leave."

Thalia says, "Henry can stay. He knows what happened. And I mean *ev-ry-thing.*"

Leif closes his eyes, returns his Dodgers cap to his head, pulls it low on his forehead, and exhales an exasperated breath.

"He's my adviser in all matters," Thalia continues. "Didn't you think it would come out sooner or later as we both tried to figure out what went so wrong?"

Leif stands. "I get it," he says. "'What. Went. So. Wrong.' That's all I needed to know. Thank you. I'll see myself out."

Henry says, "Now wait a minute. Thalia? Would you like to rephrase anything you just said?"

Leif, already in the doorway, does not sit down, but stands his ground, his back stubbornly turned to his host and hostess.

Henry says, "I have to confess, I'm totally baffled. The corporate lawyer in me would say, 'This was a contract for six full months, so what happened? We never discussed or agreed to a trial period during which the company would assess whether its publicity goals were being met.'"

"Nice, dry point," says Thalia.

"On the other hand, when I see this through the eyes of a divorce lawyer —"

"Which you're not," says Thalia.

"I meant, as someone who has negotiated the breakups of many partnerships, there's always the personal side that needs to be addressed. And when it involves my daughter —"

"Miss Blabbermouth," says Leif. "Miss Kiss and Tell."

"Please turn around," says Thalia. "It's very annoying to talk to someone's back. And by the way, nice suit."

Nice suit! Henry watches Leif closely. He thinks, *However that strikes him, whatever expression I see on his face will tell me exactly what I need to know about Leif Dumont.*

Leif does turn around in a manner that enlightens, in a manner that Henry will later describe to Todd as key. What he witnesses is a pivot and a smile — not a military about-face but a showman's spin — and without question it makes Thalia laugh.

36

A Little Mea Culpa

DENISE SENDS HENRY a cactus dish garden. The card accompanying it says, "9B officially mine. I'm very grateful. Love, Your Enemy. P.S. Can't people compartmentalize?"

He calls her and asks what her cryptic postscript means.

"First of all: Hello. I didn't know whether I'd ever hear from you again. And secondly, I thought it was obvious: There's me, there's you, there's the various satellites in our lives —"

"Do you mean your boyfriend?"

"And yours and Thalia's. No one's aiming for one big happy functional family or even one big Thanksgiving dinner. If you don't see what I see in Eddie, fine. He's sensitive to that. He can have a night out with the guys while I roast a chicken for you and your favorite child once in a while. Not every week. Not even once a month. Well, maybe once a month. And Todd, too. How is Todd?"

"Good," says Henry. "Very good."

"You're welcome, by the way: You two are my one successful fix-up in a lifetime of disastrous matchmaking. And I hope you know how lucky you are to end up with someone whom people like. That's not so easy to accomplish in this world. Believe me, I know that Eddie's no one's cup of tea except mine—and that's on a good day—but you remember what loneliness feels like, right? A warm body, and handy around the house? And get this: The mountains came to Mohammed. Can we still say that? I let the sons back into the apartment to get some of their childhood memorabilia, and the Picasso, which I never liked anyway. And the Crock-Pot, which Glenn Junior claimed his father wanted him to have. Of course I waited until the rooms were repainted—ironically by Public Enemy Number One, Eddie Pelletier."

Henry asks, "What did you have in mind, Denise? What format for reintegrating yourself? Just roasting a chicken once a month?"

"I'm starting small. Nothing big, because I know her value system, and I know she likes stuff from the junk heap."

"Such as?"

"I've had my eyes open, style- and taste-wise," Denise says. "I've made a thousand mistakes, but honestly, don't you think I'd be a fabulous personal shopper? You don't need a degree for that, or even experience outside your own closet."

"A garment, then?" he asks.

"I found it at a vintage store on Thompson Street, which, to start with, who shops in SoHo? I went there with a mission and came back with a pair of opera gloves, black velvet, past the elbow, with pearl buttons at the wrist, only one missing, very Bette Davis. I think they say *black-tie event at the Kennedy Center, circa the Eisenhower Administration.*"

297

Henry doesn't comment or correct, except to ask, "Then what? How do you see a pair of gloves leading to a rapprochement?"

"Can you help me with that?" Denise asks. "I thought you'd come up with a really good line like, 'These had your name all over them.' Only better than that. Something a little more emotionally charged, with a little mea culpa thrown in."

Henry says, "I know it's not your style, but I would just send the gloves with a note that said, 'Thinking of you. Love, Mother.' Or 'Mom.' I can't imagine Thalia wouldn't respond, even if it's just a couple of words in an e-mail."

"I'll drop them off today! Albert Einstein loves a taxi ride through the park."

"Mail them," Henry advises. "First you might consider replacing the missing button."

"I did. It's in its own little envelope. It's not an exact match, but close enough. I hope she has an occasion to wear them. Oh, I just got a flash — they'd be the perfect accessory, something old, if she ever marries Count Dracula."

How much can he confide without betraying Thalia's trust? "I'd be very careful with that," he warns.

Epilogue

LILLIAN IS FINE with Todd's moving to West 75th Street. She is hoping for a wedding or something comparable, whatever civil thing the state of New York allows between two men who constitute, in her opinion, a match made in heaven. She expresses relief, probably an untruth, over finally emptying her nest. "People were always shocked when I told them my adult son lived at home, especially when I mentioned your age. Now? You know what I say? 'He's closer to work, living in a beautiful place with his boyfriend, or should I use *partner*? I don't beat around the bush anymore, no matter what kind of person I'm telling. I say, 'He's very happy, which makes *me* happy. Aren't I lucky to have my only child seven blocks away?'"

Besides the obvious benefits of having Todd under the same roof, Henry has gained the taste, skill, and employee discount helpful in renovating a drab maisonette. Todd doodles on graph paper in his office, Williebelle's old room, working on a floor plan that borrows 750 square feet from the laundry room, to be integrated into Thalia's apartment. She needs more space.

Henry's initial reaction was dismay that a smart, sophisticated woman would be so careless, so cavalier, so unsafe in matters expressly and contractually proscribed. Call it good luck, good karma, or the gods smiling down on Henry Archer, but all is well, better than well: The careless parties were healthy, uninfected, and best of all, one of them was ovulating. After somber discussions over the course of two tense weeks about alternatives, Thalia invites Henry to her kitchen for takeout Indian food. The first sign of hope is the half gallon of milk he spots in her refrigerator. Then, as soon as he's seated, she excuses herself and returns with a wrapped package. "Here," she says, "knowing you, you'll want one of these upstairs." The paper is yellow and mint green, and nestled inside a Payless shoebox is a receiver for a baby monitor. For months to come, she threatens to call the baby Williebelle, regardless of sex. He's learned to smile and let it go.

Henry and Todd secretly confess their worries, admittedly superficial, that the baby will be long and lanky with a bony cranium and an undetectable sense of humor, but the first astonishing ultrasound is almost photographic, revealing a round face, beatific, in the way of Thalia's baby pictures. Once Leif ascertains that he is, indeed, the baby's father, he rings the doorbell, upstairs, and asks Henry and Todd for Thalia's hand in marriage.

"Absolutely could not say," Henry tells him. "But believe me, I deeply appreciate the gesture."

"Whatever happened with the Beverly Hills girlfriend?" Todd asks, serving drinks, then ordering in paninis as the three men get a little drunk discussing potential family configurations.

Leif says — employing irony, much appreciated and later

quoted to Thalia — "It must be over. I was banished from her Facebook page."

"This Caitlin business didn't inspire great confidence in your judgment," says Henry.

"I totally agree," says Leif. "And not that I'm proud of it, but did you ever meet anyone who fixed what happened to you in high school — hot, out of your league, wouldn't have given you the time of day, then suddenly wants to be your girlfriend? Despite the little voice inside you saying, 'This is never going to work'? That's where Caitlin came from — my fifteen-year-old marooned-in-the-cafeteria self."

"Denise Wales for me," says Henry.

"Tyrone Sanborne for me," says Todd. "Who hasn't had that experience?"

"My parents want to meet Thalia," says Leif.

"That is adorable," says Todd. "And my mother is dying to meet you. Not to mention Denise, who claims to have unearthed Thalia's entire layette."

Henry says, "Gentlemen. It's early —"

"Fourteen weeks on Friday," Todd adds.

"As of now, Thalia isn't thinking in terms of future in-laws. She's very happy with the way things are."

"I know what you're not saying," says Leif. "She's not so much in love with me. But I don't think that's necessary on both sides, do you? I'm almost forty. I think I hit the jackpot. I think I can give our baby a home —"

Wrong word to use in front of Henry. "Thalia stays in New York," he says.

Thalia is, of course, the pregnant woman of the new millennium. She runs; she wears maternity clothes that might as well not be labeled as such because the bump is advertised, upholstered in clingy athletic fabrics, breasts proud. She works full-time until her water breaks.

Henry doesn't sue Estime on Thalia's behalf but finds Attorney Seth Shapiro, as predicted, ultimately sympathetic to the cause. Henry brings to the table a list of contract violations, ending with the big one: "Your client got my client pregnant, despite contractual prohibitions. We are not suing or asking for child support. We've come up with a resolution that is fitting and beyond reasonable."

"Such as?"

"Employment. Estime hires her."

"In what capacity?" asks the lawyer, pen in motion.

Henry is ready: Publicity! The perfect occupational match for Thalia's stellar communication skills, her personality, her ability to think on her feet. She will, through no fault of her own, need maternity leave in late February, the same generous few months that Attorney Michele Schneider seems still to be enjoying. Has the company ever had a publicist with an acting background? Invaluable in this field. And his personal guarantee: This is no prima donna. Between her acting gigs, she worked behind counters. Translation: No job or client beneath her dignity. The difficult and the spoiled? That can be her niche.

It takes several meetings, but eventually the terms of a settlement build from unpaid intern to assistant to junior publicist with an office, a health plan, a laptop, and a BlackBerry.

Most helpful to the advance of Thalia's career and Leif's profile is the fact that Caitlin is lashing out. She uploads her disappointments on YouTube, a forty-second virgin's lament, in a clingy tank top, naming names: Leif Dumont, award-winning actor, was stolen away by Thalia Nobody, implying *girl who steals a guy by going all the way*. It doesn't take long before a citizen journalist reports on Gawker.com that Leif and Thalia were seen on Sixth Avenue between 17th and 18th, "she in a cami, loose jeans, a hat, and sunglasses. Him in a Mets cap, and giving a dollar and a pack of gum to a homeless guy."

It spawns a blind item, Leif's first, on Page Six: "WHICH sitcom spook in town scouting locations for his new flick [untrue; Thalia's tip] and his NY publicist, allegedly friends, are actually more?" Quick study Thalia Archer posts a statement on her new MySpace page, denying the rumor that she, an employee of Estime, is violating company guidelines by dating a client. "This," she writes, "will be the last time I address this baseless allegation." Eleventh graders at Beverly Hills High School fight back, expressing their skepticism by employing epithets that MySpace blanks out. By the time Thalia's belly tells the story, The Superficial goes on record saying that the faux-mance between horror lothario Leif Dumont and Thalia Archer looks like the real thing after all.

Hidden behind the work of Hollywood makeup artists, is Leif a better actor than anyone knew? Thalia says yes, particularly after lunch with ex-teacher Sally Eames-Harlan, who claims to have advised him against taking the role of Boo in the sitcom, possibly the longest-running typecasting in the history of television. Thalia, with her new corporate American Express card, picks up the check.

"She told me he did Stanley in *Streetcar*," Thalia reports.

"He did not," says Todd.

"In college. And you know, once Sally told me that, I could see it."

"Interesting," says Henry.

"If not eloquent," Todd confirms.

• • •

At twenty-four weeks, Thalia assures Todd and Henry that she has enrolled in Lamaze classes, and okay, yes, she's taking Leif. "We've been to one. Show me a guy who's having his first kid at thirty-nine, and I'll show you a guy with his hand in the air the whole hour," she says.

"Henry was worried you'd ask *him* to be the birth coach," Todd tells her.

"Oh, he'd be just the guy I'd want down there." She raises her knees to a higher rung of the kitchen stool, suggesting stirrups in the delivery room. "'Wait, Henry! Where you going? The baby's out, but you'll miss the placenta!'"

"He'll be good at other things," says Todd.

So all that Estime wanted in the first place for Leif has come to pass, by accident or default, and for Thalia, too, not that the firm had her best interest, or any interest at all, at heart. Sometimes Henry wonders if there was some grand and brilliant scheme to get their client to where he is today: in blind items and in love.

The photo of Thalia leaving Lenox Hill Hospital twenty-four hours after giving birth shows Leif holding the baby, nearly undetectable in swaddling in the cold March air. Not shown: the car waiting at the curb, Henry holding the door open and Todd already inside, pressing a tatting-edged flannel blanket into the hollows of the infant car seat. Back in the maisonette, the plywood cradle crafted by Eddie Pelletier — since painted, upholstered, and stenciled with moons and stars by Todd — stands ready in the planetary-themed nursery. Leif will tip the driver fifty dollars for the ten-minute drive across the park.

"Wow," the man says. "My lucky day. Girl or boy?"

"*Pink* receiving blanket?" Todd answers, and clucks his tongue.

"Don't tell my wife," says the driver. "Four boys is enough."

At West 75th Street, the suitcase and baby paraphernalia are quickly unloaded by the happy driver. "Photo? Sure thing," he says. "I can do photo. Digital? This button on top?"

The party stands in front of the house, Thalia holding the swaddled baby, Leif behind them, Henry on one side, Todd on the other.

"Athena Celeste Dumont, arriving home. Day one, take one," says Thalia.

"It's cold out here," says Henry. "She's never been exposed to the elements. We shouldn't dawdle."

"Closer," says the driver, "if you want everybody in the picture."

The group narrows and shrinks into the frame. The result will become the birth announcement, Photoshopped with an inset, a close-up of Athena, delicious baby.

Lillian calls this homecoming the second-happiest day of her life, and the baby girl, indisputably hers to spoil and borrow. Eventually Williebelle's white bedroom under the eaves will be her home.

Henry will be known as Grandpa, Todd as Papa Todd, and Denise will be known as Denise. She likes to remind Henry that he can draw a straight line between her and his unforeseen set of blessings. After all, if she'd been the flawless human being they all had craved, Thalia wouldn't have needed this improvised family. Though resistant for nine months, she has found two personal silver linings in her daughter's adventures: Albert Einstein has come into his own, growling custodially at strangers who get too close to his baby. And this plain fact, which she hopes has crossed more minds than just her own: If Thalia is this good at motherhood, could Denise the role model have been so bad?

MY THANKS

To Mameve Medwed and Stacy Schiff, as ever, for editorial wisdom and prize-winning friendship every step along the way. To Anita Shreve: Who better to recognize where a story should begin? To my helpmeets at William Morris, starting with beloved ace Suzanne Gluck, the indispensable Sarah Ceglarski, and my West Coast champion, Alicia Gordon.

To Andrea Schulz, fabulous and heaven-sent editor. To the indefatigable Megan Wilson, Lori Glazer, and Bridget Marmion, and to everyone behind the scenes and on the road for Houghton Mifflin Harcourt.

To Todd Shearer and George Romanella for sociological guidance and nomenclature (surely a coincidence!). To Meg Wolitzer and Bob Hughes for early reads at the right time. To Howard Medwed for fictitious legal complications; John P. L. Kelly, Media Relations, NYPD, for guidance on Leif's transgressions; and Keleigh Thomas of Sunshine, Sachs for tips on the hip.

Enduring thanks to Jane Rosenman, Harry Gittes, Benjamin Austin, and Robert Austin.